I0823950

DEAD FIRST

Also by Johnny Compton

The Spite House
Devils Kill Devils

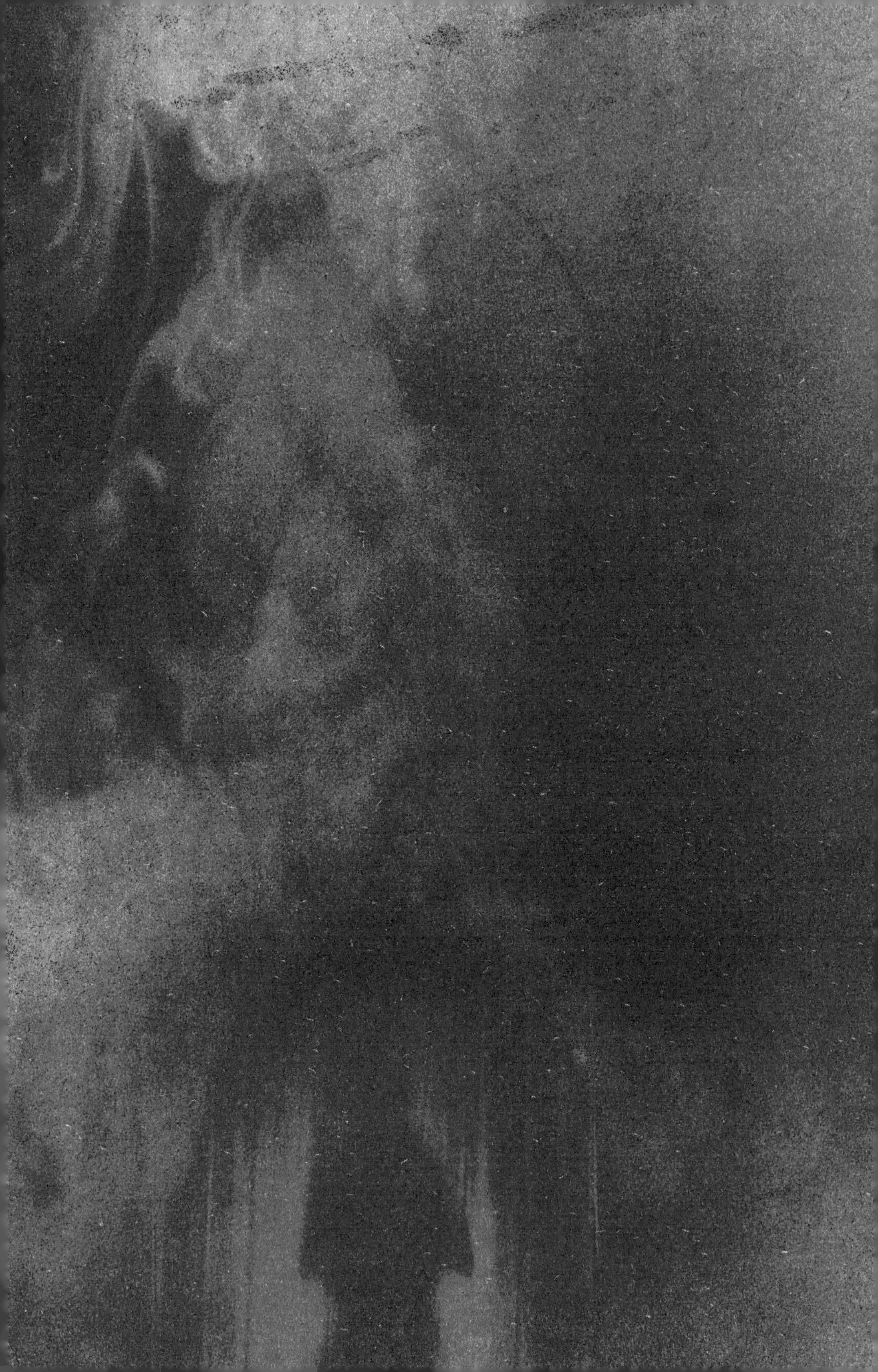

JOHNNY COMPTON

DEAD FIRST

G. P. PUTNAM'S SONS
New York

PUTNAM
— EST. 1838 —

G. P. Putnam's Sons
Publishers Since 1838
An imprint of Penguin Random House LLC
1745 Broadway, New York, NY 10019
penguinrandomhouse.com

LIBRARY OF CONGRESS CATALOGING-IN-PUBLICATION DATA
has been applied for.

ISBN 9780593854310 (hardcover)
ISBN 9780593854327 (ebook)

Printed in the United States of America
1st Printing

The authorized representative in the EU for product safety and compliance is Penguin Random House Ireland, Morrison Chambers, 32 Nassau Street, Dublin D02 YH68, Ireland, https://eu-contact.penguin.ie.

To my mother, for watching PBS *Mystery!* with me

To my father, for telling me about *The Norliss Tapes*

DEAD FIRST

1

As Shyla Sinclair approached Saxton Braith's manor, which was not atop the hill so much as it *was* the hilltop, she could not decide if it looked like it was too much *of* or *apart from* the world. With its stony façade and unevenly parapeted roof, it looked like a floodlit fort.

The car Braith had sent for her rounded a turn, and as it came closer the home's shimmering black windows and superficially burnt, tall double doors told a different story. That this place turned into a dark church after sundown, one large enough to keep you lost and trapped inside until it decided you were faithful enough to be shown an exit.

It was a place made for someone who did not have to choose between extravagances, who might pick luxury over taste ten times out of ten just to make a point. *I don't need taste. I don't need to be discerning. I don't have to have a "good eye" for anything. Whatever I choose and whatever I do is automatically the best because* I *bought it and* I *paid for it, the end.*

Now, again, she tried to weigh whether the security holstered beneath her light, red jacket would be enough, should this meeting—this incomparable opportunity—turn into something else. Said security, a subcompact Glock situated comfortably against her ribs, would prove especially ineffective if it was confiscated.

Shyla had expected the driver who came to pick her up—a tall, auburn-haired woman in her late thirties or early forties who introduced herself as Remy—to frisk her before welcoming her into the back of the relatively unassuming silver Lincoln, but that didn't happen. Maybe after the Lincoln pulled to a stop in the arched driveway leading to the front of the manor. Which would leave Shyla with only the backup security of having told a friend where she was going, as well as the instruction to follow up with her first thing in the morning if she hadn't heard back. This wouldn't be much good to her if Braith—along with Remy, and anyone else who might be present in the house—planned to do anything that would take fewer than eight or nine hours to finish.

Her past gave Shyla cause to be paranoid, and vigilant, and a glance at current world events or a general understanding of history could give anyone reason to believe a billionaire might be capable of anything, but Braith's invitation worked both to fuel and to dispel her paranoia. It was disconcerting, delivered as it was by hand to the mailbox hanging beside the door of her newly purchased cottage-style house. No postage, no return or mailing address, just her first name written in black ink. The envelope hadn't even been sealed. A small, folded letter, handwritten, was inside, telling Shyla that Saxton Braith was aware of and impressed by her work, and was interested in interviewing her for a job. It ended with a phone number, and a code she could use in a private message to any of his verified social media accounts if she needed proof that this wasn't a scam or prank. She'd used that code, sent a message, and received a simple response: *Hello, Shyla. Looking forward to speaking with you.*

Then she called and spoke to Remy, thinking, *Well, he already knows where I live. If this was something shady, some kind of setup, he could have just sent for me instead of bothering with any of this stuff that could leave a digital and paper trail.* That was encouraging in a way, although she understandably couldn't shake the discomfort of knowing someone—Remy, she presumed—had walked up the steps of her porch while she was either away or unaware, possibly at night, and left that envelope in her mailbox.

So here she was now, still thinking of how Braith had sent a silver sedan and not an unmarked black SUV. A lone driver and not a team. Someone to send a message, not "send a message." All things she could point at to reassure herself she was in no danger. Enough to make her think it was safe to make the call, accept the invitation, get in the car.

Then she'd seen the house.

That wasn't the right word. "Mansion" or "manor" felt inadequate, as well. "Estate" approached what felt appropriate, but even that felt a little too normal.

"Relic." That felt closer to what this was. Braith lived in the last-standing ruin of some ancient calamity.

Remy parked in front of it, stepped from the vehicle. Shyla got out of the car as soon as Remy opened her door, without thinking, almost as if anticipating being ordered out at gunpoint. Remy, with her dark suit and tight expression, engineered her own level of distrust. Shyla had asked Remy to keep the partition lowered during the drive, and Remy had obliged, then deftly stifled Shyla's attempts at conversation.

"Where are you from?"

"Nowhere important."

"How did you end up working for Braith?"

"I applied."

"Do you enjoy what you do?"

"I am paid very well."

Shyla hadn't really been pursuing a deep discussion. She had been assessing how disciplined, practiced, or spontaneous Remy sounded. From the moment she'd seen the square-shouldered woman standing outside her house, Shyla had evaluated all she could about her. She noted the scar on Remy's chin, almost invisible on her fair skin. The controlled gentility of Remy's handshake reminded Shyla of her jujitsu instructor, a man who'd suffered his share of "boxer's fractures" and ligament tears during his mixed martial arts career. Remy's blunt responses, wrapped in crisp, steady professionalism that almost felt like a challenge—*I can outlast you, I promise*—removed any doubt that she was a fighter. A proud one who might not ever look for a reason to show her skills, but was always happy when the world provided one.

Even the way she opened the door for Shyla had a strict and performative quality to it. As Shyla stepped out, she presented Remy with a fifty-dollar bill she had slipped from her inner coat pocket, opposite her gun. Remy looked at it like it was a suggestive Valentine's card from her brother.

"You're joking."

"Only a little," Shyla said, continuing to hold the bill close to Remy's hand. "If you really don't want it, just give it to somebody else for me." A few more seconds passed before Remy accepted the tip, and Shyla smiled while updating Remy's unwritten dossier.

She followed Remy up the stairs leading to the front door. *Stay ready,* she thought. *Trust your instincts; they've never let you down.* Which was true, notwithstanding one- or two-dozen exceptions she could recall offhand, ranging from "The timing is right, kiss this boy," to "You can get away with cheating on this one test," to "Dad and Momma wouldn't lie about something *that* serious."

Hell, overriding her shifting instincts–which couldn't decide whether to suspect or trust–and following facts and clues had brought her to the truth that altered her life.

Shyla stepped into the house, and as the door closed behind her she realized she should have turned around and asked to be taken home before coming in.

Heavy, dark sheets covered various wall hangings, as well as a few statuesque figures freestanding amidst the furnishings. She fixated on the wall décor. Portraits and paintings?

Mirrors, she thought. Covered mirrors. She'd heard of that sort of thing before, from a few family members she'd connected with in recent years, folks from Louisiana she'd met at a funeral, who told her that covering the mirrors in the house where the dead had died was a priority. One of the first things to be done, even as you grappled with your immediate mourning, almost like the deceased had a disease that would go airborne if you didn't take this step.

Not every mirror she could see in Braith's home was covered, however, which made Shyla wonder whether she was missing something or reading too much into what she saw. The latter felt impossible to her, and not just because of her previous case, the one that presumably put her on Braith's radar. Even with no previous experience working with someone who believed in demons and spirits, she would have guessed Braith had arcane and occult interests. Or, at minimum, was interested in making others think he was curious about such things.

Along the wall of the mezzanine that hung like a darkened halo over this first chamber of his home, four life-sized chiaroscuro portraits of men had been mounted in recesses between massive bookcases. She scanned each one and started to wonder if they were depictions of different men, or of the same man just wearing different, decade-appropriate fashions or uniforms dating back a century or more. In one the man wore an officer's uniform that Shyla surmised was from the First World War. In another he appeared to be wearing a white-capped pilot's uniform. The moustache and rounded glasses he paired with a Gatsby-reminiscent tuxedo made him look older than in the painting where he wore a classically 1980s "corporate shark" Armani suit.

In every picture, the man—or different men, surely related, with uncanny resemblances—stood alone against darkness, lit from below and to his left, like he stood over a white flame. Shyla felt watched by them all as she followed Remy closer to the center of the room, toward the stairs that led up to a blank black canvas framed by the same inornate wood that housed the other paintings. The blackness of the otherwise unpainted canvas was so deep, Shyla wondered whether it was a canvas at all, but instead an open space to a hallway that repelled light. Just as she was convincing herself that this was the case, the canvas split, revealing itself to be double doors in disguise that Braith opened, walked through, then closed behind him before waving hello to her.

He could have met me anywhere, Shyla thought. *I bet he owns a yacht. I bet he owns five. A private plane or two. Or he could have just picked a hotel room—bought out a whole top floor for extra privacy if he wanted to. There are a hundred other places he could have picked, and he chose to bring me here. He wanted me to see all of this. Save the note; suss the reason later.*

There would be a "later," she was sure now. She hadn't made the worst mistake of her life by coming here. She couldn't know exactly what was on the man's mind, but she was sure he wanted her to see and know something, and to carry it with her. That was why he met her here.

When he made it down, he motioned for her to join him near the huge hearth behind the staircase. *First time I've ever seen a walk-in fireplace,* she thought. She accepted and sat across from him in one of two matching, antique, cushioned chairs.

"I can't express how happy I am to have you here," he said. "Would you like anything to drink?"

"No thanks, I'm good," Shyla said.

"You're sure? Not anything?" He put an emphasis on *anything,* and stated the question like it was a dare. Try to come up with something we wouldn't have, we couldn't make, and I promise I'll surprise you. Not only will we have it, but a version of it so good it will ruin it for you. "I have a house tea, specially brewed. You won't get it anywhere else, I assure you. If nothing else comes of this meeting, you can tell your friends you drank Saxton Braith's exclusive, home-brewed tea."

"That sounds dirty."

"Oh. Yes, I didn't realize that until you pointed it out."

"Yeah, no thanks," Shyla said.

Braith nodded, then flicked a glance past her. She looked back to see Remy moving from behind her to the side of the fireplace, near the large, traditional tools you'd expect to see. Tongs, a poker, a broom, and a shovel, all black.

"I appreciate your time and don't intend to waste it," Braith said, stealing back Shyla's attention. "I am compelled to ask, what led you to accept my invitation?"

His voice matched his appearance. Strong and sturdy, but not overly so. He was nearly six feet tall. Dirty blond hair, firm brow, a nose not quite aquiline but close enough to look like the model for classical sculptors. Certainly the model for the mezzanine paintings.

He had good shoulders, a waist that was a little slight for his frame, but legs and feet that fit him. He wore a buttoned-up shirt, suspenders, casual slacks, and hard-looking dress shoes.

Shyla wondered whether he'd done his due diligence to research her, or if he was basing his impression of her on presumptions and superficiality instead. She was Black, stronger and thicker-looking than what he might consider the "average" woman to be. She wondered if he could guess her age accurately. People who barely knew her often commented that she looked younger than twenty-seven, but anyone who had a chance to talk to her called her an "old soul," and was surprised that she wasn't in her thirties. It surprised them even more to find out she'd been in this business since she was twenty-three, with seventeen cases under her belt, even if most of those had been relatively light work. Finding proof of adultery, proof of insurance fraud, a few instances of digging up old, controversial social media posts from burgeoning politicians and businessmen. Nothing close to what Dante had hired her for. That case was different. Some PIs go their entire careers without someone asking them to confirm their paranoid, paranormal delusions.

Braith knew about that job, at minimum, but as to the rest—what was true about her—he might not even be that interested.

Virtually anything of significance that Shyla could learn about Braith would be a surprise not just to her, but to the world. Saxton Braith was, as far as anyone knew, an eccentric billionaire who was content to keep his mouth shut and life secret. No one knew anything about his parents or how he had amassed the money necessary to take ownership of Daedalus Shipping before its abrupt ascension as the favored vendor in a world where "overnight shipping" increasingly became the standard, rather than a luxury.

Having lost herself for a moment, Shyla took an extra second to remember what Braith had asked her. *What led you to accept my invitation?*

"Money."

"That's all that motivates you?"

"Why else do most people work? Some love their jobs, but even most of those would stop showing up if the checks did. I bet you'd stop doing whatever you do if it stopped making you anything."

His false frown dissolved, a wry smile taking its place. "You're honest."

"If I wasn't, I'd tell you."

"So, tell me about your experience with Dante. What was your impression? Did you ever believe he was what he said he was?"

"That's confidential between me and my former client," Shyla said.

"Sure. Of course it is. But what if I told you I'd give you a million dollars, cash, just to tell me about him and your experience with him? What would you say then?"

Shyla shifted in her seat and felt uncomfortable with how much space she had to move within it. "First I'd say those are just words."

Braith held her with his eyes for a while. "And suppose I had Remy bring the money out now. Put the briefcase in your hand. What then?"

"I'd go back to what I said first about client confidentiality."

"Honestly?"

"Honestly. I'd assume it was a test, and I'd be taking a million to give up two, or more."

A clipped burst of bright laughter accompanied by a clap escaped Braith. He spared Remy a glance, and she just smirked at him. He pointed at Shyla and said, "Smart. You're a smart one. I like that. I *love* that."

"So was that whole question a test? Part of the interview?" Shyla said.

"Well, yes. Every single thing you've done since you came to my attention has been part of my evaluation of you. But I also really wanted to know. I've got my own opinion of Dante, based on the few meetings I've had with the man, and I wouldn't blame you for holding on to your skepticism, if that's where you are. He's not a very serious person."

Braith stood and walked a few feet closer to the fireplace before turning to face Shyla again. Before he could speak, realizing the implication of what he'd said, Shyla interjected, "What do you mean, everything I've done—"

"I've had someone watching you since before you were done with Dante. Is this a surprise to you? Clearly I knew where you lived, at minimum. You knew this."

Yes, she did, but there was something unseemly to her about the casual way he'd brought it up, like it was so acceptable she'd be out of line to voice objection to it. Besides, while she knew he had her address and could send people to her home, she hadn't known he'd had people tailing her. And since *before* the Dante case was finished?

"It's news to me that I was being followed. You're over here talking about me being honest with you, like I'm earning your trust. Having someone track me without me knowing is shady as hell. Why should I trust *you*?"

He chuckled at her assertiveness and challenge. Was he more impressed than indignant, or the other way around? she wondered.

"Because I can pay you enough to make you forgive that I've upset you."

"I wouldn't be too sure. I'm not exactly the forgiving kind. And you didn't just 'upset' me, you *stalked* me."

"Well, *paid* someone else to—"

"I think this was a mistake."

Another measured look, and she could feel him weighing her words, sizing up her tone, her expression, determining how serious she was.

"This is negotiation," he said.

She shook her head. "It's how I feel."

"Same thing. Or related. Okay, instead of saying that I apologize, prideful as I am, I'm going to *give* you my apology in the form of double what I originally intended to pay you."

"And how much was that?" Shyla said before she could stop herself.

Braith's smile looked like a trap that had already caught something. "A little bit more than you thought, based on what I heard earlier."

It took her a moment to recall dropping the two-million figure ("or more") moments before, which was already quadruple the life-altering payout she'd received from Dante. And now Braith was talking about doubling that. For one job. It was preposterous. She hadn't said it sincerely, but as a figure of speech.

She said, "I'm pretty sure you're just saying that."

"You know, I didn't have to admit to having you followed. I could have kept that to myself. That I was so forthcoming with you should engender a modicum of trust, I think."

Forthcoming? Shyla thought. *Yes, I surreptitiously surveyed you for an extended period of time, but now that part's over, so let me be up front in retrospect about the sneaky shit I did. Doesn't that come around to qualify as honest?*

Was she really going to sign up for this again? More rich man "logic," which boiled down to thinking truth and sense could be altered for a certain price? With Dante, at least, his sincere belief in what he hired her to prove, coupled with their slightly shared histories, made it easier for Shyla to sympathize with him, despite his self-centered and ultimately self-destructive behavior. Braith struck her as less eccentric—his odd home décor notwithstanding—and less troubled than Dante, and therefore less forgivable. Just a man likely born into barely imaginable means, who on first impression believed himself a charmer and reasonable person.

"She's going to need to see it," Remy said. "Let's just show her."

He looked back at her, sighed. "Fine." He returned his attention to Shyla and said, "*Fine.* I was trying to lead up to something here, build a little rapport with you on the way, but it looks like instea—"

Braith's head jerked forward. Blood, lightened by an instant rush of saliva, spilled over his bottom lip, down his chin. He couldn't close his mouth because the point and hook of the fireplace poker that Remy had stabbed through the back of his skull had dislocated his jaw.

I didn't even see her pick it up, Shyla thought, with a degree of embarrassment that acted as a minor sanctuary, because it meant she wasn't completely mad with fear. Not yet.

The violence had startled her, but it wasn't what pulled her near the edge of sanity. It was that Braith—though his knees briefly buckled and his body shuddered—remained standing. His eyes hadn't gone blank, much less dead. In fact they remained focused on her. And blinked. How in the world was he still on his feet, still looking at her, blinking? And . . . God, was he smiling now? Trying to smile? Or was that just how it looked as his jaw tried to reset itself.

Braith reached with both hands for the poker handle jutting from the back of his head and, with an assist from his assailant, jerked it out. A throaty hiss and second shudder spoke to his pain, and he turned fully around to tell Remy, slowly, "I wasn't quite ready that time."

Shyla barely heard this. She was staring at the pulsing wound, matted with wet hair, in Braith's skull. For a moment she had a fairly clear view of brain matter but this closed quickly. Intense nausea immobilized her, and she knew trying to stand would leave her doubled over, heaving, and even more vulnerable than she already was.

Vulnerable to what? What the hell is this? Is this real? Please don't be real. Please be a trick. Please be anything else.

Stop begging for something that can't be true to save you.

SAVE YOURSELF.

Ignited by these thoughts, Shyla found the strength not only to stand, but to squelch the urge to vomit, which tried to rise faster than she did. With Braith's back still turned, she ran to the front door.

2

Locked.

The smooth black door handle would not budge. Shyla looked for a button to press or lever to turn to unlock it, and instead saw only a small pinprick of a red light.

Smart lock, she realized. Something else she had failed to notice, along with Remy grabbing a poker before skewering her boss in the head.

Was this all a setup? She thought it had to be. To what end, though?

She turned, saw Braith lurching toward her. He was about thirty feet away, she estimated, and looked a little unsteady on his feet, his motor skills still affected by the brain injury he had impossibly survived. Remy lingered behind him, as though she might attack him again. Shyla couldn't tell if Remy was still holding the poker, or anything else.

Braith raised his hands, a show of peace. "Shyla—"

Shyla drew her pistol on him. "Unlock the door."

Following a huff of laughter, he said, "Now, what do you think that's going to do to me?"

Noticing Remy move away from Braith, out of the line of fire, Shyla aimed the gun at her instead. "What'll it do to her?"

Remy froze, looking unafraid but cautious, while Braith glanced her way, then back to Shyla. He'd stopped approaching.

"Let me out," Shyla said.

"You know," Braith said, shaking his head, "I welcome you to my home with plans to offer you millions of dollars just to do your job. Then I offer to double that after you indicate you're maybe feeling a little put off. Then to show you how much I trust you—even though you don't trust me—I let you in on my biggest secret, which might be the biggest secret anyone has in the world. And in return, you point a gun at me and at my closest confidante, when neither of us has done a damn thing to you. Some people you just can't be nice to, I suppose."

Now it was Shyla's turn to shake her head. "You . . . she just . . . I just want out. I don't care what this is. I won't say anything to anyone. I just want out."

"Okay. I unlock the door, and then what? You're going to walk home? Hard to get an Uber way up here, especially at this hour, and I don't know how Remy's going to feel about driving you home after—"

"Stop fucking with me. You think I won't shoot?"

"Oh, I'm sure you will. You've done it before, haven't you? And taken a life?"

"How—" she said before she could stop herself, though she managed to choke down the rest: *do you know that?*

"I'm a resourceful man," Braith said. "I know where you live. I know who you last worked for, and how that went. I know as much as I need to know about you, Shyla."

"I . . . I don't want any part of this," Shyla said.

Remy spoke up. "Then you should have stayed your ass home."

Braith waved toward her to quiet her. "Don't. Let's be fair here. It's understandable for her to be upset by what she saw. And had you given me an extra second or two, I could have explained things to her, maybe walked her into it a little bit more."

"I'm sure she would have handled it a lot better if you'd just gotten through your presentation."

"A lot, a little, any amount of better would beat where we are now."

"Or we could have just left her out of this. I told you how it would go, but you never listen."

"Remy, for God's sake, can we talk about this later?" Braith said.

"Think you know everything."

"Remy—"

"*Hey,*" Shyla said. "What the hell did I see? Was that some kind of trick?"

"No," Braith answered, regaining some composure after the brief *Who's Afraid of Virginia Woolf?* exchange he'd had with Remy. "No tricks. What you saw was a product of my condition. I can't die, and I don't know why. At least I'm pretty sure I can't. I've tried a lot of ways, and had Remy try everything I couldn't do to myself. You want to empty every round into my head? She's already done it, with a higher caliber. Left a hell of a mess, and it took a little while for me to get back to my feet, and get myself back together, as it were, but I did. If you want to try for yourself, well, I won't enjoy it, but I'd still rather that over you pointing your gun at her."

"This is insane," Shyla said.

"Any crazier than Massimo Dante believing he's the Antichrist?"

"*Yes*. That wasn't real."

Braith tilted his head. "Sure. But this is. Think of how quickly you've accepted that, Shyla. You know how many people's brains would have broken already? Yours is still working, processing. This is why I brought you in, why you were recommended.

"Look at me, Shyla. Focus for a second. Listen. Your heart is beating fast, isn't it? I bet you can hear it if you really listen. I bet you could spot a rhythm in it. That's a good thing. It's a reminder that you're alive, and not just conscious, but thinking more clearly than you realize. So how bad can things really be? You can handle this."

Shyla blinked hard, seeing the poker's blade jutting through Braith's mouth again. Her vision blurred for an instant, then reset, turning her focus on the blood drying on his chin, on his shirt. Some had trickled from his nostrils as well. An easy detail to miss if this was, somehow, an elaborate effect, an illusion. She knew it wasn't, though. In her core she knew, the way she imagined someone from ancient times observing a natural disaster for the first time instinctively knew they weren't hallucinating or dreaming. This was similar, in that way, to people in prehistory seeing a tornado's funnel descend from the clouds, or a mountain's peak blown off from the inside, or a wall of water overtake the coast. It was nightmarish and captivating. Something to be fled, but also watched, documented. Learned from.

She *could* handle this.

God, she couldn't be starting to consider this, could she?

"Recommended?" she said. "What do you mean, 'recommended'? Who did you talk to?"

"Your friend Jinh. Who else?"

A distinct fear, unlike the rush of urgency and bewilderment powering her to this point, gripped her. This was a clearer, more practical and anguished kind of concern. "You talked to Jinh?"

Braith nodded.

"What did she say? She . . . she wouldn't have told you–"

"She said you could handle this."

"You showed her?"

"Only had to tell her. Over the phone, too. She's considerably more trusting than you are. Then again, she's more of a believer."

"What else did she say?"

Braith answered, "She's not how I knew about what you've done. I found that out on my own."

What exactly do you think I've done? Shyla wanted to ask. It felt important to know exactly what he knew, to be sure he wasn't trying to trick her, but she thought it safer not to encourage him to say it, in case he was recording all of this. It would be easy enough for him to edit any audio to hide his secret, while keeping the things that already incriminated her, such as the fact that she'd pointed a gun at him and Remy unprovoked, something he'd made a point of mentioning aloud. Shit, he probably *was* recording everything.

"Listen," Braith said, in a quieter tone that nonetheless startled her by its closeness. Had he been inching toward her the entire time and she only noticed it now, or had he just closed the distance between them while she was distracted? In any case, he was close enough now to lunge for the gun if he wanted to, but he did not appear tense. There was a relaxed looseness in his body language, like he was more apt to slow dance than fight with her.

"Obviously I want to talk you into staying and hearing me out," Braith said, "but, of course, I'll let you go if you insist. You're not trapped here. But I just want you to understand that, in my estimation–and I'm usually right about this kind of thing–you'll just be delaying your eventual agreement to work with me. And sacrificing, let's say, one million dollars. There'd have to be a penalty for wasting my time, as well as yours."

"What about one for threatening to shoot me?" Remy added.

Braith side-eyed her without really looking at her, then went on. "What I'm leading to is that even if you leave now, what you saw will stay with you. You won't be able to forget it, and if you try to, it will just become that much more of an obsession to you. I've already done the worst thing I could to you. I've shattered reality for you, without being able to give you an answer as to why things are the way they actually are. In my defense, that's what I'd like to hire you for. Again, I don't know *why* I can't die."

"How long have you been this way?" Shyla said, then shook her head at how stupid she thought this question was, but it had raced ahead of others fighting to get out first.

"As long as I've been alive, I presume," Braith said, "though I guess I could be wrong."

"How long has that been?"

"I don't know. But if you accept the job, I'll be happy to tell you my earliest memory."

"Why . . . why do you even want to know?"

He looked at her perplexed, like an alien had asked him to explain love through an equation.

"Why *wouldn't* I want to know?"

This made immediate sense to her. Whether he was tired of living or wanted to ensure he was indeed invulnerable and possibly immortal, it would benefit him to know what made him the way he was.

She lowered her gun, out of an onset of fatigue as much as a fraction of trust that she would not be attacked. When Remy moved, Shyla almost reflexively raised the weapon again before she noticed Remy was moving back toward the fireplace. She wondered if Braith would join them for the drive home. It would be an awkward ride either way, but especially so if she was alone with Remy in the car.

A sudden notion–what her younger, newly met cousins had taught her was called an "intrusive thought"–jumped into her like it wanted to steal her for a joyride. *Shoot him,* it said. Not to defend herself, but to see if what he said was true. To make him prove that defying a deadly injury and instantly healing from it wasn't a one-off thing. A single miracle he'd been storing and cashed in just to impress and compel her, specifically, for some reason. *Put one through his head, call his bluff.*

And then what? If he's really lying you have a dead billionaire with your bullet, your gun, tied to his murder, and you probably have to kill Remy, too, so double those problems. Big difference between killing someone who'll be missed and someone who won't. And that's if he even dies. If he doesn't, you're just going to piss him and Remy off. What good is that?

And if we're past the point of thinking about shooting him, I guess we should go ahead and say yes to the offer.

She opened her mouth to do just that, and threw up instead, so hard it brought her off her heels before folding her at the waist. She struggled with, then succumbed to, a second spasm before feeling confident that she was empty. Shyla wiped her mouth with the back of her free, left hand, and stood upright.

"Sorry," she said.

Braith laughed, gestured back toward the fireplace where splats of his blood and bits of his brain matter were on the floor, fast-drying under the heat of the flames. "I was going to have to clean up, anyway."

3

Why didn't you tell me?"

"I'm sorry," Jinh told her.

"That doesn't answer my question," Shyla said.

She was home, in the three-bedroom house near the historic district downtown that she'd moved into shortly after the money from the Dante job came in. The ride alone with Remy was even more uncomfortable than she had expected, magnified by Remy keeping the partition lowered, as if she was wary of what Shyla might do. As if Remy had been entirely innocent, hadn't played a specific critical role in this traumatic episode. This fertilized Shyla's agitation, so by the time she was ready to call and confront Jinh, a few minutes past midnight, she was in a mood.

Glad you're still up, she'd told Jinh after she answered. *Did you know I was going to call? Psychic powers told you to wait up for me?*

Jinh hadn't taken the bait, instead just saying she was happy to hear from her before asking why Shyla had called.

"Why didn't you tell me?" Shyla said again.

"I didn't think it would do any good," Jinh said. "Would you have believed me if I told you?"

"That's bullshit," Shyla said. "You're going to lie to me, too, now? On top of everything?"

"Look, I didn't–" Jinh paused, evidently catching the aggression in her tone and resetting. Shyla could picture Jinh passing her fingers over her lips, a small vertical swipe she used to remind herself not to contribute to any argument's escalation. A gesture that Shyla had seen too often considering how briefly they'd been together.

"You're right. I should have told you. But I won't lie, I thought it would make you less likely to take the job."

"And you wanted me to take it."

"I figured . . . I hoped we could work together again."

"Unbelievable."

"Listen, if I had known it would make you this upset–"

"You didn't know? *You?*"

"Please stop," Jinh said, and even after three years apart, even now after her world was inverted and Shyla felt like she could fall skyward at any second, those two words, spoken by this person, made her dizzy enough to want to lie down. Shyla stayed where she was, though, seated at the simple wooden desk in her bedroom, where she had laid out the contents of the folder Braith had given her before sending her home. For a moment none of the words in the clipped newspaper columns or handwritten notes were legible, because she could only see the words "Please stop" printed over them. Feel Jinh's confusion and desperation as she pleaded with Shyla not to drive away, to tell her what she'd done to make her want to leave.

"Talk to me," Jinh said, and Shyla had to remind herself that this was her in the present, not a vivid memory. "What happened?"

"How don't you know?" Shyla said, unable to contain herself. "Did you forget to push your psychic power button? Are your batteries dead? Have you checked?"

The oddly cheerful "all finished" *boop-boop-boop* sound her phone made when the person on the other side hung up startled her. She looked at the screen, saw the CALL ENDED message flash a few times before the home screen popped up. She set the phone face down on the desk and tried to move on to the material she had to work with, what she ought to focus on. What she anticipated falling asleep atop of, crashing after her body eventually overrode the nervous energy keeping her so awake it felt like sleep might never come again.

The text on the paper was visible again, at least. The centerpiece was an article covering a plane crash from 1958 on a stretch of beach near Galveston, Texas. It mentioned a dead pilot, World War II veteran Garrett Schramm, but spent more time on an unidentified "miracle survivor." The photos splitting space atop the article displayed the deceased, in uniform, and the survivor (*Could be Braith's twin,* she first thought) in his hospital bed. It was written a few days after the accident. Another article, shorter and sans pictures, was from the day of, and three others followed up on the miracle survivor, two attesting to his "unprecedented," "remarkable" recovery, so "literally unbelievable" that the doctors and nurses the reporter spoke to were unwilling to attach their names as sources for fear of being disbelieved and ridiculed.

The final article, again featuring the first picture taken from his initial entry into the hospital, reported the survivor's escape from the hospital and asked readers to notify the paper (and, next, authorities) if they saw someone resembling the man in the photograph.

It would have been a lot to absorb under any circumstances, but with the tumult of altered reality, remorse, and past problems tossing her thoughts around like a particularly acrobatic juggling act, Shyla struggled to lock in on what should matter most.

Under her breath, and out of the corner of her mouth, like she didn't want her opposite ear to eavesdrop on what she had to say, Shyla muttered, "Shit."

She picked the phone back up and hit redial.

She saw Jinh in her bedroom, watching the phone light up and ring, not just vibrate, since Jinh was one of the few people in present day who didn't have their ringtone muted. She knew Jinh would let it go for a while, until just before it kicked the call to voicemail.

I know that much about you, and I can't even read minds, or the future, or the past, or anything. I know that about you, but you can't even guess why I'm upset?

Thankfully, Jinh behaved as predicted, giving Shyla enough time to process and purge this sentiment before Jinh answered.

"Yes?" Jinh said.

"I'm upset because he showed me."

"What? What do you mean he–"

"He said he just told you. But he *showed* me."

Shyla fell silent, counting on Jinh to pick up on what she meant.

"Holy shit," Jinh said. "*Holy* . . . what? *What?* Wait . . . how . . ."

"His assistant or partner or whatever put a fucking fireplace poker through his skull."

"*Through* his–?"

"*Through* it, Jinh. I saw it. I can *still* see it sticking a little out of his mouth. I can see the blood on his lips and chin, and that's not the worst of it because . . ."

Shyla turned from the desk, afraid she would throw up again and not wanting any of it to get on the articles–the handful of leads she had to work with. *That's everything I know about myself,* Braith had said, which had struck her as bullshit, but she'd kept that to herself. "Because he turned around after he pulled the poker out, so I saw where it went in. I saw into his head, Jinh, and then I couldn't anymore. I feel like I sound crazy saying this out loud, but . . ."

"But you know I believe you," Jinh said.

Shyla nodded and felt she didn't need to vocalize this affirmation. *You know. You know that I know.* Shyla clung to her skepticism of Jinh's psychic ability, despite evidence of its legitimacy, because she simply didn't want to believe in it. She didn't want to believe and she couldn't forgive.

Even so, Shyla also understood that no one else knew her the way Jinh did. They'd loved each other in a needed way, at a time when Shyla was at her most open.

Jinh Gang had grown up believing in the supernatural, for reasons that were arguably good, and inarguably understandable, but she believed even more, still, in Shyla Sinclair.

"Oh my God, I'm . . . I'm sorry," Jinh said.

"You didn't do it."

"I should have told you. I understand now."

"You really don't."

"I do. I can feel it now, Shyla."

"Okay. Well, that's why I'm so upset. So now you know that, too."

"What . . . what can I do to help?" Jinh asked. "What are you going to do next? Should I meet you somewhere?"

"I'll let you know," Shyla said, and they both understood that this was the end of the conversation, so exchanged goodbyes and ended the call.

Shyla returned to the materials on the desk. It took her more than a minute to refocus. She first had to fight the urge to leave the house and run giggling through the streets until the sun rose. She had just got off the phone with her self-professed clairvoyant ex, who had referred her to an unkillable man whose scant history she was now looking over. Were it not for her own past and the comparatively ordinary things she had seen and remained sane through, she might still be in Braith's house now, gun as spent as her faculties.

The bottle of bourbon in her kitchen called to her, but she ignored the temptation and stared at the articles. If she watched long enough, would it piece itself together for her? Where should she begin? When it clicked for her, it was so obvious that it felt like a trap. There was nothing really to go with if she started with the man Braith used to be. Just a couple of grainy old pictures and a mystery. No name, since he'd adopted "Saxton Braith," if he was being honest with her. She would check on that anyway, just to be sure, but expected to find nothing going past his emergence as a public figure in the early aughts, much less anything dating back to the crash, or preceding it.

Garrett Schramm had a name, a service record, and a death date, at absolute minimum. She took out her laptop from the desk drawer to commence a web search with multiple browser tabs open. A couple dedicated to different newspaper and magazine archive services, one to the San Antonio Public Library's "Research & Databases" page, one to an ancestry site, and another to a practical, ad-free search engine she subscribed to. She spent the next two hours digging past dead links, taking notes of better leads, reaching out to a few strangers from the ancestry website who might have better information than she was able to obtain, and fighting sleep that promised to deliver nightmares. At a little past two in the morning, her shoulders slumped in concert with a slow blink and sleep finally won.

She left off looking at a web page about a downtown boutique hotel, Inspiration Sweet, named after a band that Garrett might have played with after returning to San Antonio.

She dreamt of being in a house without doors, and with windows that turned into paintings when she came close enough to open one.

She woke to a new text message from Jinh:

You're not going alone, are you?

4

The old article she'd found about the Inspiration Sweet Hotel only used Garrett's first name, but referred to him as a "former flyboy (and present playboy)," and included a picture of partygoers dancing before a stage that appeared to show Garrett playing drums for the house band. Based on his birthplace of Boerne, Texas, just northwest of San Antonio, and his funeral service at the Fort Sam Houston cemetery, it made sense for him to have made a home in the "Alamo City."

One of the enthusiasts she'd contacted on the ancestry site had already messaged her back with a document that seemed to verify that Garrett was discharged from the Army Air Corps in 1946, after he was stationed briefly in Korea.

The more she looked at Schramm's pictures, the more she felt like he was smiling at her, waiting for her to turn before narrowing his eyes and contorting his mouth into a sneer. Paranoia brought about by last night's experience, probably. She was aware of that, but also didn't feel like she could dismiss the sensation entirely.

Now foresight and insight were telling her that Garrett Schramm hadn't been a good person, based largely on the way his brow shaded his eyes, and how he looked like he was smuggling a smirk under his moustache even with the corners of his lips turned down. Poor reasons to think negatively of anyone, to be sure, but she simply didn't want to like the long-dead pilot. It was better, safer, to presume something unsavory about him.

Jinh's ominous text only supported this intuition, although Shyla was reluctant to admit it. She wanted to text back, *Go where alone?* As if she didn't know. Maybe Jinh was having a vision or whatever about an entirely different place than the Inspiration Sweet Hotel. A place Shyla didn't even know of and had no intention of ever visiting.

Or somewhere you don't know about yet, but you'll have to go to.

That last thought wasn't hers. It sounded like Jinh's voice. And it didn't sound like it was in her head, but behind her, just over her right shoulder.

Shyla felt a sudden tension in her back like a cattle prod had stuck her. Jinh's voice was as imagined as Garrett's glare across time, but the ache in her back was real, and the fact that she'd slept all night in her office chair probably worsened it. After waking up from too little rest, she'd only left to go to the bathroom and then grab a bottled iced coffee from the fridge before sitting back down to keep working.

She stood again now, to stretch, then turned around just to prove she was alone in her bedroom. Nothing but her and sparse décor, not even enough for a ghost to hide behind. A large, simple clock. A couple of tall lamps, two thin sentries on each side of her headboard. Shelves stocked with enough books on psychology, history, and criminal investigations to make an aspiring cop—or serial killer—envious. A trio of snowy landscape paintings she'd spoiled herself with after the first deposit from Dante hit her bank account, before she'd even made enough from the final payment to buy the house.

She had a romantic idea of snow, although the most recent of her rare experiences with it came from the disastrous winter storm that paralyzed most of Texas in 2021. She still thought it beautiful and wondered what it would have been like to grow up sledding or getting into snowball fights, or having snow days. Her cousins and Aunt Teonna in Minneapolis promised her that snow was overrated.

Staring into her favorite of the paintings—with its barely overcast sky and fenced-in, cozy cottage, similar to the one she'd bought for herself—Shyla massaged the last knots out of her muscles. She stored this sensation with the hope of being able to use it later. Given last night's show, she figured she would have to brace herself for something as bad or worse to come.

Knowing that other, parallel phenomena could happen, and trying to anticipate them happening, made her feel like there was a bomb in her pocket that she couldn't get rid of, that might go off today, tomorrow, or never at all.

She lifted the lever on her desk to elevate it to standing mode and resumed her research, now pulling up the Inspiration Sweet Hotel's website to see if it had any more pictures of the house band with Garrett Schramm in them. It would be good to know whether he was a permanent player, or just sat in on drums a few times. If he was a full-time member of the band, the hotel might have additional records or stories that could lead her to more information about him. She navigated to the "Our History" page, which was sparer than she'd hoped it would be. Five short paragraphs that started with an explanation of the hotel's name, being the place where a locally beloved jazzman named "Sweet" Jordan had recorded his first songs, and formed the band and nightclub the hotel was named for. It spent the next few sentences on the word "suite," how it could mean a musical piece, or a space within a building, and how this connection, along with how it matched his name, surely must have made the man nicknamed "Sweet" feel that much more inspired.

Beyond that, it only hinted at the location's possibly sordid history dating back to San Antonio's "sporting" era, when it had one of the nation's largest red-light districts before America's entry into World War II.

Shyla had come across part of this history in an old *Texas Monthly* article, but not as much as she would have liked. Some establishments would have leaned into this sordid past like it was a crutch keeping them upright. There was a chance the Inspiration Sweet's current owners were enamored with its history and just didn't want to give away something they could charge for. The "Our History" page closed with a boast that the library in the hotel's exclusive, top-floor "Inspiration *Suite*" contained "diaries, confessions, interviews, and more that would make the madams who ran the Chicken Ranch blush, and the gangsters in Galveston's Balinese Room call the police!"

Online booking options were grayed out for the exclusive suite. "Call for Availability. Serious Inquiries Only, Please."

Shyla called and a chipper voice cut off the second ring just after it had started. "Thank you for choosing San Antonio's historic Inspiration Sweet Hotel, how may I be of service?"

"I was calling to check the availability of the actual 'Inspiration Suite' on the top floor."

"And what time frame were you looking at?"

"As soon as possible," Shyla said. "Tonight, if it's open."

"Oh, I'm sorry, ma'am, but it's booked up through the end of October. We have immediate availability after that, though. Would November third be good for you?"

Shyla shook her head like the woman with champagne bubbles in her voice could see her. "No, I was looking for something sooner. I'll have to recheck my schedule and call you back."

"Understandable. The room tends to get booked fast, though, so please call us back as soon as your scheduling is sorted out. I'd hate for you to have to wait even longer if someone else scoops these earlier dates up."

"Thanks for letting me know. One more quick question, can you give me the rate?"

"It currently ranges from around eight hundred to twelve hundred per night to stay in our namesake suite, depending on if you're looking at weekdays or weekends, as well as peak points in the year. The demand is highest around Halloween, the holidays, Valentine's Day, and then early spring, when it's Fiesta season."

Shyla thanked the agent for this information, told her she had no more questions, then said goodbye and ended the call. She had no intention of calling back. Instead, she was going to grab a quick shower before heading to the bank on her way to the hotel. She figured fifteen grand would be enough to show that she was serious enough to buy the current occupants of the Inspiration Suite out of their stay, or bribe the manager of the hotel to bump whoever was booked next to fit Shyla in.

If neither took the offer, she would call Braith at the number he provided to see if he could step in. She was tempted to start with that idea, as much to gauge his response as to actually solicit his assistance. She preferred not to speak to him again, however, until she had information he didn't already have.

5

Fifteen grand in hundreds was a thinner stack of money than she would have guessed just a year ago, before the per diem she received working for Dante made her more familiar with these quantities of cash. It fit in a standard #10 envelope. She brought a rolling suitcase with her and put the envelope with the cash in that, instead of keeping it on her. In her limited but definitive experience, arriving in hotels without any luggage in tow garnered second looks, if not outright suspicion. She also didn't like having that much money just hanging out in her inner coat pocket, not unless she knew she was going to be handing it to someone in the immediate future. A zippered suitcase with a combination lock wasn't exactly a safe, but it made her feel like the money was more secure, and couldn't just slip out and get scattered if she needed to take off running.

The small rolling suitcase made her look official yet unassuming, innocuous. She counted on this as she walked through the front entrance of the Inspiration Sweet Hotel and gave the woman at the front desk a clipped smile and nod that was more raised eyebrows than head movement. A look that indicated she preferred to do the bare minimum when it came to basic greetings and courtesies.

The clerk returned her smile, looked like they were going to say something, probably a practiced welcome, possibly coupled with a question of whether Shyla was checking in if the clerk didn't recognize her. Shyla figured that with shift changes no one at an even relatively small hotel could presume they knew every single face that came through the door.

The online video tour of the hotel on its website told Shyla the elevators were straight past the front desk and slightly to the left, just past the library that doubled as a "business center." Being able to walk straight to the elevators like she'd already been here helped her look like she was a guest, and in her periphery, as she passed, she saw the clerk offer a slight wave and a "Welcome back," then return to whatever they were working on behind the counter.

"Thank you," Shyla said before reaching the elevators. She was taking a chance that the elevators wouldn't require a room key. A place with this aesthetic, this vintage, transportive ambience, felt like it wouldn't have such a feature. If anything, now that she was inside the hotel, with its rich oaken smell deep in her nostrils, and its dark metal-and-mahogany furnishings, she was surprised the elevators didn't have gated doors.

When the doors parted and she stepped inside, she was proven right. This probably wasn't a place that ran into many—if any—issues of unwelcome visitors. It was positioned on a side street just far enough from San Antonio's bustling downtown River Walk to receive comparatively little foot traffic. Its front, while four stories tall and unusually wide, still presented more as an old, elaborate home, with its wraparound porch and lack of signage, than a hotel. Being where it was, anyone who saw it could likely guess it wasn't a house, at least, but might think it was an apartment building, or a storefront for mundane businesses–insurance companies, investment firms, and law offices. Because that was the case so often in the city. Quirky bookstores or cool artist enclaves couldn't typically afford the rent of a place that looked this good but was a little too far off the beaten path. You had to know in advance something interesting was there in order to find it.

On the way up to the fourth floor, Shyla realized what the semisweet woody smell reminded her of. She hadn't been able to place it until something in her brain joined it with the imagined scent of cheap sugary cereals, and a fresh pot of instant coffee. The old home in Mississippi she had lived in as a child, from around four to seven years old. The place that housed her worst memories, because they were supposed to be good memories, wholesome memories. Christmases, with few gifts, sometimes just one, but one that told you people cared about you and listened to you. The kind of neighborhood friends you could fight with and laugh with in the same afternoon. Where she'd learned to ride a bike, started learning how to work on cars, learned to shoot a BB gun.

A great, terrible lie smothered it all, though, like an eclipse that did worse than hide the sun, but swallowed it, stole its heat but none of its light. Altering the world.

A bell chimed. She was at the fourth floor. She'd waded so far into her memories they'd made her buoyant, and she hadn't felt the elevator lifting her, so for a moment it seemed as though the fourth floor had come to her. The dark corridor that greeted her when the doors opened added to this disorientation. She hadn't known what to expect when she arrived. The video tour hadn't provided a look at the fourth floor, much less the lone suite that occupied it. Small glass gas-powered candles lined the walls, lighting the path to a gently haloed door at the end of the hall.

It was a clear, bright day outside, and the warmth of the light framing the door told Shyla that the curtains inside the suite were open. It didn't mean much except that the people occupying the suite probably weren't asleep, getting a late start to the day, or taking a midmorning nap. They had been up and had let the sunshine into their space. That didn't mean they were there right now, of course. But at least she wouldn't be waking them up when she knocked on the door.

She tried to tread lightly after exiting the elevator car and approaching the door to the Inspiration Suite, but the hard plastic wheels on the suitcase killed any hope she had of remaining stealthy. Had that not been enough, the *ding* that accompanied the closing of the elevator doors went up and down the hall like a rambunctious child with nothing fun to do but run.

Shyla moved quickly, wishing she could outpace the rumble and skip of the wheels over the floorboards at a brisk walking pace. Just fast enough that, though she knew this had to be a psychosomatic illusion, Shyla was sure she saw the streaming flames on the walls lean and flicker as she passed.

At the end of the hall, in front of the door, she stood on the light coming from underneath it and felt like she had spit on someone's welcome mat, but knocked three times nonetheless. She was here to work. Following the third knock she dropped her hand and listened for any movement behind the door. Rustling, footsteps, whispers. Seconds passed, and she counted in her head, knowing that fifteen seconds of silence could feel like a minute if you weren't keeping track. She gave them thirty seconds to answer, figuring that in such a small space it wouldn't take that long, provided that everyone inside (which could be just one person for all she knew) wasn't in the bathroom.

She knocked again at the half-minute point, then added,

"Housekeeping," in her least offensive, generic, *this is one of the few words I know in English* tone.

Ten more seconds.

Fifteen.

They could be out, she thought. *They're* probably *out.*

A shadow spilled over the light bathing Shyla's feet. She looked down to confirm this, having only felt it initially, like a sudden cool tide rolling up over her ankles. The shadow coming from under the door was narrow at first, and centered, fitting the person on the other side who had come to look. Before Shyla could begin her pitch, try to balance between the lie she'd told to summon the occupant and as much of the truth as she wanted to share, she saw the shadow expand. It washed over the rest of the light on the floor, then rose to envelop the light surrounding the door in its frame.

This onset of darkness itself isn't what made Shyla take half a step backward. The way it *moved* did.

"Hello?" she said, feeling stupid and, worse, helpless as the word came out.

Silence ensued and then, on autopilot, Shyla resumed counting in her head, unaware of how many seconds she'd lost, but knowing she got to fourteen before the doorknob turned. Slowly, like it was an old, rusted automaton, long overdue for a recharge.

Shyla had to remind herself to breathe.

The door cracked open, both in terms of the sound it made, surprisingly loud, and the sliver of an opening it gave Shyla to look inside, in which she saw darkness that felt impossible. She heard the door chain tighten and *clink* but couldn't glimpse it. Couldn't see anyone inside, although she heard breathing. Faint at first, though clear, then increasingly and deliberately heavy, even as it remained steady.

It took her a moment to realize there were words buried under those breaths, no more than three syllables hidden in every exhalation, and even some of the inhalations. Words spoken softly and carefully. Words that were distinct, forceful, and entirely unrecognizable. Shyla felt something stir within her, a deep understanding of the clear distinction between human languages and others. Something that made sure you never mistook a growl for a word. She heard something that should have been more easily mistakable for a foreign tongue, but was instead altogether removed from what humans should be able to replicate. It was close to a chant, but closer to a musical note trying to imitate something natural but hideous. The vocalization of a string instrument duplicating the whine of prey mid-slaughter.

Behind her, a pair of flames across from each other died. This new darkness glanced across the back of her neck before reaching her eyes. She turned just in time to see another pair of the lights fade. Now she was counting how many there were, still lit, between her and the elevator. Four more pairs. Eight total.

Seven.

Six.

"We know he sent you," whispered the voice behind the door, while impossibly sustaining its eerie prayer.

Or darker than a prayer. This was more sinister. An invocation.

Five flames, then four. The voice seemed to recede behind her, which made Shyla feel like the hallway had tilted and she had slid unknowingly toward the elevator. She turned back to the door to be sure it wasn't farther away than it had been a second before. It was still there, as close as it had been. But the voice felt like it was seeping through the outer walls of the hotel. So quiet she could hear the hush of more candles snuffing out. The familiar, single ring of a struck bell was louder. She turned again, feeling like the unwilling participant in a party game, and saw that all of the candles were out, and the elevator doors had reopened.

The ceiling light inside the elevator car wasn't half as bright as it had been when she'd ridden it up to this level. It ebbed, fading nearly to nothing. Behind her, the voice was thinner still and seemed to prick a deeper space inside her mind. She felt like it poked holes in the walls of her eardrums.

The silence was short-lived, broken first by a heavy footstep, then by a groan, both coming from near the elevator. She reached into her jacket for her gun, despite having no intention of pulling it out. She thought of the man sitting one seat over from her on her last flight from Minnesota back to San Antonio. There had been heavy turbulence, and the poor guy, who'd fidgeted even while the flight was steady, gripped the seat ahead of him as though he could force the entire plane to quit shaking and bouncing.

That's what she was doing now, holding the gun and pretending it could do something, like a younger sibling with an unplugged controller watching big bro actually play the video game on the screen. Except even babies couldn't be fooled by that one, at least not more than a few times. Here she was, acting like she could fool herself.

The footsteps thumped forth, along with a dragging sound that didn't emanate from the floor, but from the wall to Shyla's left, as though the invisible figure shuffling toward her had to lean against something to keep from falling. Its next groan was interrupted by a wet cough that was cut off by a second set of footsteps, louder, heavier, more measured, playing a call-and-mock duet with the first set. The laughter of the second phantom was terribly ordinary. Almost half-hearted. A polite laugh offered on a first date that's barely worth continuing.

A few more steps from the first figure, and a final moan, preceded a hard, flat thud that rattled the floorboards. Shyla stared ahead, fully alert, waiting, bracing herself to see something terrible. Something worse than what she'd seen last night.

Not possible, she thought.

Yes, it is.

No, what I saw—

Wasn't any worse than what I've seen before. Might have been better, because Braith survived. How is that worse than seeing a body? It's not. And whatever I see here won't be—

The door slammed behind her. She jumped, turned, opened her palm wide to be sure her fingers were nowhere near the trigger when she withdrew her empty hand from her jacket.

It was oddly surprising to see the door closed. The bigger issue, she instantly realized, was that she had turned her back on who- or whatever was in the hallway with her. As if sensing her realization and wanting to reinforce it, the laughing phantom snickered again, sounding satisfied this time. Like he—it was definitely a "he"—was fondly reminiscing about something.

Something he knows he shouldn't have gotten away with.

I'm getting out of here. She forced this thought to the front of her mind, then stretched it to wrap around everything behind it. Nothing else could matter right now.

I'm not turning around. I'm not going to look. I'm not going to see it. It wants *me to see it.*

She was painfully sure of this. It was knowledge that could leave a scar. That she could tell a doctor about, only to be told it wasn't real, that she was only imagining it, until it metastasized into something they would catch and diagnose too late. She wasn't going to ignore it.

She barely remembered to grab the handle of the suitcase—which she'd released after the first flames went out—then started walking backward, her eyes half closed. She was ready to snap her lids shut at the first hint of something that shouldn't be there. But it was a sensation, not a sight, that came first. A piercing coldness struck her, but the sensation that almost froze her in place was the tingling, so strong it felt like her blood was vibrating.

A high came with it, one belonging to a trip you couldn't exit from. The feeling of being dosed with inescapable hyperreality, able to see everything you're capable of, every consequence of any action you could take, almost dropped her to her knees. Not only because it was unpleasant, but because it was not *entirely* unwelcome. Because it was familiar. She hesitated only a second, then kept going, eyes fully closed now, until she passed through it all, feeling like the saint of sunlight had pulled her through a blizzard.

Reflexively, she opened her eyes.

The door to the Inspiration Suite was open.

A figure stood silhouetted by the light blazing through the large, uncovered windows behind them.

"We know he sent you," the figure said. A woman's voice? A single voice or two? Shyla couldn't quite be sure.

"We know he sent you," they said again, and Shyla felt almost compelled to confess that, yes, they were right, Braith had sent her, Braith had paid her, and she had agreed to do this because she was concerned that he might know something about her that no one should know.

To her right was the door to the stairwell. Foregoing the elevator, she picked up the suitcase, clutching it partly like a shield and partly like a makeshift life preserver, and escaped into the stairway. She switched to carrying the case on her shoulder to make it easier to take two or three stairs at a time on the way down. She didn't feel out of breath until she made it to the bottom floor, opened the lobby door, and took a seat on the first chair she saw. This allowed tension, more than exhaustion, to catch up and suck a little air from her lungs, leaving her panting for a moment.

"There she is," she heard someone say.

Not now, damn it, just give me a moment. Give me ten seconds to get a story straight before you come over here asking who I am and what I'm doing–

"Babe, over here!" It wasn't the front desk clerk talking to her. This voice was familiar. She hadn't recognized it at first, the fog of fear and fatigue in her head had distorted it. Now that she knew who it was, she had an interrogation of her own brewing.

She looked over and saw a familiar face standing at the front desk. Jinh, smiling her tight-lipped smile, offset in visible enthusiasm by raised eyebrows that looked like they wanted to invade her hairline. She waved at Shyla and said, "Did you go up looking for me? I told you I was running a little late. I'm just getting us checked in," she said.

What the hell are you doing here? Shyla thought. *Did you follow me? Did you set this up somehow? Do you know what happened upstairs?*

She was nowhere near asking any of these questions aloud. Who would she be kidding? Like she'd ever been happier to see Jinh in her life.

6

I told you not to come here alone."

"No, you just asked if I was," Shyla said.

Jinh rolled her eyes. "Stop. The warning was implied."

"Yeah, well, you didn't say why, or what would happen," Shyla said. "Or how about, 'Wait for me'? Yeah, you probably couldn't say that one because then it might give away that you were closer than you wanted me to know."

"Give it away more than me actually showing up? Sure," Jinh retorted. Her use of sarcasm was a sign that she was genuinely upset, which concerned Shyla, since Jinh wouldn't be so aggravated with her unless she felt Shyla had really put herself in danger.

Shyla sat at the foot of the bed in the first-floor room Jinh had reserved online. She felt like Jinh should have been holding an ice pack to her forehead while another person removed boxing gloves and tape from her hands. Instead, Jinh stood across from her, leaning back against the dresser, arms folded across her chest.

"You going to tell me how you knew I'd be here?"

Jinh shook her head. "How I usually know things, Shyla. You still need convincing?"

"I guess not. Not really."

"You 'guess'? What else do I need to—"

"I *just said* 'not really,'" Shyla snapped. "And if you know what my last two days have been like, maybe give me a fucking break right now, huh? It hasn't *even* been two days. It hasn't been twenty-four hours."

Jinh unfolded her arms and came over to sit beside Shyla, which was enough of a mea culpa for the latter to let her aggravation go. Mostly.

"Do you know how annoying you can be sometimes?" Shyla said.

"Weirdly, I don't get visions of that. One of my blind spots. What happened?"

"I ran into something . . . I don't know. Something weird up on the fourth floor."

"Explain 'weird,'" Jinh said.

"Voices, and . . ." Shyla drew a deep breath. She was being silly, clinging to denial like there was any refuge in it, and being coy as though Jinh, of all people, might ridicule her. "I heard voices and things happening right in front of me in the hallway, but nobody was there. The lights went out. The candles, I mean. There was this person, I think, inside the suite. I went up there to see how much it would take to buy them out of the rest of their stay so I could get to the books and whatever else is in there. Whoever was in there, they said . . . they said they knew 'he' sent me. They said some other things, too, but I couldn't understand any of it. But I think whatever it was might have called up the . . . whatever was there in the hallway with me."

Jinh rubbed Shyla's back, a simple, always effective calming gesture that threatened to put Shyla to sleep.

"That's all?" Jinh said, relief lifting her tone.

"Nothing impresses you."

"That's not what I meant. I meant did you go anywhere else?"

Shyla shook her head. "Was there somewhere else you thought I'd go?"

Jinh hesitated before answering. "I'll only tell you if you promise not to go off by yourself. You're stuck with me now."

"Uh-huh. So, how long have you been in town?"

Jinh rubbed her own arms as if the thin sweater she had on was only for show. "I just got in this morning. I was already in Houston. I was there last night. After I talked to Braith about you and thought you'd take the job, something came to me, showing me the water and a city by the coast in Texas, so I flew in. I figured we'd end up there. But then I spoke to you last night and saw you in here, clear as anything I've ever seen. Most of the time there's more of a blur, or a haze, flashes of things that are true and a lot of things that aren't. But this was . . . *present*. Shook me out of my sleep. I booked the earliest flight I could hoping to beat you here."

"You must've seen something pretty bad," Shyla said.

Jinh nodded. "But I'm here, so it can't happen that way anymore, so don't ask me to tell you what it was."

"I don't want any details. It sounds like you were worried about something worse than what was upstairs."

Again, Jinh nodded. "Downstairs."

"The club?"

"Under that," Jinh said. "The sub-basement."

The hotel's website, and Shyla's limited research into the building's history, hadn't mentioned anything about a "sub-basement."

The old nightclub had been underground in a literal sense, as were many places in or near downtown San Antonio. A different, nearby jazz club that Shyla was fond of was located below street level, and she sometimes dreamt of opening her own place with more of a blues influence, a chill juke joint she'd call "The 414," after the number of the hotel room where legendary guitarist Robert Johnson made his first recordings. The Inspiration Sweet's nightclub, with its house band, was the kind of place she sometimes daydreamed of hanging out in. Of wishing she could time travel back to, its music and atmosphere making the dangerously regressive attitudes of the era endurable, because here was an oasis. Music, dancing, drinking, and maybe a little smoking equalized them all, onstage, on the floor, at the tables, at the bar.

But under it all there was another space. Something else. Something Shyla ought to be afraid of.

"What did you see down there?" Shyla asked.

After a moment, and heartened by a deep breath, Jinh said, "I saw blood pooling near my feet. I couldn't make myself look up to see what was happening. I heard people screaming. Awful, *awful* screaming. And crying. And laughing. Just hopeless, horrible noises. And I heard you in the middle of it all. I could pick your voice out through anything."

Shyla's mouth hung open, waiting for the right question to fill it. "Well, did you hear me screaming or crying? Or laughing?"

"It doesn't matter now," Jinh said.

"Come on."

"You know, I told you something once without realizing that you didn't want to know. And then you left me, and never told me—*still* haven't told me—exactly what I did wrong. If I can help it, I'll never make that mistake again."

Shyla stood and suppressed an outburst. *After everything I just told you, this whole situation that you damn near set me up for, you're still bringing up old shit? You're still hung up on back then like it's supposed to matter more than right now?*

She kept this to herself, not because she didn't want to run Jinh off (she would have to say something considerably harsher to do that), but because she wanted Jinh clearheaded and ready for whatever was next. It wouldn't do Shyla any good to deny that she needed Jinh. And it was past time she acknowledged what Jinh was. What she could do.

After taking a moment to compose herself, she came to the answer she sought, anyway. "You heard me laughing."

Jinh ran her hand over her dark hair like she was smoothing out wrinkles from forehead to crown. She did this when she was nervous, or sometimes when she was tired and fighting to stay awake. When she did this while at the wheel on a long road trip or during a late night, Shyla knew it meant she needed to take over. When Jinh did it during conversations, Shyla knew a lie or a dodge was coming, and the only thing that annoyed her was that, by now, Jinh should be aware of her tells. Shyla had told her about it more than once when they were together—hell, she'd spotted it and made mention of it during their first meeting, after Jinh invited her to guest on her podcast—but Jinh would try to slip the lie past her, anyway.

"That wasn't it," Jinh said, shaking her head as she finished, almost like an afterthought.

"If I was screaming or crying, I'd either be hurt or in trouble, and you'd tell me about that. That only leaves the other one. But you wouldn't want to tell me about that because you don't know what it means."

Jinh started to reach for her head again, then stopped herself midway. Not having another objection chambered, she just stared ahead and shrugged.

"Okay then," Shyla said. "Let's figure it out."

"The bar doesn't open until four. I checked before I came. We've got time to kill, unless you want to try to sneak in."

"Not worth the risk of getting caught and kicked out."

"Yeah," Jinh agreed. "We could go back upstairs. Try that again. Except you wouldn't be alone this time. Maybe with me there—"

"No, fuck that." The idea of being stuck in that hallway, pinned in on either side by people she couldn't see, made her queasy. As she thought back on it, the part that should have been the worst of it wasn't. What she'd heard from the ones who came out of the elevator, what she'd felt as she passed through them, had chilled her, literally and figuratively, but it was the voice behind the door that would have made her quit if she could convince herself that this horror hadn't already grafted itself to her life.

We know he sent you.

This altered the landscape like an artillery barrage. She wasn't just looking into something strange, uncovering a deep, uncanny mystery. She was up *against* something, or someone, wasn't she? Someone who was at least a step ahead of her, and not only wanted to have it that way, but wanted her to know it.

"You know, whatever's in the sublevel could be worse than what's upstairs," Jinh said.

"Right, blood at your feet and all that. Any chance you were wrong about that? Don't the signals get crossed sometimes?"

"Happens all the time, which makes it stand out that much more when it's a clear vision."

"Damn." Shyla thought on it for a moment longer than necessary, already knowing she was going to find any excuse she could to not go back up to the fourth floor. Not today, and hopefully no time soon. "Well, if I'm going to have to go through shit like this, I should be looking for something new whenever I can. Not going back to where I've already been. I might have only so many of these in me before I snap, or drop from a heart attack. No sense revisiting somewhere unless we're sure it'll do some good."

The exaggerated eagerness in Jinh's nod told Shyla that Jinh didn't agree but wanted to comfort her. Shyla was fine with it.

"So then what do we do?" Jinh said.

"You hungry?"

"I could eat something."

"Me, too," Shyla said, though she actually didn't have much of an appetite. She just knew it had been a while since she'd eaten and was looking for any excuse to leave the hotel. "Let's get out of here and figure it out from there."

They found a Thai restaurant around the corner that served the entrées faster than Shyla would have preferred, so they were only able to kill a little over half an hour there before giving up their seats to lunch-rush patrons waiting for a table.

From there they caught a rideshare to the city's Central Library, each taking a computer and searching for more information about the hotel, the club, the band, anything that might be related to Garrett Schramm, and by extension Saxton Braith. Shyla found nothing new worth looking into. Jinh clipped a couple of filler articles from the summer of 1951 about missing persons that she said gave her a "tingling sensation," and Shyla had to suppress an urge to joke about Jinh having disturbing kinks.

Jinh also found a lengthy editorial written in 1948 by a Reverend Germain Carol of the Calvary's Castle Revivalist Church, lamenting the city's "tolerance of wantonness, worldliness, and wickedness," and suggesting it was another sign that end-times were near. He reserved particular ire for a place that dared use the word "Inspiration" in its name, a word that belonged to God, the reverend declared. "More than once I have stood before the doors of this particular den of sin, clad in the armor of the Lord, singing mightily in His honor until the Lord demanded I rest and save some of my voice for the next day's work." Shyla thought the article was worth summarizing, linking to, and highlighting in the Notes app on her phone. Nothing came from a further search of the reverend's name. A search for "Calvary's Castle" limited to the same time frame as Carol's article, however, turned up a brief article that stated the church had voted out an unnamed leader a year after Carol's diatribe. Per that article, the remaining church leaders had described this unnamed pariah as a "false shepherd," and "wanton, wayward lech."

"Getting anything from that?" Shyla asked Jinh.

"You know I hate when people put it that way. I'm not turning dials or flipping channels in my head to get a connection."

"Well, how else should I say it?"

Jinh shook her head, shrugged more out of mild aggravation than actual concession.

"Do you think they're talking about him?" Shyla asked.

"Maybe," Jinh said. "I don't feel anything from it, but, you know, it's hit-or-miss."

Shyla found herself respecting this explanation of Jinh's inexplicable insights more now. She used to see it as a cop-out, a psychic's way of hedging against inaccurate predictions. Jinh always spoke of her limitations sheepishly, however, almost as though it was a source of shame. Like she blamed herself for not being better. Not having mastered this skill she didn't know how to develop and had no way of practicing.

They printed the articles about the missing persons and the two related to the reverend, and Shyla sent digital copies to her email. They returned to Shyla's car in the parking garage across the street from the Inspiration Sweet. Shyla said she wanted to grab something out of her trunk, but when they got there admitted that she was exhausted and wanted to grab a nap in the car before the hotel bar opened. The thought of falling asleep inside the hotel made her nervous.

Jinh didn't object, though she looked like she wanted to say something, ask something, probably apologize again for getting Shyla involved, or at least try to explain her reasoning and motivation. Instead, she accepted the driver's side so Shyla could have a little more legroom in the passenger seat, which she pushed all the way back and fully reclined in before shutting her eyes. Even without seeing her, Shyla could picture Jinh pretending to reread the materials they had left the library with, while actually keeping watch.

As if to be sure Shyla wouldn't be possessed in her sleep and wake up as something else.

7

The bar was dimly lit, and the tea candles on every table and at each end of the bar had to carry more of the workload than they should have had to. All of it was half eaten by the dark red and coffin brown decorative scheme, intermittently broken up by bronze inlays.

It looked empty, save for the bartender, who wore a white button-up shirt with sleeves rolled above his elbow to reveal his tattoos. Red suspenders and tan pants completed the ensemble, although his moustache, curled at the ends, looked like it could have come with the outfit. Shyla was almost disappointed that he wasn't wiping out the inside of a tumbler as they entered.

He gave her a smile as she approached and took a stool, but his expression changed when he looked to Shyla's left. She followed his eyes and saw that Jinh had stopped, frozen, several steps back, staring past Shyla and the bartender. Shyla couldn't bring herself to turn toward whatever transfixed Jinh, so she turned back to the bartender, whose expression she now read as a blend of concern, pity, and a pinch of irritation.

He spoke up before Shyla could think to ask him or Jinh what was wrong. "You're sensitive," he said to Jinh.

Jinh nodded like she'd been ordered to answer under hypnosis. Then turned to the bartender and said, "What? What do you mean?"

He glanced between Jinh and Shyla before telling the latter, "Listen, don't take this the wrong way, but maybe you ought to get her out of here."

"Maybe you should tell us what you mean by that," Shyla said, "before we do take it some kind of way."

"I'm just trying to help. I've seen people down here with that look a few times before."

Jinh's nostrils flared briefly before she marched to the bar, took the stool beside Shyla, and said, "Can I get a bourbon, please? Whatever you'd recommend. Double."

The bartender turned to Shyla for her order. "Water for me." She retrieved the envelope in her jacket's inner pocket, took two of the loosened bills out and placed them on the bar, pinning them down with her fingertips like they might escape. "What'd you mean when you said my friend was sensitive, and that we should leave?"

He leaned toward the bills, visually inspecting them, then reached for them. Shyla slid them to her right, out of reach. He raised his hands, a show of innocence and silent apology. "I just wanted to check. Those could be fake."

"And you could be about to lie."

He sighed, took a bottle, a glass, and a tumbler from under the bar, and started talking as he poured. "I just don't want anything bad to happen to anyone, okay? I'm going on my third year working here, and I've only seen that look on someone's face three other times while I was working down here. One of them, this guy basically had a seizure. The other tried to tough it out, fainted on her stool. The last one got the look and immediately turned around and left. The one thing in common was what I caught each one of them looking at."

Listening to him lowered Shyla's guard enough that she looked without thinking to where he pointed. She saw what had temporarily petrified Jinh. A door. Flush with the paneled wall, its black handle almost invisible. Its most ominous feature was how evident the attempt to conceal it was. Shyla wondered if she might have spotted it sooner, were she not distracted by the curtained-off corner. She guessed she thought that only because the door looked so conspicuous to her now.

"What's back there?" Jinh said.

The bartender shrugged.

Shyla asked, "You really don't know?"

"Well, I know what *I* see down there," the bartender said. "Boxes, bottles, extra glasses, cleaning supplies, a couple of stools and chairs we had to retire stacked to the side. Just stuff we have in storage. But what you really mean is 'What's wrong with the place?' I don't know. I'm just glad I'm not the 'sensitive' type.

"You know, before I took this job I didn't believe in any of that. The people who'd been here longer than me told me I'd be really lucky or clueless to stay that way. Learning how to be hospitable and lean into the lore of the place with all the ghost hunters, the hobbyists, and supposed psychics who come through was part of my training. But they also gave me the heads-up that probably, once in a while, I'd see somebody have a strong reaction to that door. I was like, 'Okay, sure,' and waited for them to prank the new guy, lock me in the storage level, make some noises, flicker some lights or something. Instead, about four months into working here, I saw a man get this terrible look on his face and kind of drift toward the door before he tensed up. But the way he seized, it was like all of his muscles locked up specifically to force him not to take another step. And the fear was, like, bursting out of his eyes. When I started bartending I worked some bad spots on the west side, near where I grew up, and I saw some brutal fights, people getting stabbed, people pulling guns. I saw a guy almost bleed out once, had to hold a towel to his neck to help him, and I saw on his face that he understood what was happening. And even that didn't measure up. The guy I saw here, his eyes were trembling in their sockets like they wanted to run away. His jaw was so tight I heard a couple of his teeth crack, and that was before he really started shaking. You looked like you were pretty close to that for a second," he said to Jinh.

Jinh took a drink, started to set her tumbler down, then raised it for another swig. Shyla eased the two bills toward the bartender, then tapped the stacks hidden inside the envelope.

"Give you more if you let us get down there," Shyla said.

The bartender shook his head, scoffed. "No fucking way."

"I'll be fine," Jinh said. "The people you're talking about sound like they were having their first ever experience down here. They wouldn't know how to cope. I had my first when I was sixteen, and a lot more since. I'm prepared. I can take it."

"Yeah, I don't know anything about all that," the bartender said. "All I know is I've seen people so scared it hurt them, and it shook me up to see them that way. But apart from that, we don't even let the people who officially book the place go to the storage level. Even if I didn't care about what I think could happen to you, I'd care about staying employed."

Shyla nodded. "I can respect that." Then she pulled the three remaining stacks from the envelope. "Excuse me if this is a little bold, but I'm guessing we won't have much more time to talk about this privately."

The bartender shook his head. "Doesn't matter however much that is—"

"Fifteen thousand," she said. *What you make in two months, at least,* she wanted to add, but didn't. *And that's if you're doing exceptionally well here. Don't try to tell me otherwise, you're not the first bartender I've had to bribe in this city. Not the second or third, either.* What she said instead was, "Kind of doesn't look like it, right? A hundred-fifty sheets of paper. Like a notebook."

"I . . . I don't . . . I still shouldn't—"

"What if we call this half, and I can get you another fifteen?"

"Seriously? You're not lying to me?"

"If I was, I'd tell you."

It took him a second to get the quip, another to remember to smile, out of politeness if nothing else. "It would, um . . . it'd have to be later. I close tonight. I could probably let you in after hours."

"Day or night isn't going to matter," Jinh said.

The bartender jumped in to add, "You won't be able to stay long, though. I can keep it clear here for thirty to forty-five minutes, probably, but that's it."

"That should be good enough, right?" Shyla said to Jinh.

"It better be," Jinh said. "I hope it won't take half that."

Shyla gave the bartender a smirk she hoped was equal parts reassuring and assertive. "All right. Thirty minutes for thirty thousand. When else are you going to make a grand a minute for doing damn near nothing?"

He looked away, like he'd find a good reason to decline, or maybe just a deeper set of principles that fell out of his pocket.

"You two came here exactly for this, huh?"

"Just need to know a little bit more about the place," Shyla said.

"And if you don't find what you're looking for? Are you going to cheat me?"

"We're paying for access, not intel. You'll get yours either way. See you tonight."

After just enough hesitation to make Shyla think for the first time that he might actually reconsider and turn down the offer, he said, "Okay. Come back around two. I'll get you in, but once y'all are down there, you're on your own. If anything happens, I swear I'm going to say you snuck in, or broke in or something. I'm not—"

"Relax, nothing's going to happen." As soon as she said this, in her periphery, Shyla caught Jinh flinch. Somehow, she found it silly to be psychic but still superstitious, almost like a doctor trusting a faith healer. Then she was reminded of medical professionals she knew or had spoken to, paramedics and emergency room personnel whose experiences had taught them to be wary of full moons and avoid saying, "It's been quiet today."

With that in mind, Shyla thought it would be prudent to be more mindful of her words and defer to Jinh's ability. If nothing else, she needed Jinh to feel as confident as possible about returning tonight to find out what was behind the door, because Shyla had just spent almost all the false bravado she had in reserve.

After going to the bank to get the other half of the promised money, they came back to the hotel room, where they reread and traded thoughts on what they had researched in the library. They focused on Reverend Carol and his defunct church. Shyla pulled up old maps of the city on her computer and found the former location of Calvary's Castle, which was now a strip mall. With nothing to do but wait, they drove there to see if Jinh would be able to sense anything at the site. Nothing came to her, so they ate at a nearby restaurant, then drove to Shyla's house so Jinh could rest. Unable to even pretend to sleep, Shyla had found herself back at her desk again, her vision burning under the glow of her laptop as she searched for another clue, another path to Garrett Schramm's history, and Saxton Braith's by extension. Any reason not to return to the hotel.

As midnight approached, she felt and fought an urge to call Braith and tell him she had changed her mind. He still probably had another business day at least to cancel the wire transfer of her first payment.

It would be worth it to test his response, wouldn't it? If it was, it would be the easiest way out of this. No more immortal billionaire, no more psychic ex-girlfriend, no more haunted hotel. No chance to discover more troubling things. Not if Braith let her out.

What's in it for him? she thought. He needed her for something. Scouted her, invested in her, and implied he might somehow know enough to blackmail her. He had nothing to gain by letting her walk. She would be asking a favor of a man who had incentive not to grant it. And she'd be revealing a weakness, a fear that might be too valuable to him not to use against her. Best-case scenario, he might think she was shaking him down for even more money. Indirectly demanding hazard pay. At worst, he'd lose some faith in her, while gaining an equal or greater amount of power *over* her.

Instead of calling him she kept doing what she had been doing, looking online for anything that might be of interest related to the only lead she had regarding Braith's past. Garrett Schramm and the plane crash. She searched for anything related to pilots and aircraft near San Antonio in between Schramm's birth year, 1918, and the date of the crash in '58. She had just stumbled onto an article about suspicions of planes transporting contraband when Jinh's alarm went off, informing them both that it was time to go to the bar and discover what was underneath it.

8

Day or night isn't going to matter.

Shyla knew it would be unwise to bring Jinh's words back up to her, but she couldn't help dwelling on them now that the time had arrived. As a practical matter, Jinh had to be correct. It was no darker inside the basement bar of the Inspiration Sweet Hotel at two in the morning than it was at two in the afternoon.

Nonetheless, night pervaded. Shyla felt it. The truth of it. They were on a side of the world that the sun couldn't reach, and even when that shouldn't matter, it did. Things that existed solely to be hostile to human life thrived in the night. It was easier to take daylight for granted, say it wouldn't be of any use, when it was just an exit away, as opposed to several hours.

The only thing that kept her from delaying this until morning was the probability that this was their best opportunity to get into the sublevel.

To settle her nerves, Shyla focused on something else Jinh had said. That thirty minutes ought to be enough. Well, "better be" is what she'd actually said, and then that she hoped it wouldn't even take half that time. A quarter hour or less. That's all it would take. Shyla could hope for that, too, and maybe if they both focused on that hard enough, it would have some kind of effect.

The bar was as empty as it had been when they had come earlier, but felt oddly larger, and that much more vacant because of it. Every pop or creak from the building settling, or series of thumps from someone moving around upstairs, made Shyla listen for an echo she was sure ought to follow, but never did.

The door to the "storage level," as the bartender insisted on calling it, was open to them. A lit white bulb with a pull cord hung just inside, lessening the safety hazard presented by the steep wooden stairs.

"I'll, uh . . . I'll have to close it behind you, in case somebody comes down here," the bartender said. "In case y'all make any noise, or just so they don't ask why–"

"I get it," Shyla said without looking his way. She stared down the doorway like it was looking back and challenging her. She wanted to feel something. Tried to feel it. When she peeked at Jinh and saw how ashen she was, it made her feel unprepared. Inadequate to the task. Things had to be made obvious for Shyla to be aware of them. She wasn't like Jinh, who could see things before they happened, in her sleep from two states away. Who could feel the presence of something from the floor above. This left Shyla at a disadvantage, didn't it? Jinh, too, since Shyla was her backup.

There has to be a different way, she thought, and was about to say this when Jinh took her hand and led her toward the door. Her grip tightened enough to be painful when the first step croaked underfoot, became stronger still when they heard the door ease shut behind them when they were halfway down. A blank brick wall faced them, along with a soft splash of light from the opening at the bottom of the stairs, to the left. A decent hiding space for anyone lurking.

With four steps left, Jinh shivered so hard Shyla thought she'd lose her balance and fall, and that they'd have to turn around before they even properly entered the sublevel, but Jinh remained on her feet and quickly descended the rest of the way. She turned the corner ahead of Shyla and was out of sight just long enough to make Shyla feel desperately alone. If given another second, she'd have shouted for Jinh to come back and not leave her sight again, but she followed quickly and caught up to her three steps into the larger-than-expected storage space.

Assorted boxes and crates branded with the alcohol they contained were stacked halfway up the far wall. Shelves lined the wall to the left, while old stools, a few faded paintings, a bent metal structure of a martini glass, and Christmas decorations lined the wall to the right. Something that felt out of place, embedded in the right wall, stole Shyla's attention. An old brass spigot.

The sound of metal tapping concrete brought her back to Jinh, who had stepped on something Shyla had overlooked. A metal grate in the floor. No, not a grate. What Jinh stood over and stared down at was a drain.

Used to be a laundry room or something, Shyla thought, because that's what she wanted to think even as another side of her brain was dredging up images from a documentary about slaughterhouses she'd watched a few months ago.

What was it called? It was named after a specific place in the butchering plant. What was it?

Stop. Don't think of that.

She wasn't "sensitive" in the way that Jinh was. Whatever she'd experienced on the fourth floor must have been deliberately conjured, brought to her by the people behind the door of the suite.

Lacking Jinh's sight, Shyla had to trust her instincts, which were not flawless, proven by the fact that she found herself involved in Braith's business, but still sharp, honed by the niggling sense of wrongness she'd lived with since childhood. Right now, she instinctually understood that this space housed grim history. Things had happened here that the current proprietors wouldn't want known to anyone, including themselves.

Underneath the old nightclub that was already underground, there was a room, private and possibly secret, that even decades later made certain unfortunate individuals sick with terror. A room with a spigot for a hose, and a drain in the center of the floor.

There's a name for a place like this. What is it? What's it called?

"The killing floor," Jinh said. She was statuesque, her spine straight as a beam of light. Her voice reverberated off the walls, and it was impossible for Shyla not to think of her as possessed. She reflexively took a step backward before reminding herself that this was Jinh. Yes, she had plucked a thought right out of Shyla's mind to answer a question Shyla hadn't voiced, but that didn't at all change who she was. Didn't make her any more or less frightening than she'd always been. Shyla wasn't going to abandon Jinh here, of course, even though her body had reacted as though escape—from this room and from Jinh—was the priority.

"What do you see?" Jinh said, and it took a moment for Shyla to realize she was speaking to her.

"Um . . . boxes. You're standing over a drain. There are some stools against the—"

"You don't see them? Any of them? Not even their shadows?"

"Jinh, I can't see anything that isn't in the here and now with us."

"They *are* here," Jinh said, squeezing the words out as though they were fighting to stay in her throat.

"What are *you* seeing?" Shyla said, coming closer to Jinh. What would be the sign, she wondered, that things were going too far? How would she know when it was time to pick Jinh up and carry her over her shoulder like a firefighter, if needed, to get them both up the stairs and out of here?

"They're standing around us," Jinh said. "Standing back, just watching. They're not . . . They don't have anything. I don't see anything in their hands, but they could stop us from leaving if they wanted to. But they're just waiting . . . they're waiting for him to . . . no. *No. Don't make him—*"

"Who are you talking about?" Shyla barked. "Come on, Jinh, don't get lost in this. I can't see what you're seeing. You have to tell me."

"*Don't make him do this. I won't let you.*"

"Jinh!"

"*Stop!* Don't say another word." Jinh whipped her head around. There was a startling frenzy in her eyes, a look of hate fused with fear. She raised her hand, pointed, revealing she was not addressing Shyla, but something behind her. Something near the foot of the stairs. When she spoke again her voice was low, sincere, and sodden with worry. "Don't you say anything else about her."

"Jinh, talk to me. What's going on?"

"Stop laughing."

"What the fuck, Jinh, *what's behind me?*"

"Garrett Schramm," she said, speaking urgently as though she only had a few seconds before communication would be cut off. "He's here. He says he saw you upstairs."

"He can see us? He's talking *to* you?"

"He says that if you could see what I could . . . Oh God. He's lying. He has to be lying." Jinh put her hands over her ears, folded her legs beneath her, and sat on her heels.

"Goddammit, Jinh, what is happening?"

"Shyla, *move.*"

"What?"

"Move, *now*!"

Before she could, the strange sensation that overcame her on the fourth floor was upon her again. It was more intense now, and she could no longer feel the floor. A hideous high that came from witnessing something awful, but knowing you were somehow safe. Sickened, but safe and somehow powerful. Like floating above a crashing flood, watching people pummeled by tide, by parts of houses and trees, by other bodies tossed around by the waves.

It was difficult to reconcile feeling genuinely guilty, blessed, fortunate, and victimized. Shyla had struggled to find a healthy balance among these sentiments ever since she'd discovered the truth about her parents. The spirit inhabiting her found this conflict within her and accessed her deeper secret. Something she hid from everyone. The secret she thought Braith might know.

How could he know, though?

Because he felt it in your soul, same as I do. Garrett's voice in her head. It matched the narrow eyes and wicked smile she couldn't see but had sensed in his photo.

You shouldn't feel shame for surviving, girly. Or for killing. You took control. Tell me it didn't feel good.

"Get out," she said through gritted teeth, wanting to scream it but having no strength to.

She heard Jinh's voice from too far away to understand what she was saying, and realized then that she could not see. A field of red covered her vision, so thick she felt it plugging her ears. She was thankful for this when the crying started, followed by screaming. She thought she saw a face, mouth agape, trying to push through the red. She saw something else trying to come through. An object that looked almost rectangular before enough of it bled away to reveal a handle and barrel.

Shyla reached for it without thinking. It could help now, couldn't it? It had before, when she'd needed it.

Needed? Schramm's snickering felt like burrs prickling the grooves of her brain. *You're going to make me point to that mirror, ain't you?*

I had to. I thought I needed *to do it.*

You wanted *to. No shame in that. I'm not judging. I admire it. Reminds me of me. You would have fit in well with the rest of us.*

I'm not like you.

Well, you can't say that without knowing what I'm really like, can you? I, on the other hand, can feel what you are, through and through.

"Shut up," she said, and heard Jinh speaking indiscernibly again, her voice barely reaching Shyla through the growing cries and screams. Shyla grabbed the red gun she was reaching for, and it nestled into her palm like it was reaching back for her. It felt good against her skin. She felt so charged, so empowered, that the numbing tingle turned almost ticklish, and she did something unexpected.

She giggled.

The recognition of how absurd it was to do this prolonged her snickering, and when the gun unexpectedly pulled her forward it also pulled a heartier laugh out of her.

A frightened shout that she was mostly sure came from Jinh penetrated the red and her own laughter, which was paired like a duet with Schramm's laughter. It briefly silenced Shyla as she let the gun guide her.

You know it felt good. You did it. And liked it. Schramm, coaxing her, challenging her. Schramm had found a connection between them and thought he could manipulate her with it. She felt the thin shell of his confidence, tapped on it, and heard it crack.

It felt necessary, not good, she said. *We are not the same.*

You're a liar, he told her. *I know your type. You'd have been one of us had you been around then. Either that or we'd have used you up just like—*

Shyla could not help but laugh.

Just like those saps you hear crying and carrying on right now, Schramm said, becoming more pathetic to Shyla the louder he got. *You're either just like them, or just like me. That's all there is in the world.*

The more Shyla realized how wrong he was, how idiotic, the harder she laughed. It amused her in a way she couldn't explain. She should have been more frightened than she was, but this *did* feel good. Killing hadn't pleased her, but breaking the soul of a man like Schramm by making him feel like a joke was close to exhilarating. It was so much *better* than killing. Someone could only die once, after all, but the weakness and shame he was suffering now could go on endlessly.

The temptation to stay here, trapped within this high, punishing Schramm with her laughter forever, became frighteningly real. Shyla tightened her hold on the gun that guided her, trying to focus on Jinh's voice.

There was nothing more pathetic than the desperate efforts of an evil man. Why would Schramm try so hard to convince her they were the same if not because he needed something from her? Even as he lived beyond death in the eternal replay of what he had done on the killing floor, he needed to know he was not alone. His spirit remained here, reliving the grisly events that had defined his existence, but whatever sadistic gratification he sought from it was not enough.

He needed to *share* this with someone. To feel a dark connection, even to someone born decades later into a very different world, with a different set of values. Connected in taking a life.

I'm nothing like you, she told him. *You're like the man I had to kill. Just a coward.*

"Who are you talking to?" Jinh said.

The red murk fled Shyla's vision so abruptly she flinched at the reality that supplanted it. The gun was gone as well, replaced by Jinh's hand.

"Where . . . ?" Shyla started to ask, but she glanced at her surroundings and quickly pieced together the answer. They were in an alley beside the hotel, at the top of a stone stairway wet by a light rain continuing to fall. The bartender stood at the bottom of the steps, by the open door to the back exit Shyla had spotted earlier near the curtain-concealed booth. Jinh had broken from whatever spell had gripped her in the sublevel to hustle Shyla up those stairs, then out through the back to where they were now.

The bartender locked eyes with her for a moment, his face confessing to many things.

He saw or heard something that made him more of a believer than he'd been before.

He didn't want to subject himself to it again.

He never wanted to see Shyla or Jinh again.

He didn't want to be anywhere near this place again.

After a final glance back inside that made him wince and turn his head immediately, he rushed up the stairs, past Jinh and Shyla, and down the street, toward anywhere that wasn't the Inspiration Sweet Hotel.

"We should probably leave," Shyla said. When she tried to stand, Jinh tightened her grip on her hand.

"Who were you talking to?" Jinh said.

Shyla remembered that this question was what had brought her out of whatever state she'd been in while infested by Schramm's presence, and back to reality, although escaping the killing floor and the building itself had probably contributed to this, as well.

"I was talking to him. Garrett Schramm. He was in my head. Was I talking out loud?"

"Yes."

"The whole time?"

"Yes."

"Shit." She tried to recall what exactly she might have said, if any of it might have been incriminating. If so, she needed to get on her feet and chase that bartender down, get his name, which she'd deliberately avoided asking to this point, to keep him at a distance. Then get his agreement, at gunpoint if necessary, to keep his mouth shut about whatever he'd heard. If she'd let the worst of her past slip, he'd be apt to believe the gun wasn't for show.

"Why did you say you weren't like him?" Jinh said. "What were you talking about? There was something you said you needed to do. Was it something you've already done? What was it?"

"Let's get out of the rain," Shyla said, a little too loud. She squeezed Jinh's hand back, the pressure making Jinh release her like pushing in on a finger trap.

She stood, less alarmed than she'd been just seconds ago. If Jinh still had questions about what Shyla had said to the spirit of Garrett Schramm, the bartender had the same ones, and he wasn't going to come back around to ask. He was probably going to try to forget her, everything he heard, everything about this night.

Shyla walked toward the parking garage across the street, not bothering to turn back when Jinh said, "Shyla, I need to know what you did."

She was halfway across the street before she heard Jinh following, her shoes splashing shallow puddles. Shyla picked up her pace and made it through the entrance of the garage before Jinh ran just ahead and faced her. "I need you to talk to me, damn it."

"Why? It's got nothing to do with you."

"I just . . . I need to know. If you want me to keep helping you, I need to know some things. I think maybe he was able to get to you because of whatever you've done. I can't really think of any other reason right now. And I can try to help protect you from that happening again, but not without knowing what I need to know."

From her quavering voice to her shaking hands, to the way her eyes looked like they wanted to spin back in their sockets to darken her world, it was clear that Jinh wasn't entirely over her part of the ordeal. Shyla was thankful that she had summoned enough courage and control to get them both out of that awful place. But none of that entitled Jinh to know about things Shyla never planned to volunteer. Not to anyone. And she resented—or quickly manufactured resentment about—what she took as an attempt to get her to talk while she was still pulling her mind back together after what Schramm did to her. If not for the hardening effect of past experiences, she would be telling Jinh everything, like she was a divine savior she was praying to for deliverance. But that was not who she was. She was Shyla Sinclair. She'd done difficult, necessary things before. She could do them again. What she had to say next, for example.

"I never asked for your help. I'm glad for it, I've thanked you for it, but don't act like I owe you, or asked for it, or like you don't know damn well I can save myself."

"That's not what I said. I'm not saying you ever *needed* me, but this is different."

"You're the one who came to me. From day one. You heard about my story and came to me. You asked if I wanted to be part of your whole thing and I said yes. *You* asked, not me."

"Shyla—"

"Don't talk to me about if I want you to keep helping me. Like I'd be screwed on my own, without you."

"You'd be dead or something worse if I hadn't got you out of there just now," Jinh said. She had reached for a colder tone, but it melted before she finished the sentence. She cared too much.

Maybe that's the sensitive part of being "sensitive," Shyla thought.

"Fuck you," Jinh said, maybe because she'd read Shyla's mind, or maybe out of general frustration. "I'm sorry. I'm sorry. You know I don't mean that, I just—"

"You're wrong," Shyla said. "You think Schramm could have done something to me? I was already chasing him off on my own. That's why I was laughing. Because I made him understand what makes me different from him, even though he tried to say we're the same. And I felt how weak that made him feel, and I think if I got to spend more time in there, I could *really* make him feel it."

"What does that even mean?"

"I'm telling you, Jinh. He was afraid of me. I felt it." She had, right? She wasn't deluding herself? Misremembering? Coping in the immediate aftermath of trauma? She knew what all of that was like, and this didn't feel completely dissimilar, but different enough. It had to. Or she at least had to believe it did.

Jinh, reduced to pleading, asked, "Why, though? Tell me, please, *why*?"

"Because he's not the kind of killer I am."

9

Shyla and Jinh returned to her house and slept in separate rooms, saying nothing to each other. A little after nine in the morning, Shyla woke from troubled sleep to the rapid tapping of Jinh's fingers on the laptop at her desk.

I never changed our password, she thought, *and, of course, she still remembers it.*

Jinh finished whatever she was typing before she looked back to see Shyla getting out of bed, and said, "I hope you don't mind, but I might have found something."

"About Braith?"

"Schramm."

Shyla shrugged. "If that's what we have, let's keep going with it."

Jinh said she had been up since seven, reviewing something sent to her by contacts she had on the other side of the world. Her podcast, a blend of true crime and supernatural lore, hosted by an honest-to-God psychic investigator with fairly unique legitimacy, had an international fandom, and was even bigger overseas than it was stateside. She'd collaborated with podcasters and vloggers from Japan to Peru, and had a couple of well-connected family members who were happy to help her with research when needed. She had reached out specifically to her eldest cousin, who was a retired detective in Seoul, and to his daughter, who was a journalist. Each assisted in different ways when she needed details about a local haunting, urban legend, or murder that her American upbringing didn't make her privy to. Jinh had messaged them last night while riding silently in the passenger seat. Shyla had noticed the phone in her hand, but presumed she was booking a flight back home to Seattle. Instead, she was taking steps to prove yet again that help not "needed" was still useful.

Recalling Schramm's early discharge from the military, she asked both cousins if it was possible that any American soldiers had ever been suspected of something criminal, something awful, during the period when Korea was caught between wars.

"Beyond possible," her older cousin had written back. "Especially after the uprising in '46. Although probably before that as well. I remember when I was young, just promoted, I helped interrogate an older woman who had killed her husband. She had a world of scars on her arms, some on her neck, and even her face. We asked if her husband had abused her. She denied it, and then told us this strange story.

"She said the scars were from a 'club' she had joined when she was younger and coping with an opium addiction. When she couldn't pay for it anymore, she was brought in to be part of a secret club where night after night she was asked to do dangerous, horrible things. Russian roulette, for instance, except instead of pointing the gun at your own head, you pointed it at the person in front of you. Not usually at their head, she said. The ones in charge didn't mind if you died, but wanted to keep you around for more games as long as they could. So, you targeted a hand, an arm, a foot, a knee. Only on special occasions, with the ones who were close to worn out anyway, did they let you aim for the stomach or heart. But the roulette itself was rare, anyway. Most of the time they were forced to play games that involved fire or branding irons or an electric shock. Sometimes the people running things made them play with knives, with a little bit of salt or green mandarin juice for the wounds. 'Games' built around how much pain you could tolerate, and how much suffering you were willing to inflict on someone else to get what you wanted.

"The 'winners' would receive whatever their drug of choice was. The losers, if they didn't die during the game, might die from withdrawal later. I suppose some of the winners probably OD'd, as well. She said she was there by choice, although it sounded to me like the opium was making the choice for her. Either way, she wasn't so sure about that for everyone else. Some of the others she shared a small apartment with swore they hadn't been addicts before. They were stolen from their homes or off the street. People who wouldn't be missed. A lot of people had close to nothing after what the Japanese did, and lots of others couldn't sympathize because 'close to nothing' was better than what they had. The point I hope I'm making is that it would have been easy to find people to take and keep and dump when they were used up.

"She said a small crowd of men and even a few women gathered to watch them several nights a week, moving around from one empty warehouse or field to another. After the war there were many places that no one but the wicked would be caught dead or alive in. She said some of the men were American, so obviously military, especially based on their haircuts. She thought that was also part of why they could get away with what they were doing. She said there were probably local police and Korean soldiers present, too. Some placed bets on who would be the first of the 'players' to pass out, which one might chicken out, and which one might die. It wasn't the same bettors and watchers every night, but mostly familiar faces over time. And there was one man she especially hated.

"He was an American, and she couldn't describe what he looked like even though she told us she could see him when she closed her eyes. She hated him most because when he would get impatient with them, he would snap his fingers at them with this rhythm, like he was trying to teach them a song. Sometimes he'd clap his hands, but with the back of one hand hitting the palm. He would say, 'Come on, come on, come on,' to them, over and over, to the rhythm he made, like he was singing it, and he would even bop his head like he was ready to dance. 'Come on, come on, come on.' Snap-snap-snap-snap, clap-clap-clap."

As Shyla listened to Jinh recap this, she could imagine Garrett Schramm on the drums for the Inspiration Sweet's house band. Grinning like the devil's favorite demon. His mind in three places at once. There in the moment, and in the past as well, thinking of the things he'd done, and also in the future—the near future—where he'd get to do it again. This pernicious pastime he'd brought home with him. Or maybe that he'd brought from Texas to Korea and then back. This thing he'd lived for. He was a man with talents. He'd learned to fly, learned music, but after he died, did he haunt an airfield? Did he haunt the stage? No. He was down there on the killing floor.

"After we were done talking to the lady," her cousin had continued, "I told my superior that I thought she made it all up. She just wanted us to feel sorry for her, wanted us to think she had an excuse for killing her husband. But the boss told me not to be so sure. He said he'd heard similar stories. Especially about a certain American in Seoul who was one of the ringleaders of this whole business.

He told me to ask some of the vets about it. The stories went that when the American's commanding officers found out, some wanted to ship him back home, but he was so good at his job others wanted him to stay. The only thing they all agreed on was that they couldn't afford to embarrass their country by publicly acknowledging their findings. So, they sent him to Gimpo, hoping a smaller city would make it too difficult for him to get up to the same trouble.

"A few months after he arrives in Gimpo, rumors kick up there. People start going missing. The few that turn up are either dead or close to it, and so high it's hard to get them to say anything that makes sense. The ones that can talk keep going on and on about this frightening white man, a 'dancing man,' who likes to watch others play his favorite game, called 'How Many Cuts?'"

10

Braith called back less than a minute after Shyla left a message with Remy.

"You have something already?" he asked.

"Yeah. Your pilot friend was into some sick shit." She hoped her accusation by association came through clearly.

"Sick like what?"

"Kidnapping. Torture. Maybe worse."

"Worse? That narrows it down to a thing or two."

He sounded too nonchalant, like he was expecting to hear something like this.

"None of that is a surprise to you?" she said.

"Anything you tell me is going to be equally surprising to me. If I don't sound shocked enough for you, it's because I've had to teach myself to stay even keeled when I get new information. Apart from that, I've had to learn that I could be sawed in half like a magician's assistant and just pull myself back together again. I don't have much shock left in me."

"But you hadn't found out any of this on your own when you looked it up?"

She could see his smile through the phone, oddly admiring. "I never truly tried to dig into my history before I found out about you. I didn't know where to start, and I might have been more afraid of finding things out than of never knowing. That's why I hired a trusted professional."

"That's not what you said before, at your place. You told me you'd looked him up," she lied.

A brief hesitation and small huff preceded his reply. "Has that worked on many people?"

"Not one. Not yet," Shyla said. "Listen, at the hotel, there were people there who said they knew you sent me, and they seemed pretty upset about it."

"What? What did they say?"

"They said they knew you sent me."

"Did they threaten you?" Braith asked.

They snuffed out every light in the hallway and trapped me between them and the ghosts they summoned in the elevator. I feel like that counts.

"They made it known they could do some harm," she said.

"Do you need me to send Remy to accompany you?"

"I need you to tell me why anyone would know I was coming, and that you hired me."

"Shyla, I don't even know my birth name. I don't know my past. I remember only one man, who you just told me did terrible things while he was alive. I don't know who else might have known me then, or what they told anyone else. I would have stalkers to spare as it is, just being a rich man in this world. I have no idea who knew you were coming, or how they knew where you'd be."

Pity poor you, "just being a rich man in this world," Shyla thought.

"Behind every fortune is a crime." So went the misquote, which in its entirety, from Balzac's *Le Père Goriot,* read, "The secret of a great success for which you are at a loss to account is a crime that has never been found out, because it was properly executed." What greater success could there be than becoming bulletproof, blade-proof, presumably fireproof?

Kill-proof.

And he was wealthy on top of that. He hadn't discovered his immortality and decided to lay low, wander the earth, live off the land. He made himself as rich as he could. This belied any notion that he was as hapless as he tried to paint himself.

She asked, "So, just to be clear, you don't know why anyone would know about our arrangement?"

"No idea."

"Well then, how am I supposed to go ahead?"

"However you think is best," Braith said. "Which might be not at all if you're willing to step away from my offer, although I'll be very, *very* disappointed, and can't honestly promise I wouldn't be sour about it. But I feel like it's worth reminding you that my offer is in the *millions,* commensurate to the task. I'm not some cuckold asking you for pictures of my wife with her lover. This is much bigger than that, and I would have assumed someone as smart as you understood that when you accepted the job."

"Well, to be fair to me, I accepted it under duress."

"Duress? By all means, explain."

Shyla held her tongue. The obvious answer was that she felt pressured after learning his secret, but what had concerned her at least as much at Braith's house was that he knew hers. What she had confessed to Jinh.

That she had killed before.

If Braith had somehow unearthed details about what she'd done to Rodney Hewitt and was feeling sour enough about her wanting no part of this case anymore, he could use that against her.

"If you're talking about my demonstration with the poker," Braith said, "while I'll concede it must have been traumatic to see, it was harder on me. What doesn't kill me doesn't make me stronger, it just hurts worse. I don't think it fits the definition of duress to give *you* a fortune for watching *me* get stabbed in the head."

"What if I'm not talking about that?" Shyla said.

Several seconds ticked by before he answered. "Then I'm at a loss."

His hesitation made her think of playing chess online with those time limits. Most people took it as an independent challenge to make moves as quickly as possible, while some seemed to strategize using as much clock as permitted. And a few toggled between both techniques. Part-time plodders who were occasionally up-tempo. Sometimes Braith had a ready response and other times he paused longer than she anticipated, but at all times it felt like he was in complete control of whatever move he wanted to make.

"The offer for Remy to accompany you is still there," he said.

"I don't need her," Shyla said.

"You mean you don't trust her."

"I mean what I said. But the other thing, too."

"Well, I trust her, so if you don't, what does that say about what you think of me?"

"Maybe I think you ought to double-check who you put your faith in," Shyla said.

"Hm," Braith said under a chuckle. "Okay. If anything else comes up, please call. In the meantime, I'd like to send you something that's helped me a lot. If you can imagine, I'm a man living with considerable stress on a daily basis, but I've studied some techniques to help me manage it. Breathing, focus, meditation. It might sound like nonsense to you, but a couple of days ago you'd have thought the same of ghost stories in haunted hotels, among other things. So take a look at it, and give it a chance. I think it can help next time you find yourself 'under duress.' And if anything *too* crazy happens, just know I'll probably insist on Remy coming with you. Just in case."

"In case what? I can handle myself."

"Oh, I know that. But, then again, I could be wrong," Braith said.

No, you know, Shyla thought. *You just said it. You know I can handle myself. If you were still trying to pretend like you're underestimating me, you just gave it away.*

He knew that she would go to certain criminal extremes to protect herself if she had to. He'd seen her pull a gun on him when she couldn't get out of his house, and even threaten to kill Remy after he pointed out that shooting him wouldn't keep him down. But he was still talking like there was a chance Shyla wouldn't actually pull a trigger if it came to that. And that worried Shyla as much as anything she had faced at the hotel.

11

As soon as Shyla hung up with Braith, Jinh came from the bedroom to join her in the living room, like she'd been listening in and waiting for the end of the call. They were separated only by a wall and the open bedroom door—not even a hallway divided the house's primary bedroom from its living room—so it was understandable for Jinh to *hear* that Shyla had been on the phone with someone. Being able to jump up from the computer desk and come to Shyla as soon as she heard silence seemed like clear evidence she was actively *listening,* however, and Shyla decided to take that as a good sign.

Apparently, Shyla's admission to having killed someone hadn't scared Jinh off. Had Shyla believed three years ago that Jinh wouldn't view her too differently, knowing she had taken a life, maybe she would have stayed. Probably not, though. Fearing how Jinh would react to knowing that Shyla had killed one of the people who'd abducted her had been only one reason she'd left. There were at least two others that outweighed that fear. One was that the unwanted truth Jinh had dropped on her had instantly changed the way Shyla felt about herself. And she couldn't stamp out the anger she held toward Jinh for giving her a truth she never asked for, even though Jinh had meant well. Hell, especially because Jinh had meant well. Somehow, that made it worse.

"Okay, so, long story short, I might have a new lead," Jinh said.

"Give me the long story," Shyla said.

Jinh explained that a friend of hers from Mexico, with whom she'd collaborated on an episode about a phantom ambulance, sent her a story about a strange, wandering white preacher from San Antonio who roamed different parts of Nuevo León in the late 1950s and early 1960s. He was haggard, almost a walking skeleton, which made his beard stand out that much more. His sun-leathered skin probably protected him from the elements more than his loose-fitting shirt and pants. Some people saw him in shoes that were "beaten beyond mercy," and others said his oversized bare feet were the only strong-looking part of him. One person joked that he must have robbed the oldest grave in Mexico for his clothes. He called himself "Father Villancico."

He went around proselytizing in broken Spanglish. He was somewhere between a doom prophet and a hopeful penitent. He told any who would listen–and many who would have preferred not to–about his time in San Antonio, where he had fallen in with a man he believed to be the devil incarnate. A master of torture and king of lies whose only love was blood on a blade. He had promised the old preacher extraordinary delights but led him instead to his downfall. The abandonment of his "flock," the brink of death, the doorstep of hell.

"Father Villancico" boasted as humbly as he could manage that he had clawed out of the dungeon of drug abuse, perversion, and worse, and was now paying his penance through a pilgrimage in "harsh, helpless lands." It was difficult for any of the "helpless" who fed and clothed him to be too angry with a man insulting their home, given he was likely delirious from heatstroke. The ones he visited with expected him to be dead soon, anyway.

But he didn't die, at least not before his final sighting at the north end of the state, near the border, where he told the last man to meet him that his penitence was finished, and the Lord was calling him home. He would return with his head held low, forever bowed, understanding he would never again deserve to think of himself as he had before, as a "warrior of the Lord." He would gladly be known, instead, as the example of what not to become. A fool to be mocked and ridiculed in the court of the King of Kings.

"El Bufón del Castillo del Calvario," Jinh said, finishing the long version of the story. "The Fool of–"

"Calvary's Castle," Shyla said. Jinh nodded.

Shyla went on, "And my Spanish isn't quite immaculate, but I'm going to just guess that *villancico* means *carol*."

"Also correct."

"The preacher we read about earlier, right? The one who got excommunicated, or whatever they call it on the evangelical side."

"I think they just kick you out."

"They should really get a word for it. All right, Reverend Carol . . . he said he actually went to the Inspiration Sweet a couple of times," Shyla said, checking the notes she'd added to her phone after reading Carol's editorial. "Then the church kicked him out . . . well, they kicked someone out, but the article didn't say who. Had to be him, though, right?"

"I'd say so," Jinh said, "given what we have now. If that was him in Mexico, back then, then the reason he fell out with the church is because he fell in with a man who loved torture and knives."

"Yeah. After a while the reverend stopped going to the Inspiration Sweet to sing hymns and started going to listen to the music. Dance a little, drink a little, next thing you know . . ."

"You say it like that, you make it sound like jazz and dancing are actually gateway vices that'll take you straight to hell," Jinh said.

Shyla smiled. "Well, if you're especially repressed, maybe dip a toe into Beethoven before diving headfirst into Basie. That's all. Anyway, we're both thinking the man he started to run with was Schramm?"

Jinh nodded.

"Okay. And what's the leadoff of that?" Shyla asked.

"Carol's granddaughter. Luisa. I pulled up two different interviews she's given to Christian magazines where she alludes to growing up hearing 'intense' stories from her grandfather."

"Well, damn. That really could be something."

"Yeah. And you didn't even have to ask for my help to get it."

Shyla sighed. "Right. About that."

"You're sorry?"

"*Very* sorry. Are we good?"

"We're good," Jinh said. "As long as you can be less of a dick."

Shyla started to respond with a verbal jab, something not as harsh as the worst things she'd said last night, followed by the observation that Jinh had only wanted her to be *less* of a dick. Before she could, though, her phone buzzed in her hand and she glanced at it. Braith's text message was accompanied by an attachment.

Try it, the message read. She scanned the preview image of the attachment and saw it was an electronic booklet on "Deep Meditation." Bolded terms like "reshaping consciousness," "power listening," and "rhythmical pulse" immediately put her off and she didn't bother opening the document.

"Do you have an address for Luisa?" she asked Jinh.

"I have an address for an office in Castle Hills. She's a Christian marriage counselor. I think she works out of her house."

"All right. Let's go see her."

12

A modest sign in the front yard read, LORD'S LOVE COMMITMENT COUNSELING, with Luisa's faux-signature printed underneath the slogan. The place looked cuter and quainter than the surrounding houses. Low picket fencing lined the perimeter, barely high enough to keep out a big dog, provided it wasn't fairly athletic. It was so traditionally styled it didn't even have a garage, and its driveway was set with fine gravel. It had a higher-than-necessary peaked roof and a small porch with a loveseat swing set. It reminded Shyla of certain shops and businesses off the main strip in more-touristy towns like Fredericksburg, or in college towns like San Marcos. She'd visited a lawyer's office with a similar, overly homey appearance in Boerne while hunting down Dante's ancestry. Based on that experience, she was prepared for the proprietor to answer the door with a big smile and proceed to be as unhelpfully amiable as possible.

What Shyla did not expect was for Luisa to open the door wide, lean into a hard look at her, bulge her eyes like she was adrift at the edge of space, and say, "I'm not supposed to talk to you."

Shyla took a step back while Jinh stayed firm where she was, ready to put a foot in the doorway like a reporter in a movie.

"You're not supposed to talk to who?" Shyla said, the question already out before she realized it wasn't what she needed to ask.

"*You,*" Luisa said. She was a perfect match to the picture on her website. Dusty blond, lean, and kind-faced even as her startled eyes, tone, and words effectively told Shyla to leave her property and never come back.

Jinh took a half step to her right to occupy more of Luisa's sight line, then asked, "Ma'am, you don't even know who we are."

"Not you, but I know her," Luisa said, pointing at Shyla. "They told me about you. They told me you'd be here, and . . . no, no. You need to leave."

She started to close the door, but Jinh really did put her foot against it, along with her knee, to keep it open, and Shyla put her hand to the door and leaned in to assist.

"Hold on," Jinh said. "Now, you didn't have to open the door to us, but you did, so I think you actually do want to talk."

"I just needed to see if she was really real," Luisa said, still looking Shyla over as though she might indeed be an illusion.

Shyla sighed. For someone whose entire career was built around fostering better communication, Luisa seemed to be going out of her way to be vague. Then again, her distress was evident, and the simple arithmetic of the situation told Shyla that someone else had arrived ahead of her and told Luisa she would be coming. This would mark the second time in two days that she found herself standing outside of a door, talking to someone who had advance knowledge of her arrival. Braith had to have some idea of why this was. He might even be behind it, and this was all part of a strange game he was playing.

"Who told you about me?" she asked Luisa.

"You need to go *now*. If you don't–"

"Just answer that question and I'll leave."

"I'm going to call the cops."

"Who told you about me?" Shyla said again, more demanding this time.

Luisa looked and leaned to her left, like she might have reached for something. "I've got a gun here. I know how to use it. I've been shooting since I was six years old."

"Did your grandfather teach you?" Shyla said. "I hear he was better with knives."

Luisa looked like someone who believed she'd seen a ghost, only to realize as it reached for her that it was actually a demon. The fear she'd already felt at the sight and recognition of Shyla Sinclair bloomed into its truer, larger form, finally removing the last natural traces of kindness from her face.

Instead of pretending again to reach for a gun, Luisa's hand went into the front pocket of her pants to take out her phone. Her thumb tapped the screen as quickly as it could, which wasn't fast enough to keep Shyla from snatching the phone and shoving Luisa back into the house, if she wanted to do that. She thought about it, then decided against it. Instead, as Luisa made good on her threat to call the police, Shyla put a hand on Jinh's shoulder and motioned for her to walk with her back to her car, parked at the curb.

Behind them, they heard the dispatcher answer–Luisa apparently having placed the call on speaker–and ask for an explanation of the emergency.

"Yes, there are two people at my home harassing me," Luisa stammered. Shyla couldn't make out what the dispatcher said next as she made it to the car, but just before she opened the door and got inside, she heard Luisa say, "No, no. Two different people this time."

Inside the car, she looked past Jinh through the window to

watch Luisa, who remained outside to watch them leave. She could not help catching Jinh's eye, however, and when she did, Jinh said, "You heard that, too?"

Shyla nodded.

She started her car, put it in drive, and took off feeling like she knew more now than when she'd arrived, but not enough to know where to go next.

13

They stopped at a taqueria in a strip mall close to the highway, near where the Castle Hills city limits ended and San Antonio's began. Shyla didn't realize how hungry she was until she walked in and smelled the chicken and steak grilling in back. Right after their waitress sat them, they ordered, then waited silently with their complimentary chips and salsa for a little while. They found no foothold in the conversation they needed to have until after the waitress came back with two waters and a saucer with lime wedges.

"Somebody got to her," Shyla said, stating the obvious and feeling doubly ridiculous for how conspiratorial she sounded. They sat in a booth near the back of the restaurant, two tables removed from anyone who could have eavesdropped on their conversation. The window just above and to the left of her had two unlit Guadalupe candles resting on its sill.

"You think we ought to go back?" Jinh said. "Because I think we should. I don't know where else to go or who else to talk to that might get us somewhere."

"Yeah, and she knows more than we could have guessed. She knows enough that whoever's ahead of me thought she needed a visit."

"All right. So we go back, but how do we get her to open the door this time?"

Shyla shrugged with her eyebrows. "You don't have any experience with this?"

"No. If anything I have people who want to talk to me *too* much. I take it you're not practiced at this, either."

"Eh." While most of her work was done from behind a desk, Shyla had engaged in a few of the more adventurous and stereotypical investigative activities on occasion. She tailed someone from her nondescript silver Civic a few times, and found the car so useful for the job she didn't bother to "upgrade" after Dante's payments came through. She'd successfully broken into someone's home once, and someone else's office. She had talked her way past a bouncer to crash a private party before, and another time she convinced a motel clerk to give her the key to someone else's room. None of this felt like it would be useful to her and Jinh now.

Luisa had called the cops on them already, *and* she'd recognized Shyla, somehow. She might not know Shyla's name, but it was certainly possible that she did, and not only because whoever had come to see her had told her.

Using aliases on Jinh's show hadn't been enough to completely protect Shyla's identity. Once her story was known to Jinh's hundreds of thousands of subscribers and others who read or heard about it later, mass amateur sleuthing began in earnest. As much earnestness as one can reasonably expect from the story of a stolen Black infant.

It didn't take long for people to figure out who she was, what hospital she'd been taken from, when she'd been taken, who her kidnappers were, and who her parents were. Now Shyla was an entry in the online Crime Library. She was the subject of several other true-crime podcasts or short videos on social media, which largely regurgitated what Jinh had already shared with the world. She wasn't "famous" in any real sense, but she was easier to look up than the average person was.

So, it was possible Luisa had already given the police Shyla's name. Not just any police, but the ones in the San Antonio enclave of Castle Hills. Shyla liked to think her savviness was why she'd had few dealings with cops during the handful of years she'd been an active investigator. Luck played a role as well, as it did with everything, but she also knew how to keep a relatively low profile, appear unassuming, unconcerned and not concerning. She dressed in simple colors and outfits, but never anything so dark or stark it made her look like she was trying to avoid attention. Trying too hard to look inconspicuous was a great way to achieve the opposite effect.

Nonetheless, occasional run-ins with law enforcement were unavoidable. Her informed opinion was that city cops were worrisome, and country cops were a coin flip, but the ones from the suburbs were her least favorite. They were as quick to take offense as they were to antagonize. She knew some cities housed cops who seemed to believe the department had an annual kill quota, and some county sheriffs actually subscribed to a fringe, extremist notion that they were the highest authority figures in the country, which meant the law was whatever they determined it to be. Even with that in mind, Shyla felt more anxious around suburban cops than the rest. Basic boredom combined with a desire to feel powerful and essential drove the worst of them to mistake abuse for productivity.

She'd already had one run-in with a Castle Hills cop, who had pulled her over for expired tags that were no longer expired. She'd had it taken care of a day earlier and put the sticker up, but apparently it took longer than that for the official database the officer was relying on to catch up. He'd followed her since she'd pulled out of the parking lot of an antiques store where she'd picked up a couple of lamps. He saw those in the backseat after he pulled her over, then questioned why she had them, where she'd gotten them, if she had a receipt, and what she wanted to do with them. "Light a room," she'd said, and he'd snorted like she'd said something sarcastic.

He returned to his car with her ID and insurance card and kept her waiting a few minutes before coming back to tell her why he'd pulled her over, adding, "I guess it's just good luck I didn't get you a day earlier, huh?" His tone betrayed his disappointment, as well as an accusation too absurd to be spoken. He made it sound like she'd done this deliberately, baited him into pulling her over just to waste his time. "You working over here today, Miss Sinclair?" When she shook her head, he'd said, "You *are* that P.I., though, aren't you? The one with the psychic girlfriend?"

Knowing that he'd looked her up—over the web, not just in his open-warrants database or anything else that would be relevant to his job or the situation—gave her a sick feeling, like something was swimming laps through her stomach. Instinct and practice told her to tell him nothing, stay dead silent if she couldn't think of the safest way to say that if she wasn't under arrest, she wasn't answering anything. Instead, she said, "The one working for Massimo Dante, yeah."

She was actually off the Dante case by then, and figured out even sooner than that, within a week of taking a job that would last almost three months, that Dante needed a psychiatrist and a few genuine friends, not an investigator. She had kept that to herself, though, and saw things through as he wanted her to, producing evidence that proved he was indeed the illegitimate son of another illegitimate son, and could call Jack Parsons, the rocket scientist / occultist, his grandfather. From that he extrapolated that he was the Antichrist, based on letters and codices he'd inherited from a grandmother he'd never met. Shyla'd had nothing to do with that part. Other occultists she met during the investigation said all these texts were either forged or nonsensical. Dante was sure he had cracked the codes within those documents, however, and was convinced, after learning his ancestry, that he was the devil on earth. He'd told Shyla he was going on a "spirit quest" to determine if he should live up to his destiny or resist it. Then, to Shyla's knowledge, he'd gone off the map. Dante's assistant called after the job was over to confirm Shyla had received her last payment and ask if Dante ever mentioned any places he might disappear to. When Shyla had asked if that meant Dante was missing, the woman had just wished her a good day and then hung up.

The cop needn't know any of that, any more than he needed to know why she'd bought a matching pair of bronze lamps, or about her relationship with Jinh.

The officer's lip curled. He knew why Shyla had dropped Massimo Dante's name, but didn't want to concede that she had an upper hand. "Are you supposed to be telling me that? Feels like it takes the 'private' out of PI."

"Let me call him to see if he's okay with it. Give me your name and badge number so I can tell him who's asking."

He looked away with a scowl, like he was scanning to see if anyone had seen him trip and was ready to cuss them out for laughing. "You have a nice day," he said on the way back to his car.

That hadn't even been her tensest experience with a cop convinced he was a paladin of suburbia. The last line of defense dividing sterilized civilization from the disparate colors of a lawless world.

That same officer could easily still be with the Castle Hills PD. If he was the one who took Luisa's call, she might have given him Shyla's name. Or the description alone might clue him in to who had arrived to "harass" a poor, wholesome, frightened local woman.

One of the pitfalls of pairing with Jinh was that they made for a memorable couple. Working alone, Shyla wasn't exactly forgettable, but a solo Black woman, despite being of above average height and weight, didn't stand out as much as one with a lean, lightly freckled Asian colleague.

How do we get her to open the door? Jinh had asked, but Shyla was starting to rethink revisiting Luisa at all. Not all good leads were pursuable.

She felt something light flick off her face, under her right eye. The small white projectile landed on the counter, beside the puddle of condensation forming under her glass of water. It was the wrapper for Jinh's straw, balled up and punted Shyla's way with Jinh's middle finger. Shyla glanced up and noticed that the shareable nacho plate they ordered was in the middle of the table.

"You zoned out there," Jinh said.

Shyla shook away the cobwebs in her head. "Sorry."

"Think of anything useful, at least?"

"Not really. Except maybe we need to go with something else."

"What do you mean?"

"I mean see if there's anyone else we can talk to. Give it another go searching online for things connected to the reverend, or Schramm," Shyla said. "Now that we know better what we're looking for—"

"No, this is good. This is—" The buzzing of one of Jinh's phones in her purse interrupted her. She kept two phones with her, one that was personal and one for business. The latter was actually a "hotline" where fans of her show could call in or message her. Some wanted to share their crazy stories of the supernatural. It was a testament to how much people revered her. Even the people opposed to Jinh generally didn't regard her as a grifter, but a menace. A threat not just to their beliefs, but to their reality, like she was a living gateway through which horrible forces might emerge.

Jinh cherished her fans and didn't mind the haters. The only people she didn't like receiving calls from were those seeking help. People hoping—*pleading*—for her to solve some personal mystery.

Tell them where their missing daughter is.

Tell them who ran down their father in a hit-and-run.

Ask their deceased son if he *accidentally* overdosed. Couldn't she at least do this? Please?

They pleaded as though Jinh chose who to help based on who sounded more earnest, more desperate. No matter how often she explained on her show that she had limited control over this thing that altered her life and worldview, that it brought visions to her to parse out as opposed to her summoning them, many people refused to understand. All they knew was that she had a power that they didn't, and a more legitimate backstory than almost anyone else also claiming that power.

Jinh was accidentally "outed" as a psychic by a well-meaning YouTuber with millions of subscribers, Serious Circus, who specialized in "Stories of the strange, weird, and abnormal." Few people outside of Tumwater, Washington, had known about her story. Then Serious Circus, in their signature, semi-misleading-for-the-sake-of-preserving-a-plot-twist style, shared the story of the teenage girl who'd entered a police station, against her parents' advice, to tell them she knew where to find a missing classmate's corpse.

When the police initially dismissed her, she had gone into the woods herself to find the poor girl, Sarah McDaniels, and tried to call from the site but couldn't get reception, so she took pictures and trekked back to show the police firsthand what she'd seen. They promptly arrested her, despite evidence indicating the victim had been abducted near her home at a time when Jinh would have been at work on the other side of town. The police then altered their previously established timeline to open a wider window through which Jinh could have abducted Sarah, or "more likely" gone into the woods to meet her accomplice—since actual evidence indicated the culprit was a male—and participate in the deed.

She'd been interrogated and held for two days while her parents tried to arrange for bail before two friends of the actual killer told police that he had bragged about it while drunk, at a small party they were having. The murderer was the stepson of the recently retired police chief, and the scandal swept Jinh out of the spotlight, which she and her family were so grateful for they didn't even pursue litigation.

Six years later, Serious Circus picked up the story and highlighted Jinh's stated reason for knowing where Sarah McDaniels was. She'd had visions of the girl. Painful, awful visions not just of Sarah's body, where it was located, but of Sarah's spirit, screaming to be heard. Crying for her mother and father to come find her.

Jinh endured this as well as she could for weeks before telling her parents about it. They traded a long knowing look, before telling Jinh the truth about one of her great-uncles. The one her family seldom spoke of, who went mad in Seoul and killed a neighbor he accused of being a monster and was sentenced to death for it, who died of starvation in prison before his execution date, because he'd gone too mad with his professed "visions" to eat anything. Who was exonerated in the minds of many when six infant skeletons were unearthed on his deceased neighbor's property after the new owners started to renovate.

Jinh's parents gave her sedatives to help her sleep, brewed teas to soothe her nerves, said prayers to invite divine intercession, and told her to try to suppress the images. They were terrified for her and, to be fair, unequipped to handle their daughter's ability. Jinh knew, or felt, that her only hope would be to unburden herself. It kept her from going mad and eased her pain, but didn't eliminate it, and didn't grant her any significant control over her power. At best she had a large but fragile cage around it now. Some people understood this, but those who didn't still called, begged, bargained, and sometimes made threats to try to get her to help them.

Jinh kept the phone number on her website open to the public nonetheless, because she'd found it more controlled that way. Before she had activated that line, strangers had found her personal line and called there. A few still did, but it was much rarer now. And she was successful enough to staff three people who helped screen her messages. Even so, she liked having the phone by her side. Despite the negative experiences, most of her fan interactions were encouraging.

Now, however, she took the phone from her purse because it pressed against her keys and the added jingling annoyed her. She set the phone face down on the table.

"This isn't something we should just move on from," Jinh said of Luisa. "Not after the first speed bump."

"She called the cops, Jinh."

"Fine. First roadblock."

"She called the *cops* on *us*."

"Yeah. And here we are, eating nachos a few miles away, with not a police raid in sight."

Shyla knocked twice on the wooden table.

Jinh said, "We're not nearly as known as I think you think we are. And anyway, if we got jammed up, don't you think Braith would–"

Her phone vibrated again on the hard table, sounding like unmanned construction equipment someone forgot to power off. Jinh flipped her phone over to set it to DO NOT DISTURB, then stared at her screen like she was trying to be sure the winning lottery numbers matched her own.

"What's up?" Shyla said.

Jinh turned the phone to show Shyla the name on the caller ID.

LORD'S LOVE COMMITMENT COUNSELING

"Should I answer?" Jinh said. "Do you want to?"

"Let her leave a message," Shyla said. Overly cautious, bordering on paranoid? Probably. Even if Luisa was calling to bait them into some kind of trap, and even if that trap somehow only required hearing Shyla's or Jinh's voice, there was little chance it would be effective, and even less chance that the police were involved in it. Still, why take any chances? They could always call her back.

Shortly after the buzzing stopped, Jinh's phone pinged. She turned the phone sideways on the table so that they could both read the transcribed voicemail at the same time.

I got your number from your website. I looked you up after you left. This is Luisa Carol. You were here earlier. Look, that thing your friend said about my grandfather and knives, I need to know how she knew that. No one's supposed to know about that. Call me. I want to talk.

14

They took their time before returning Luisa's call, much less returning to her house. In the interim they talked about what to do if this was a setup, and Castle Hills police cars were waiting for them when they turned down Luisa's street. They settled on Shyla using Braith for her lone phone call, and even dropping his name on the spot to see if it made the cops jump. Braith was arguably more well-known than Dante, especially since his purchase of a huge social media site a year ago.

Not wanting to leave it to chance, however, or annoy Braith by surprising him with a bail request should they get arrested, Shyla phoned Remy and asked what the protocol was if her investigation put her at odds with law enforcement.

"Why?" Remy said. "Are you planning to do something illegal?"

"It's never a plan. Always a possibility, though."

"Always?"

Shyla sighed. "Like everything you do is so clean. Is he going to back me up or not? I feel like if he wants me to push this, he'd have a contingency for run-ins with cops. Or he didn't think that far ahead?"

"We'd just rather you not do anything to bring us negative attention, if at all possible. Is four million dollars not enough incentive to do your job well and legally? You need a legal fund per diem, too?"

"Gotdamn, you sound salty today. What is this?"

"I guess talking to someone who just pointed a gun at me puts me in a weird mood," Remy said.

"I didn't *just* do that. It's been—"

—a couple of days, Shyla kept herself from saying, realizing just in time how stupid she would sound. "You know what, I'm sorry about that. Okay?" She took a big breath that smothered her unwarranted, useless aggravation and tried again with a more appropriately apologetic tone. "I actually am sorry about that. In my defense, I was under some unexpected pressure. I think you can understand that."

She heard Remy huff into the phone, then waited out a few seconds of silence for Remy's response. "We've already set aside funds to address any legal matters that come up. We also have other contingencies in place that you don't need to worry about now, but they should keep you from having to point a gun at another unarmed person."

Shyla smiled. "Unarmed?"

She thought she could feel Remy begrudgingly smirking through the phone. They both knew Remy had been carrying when Shyla drew on her. Probably more than one piece. Different calibers for different occasions, most likely. And had she really believed Shyla was about to shoot her, she would have just stepped behind Braith, and shot through him to down Shyla. She probably preferred dum-

dums, expanding bullets that minimized the risk of accidentally hitting the person standing behind your target, but Remy likely had something military grade for better stopping power. By the time her Big Bore Magnum smashed through Braith, its velocity would fire fragments—metal and skeletal—deep into Shyla's body.

Neither here nor there now. The important thing was that Braith had budgeted and planned for "any legal matters." Which sounded to Shyla like more than just bail or lawyer fees. Obviously Braith didn't have to "budget" for anything short of a trip to the moon, and maybe not even that. This all meant they'd set aside money in case things went bad, for cops, press, witnesses, judges, and whoever else needed to be paid off. This might have set a different person at ease. For Shyla it reminded her of the kind of people she was professionally wed to.

Jinh's fault, she thought as she contemplated this on the way to Luisa's house. When she waved that thought away, Jinh looked at her, puzzled, and Shyla lowered the window and waved again, pretending to rid the car of a gnat.

Luisa was waiting for them at the stoop of the walkway leading to her front door. The tip of her cigarette glowed under the shade of large oaks stationed on opposite sides of her lawn, and the way she bounced her knee and blew the smoke with the breeze told Shyla she was both a seasoned smoker and a relapsing quitter. She was anxious, and not because a bunch of cops were waiting to ambush Shyla and Jinh. They were in the clear, no laws in sight. And Shyla doubted Luisa was nervous about being alone with Shyla and Jinh.

No, Luisa Carol was stressed about what she might learn.

That thing your friend said about my grandfather and knives . . . No one's supposed to know about that.

When Shyla parked, Luisa stood, dropped her cigarette, stepped on it, then walked into her house, leaving the door open. Shyla got out and marched forward while Jinh was more hesitant. It took Shyla a moment to consider how Jinh might feel about walking through an open doorway into unknown, confined space, given what they'd been through at the Inspiration Sweet.

What she pulled me out of, Shyla thought.

She looked back to Jinh. "You feeling anything?" she asked.

"Just . . . just what I felt earlier."

Shyla frowned. "What do you mean?"

"Not like that." Jinh shook her head. "Not like this is the same. Just a bad memory."

Shyla walked back to her, put a hand on her shoulder, and that was enough. Jinh came with her to Luisa's front door.

Luisa had moved past her living room through a pair of French doors that led to a cozy office space made for three. Shyla and Jinh followed as Luisa took her place behind her desk and they sat in the twin chairs across from her like a couple of clients. Shyla wondered if, being a "Christian counselor," Luisa had ever had two women sitting across from her for an official visit. Just a few months ago she had driven past the old brick church near her favorite park and seen pride flags over the marquee inviting everyone to the nine A.M. Sunday service. She'd been startled enough by this to visit the church's website and watch the sermon they'd streamed from the previous Sunday, and felt oddly comforted when the camera panned to a congregation of mostly white, mostly older Lutherans nodding in agreement to a message of "tolerance." She wasn't the biggest fan of that word. It reeked of begrudging arrogance (*I suppose I'll let you folks exist. If I must, I guess I'll tolerate that you are who you are*), but sometimes small wins felt big enough.

Maybe she was wrong about Luisa, and she accepted clients of all kinds (well, save for throuples and beyond, given the seating arrangements). And it probably wouldn't matter one way or the other. But Shyla tried not to dismiss anything that crossed her mind as immaterial until it was proven so.

"You two are together?" Luisa abruptly asked.

Jinh flinched at the question and looked at Shyla to answer.

"Does it matter?" Shyla said.

Luisa looked embarrassed and shrugged. "I just . . . I pride myself on being able to tell a lot about most people when I first meet them."

"Just based on how they look?"

"Not like that," Luisa said. "I know what you mean by that and I don't . . . I shouldn't have worded it that way. I just believe having a good gut instinct is important. A good feel for people. That feel is what told me to tell the police I didn't want to pursue charges when they arrived. Then it told me to track you down. I had your name," she said to Shyla, "and that eventually led me to your website," she said to Jinh. "And the feel told me to go ahead and call you instead of letting this go, or even just sleeping on it."

"What else did it tell you?" Shyla said.

"That I should trust you more than the other two who showed up."

"They give you a bad vibe?"

"Oh, more than that," Luisa said. "I didn't need a feel for that. Those two were . . . They made it very plain who they were."

"They threatened you?" Jinh said.

Luisa bit down on what to say next, then relaxed enough to let it out. "They promised bad things—very bad things—would happen to me if I helped you. They said it like prophets. Like God sent them to warn me. And I know that's not true, but I believed it a little, especially when you showed up at my door."

"Did they do anything else? Make you see things?"

"What do you mean by that?" Luisa answered a little too quickly, like she'd been expecting that question, preparing her denial in two or three stages.

Shyla smiled softly and then gave her an out. "You'd know exactly what I meant if they did. It's okay. Not really important." She didn't necessarily believe that last part. It would be good to verify that the couple who'd come to see Luisa were the same as the ones from the Inspiration Suite, although as it was Shyla couldn't imagine they were anyone else. It would also be good to know if they were only able to darken the hallway and summon the spirits there because the hotel was teeming with ghosts and was the site of horrible sins.

What little she knew about this sort of thing she'd learned from Jinh, either through observation or lessons that Shyla now wished she'd taken more seriously. One thing that seemed certain to her, though, was that proximity to traumatic, psychically scarring events amplified what Jinh could do. Maybe there were levels to this, and Jinh was a comparative yellow belt while these other two were full-fledged senseis.

"Could you answer my first question?" Luisa said. "Are you two together?"

Shyla started to roll her eyes, then remembered Luisa's reasoning for asking, and figured if it would help them get answers from her it was worth it.

"We used to be. Now we're just work colleagues."

Luisa nodded. "I thought so. See? I can read people pretty well. I'm not judging you or anything. I've actually had a couple of queer clients."

Good for you, Shyla thought wryly.

"I converted to the Episcopal church four years ago. We have a strong stance on loving all. And that led me to my work today. I thought it was a better way to make a difference, without . . . Well, when I was younger, I took more after my mother, who took after her father. We were a little more extreme."

"In what way?" Jinh said.

Luisa nibbled the corner of her bottom lip nervously. "Grandpa Carol said he used to know the devil. He said he'd been disguised as a musician who played sinful music that was the first step down the road to damnation. This 'devil' tempted him and took over his mind. He said the devil showed him something he thought we had to know but was afraid to tell us. When he came back home, after his 'pilgrimage of penance' in Mexico, he finally told my mother everything. What he'd done and seen. She was already the most passionate of his 'missionaries' by then. She'd carried on without him while he was away. When he told her what he'd been through she went away for a while herself. I think she needed some time to process who her father really was, because she'd followed and trusted him her whole life while he'd been holding this ugly secret of his past all along.

"When she came back, she said she'd save the whole story of what he'd done for when I was her age. She was thirty-six at the time, and I was thirteen, and I think it was around then that I started telling myself I needed to get away from all of that when I got the chance. I saw how Grandpa was, and what Ma was becoming, and I realized I didn't want to be like them. She must have felt it, because she started telling me things here and there before I got out of high school. She made it sound like she was trying to prepare me a little bit at a time so I wouldn't be hit too hard by it like she was. But I don't know if there's a way to tell any of that to someone without it being too much. Just the little bit I learned—she never got around to telling me most of it—gave me bad dreams. I still get them once in a while.

"She told me that the devil, dressed like a man, taught Grandpa 'how to play a body with knives.' Her exact words. She said it to me more than once. She used to say, 'Your grandpa knows things you never should have to learn, like how long it takes a man about twice your size to bleed out after they've been stuck.' She said he knew how to play with fire and guns, too. Even knew how to play 'falling games,' she called them. But the main and worst thing he learned was how to play with knives."

One thing Shyla had learned from Jinh, with regard to questioning anyone, was to defer to asking about the person in front of you and not about someone else whenever uncertain. So as eager as Shyla was to ask Luisa two or three questions about the reverend, she instead followed up with "How were you able to get away?"

Luisa looked at her like she was surprised Shyla could speak and responded, "Hm?"

"You got away from her before she could tell you the rest, right? And before your grandfather could, either."

Luisa nodded, but less in the affirmative than as though she was pretending to remember something in the hopes it would help her actually remember. Then she shrugged. "I don't know if 'got away' is the best way to put it. It's how I think about it, but really . . . really, they went away. Both of them ended up in Yorktown, in the old mental care hospital there. The memories and nightmares got to Grandpa too much when he got into his eighties. He took to drinking, and overdoing some of his pills, and sometimes cutting himself either to make up for what he'd done to other people, or to try to get the last of his demons out of him. He could never make up his mind which it was when you asked him. Ma tried to fix him with prayer, but he put the knife to her a few too many times when he was at his worst, and she finally had enough. It was only ever shallow cuts, nothing life-threatening, but . . . well, that's a really worthless 'only,' isn't it?"

She sighed and looked like she would flatten thinner than the throw blanket she sat back against, but then puffed herself back up with a healthy inhalation. "Anyway, the sadder thing was how soon Ma followed him into the same institution. When he got inside he got better enough to write her letters, and within a month she was visiting him, and it was like every time she went to him she left a little of her sanity with him. Which I assume he chewed up, spit out, and stepped on as soon as she left. She tried to keep preaching, but her sermons turned into rants. Pagan things she tried to claim were the oldest truths of the church. She'd go on about this thing called 'the hand of glory.' You ever heard of that?"

Shyla looked to Jinh, who nodded. She probably had three or four books dedicated to the hand of glory in her library back in Washington. "The severed hand of a dead man," Jinh said, clueing Shyla in. Then she clarified, "A hanged man, actually. Either his left hand or, if he was a murderer, whichever hand he used to kill. It's supposed to have powers."

"Right," Luisa said. "Although, the way Ma told it was different. It wasn't the hand of a killer, although she didn't explain past that. She said this hand of glory was kept in an unused part of the hospital where Grandpa was. It was kind of a perfect spot for such a thing to be in, I guess, considering all the other stories people told about the place, you know?"

"I don't," Shyla said. "What stories?"

"Huh. Maybe the stories just made it my way more because I went there so often to visit Grandpa. I heard it from people at church and around the town that they were building a new chapel for the hospital, but either found old secret graves there, like some murder victims or something, or kept finding dead animals on the site with no explanation. Something like that, something that stopped the construction. I also heard it was a secret temple for devil worshippers, that it was actually a new mortuary and there was supposed to be a 'death tunnel' connecting it to the main building. All types of nonsense. I think whoever told me that last one stole it from a movie or something."

"It's from a legend about a hospital in Kentucky," Jinh said.

"That sounds about right. It was all silliness. A bunch of rumors picked up from somebody else who picked it up from somewhere they can't remember. But Mom's 'sermons' about the hand really put people off. You know, a lot of people talk about things they claim to believe, that they've heard about, but really they just want to gossip. Ma had conviction. That can be a little scarier. Our tiny congregation was already made of people closer to the fringes than the center of Christian beliefs. They were the last ones hanging on to what was left of the old Calvary's Castle. They were comfortable with us singing strange old hymns that sounded more like chanting. They were okay with us not having a single building to call home. Sometimes we had service in a field where no one would bother us. It took a lot to put them off, but Mom's hand of glory preachings did it. When she realized she'd lost all of them, and lost me, that's when she checked herself into Yorktown, to be with people who she said already knew the truth."

"It sounds like she never recovered," Shyla said.

Luisa smirked sadly. "No, but she never had much of a chance. She passed less than a year after checking in. Things were bad in there, all the rumors aside. Lot of neglect and abuse."

Shyla let silence hold the room while she contemplated what to ask next. "You know, you haven't asked about why we showed up here, why any of this matters to us. You don't want to know?"

Luisa shook her head. "In fact, I'd be quick to get my gun and ask you to leave if you started trying to tell me. Listen, something about you all told me I could trust you more than the other two. And I figured I only had a few ways to go about it. Keep quiet, get the police involved to keep you away, or follow my instincts, take this opportunity to unburden myself. These old family secrets have been heavy. Now part of that weight is with you, and I don't know why you wanted to know any of it—and I truly don't care—but I trust that now you'll leave me alone."

"We will," Shyla said. "But what about the other two? They don't worry you?"

"Oh, they terrify me. I know I'm going to dream of them. Only for tonight if I'm lucky, but I doubt I will be. But you were right about them being able to make me see things. That's part of why I'm trusting you over them. Anybody that can do what they can . . . You know they're willing to do wrong, because what they made me see . . ."

"Was it Reverend Carol? Or the man—the 'devil'—that he talked about?"

Luisa glared at Shyla like she and Jinh were going to peel away their false faces to reveal themselves as the pair who originally visited. *This was a test,* they would say. *Do we even need to say that you failed? Do we need to remind you of what we said would happen to you if you talked?*

"Lucky guess," Shyla said with a shrug. "I'm not too bad at reading people and situations myself."

"Well, it wasn't just Grandpa," Luisa said. "And it wasn't just that other man, either. They showed me my mother in her last days. That was the worst of it. The way she looked and sounded and *smelled,* it was . . ."

Shyla waited for Luisa to elaborate, but then realized she, of course, wouldn't. Hearing Luisa's nondescription made Shyla think of reading "The Monkey's Paw" in the school library when she was probably too young, from an older anthology with a kid-friendly cover and less friendly stories. She thought of the couple's dead son, wished back to life after being "caught in the machinery" at the factory where he worked, now knocking on the door. The exact nature of his accident, his specific injuries, and the condition of his body never told, leaving Shyla to think of every scenario she could, every kind of mutilation her mind could conjure. She did that now, with the reverend and Luisa's mother. It made her want to apologize, not for what Luisa went through, but for even bringing it up.

"So that man, the one who tempted my grandpa, I take it that's who you're really trying to learn about," Luisa said.

Shyla nodded. "Do you know if he ever made it around to Yorktown to visit the reverend? Did your mother ever meet him?"

"Not that I know of. But in that vision or whatever I had from the other two, that man was there in the hospital with Mom and Grandpa. At least I think he was. It's hard to say. I can still sort of see it. It's burned into my brain, but in a way where it's kind of melted together, so some of the details are tough to make out."

Jinh asked, "What about the couple? Do you think you could tell us what they looked like? So we can look out for them?"

"I wish I could," Luisa said through a soft, sad chuckle. "This whole time I've been sitting here I've been trying to remember their faces. They were right here in this house, talking to me. I know they were. I remember hearing them knock on my door, telling me to let them in. I felt like I didn't have a choice. I remember the house getting dark. I remember thinking it was strange and disturbing how their voices seemed to be coming from under the floor, right under my feet, even though I was looking right at them standing in front of me as they spoke. I watched their mouths, I stared into their eyes, I can tell you verbatim what they said, and

I'll know their voices until my dying day, but I couldn't tell you a thing about what they looked like. Not height, not race, not whether they were fat or thin, or male or female. It's like they weren't really here. But I know they were, and there were two of them. The rest, I don't know. It's like they made me forget."

15

Back home, while Jinh reached out to different contacts she thought might help her sift facts from the legends about Yorktown Hospital, Shyla decided to make a phone call.

The meeting with Luisa had left her tense, feeling like there were eyes in the trees and watchers behind every window on the drive to her house. She brewed some lavender tea, put on a lo-fi beats playlist, and tried to think of her journey. Things she had survived. Abduction, discovery, deliverance. Making it through her first seventeen years wasn't something she thought to credit herself for until her aunt Teonna told her to.

"That was my sister's spirit in you," she'd said. "Just think back, I bet you'll find more than a few times where you had to say or do the right thing to save yourself from those people doing something worse to you. That was something you got from Jackie."

Shyla actually couldn't find any of those lifesaving occasions. Linda Montgomery and her boyfriend, Rodney Hewitt, had never posed a direct threat to her until her final few months with them.

Until Shyla started to suspect they might resort to drastic measures to keep her from running to the police. Before that, they'd barely ever raised their voices to her, much less a hand. She remembered joking with the few friends she'd made while in Mississippi about having the only Black parents that didn't even talk about disciplining their kid.

She had made it easy on them, being the quiet type, too risk averse to be tempted by underage drinking or smoking, or to even talk back to teachers. Of course, Linda and Rodney had likely instilled this caution in her since before she could form memories. A reserved, safe child was less apt to injure herself, for instance, minimizing the number of trips to the hospital, where discrepancies or irregularities with personal records might be uncovered. As she got older she wasn't the type of kid who would get busted using a fake ID to buy alcohol, or be with a friend who stole their mother's car for a joyride. She wasn't going to jeopardize the situation they had put themselves in when they took her. Or rather, to be accurate, when Linda snatched her and Rodney agreed to help raise a stolen infant.

To hear Aunt Teonna tell it, however, Shyla's instincts had served her well early, because some part of her knew something was amiss. Knew that she didn't share enough physical features with the people claiming to be her parents. Knew it was strange that they had to move to a seemingly random place every two or three years. And also knew, according to Teonna, that Linda and Rodney would treat her as incriminating evidence they had to get rid of if that's what it took to keep them out of prison.

The one thing that might support her aunt's belief in her instincts, Shyla thought, was her ability to feign sleep, which she had developed at a very young age. Her earliest memories of doing so successfully came from when she was five years old. For years afterward she thought this was just something most kids did, and it wasn't until her late teens that she learned, on social media, that a lot of kids *tried,* but that actually getting the breathing rhythm correct, slacking your jaw a bit, lying in a position that might not be comfortable to you if you were awake, perfecting the stillness, these things didn't occur to them. They just thought closing your eyes and not moving was enough, and if that failed they didn't care to learn how they could mask it better in the future.

Shyla initially thought she was motivated by her hatred of assigned nap times. Whenever Linda and Rodney tried to put her to sleep right after lunch, her instinct was to fight it. After the first few attempts to argue that she wasn't tired were met with some variation of "Try anyway," followed by them waiting in the room to see or hear if she was doing as she was told, she realized she could get her way sooner if she could effectively fake her sleep. If they were convinced she was out for the next couple of hours, they would leave her in the room alone, and sometimes leave the house entirely, and she would be free to do what she wanted. She started practicing every morning when she woke up, and every night as she actually became drowsy, paying attention to how she lay and how she breathed.

She remembered the first time it really worked for her because before she left the room, Linda said, "Are you asleep, princess?" She'd said it softly, like it was a pleasant secret. Like she was whispering the gift she had bought for her birthday, sure that Shyla couldn't hear her through her dreams. And it had tested Shyla, because she wanted to giggle. How could she answer that she was asleep if she *was* asleep? She was tempted to say yes just to see how Linda, the woman she believed to be her mother, would react. See if she found it as funny as Shyla did. But Shyla knew if she got caught tricking Linda, she would never be able to try this again.

If Aunt Teonna knew about this, she would say, "You see?

Some part of you knew even back then you couldn't trust them. You taught yourself that so you could spy on them. Your mother would have been proud."

With the tea and music failing to soothe her, Shyla thought she could use some of her aunt's encouragement at the moment. She went to place the video call in the back guest room. It rang twice before Teonna answered, her eyes low, chin high, and her casual *I knew you would call* smirk barely perceptible on her face, yet filling up every corner of the screen.

"Girl-Girl, how're you doing?" Aunt Teonna said. She always sounded like she knew the trouble you were going to get yourself into before you even got the idea that would lead you to it. And like she was resigned to you not taking her advice, loading up a *Didn't I tell you?* to be fired when the time came. Somehow, Shyla found this comforting. It came from a place of love and understanding, part of that understanding being that you were going to be okay, you were going to survive your self-made troubles, and while she might give you a hard time about not listening to her, she was never going to give up on you.

"I'm doing better than most. Not much more to ask for."

From offscreen, she heard someone ask Teonna who she was on the phone with. Teonna told them, "Girl-Girl," the nickname Teonna had given her, although to some, being their older cousin, she was "Big Cuz." Teonna turned the phone to face the ones asking, revealing a card table where four of them were playing a game, Spades most likely, and two more were hovering nearby, probably talking shit. They all waved at the camera and offered their greetings.

"What's up, Big Cuz!"

"When you coming back up?"

"Hey, Girl-Girl!"

Shyla just smiled and waved back. Teonna took her calls on a tablet, not a phone, so the screen was probably big enough for them all to see. Shyla still didn't know how to respond to being the "Big Cuz" to anybody. Even a few of her cousins who had her by a couple of years treated her like she had seniority because of some of the things she had done for the family since connecting with them, and especially after she was paid for the Dante case. She had covered a few outstanding bills from treatments and surgeries, helped with some tuitions, paid off a couple of mortgages, and gifted a decent little used Toyota to a recent college graduate. Things to make up for all the trouble she felt she caused by letting those people take her, as if she'd been old enough to do anything about it when it happened. Still, maybe if she'd paid more attention, spotted the clues sooner, her real mother would still be alive. Just a couple of years could have made all the difference. All she could do now was make up for that. Not that anyone was asking her to. If anything, Teonna had told her more than once to stop giving away what she'd earned.

"When *are* you coming back up?" Teonna asked after turning the camera and screen back to herself.

"I'm on another case right now, but after I'm done with that I'll be on the first flight I can find."

"'On another case.' Look at you," Teonna said, pride beaming like a searchlight. All of her family—the Sinclair kin—talked about Shyla's work like she was a celebrity secret agent. More James Bond than Easy Rawlins, tracking bad guys and keeping innocents safe, all while making a great living. Who could blame them? The only PI they'd ever met had solved the crime of her own kidnapping, been the subject of a popular international podcast, and made enough money off her last job to be a bit of a cash angel to the family she'd reunited with.

"You're being careful?" Teonna added. "I know that last one had you stressed."

You don't know the half, Shyla thought. She obviously hadn't told Teonna any of the odder, darker details about her previous client. The places she had to go, the weirdos she had to speak to. Aunt Teonna would have caught a bus down to Texas–she didn't trust airplanes–to keep Shyla away from Massimo Dante if she knew he believed he was the Antichrist, no matter how ultimately eccentric and foolish he turned out to be.

During one of Shyla's visits north, while staying up late playing cards, the conversation with her cousins had veered into spooky stories. One of them swore the old house they used to live in had been haunted, and another talked about a supposedly haunted hotel in the city, but most of them just wanted Shyla to tell them about ghost stories she'd picked up while living down south. She was telling them about the headless ghost of Deer Island off the Biloxi coast when Teonna emerged from her bedroom and let them know she'd heard enough of their conversation to disapprove of it.

"You all know better than to speak about any of that," Teonna said. "Speaking about spirits is how they can come find you. And even if they can't hurt you, they can make you hurt yourself."

If she wasn't happy about them merely discussing the idea of ghosts, she would have thought working for a man who feared he was Satan's son was an immediate intervention-worthy crisis. And if she found out that this man was why Shyla could be so generous with her money, she'd want anything bought or secured with said money–from house to car to transplanted kidney–burned on church grounds.

"I'm keeping careful," Shyla said, realizing too late how long she'd hesitated before answering Teonna's question and how weak her reply sounded. "I'm *always* careful. Part of the job."

"Uh-huh. You keeping something from me?"

"If I was, I'd tell you."

"Come on, Shyla, what's on your heart?"

Shyla thought again of that night at Teonna's house when she and her cousins had shared stories, how Teonna's bedroom was halfway down the hall, and how they hadn't been *that* loud. But she'd heard them nonetheless, because that's the way of a matriarch. And Teonna had strong observation skills besides her seemingly uncanny intuition. Once, during another visit, they'd been watching the afternoon news together—Teonna refused to miss her afternoon news—when the broadcast played footage from a news conference. A woman was pleading with whoever had kidnapped her infant son to please return him unharmed.

"That woman did something to her boy," Aunt Teonna had said. When Shyla and others in the room cast the same question toward her with simultaneous glances, she answered, "Her hair's done."

Two days later, the news reported the arrest of the very same mother who'd taken the time to make her hair look nice for the cameras while her son was supposed to be missing. She had confessed to drugging the child and abandoning him in the woods.

If Shyla meant to hide what she actually felt from Aunt Teonna, she should have gone to the car to fake a reason for this to be an audio call, instead of putting her face on video. Evidently some part of her wanted her auntie to know, or at least ask, what troubled her.

"I need to hear something good from a good voice," Shyla said.

"It's never too late to get yourself out of something you had no business getting into," Teonna answered.

"We both know that's a lie."

"You want 'something good,' or just the truth?"

"I was hoping it could be both."

"Yeah, well . . ."

"Getting out of it's not an option," Shyla said. "So what else can you tell me?"

"Depends on what we're talking about, Girl-Girl. You talking work or something else?" Teonna's eyes narrowed. "You back with that young lady Jinh?"

Shyla glanced over her shoulder, expecting to see Jinh standing behind her, having entered the room without her realizing it. That would explain why Aunt Teonna would even bring Jinh up, since Shyla had told her they had broken up three years prior. She'd also told her auntie about the two boys and other girl she'd been semi-serious about since then. Jinh wasn't there, and Shyla returned her attention to the phone, wondering how Aunt Teonna had pulled a quarter from behind her ear.

"I'm not with her. And it's not about anything like that. It's work."

Her auntie was nodding before Shyla finished her sentence, agreeing to let Shyla pretend Teonna wasn't half right. "Well, I know a lot less about your occupation than I do about love and second chances, that sort of thing."

"It's not about that."

"Sure. You know who you're talking to, right? But concerning what you say it's about, you inherited good instincts from me and your mom. We got it from your grandma and her sisters. You're smart, you're attentive. You know who and who not to trust."

Do I? Shyla thought.

"And you know when it's time to kill," Teonna said.

"Yeah, I do," Shyla said, albeit with a fraction of the confidence she hoped to project.

"Hey." Teonna turned up the authority in her voice, not quite to its highest level but near to it. She didn't have to elaborate. Shyla knew exactly what Aunt Teonna was scolding her about.

"I know," she said. "I won't let anything happen to me. I wouldn't do that to you."

"You wouldn't do that to *us*."

"Right. I promise. It won't come to it, but if it did, I'd know what to do. And I wouldn't hesitate." She managed to squelch any self-doubt trying to steal space in her voice this time and saw that Aunt Teonna was partly satisfied by what she heard. Shyla had called to hear something that would settle her nerves a little and lift her confidence, but seeing Aunt Teonna's approval of her own mini pep talk accomplished the same thing.

"All right then, Girl-Girl. I think your friend is trying to get your attention, so I'm gonna let you go."

It took Shyla barely a second to realize what this meant. This time when she turned around to look, Jinh was there, standing in the doorway holding papers, having used Shyla's printer.

With an *I'm always right* grin in her tone, Teonna told her niece, "Might as well let me say hi to her."

Shyla almost rolled her eyes but figured her auntie would be able to see it even without her facing the phone's camera. She held the phone toward Jinh, who waved like she'd just learned how to open her hand yesterday.

"Hi, Auntie T," Jinh said.

"Hey, Jinh-Jinh. You being good to our girl? Keeping her out of trouble?"

"I'm trying to," Jinh said, and Shyla flashed a hot glare at her for sounding not just uncertain, but slightly guilty, which she knew her aunt would suss out.

"Try your hardest," Teonna said. "Keep yourself safe, too. I'll talk to you two later. Love you, Girl-Girl."

"Love you, too."

Shyla hit the END CALL button, then shut off any lingering sense of weakness—of neediness—she might have carried with her before she gave her full attention to Jinh.

"Sorry," Jinh said. "I didn't hear—"

"It's fine," Shyla said. She nodded at the papers. "What have we got?"

Jinh came forward and handed Shyla everything she'd printed. "A lot. Maybe too much."

Flipping through the pages quickly told Shyla exactly what Jinh meant by this. Unlike the little-known Inspiration Sweet, the unfamiliar-to-Americans devilish escapades of Schramm, or the life of Reverend Carol, the old Yorktown Hospital was overly trodden territory. Its legend had been explored, adopted, embellished, and expanded upon by seemingly hundreds of seasoned bloggers, video essayists, and podcasters remotely interested in urban legends, "true hauntings," or unexplained mysteries. Had it shut down earlier, at least in the 1960s or '70s if not beforehand, it would have older, pre-internet sources to root and ground its more far-fetched stories. Instead, it closed in the late '90s, so its legend developed alongside the growth of internet lore. It was harder to parse out what was authentic to the site, stories that originated with former patients and staff, and what was born from and malformed by the online "real horror" community.

If not for the possibility that Schramm, their one sure link to Braith, had been there, and the certainty that Reverend Carol had died there, as well as a chance that the hand of glory Luisa mentioned might have been there, Shyla didn't think it would be worth looking through all of this. But this was where the case had brought them.

Shyla couldn't put all of the pieces together yet, but she had a general idea of where some might fit, and, at minimum, she *had* the pieces. Braith was close to Schramm. Schramm had tempted the reverend, and the reverend had ended up in the old hospital, where he spoke of the magical hand of a dead man. Shyla wasn't close to being able to say that the hand even existed, much less that it was linked to Braith's unexplained immortality, but it felt like a strong possibility to her, in part because the two mystery people with considerable power and an interest in stopping her investigation apparently didn't want her to find out about the old Yorktown Hospital and the hand of glory.

As Shyla flipped through the pages she saw many inconsistencies. Some reported the year of closure as 1996, others '98 or '99. A couple even left off at one of the earlier closure dates in the 1950s, neglecting to mention the multiple times the hospital reopened. A couple of the pictures pulled from online articles and ebooks didn't match the more recent photos of the derelict site, showing buildings that were not merely outdated versions of a renovated property, but were instead of an entirely different set of buildings. There were two mentions of the hospital being a four-story building when neither photographic depiction of the hospital was taller than two stories. One entry from a local tour book of Yorktown's history even placed the hospital on East Main Street, instead of West Main.

"I mean, we would have to go there in person to be sure about anything," Jinh said. "When I get there it should hit me what's real and what's fake. At minimum, we know Luisa's mother and grandfather–"

Shyla held up a finger, asking for a moment of silence as she flipped through the loose pages, which she started to separate into stacks on the guest bedroom's mattress. Far in the back of her mind, she saw an imaginary version of herself pinning different pages to different corners of a large corkboard, filling spaces in between with connective clues and red string. What she was piecing together wasn't that elaborate, however. She just happened upon what she assumed was the most obvious explanation for the discrepancies she'd seen.

After letting Shyla sift back and forth in silence, while the rustle of pages filled the room, Jinh finally had to ask, "What are you looking for?"

Shyla just held up her finger again, prompting Jinh to come closer to see if she could figure it out for herself. In the corner of her eye, Shyla saw Jinh shake her head out of confusion and frustration. She answered the next question—or what she thought Jinh should ask next—before it came.

"There were two hospitals," Shyla said.

Jinh squinted at the two paper stacks, one notably taller than the other. Then she gave the same furrowed look to Shyla like she was a living puzzle reconstituting before Jinh's eyes.

Shyla repeated, more firmly this time, "There were two hospitals."

"Wait, no . . . how big was Yorktown?" Jinh asked, leaning toward the papers, then sitting beside them like they'd give her an answer to reward better bedside manner. "There were only a couple thousand people living there, right? Even back when it was growing. I think there were less than two thousand. Or barely over."

"I think that's about right," Shyla said.

"So why would they have two hospitals? There were towns that size that didn't even have one."

"Yeah, there were. But Yorktown had two. Look at it."

She gave Jinh time to look it over, observe the same things she had. There wasn't just a difference in closure years, but in the years that the place opened. The more famous Yorktown Hospital opened in 1951, while its unknown predecessor opened in 1919. It was on East Main Street, a four-story building instead of the two-story structure more people were familiar with. A cursory review of its history told of its multiple closings and openings as well, going from a public hospital, to a private mental health facility, to more of a "wellness resort," then returning to a psychiatric facility before a brief stint as a nursing home, then finally shuttering in 1999. How had this been forgotten? It felt, irrationally, to Shyla as though the more notable Yorktown Hospital had been built deliberately to draw attention from the older facility.

"Oh my God," Jinh said. "There were two hospitals."

"There *were*?"

Jinh side-eyed Shyla, whose smile earned one in return. Shyla thought this might have been the first time Jinh genuinely smiled at her—not as part of a ruse, like she had when she first showed up at the hotel—since before they'd worked together on Dante's case. Had it really been that long? That couldn't be right, she had to be forgetting a moment from the past few days. Or she was misremembering how dour and distant they had been toward each other—well, really, how distant *she* had been to Jinh—while helping Dante. It couldn't have been years since they'd shared a smile.

A forceful knocking at her front door startled Shyla. She and Jinh looked at each other for confirmation that they had heard the knocking. They waited for a second set of knocks before reacting. When that came—three knocks as loud as the first set—Shyla stood and moved through the house to the front door. She wondered if she should double back to get her "house gun" from her bedroom. The moment served as an added reminder and encouragement to buy a shotgun to place in the storage closet near the foyer. For now, she decided to just go to the door and check the peephole first.

She expected to see a cop, at worst, or, more likely, one of the random door-to-door salesmen who made occasional rounds through her neighborhood. Instead, she saw Remy, hand raised to knock again before something made her lower it.

"I heard your footsteps," Remy said. "You may as well open up."

"What are you doing here?" Shyla said. To her left she saw Jinh motioning to grab her attention. When she looked at her Jinh mouthed, *Who is it?* As though it mattered whether she was heard or not.

"Saxton thinks I should step in," she said. "He said he told you that would happen if things started to get out of hand." Jinh's expression condensed, then opened as she recognized Remy's voice.

"'Step in'?" Shyla said.

"Assist," Remy clarified. "We got a call about a call placed on you. You scared someone into contacting the police."

Shyla's heart thumped like an upstairs neighbor doing God-knows-what at midnight. Hadn't Luisa said she gave the cops a different description of them or something? No, she'd just said she told the police she didn't want to pursue charges. Maybe she made an excuse that they were friends or family members and that she could handle it herself, something the cops would readily accept so they could take the opportunity to let it go.

Nonetheless, the officers would've had to file a report, and probably talked about the incident among their peers. Luisa had probably given a description of her and Jinh during the initial phone call. Through some chain of communication, this all made it back to Braith.

Not wanting to speak through the door, but also not wanting to let Remy in, Shyla came outside. Instead of stepping back, Remy moved aside, but she at least didn't try to push her way in. Now Shyla could see Remy sported a full black rucksack on her back. She wasn't here for a quick intervention. Braith had instructed her to settle in.

"We took care of everything," Shyla said, "so we don't need any assistance. Thanks for coming out, though."

"You took care of everything? How did you do that when you don't even know what everything is? You're going to get the physical descriptions on the report altered? You'll have the body camera recording misfiled? You're going to do all of that?"

"That feels like overkill."

"Thoroughness," Remy said. "It's called thoroughness. And it also applies to me being here."

"And how long is that supposed to be for?" Shyla asked, gesturing toward the rucksack.

"Until I'm called back. You'll know when I know."

"Oh, for God's sake. What am I even getting paid for if I need a babysitter?"

Remy smirked. "You really want me to take that question back to Saxton? His answer might leave you looking for different work."

"Do I look like I'm hurting for his money?" Shyla said, pointing to her house. "I promise, I'm not."

"Then why did you take the job?"

"Because I felt more than a little bit trapped. Maybe even set up to where I couldn't say no."

"Well, if that's the case, you'd have to think your friend was complicit in it, at minimum," Remy said.

Shyla shook her head, then looked over her shoulder to the casement windows in front of her house. Jinh stood in one, having pulled back the curtain to watch Shyla and Remy. She looked like she haunted the place, like neighborhood children would warn the new kids about her and the house when they moved in. *She's always in the window every afternoon at six o'clock. If she catches you watching her, she'll start appearing in your dreams.*

"We didn't set you up," Remy went on. "You could have just said no and walked away. You still can."

Shyla scoffed. She hadn't shared her biggest motivator for agreeing to work Braith's case. The fear that he might know what she did to Rodney. That he could blackmail her with this information.

And now she had confirmation that he had connections with at least one police department. The odds that the Castle Hills PD was the only one he had any influence over were too small to see with a microscope. Walking away now wasn't an option, and Remy surely knew it, even if she might not know what Braith had over Shyla. Or *possibly* had over her.

He knew she'd fired a gun before and taken a life. And he'd added something about Jinh, as well. *She's not how I knew about what you've done. I found that out on my own.* What else could he have been talking about?

Now he was sending his professional goon to her house to be a live-in spy, reminding her that he knew where she lived, and that he wasn't shy about deploying resources under his employ, from his personal mercenary to moles that might comprise an entire suburban police force. Her only exit from the situation would be to go back in time and decline Dante's offer, so as not to find herself on Braith's radar. She wasn't ready to believe this was completely impossible given everything she had been recently exposed to, but for practical purposes, she had to consider it undoable since she had zero clue how to do it. Maybe she should ask Jinh about it.

In the meantime, she believed if she finished this and got the payout Braith had agreed to, she could use that money to protect herself, and her family. Buy a house—hell, an estate—somewhere with no extradition treaty, for starters. That felt like an extreme, early step, but as she'd just heard from Remy, it was better to be thorough.

Anyway, that was only if things went bad or worse. Ideally, Braith didn't know about Rodney and had bluffed Shyla based on a tell she didn't realize she had. Hopefully he would leave her be after she helped him find the source of his immortality "curse." He struck her as arrogant, entitled, and certainly deceptive, but not necessarily an ingrate.

Then again, she imagined it was difficult if not impossible to be as wealthy as he was without developing some dearth of gratitude.

She was getting ahead of and apart from what was important.

"What exactly does 'assisting' entail?" Shyla said.

"Just about anything you can think of and, hopefully, most of what you can't. I run interference with law enforcement, security guards, bodyguards, and anything related. I help you get into places you would have trouble getting into."

"We haven't had a problem with that yet."

"Right. 'Yet.' Let's not wait until you have the problem to find a solution for it."

Stubbornness told her to keep objecting but prudence won her over. It wasn't like there was some masterful counterargument she could make that would prompt Remy to go back to Braith and report she'd failed. *Sorry, but when I got over there she started making valid points and shit, what was I supposed to do about that?* Shyla made her displeasure known with an exaggerated sigh as she walked back through the front door, with Remy following.

"Least you could have done is bring some tacos or something," Shyla said.

"If you want to order delivery, I'll pay for it. I've got a per diem."

Shyla closed the door and pointed between Jinh and Remy. "You've met, right?"

"On video calls. First time in person." Remy extended her hand, and Jinh took it like she was being handed a gun she had no intention of using. They didn't shake, just briefly clasped hands, then released. Jinh put her hand behind her back immediately after while Remy's went up to the strap of her rucksack so she could remove it.

Shyla started to explain. "Braith sent her here—"

"I heard," Jinh said.

Following the sound of Remy's rucksack thunking on the floorboards, an awkward, stuffy silence stilled the three of them. Remy finally broke it by asking, "So, what have we got?"

"Not really sure yet," Shyla said. "I'll catch you up."

They sat in the dining room. Jinh ordered dinner on her phone, Remy paid as promised, and Shyla guided Remy through all they had discovered so far. The only details she withheld were related to her behavior in the kill room of the Inspiration Sweet. The laugh she'd had at Garrett Schramm's expense for thinking he could tempt her, thinking they were anything alike. And, of course, she kept quiet about what she'd revealed to Jinh. That she was indeed a killer.

Shyla still hadn't shared the specifics of that with Jinh. She didn't know when and how to break down exactly who she had killed, and why.

Rodney Hewitt. Husband to Linda Montgomery. Guilty of aiding and abetting his partner after she kidnapped an infant from a maternity ward. Shot dead by the girl he and Linda raised as their daughter until she was seventeen. Until she solved her own disappearance, reclaimed her real name, outed her fake parents for who they were, and made sure at least one of them paid not only for stealing her, but for the death of her real mother.

16

Shyla told Jinh she'd feel better if they slept together in her bed tonight, especially with Remy insisting that she preferred sleeping on the living room couch. Presumably to keep from being locked or barred inside one of the guest rooms. Jinh had obliged Shyla's request, and they lay next to each other with Jinh's head resting on Shyla's shoulder, for the first time since Shyla had left the apartment they shared three years ago.

They did not sleep, however.

Divided, discordant images comprised of one memory tormented Shyla's mind in the dark. What should have been a straightforward narrative became kaleidoscopic. She spent over an hour awake, staring at the ceiling fan, locking in on one spinning blade and following it until it made her want to shut her eyes. This helped her remember to blink.

She was, at different moments, in the room of the last house she'd lived in with Rodney and Linda. Then she was in the field pulling Rodney's slight, limp frame toward the well. She was back in the house, cleaning up after disposing of his body.

She watched over her own still form in bed the same way Rodney had. She was awake, but he didn't realize it. Years of practice at faking her sleep had paid off.

The shattered mirror of this memory, with its shifting shards that held trapped reflections of every second of that night, abruptly mended itself and put things in proper order.

Rodney watched her in bed for so long Shyla thought she wouldn't be able to maintain her ruse. Her steady breathing belied a racing heartbeat. Years later, and likely for the rest of her life, she'd wonder what he would've done if she'd woken up. Would he have had to kill her, reluctant as he was to do so, because she'd have seen him with the gun?

She kept her eyes closed and her body still, and Rodney couldn't bring himself to shoot the girl he'd raised, so he turned his back to her and left the room without closing the door. Shyla peeked at him with one open eye after sensing he'd turned around. That's when she'd seen the gun in his right hand.

The sound of the gun hitting the kitchen counter motivated her to move. The time was now. The wooden legs of a stool skittered across tile, and that, along with Rodney's pathetic sobs, covered the sound of Shyla sliding out of bed.

She couldn't feel her legs as she walked out of her carpeted bedroom, down the hall, and into the kitchen.

Rodney was on the phone with someone. "Maybe we shouldn't do this," he was saying.

Shyla stood behind him, equal parts nervous and furious, not sure whether to lunge at him or rush for the door. His gun was behind him on the counter. Pointed at him, like an arrow directing her toward what to do.

"But if she's told anyone already, then it won't matter," Rodney said, "and we'll have just . . . we'll have killed her for nothing."

The person on the other line raised their voice now, and Shyla was sure it was Linda. Rodney wiped at his eyes and nodded along to whatever was being said, then responded, "I know, I know, I just . . . You're right. I'll do it. I'll tell her now. It's either . . . Right . . . Right. Yeah, okay. I love you, too."

This confirmed it was Linda, but more important, he had just agreed to whatever she had told him to do. Shyla couldn't hesitate another second. In three strides she made it to the gun and had it leveled at the back of Rodney's neck before he could react.

"Don't turn around," she told him.

She could have shot him right there, or asked him what exactly he'd planned to do with the gun he'd brought into her room while she was "asleep." This could have given him an out to claim he just wanted to scare her, pretend to threaten her into not going to the police or anyone else with whatever she'd already figured out.

Instead, Shyla asked him, "What did you do with my mother?"

"Baby girl, listen to me now—"

"What did you do to my mother?" she said, grief and fury pinching her voice.

"Wha— I . . . I was just on the phone with her—"

"No. Not her. My *mother*."

Rodney's back straightened and he half turned his head toward her. He put on his fatherly voice as if he had any right to do so, and said, "Linda *is* your—"

"No the fuck she's not. And you're not my father, so don't try to drop your tone with me. You're a fucking stranger who just walked into my room with a gun."

"Baby girl . . . that's not what I . . . you don't understand–"

She pushed the gun hard into the back of his neck and he seized, clenching his fists, not because he was bracing to strike, but forcing himself not to move.

"What did you do–"

"I didn't do anything to that woman," Rodney said. "She was crazy. I just told her to stay away, that's all."

"You're a liar," Shyla said, her gritted teeth almost keeping the words caged. "All you ever did was lie to me. You stole me, you lied to me, and you were just about to kill me."

"No, that's not–"

"What did Linda just tell you?"

He couldn't answer honestly without adding yet another lie to his life's total, so tried again to assert some authority. "Don't use her name. That's disrespectful. That's your momma, now."

"You killed my mother," Shyla said.

"What? What are you . . . are you talking about that crazy woman?"

"Don't call her that."

"Why are we even talking about her? Look, just set the gun down and calm down, okay? I'm sorry, now. I'm real, *real* sorry I even brought it in here. It was a bad idea, and I didn't . . . I wouldn't have used it. I would never–"

"Do you even hear yourself?" Shyla said, almost like she didn't expect him to hear her, like they weren't even in the same building. "You came in my room while I was asleep with a gun. You came into my room while you thought I was sleeping, with *this fucking gun in your hand.*"

"I'm sorry!" Rodney said, like he could shout it forcefully enough to blast away Shyla's anger. He wasn't apologetic, he was desperate.

"Sorry for what?" Shyla said. "For taking me?"

"I didn't do that! Linda was the one . . . Listen, please just put the gun down and I can–"

"What else are you sorry for, Rodney? Are you sorry for killing my mother?"

"That woman wasn't–"

"Her name was Jacqueline. Her family called her Jackie, and she named me Shyla. *That's* my name. I'm Shyla Sinclair."

"Enough of that! Stop it, goddammit. You're still *our* baby girl, not hers. That woman wasn't your momma. She didn't raise you."

Shyla's rage dazzled her. It was so pure it almost felt good. A tingling sensation enveloped her, and the gun felt like the only thing keeping her from floating away. No, not floating, firing off like a rocket that would explode when she was barely a hundred feet high.

She didn't raise you. He'd really said that. As if Jacqueline had abandoned Shyla on the side of the road, and Linda and Rodney had saved her.

That woman . . . She was crazy . . . She didn't raise you.

"You never gave her a chance," Shyla said. She pulled the trigger, and it felt so easy to do that she did it again, and once more before she realized she couldn't hear anything but a tinny ringing, and that the man who'd been standing in front of her a second earlier wasn't in her direct line of sight anymore. She thought to look around, like he might have run off to hide elsewhere in the house, but realized that all she had to do was look down.

Rodney lay on the floor, bleeding out. There was a bullet hole high up on his nape, almost through the base of his skull, another in the upper center of his back, and a third a little lower and to the right.

When the gunfire tinnitus dissipated, all she could hear was Rodney's awful whimpering.

A minute later, there was nothing.

It had been stunningly easy to pull the trigger. The aftermath, she presumed, would be considerably harder to deal with. Shyla waited for a wave of nausea to hit her, and tightened her stomach and took deep breaths to prepare for it, but the feeling never came. Similarly, she anticipated that the realization of what she'd just done would crash into her so forcefully she wouldn't be able to remain standing, so she stepped a little closer to the stool Rodney had just been on, but that sense of "Oh God, I killed someone" failed to show, as well. She was at peace with this almost immediately.

He was planning to kill you, she reminded herself, in case regret tried to find enough space to stretch its legs in her mind. *He wanted to kill me, just like he killed my mother.*

God, my mother. Shyla realized that he never told her exactly what he'd done to Jacqueline Sinclair. How he killed her and where he hid her body. This made her eyes water. She'd have to remember this when she caught up to Linda. That was the only other person she could get closure from regarding the death of Jacqueline Sinclair, or so she thought at the time.

For now, she had to consider her next step. She blinked away her still-forming tears and looked at the phone Rodney had dropped when he fell. Calling 911 seemed like the obvious move until she gave it an extra second of thought.

She'd shot him in the back. Not once, multiple times. It would be hard to explain that she felt threatened given how she'd killed him. The fact that he was one of her kidnappers might not matter, either. The news story about that poor girl who was arrested for killing the man who trafficked and abused her had just come up in school. One of her teachers introduced it as a debate topic, comparing legality and morality. If she called in and confessed to what she'd done, there wasn't a guarantee that she'd be seen strictly as a victim, or that she would be treated with much understanding or mercy.

The room was starting to tilt back and forth, so Shyla sat on the stool. She looked at the small pool of blood coming from Rodney's neck, spreading under his half-turned face. There wasn't any blood coming from under his body. Did that mean there weren't any exit wounds? She checked the far wall Rodney had been facing when she'd fired and saw no signs of a bullet having struck it. She didn't see any spatters of blood on the floor or walls, either.

Trying to clean up the scene would make her look worse if she wasn't thorough, but it might not be quite as difficult as she imagined. If she was lucky, the police wouldn't care enough about Rodney's disappearance to genuinely look into it.

During the months she'd spent researching her own circumstances, discovering how she could have been abducted and moved around from state to state without anyone finding out, she realized how many crimes remain unsolved simply because there isn't enough incentive to investigate. It wasn't like in the TV shows where detectives and forensic scientists worked late hours on every case, always with an eye toward clues that lay beneath the surface. A case that could be closed as "exactly what it looks like" wouldn't receive extra attention. Hell, plenty of cases were left open and essentially abandoned because they just weren't a priority and would require more effort and resources than authorities were willing to give.

The abduction of a little Black girl from a maternity ward in a Midwestern city, for instance.

She was in a different part of the country now, dealing with a different police force, but she thought the general principle would still apply here. Rodney wouldn't be on anyone's most wanted list, and even if the cops started to suspect something had happened to him—that he hadn't just gone on the run—they wouldn't think he was worth the investigation.

She just had to think of a place, and something would come to her while she cleaned up. When she went to look for cleaning supplies in the cabinet under the kitchen sink, she saw something that made her realize she might not need to think of a place, and that also reinforced that she'd done the right thing.

A large, unlabeled jug of thick, dark purple liquid was under the sink, next to newly purchased large brushes with visibly stiff bristles. One brush head was attached to the chuck of a power drill. A stack of thick rags and a small bucket made up the rest of the newly purchased supplies. Things Shyla had never seen Rodney and Linda buy before. They'd had to clear out the usual cleaning products that would be here, like dish detergent and disinfectant wipes, to make room for these other things, which they'd picked up for a specific purpose.

Rodney could claim he wasn't really going to hurt Shyla, and maybe he'd had second thoughts the minute he walked into her room—maybe even before that—but there had definitely been a plan in place to kill her. He and Linda had premeditated it, talked it over, prepared for it, and put money into it. All because they had suspected, accurately, that she had figured them out, and they'd rather kill the girl they called their daughter than let her live to tell the world what they'd done.

If they went through this much prep just for the cleanup, they had definitely picked a place to dump her body.

Shyla went back to Rodney's phone and unlocked it with a fingerprint from his right hand. A new message had come in from Linda. Shyla glimpsed the preview without wanting to.

It's for the best, for us and even for . . .

That was as much of it as she could read, but she could guess what kind of bullshit justification and psychotic, murderous pep talk she'd see if she opted to open the full message.

She clicked on the MAPS icon instead and checked his most recent search and travel history, and saw it right at the top. A flagged location without an address about an hour's drive away from the house, in the Hill Country. The satellite view of the location didn't provide much detail, only showing dry, rocky terrain mostly obscured by trees. No buildings nearby, and not even a paved road that could bring her to it.

Hoping to find a little more information about this place before driving there, she checked Rodney's search history, and beyond searches into stain-removing solvents, and another on frangible bullets designed to essentially disintegrate on impact with the target, what jumped out at her was one stating "caves near me." She clicked on this from the drop-down options and the first result, marked as "Visited," was an article from a spelunking website titled "With Over 3,000 Caves Near San Antonio, How Do You Know Where to Start?"

She knew what the flagged location was now. It wasn't just a place where Rodney and Linda planned to dig a shallow grave, but a different, much deeper kind of hole in the ground. One they must have been confident would keep a body hidden forever.

17

Shyla was being jostled so hard she thought the bed was moving. It took her an extra second after waking up in her bedroom, dimly lit by the lamp on the nightstand opposite her side of the bed, to realize that she'd even been asleep. She remembered lying beside Jinh and her thoughts drifting back to the night she shot Rodney, but didn't think she'd even been that tired. Now Jinh was practically roughing her up to get her out of bed, like it was an emergency.

She shoved Jinh's hands away and said, "I'm up," then remembered Remy was in the living room and lowered her voice. "What's happening? What's wrong?"

Do I need my gun? she thought.

"No," Jinh said, reading the unspoken question, and Shyla felt like invisible fingers had pulled a splinter out of her brain that she didn't even know was there. Her right eye twitched and she shook her head.

"Did you just . . . ?"

"Yes," Jinh said. "Sorry."

"Why did it hurt?"

"I don't know. I didn't even mean to. I'm sorry. I think . . . Listen, you were dreaming, and it woke me up. I saw it all. It's almost like my head is on fire right now. Shyla, was that real? What I saw you do to Rodney? Is that just what you wanted to do or is that what you did?"

Shyla's silence provided enough of an answer. She knew that, and Jinh likely did as well, but Jinh still shook her head and said, "I need to hear it from you. I need to be sure."

Shyla sighed. She'd already confessed to Jinh, when they'd made it out of the Inspiration Sweet, that she'd killed someone, but she'd spared her the specifics. If Jinh had seen it all through a replay in Shyla's dreams, though, why continue to hide anything? Why keep it from her?

Because she isn't supposed to know, she thought. *This belongs to me. It should just be mine.*

Realizing how pointless and petulant this sentiment was, Shyla relented. There was no use in holding on to this secret any longer. "Yeah, it's what happened. I killed him."

"Because you thought he killed your mother?"

"That and the whole thing about him planning to kill me first."

Jinh nodded. "I know, but your mother . . . I felt it. That was the main thing. You thought he killed her. Is that why–"

"We don't have to talk about this."

Shyla tried to slide away and lay her head back on her pillow, looking to shut off the conversation, but Jinh put her hand on Shyla's arm. High on her forearm, near the crook, and for whatever reason this was Shyla's weak point with Jinh. Something about the tenderness of it, the way it almost tickled her in that specific place, always made her at least stop to listen, even when it was the last thing she wanted to do. Jinh found this out early in their relationship but rarely exploited it, to her credit. Only when she felt it was important.

"I didn't know," Jinh said, startling Shyla back into the here and now.

How could you have? Shyla started to say, but stopped herself, because there *was* a way for Jinh to know. That same psychic ability that at the time had shown Jinh what really happened to Shyla's mother should have also shown her that Shyla had killed Rodney. He wasn't just a missing person, along with his wife. Shyla had shot him and dropped him down into a space so deep and thin it would be too dangerous to try to pull him out even if someone found him.

Jinh should have known, damn it. If she had, she could have spared Shyla the truth about her mother. That she'd died in an accident on the road, during her drive back from a meeting with Rodney. He'd had nothing to do with her death. Shyla couldn't have known this then—and wouldn't have believed it if anyone other than her psychic girlfriend had told her.

From the relatively few newspaper articles and blog posts Shyla had found at the time, Jacqueline Sinclair had never given up her search for her kidnapped daughter. At some point she had picked up on leads that brought her all the way down to Texas, but she had failed to come home from that trip.

Shyla's father, Martin, had supported Jackie up until that final leg of the investigation. He'd actually thought the latest clues Jackie had found were promising. He thought they were closer than ever to actually finding their baby girl, who would have been a teenager by then. So Martin wanted to dig a little deeper, from afar, to get concrete evidence that would hopefully convince authorities to take them seriously, at last. Jacqueline was done putting faith in anyone else to get her girl back, though, so she had gone off, and Martin let her go on her own, and it was the biggest regret of his life. One he couldn't live with soberly. Less than a year after Jackie's disappearance, Martin took four times as many sleeping pills as his prescribed dosage, washed them down with Hennessy, and left a note for Teonna to save space beside his grave to bury Jackie there, whenever they found her.

Shyla wished she'd gotten to know her father but wondered about her mother more often. She thought of how brave her mother had been to go after her child's kidnappers alone. The gall she'd had to even arrange a meeting with them. Shyla regularly wished—prayed—for an ounce of her mother's audacity. To hear Aunt Teonna tell it, she had it already. *You've got all of Jackie's heart and then some, Girl-Girl. If you didn't you wouldn't have figured out who you really were.*

Intuition hadn't been the only thing that helped Shyla conclude she didn't belong to Rodney and Linda, however. Serendipity had played a role. She happened to see a movie on television called *Running on Empty* when she was twelve. It was about parents on the run with their children, fleeing from a crime that condemned them to a half-nomadic existence. Always prepared to move the moment anyone might become aware of their secret.

It made her wonder why her parents had taken her from Mobile, Alabama, to Biloxi, Mississippi, to Alexandria, Louisiana, then to Atlanta, and then, over to Texas City, Texas, between Houston and Galveston, all before she became a teenager. Why they never gave her a good or consistent answer as to why they had to move so often. Why kids at school seemed puzzled when she told them that, no, her parents weren't in the military, they didn't work the oil fields, and they weren't migrant farmers. She didn't exactly know what they did for a living, as they were always vague about it, but she was sure they didn't have any of those jobs, which left the fleeting friends she gained and lost scratching their heads when Shyla explained all the places she'd been, despite Rodney and Linda always warning her against telling people—even other kids—about that.

She didn't lie to the few friends she was able to make in these places, knowing full well she'd have to leave them at some point. At least she could leave them with the truth about herself, something to make her memorable to them.

Running on Empty had provided the first hint as to why Rodney and Linda could never stay in one place for too long, never had many friends of their own, never brought around other relatives, and didn't let Shyla engage in extracurricular school activities. They even tried to homeschool her once, before likely realizing that the paperwork required to do it was much more intensive than what was needed—or could be faked—at an ordinary, understaffed public school with overworked administrators.

A few years after she'd seen the film, with the ideas it put in her head holding steady, they abruptly moved to San Marcos. This was the most sudden move yet. Every other time they at least waited for the school year to end, but this time they uprooted her in the middle of March. Shyla was still young and didn't know the overwhelming majority of what there was to know about the world, but she knew that something about her family situation—and her "parents"—was bizarre. That's when she started staying late in the library of her newest school, lying to Linda and Rodney about difficult assignments so she could have more time alone to look up reasons they might be on the run with her. It wasn't long until she came across stories that linked fugitive parents with baby thefts, and it occurred to her how little she trusted her parents, and that there might be a good reason for this.

As Linda and Rodney started questioning her more aggressively about why she was spending so much time in the library, why she couldn't just come home to do her schoolwork on the computer they bought for her, and what else she could be doing when they weren't around, Shyla learned to fear them.

Then she happened upon a few news stories about a newborn taken from a Minneapolis hospital, a police investigation that barely got out of bed to look around, and distraught, dogged parents-turned-investigators who had to resort to charity and crowdfunding to pay bills and keep the pursuit of their lost daughter alive. She saw a photograph of her mother, saw her own eyes, nose, brow, lips, and chin looking back at her. Right away she understood why her skin tone didn't match either Linda's or Rodney's lighter complexions.

Finally she found a thirty-second news clip about Jacqueline "Jackie" Sinclair being missing, her last-known whereabouts being the Galveston, Texas, area, about three years ago. She would have gone missing just a little bit before Rodney and Linda had moved Shyla away from Texas City, less than fifteen miles from Galveston.

With this revelation Shyla's paranoia developed new purpose, and she found spectacular anger within herself. Anger that in its purest form would be worthy of its own museum, so it could be studied and admired. She saw colors of hatred that could blind a god. In hindsight, it was amazing that she'd refrained from trying to kill Rodney or Linda until one of them came into her room with a gun.

Jinh spoke up again, returning Shyla to the moment. "If I had known, I don't think I would have told you. When I had that vision of where she was I just . . . I thought you needed to know. I thought I was helping."

"I know you did," Shyla said, then shrugged and repeated, "I know." After a moment, she succumbed with a grin to a grimmer curiosity. "You wouldn't be able to tell me where Linda is, would you?"

Jinh shook her head. "If I ever did find out . . . if I ever heard anything from her . . . would you want me to tell you?"

Shyla knew Jinh well enough to recognize a question holding a secret from her tone alone. "You've heard something from her before."

Jinh swallowed, shut her eyes, and Shyla sensed that she was afraid of saying something that would make Shyla leave her again.

"It's okay," Shyla said. "I want to know."

Jinh exhaled slowly. "I wasn't ever sure that it was her. That's why I didn't tell you before. I mean, I knew, I felt the truth of it, but I still . . . I couldn't be as sure as I wanted to be. That's the only reason . . ."

"It's okay," Shyla said again.

"It's not," Jinh said, shaking her head. "I should have told you before."

"Just say it."

This time Jinh's nod was more assured. "The first time I came to see you down here, I heard this voice every night pleading with me to tell you something. It was a woman, and she'd say over and over, 'Tell her. Tell her. I gave everything up for her. I gave up everything I could be.' And when I didn't tell you, she got angrier every night. She was shouting in my head, 'Tell her now. You have to tell her–I gave up everything just so she could be mine. That's real love. Tell her now.' The voice was far away, but it felt so strong. And something about it sounded like a trick, so I never told you. But I could feel it was Linda. I could tell. The 'trick' part was just her trying to fool me into giving you her version of things. Like she'd actually sacrificed anything for you."

Shyla chuckled to mock Linda's sentiment, as though the woman was listening, which she might be, for all she knew. "So you heard her ghost? She's dead?"

"I can't say for sure. I catch stray thoughts from the living from time to time. I just heard yours, you know."

"Yeah, but I'm close. That matters, doesn't it?"

"Sometimes, but not always. Not if I'm really thinking about you, or I've got some kind of connection to you. I sensed you were going to the Inspiration Sweet even though I was all the way in Houston, right? I caught that from about two hundred miles away. And you weren't even trying to share that with me. I've had other moments, with other people, where they knew what city I would be in, and stayed up all night trying to make me think of them and hear what they wanted to tell me."

"So you're saying Linda could've been . . ." Shyla shuddered. Not out of fear that Linda might have been close enough to spy on them, lurking to get a glimpse after listening to Shyla tell her story on Jinh's podcast. Not because that would mean Linda had deliberately tapped into Jinh's mind, believing enough in Jinh's professed empathic telepathy to try to use it to her advantage, try to manipulate Jinh into relaying a message for her. No, Shyla felt a chill because if this was true—*if* Linda was alive and nearby in those days when Shyla and Jinh first explored their feelings for each other—then that meant Shyla had missed her chance. She'd been too busy pursuing romance to keep her eyes open and her head on a swivel, when she might have caught Linda watching from a crowd when Shyla and Jinh were on dates at San Antonio's Battle of Flowers Parade, or during the Strawberry Festival in the nearby town of Poteet.

Linda might have been close enough to run to. Shyla could have had her. She could have *had* her, and just missed her.

"So she could have been alive?" Shyla said, barely suppressing her anger.

"I don't know. I can't say."

"You don't even have a clue? A hint?"

Jinh sighed. "If I did . . . if I did, would you really want to know?" Shyla felt the gravity and strength of this question like it was a rogue planet threatening to rip her world away as it passed through, steal her from the sun and moon and anything else that balanced her out and allowed life to go on. "Sure. I'd like to know. If she's alive, I want to catch up with her. Reminisce on some of the good times, and tell her it's all bygones now. We all make mistakes, right? Some more severe than others, but hey, we all need to be forgiven for something. I'd tell her it's all water under the bridge. But when I say that, it'll make me think about actual water under an actual bridge, like where my real mother's still stuck in her car, and I'll think about how even if they didn't kill her, it's still their fault she died. And then I'd say, 'Fuck forgiveness.' And then I'd go to work on her."

"Shyla–"

"No, Jinh. I don't want you to tell me. I want to know, but I *can't* find out. If she's alive, I'd like to reunite her with Rodney. But if she's already dead, I'd rather go on thinking I might catch up to her someday. So that makes it a hard no. I mean that, Jinh. If she's alive, I can't know, and if she isn't, then it doesn't matter. Do you understand?"

Jinh nodded, but Shyla waited for her to give verbal confirmation. Jinh said, "I understand."

"Good," Shyla said. "You get why I left now, don't you?"

"I think so," Jinh said, "but I'd rather hear it from you to be sure."

"Okay. After you told me about my mom's accident, how she really died, there was no way I was going to be able to keep what I did to Rodney to myself. Which would have meant asking you to lie if his case ever warmed up again for any reason. I was mad, yeah, but I was also scared of doing that to you. So I left."

"I'd have lied for you, Shyla. I still would. You think I wouldn't?"

"All I was thinking was that I couldn't put you in that position," Shyla said.

Jinh took a moment to respond, then just nodded and said, "Thanks for that."

Shyla started to turn over to try to squeeze in a little more sleep before the sun would be up in a few hours but stopped herself. There was something else she wanted to know.

"Can I ask you something?" she said to Jinh. "When you caught the vision from my dream just now, and saw how it all happened, were you able to see anything from his side of it? Or get any of his thoughts?"

Jinh shook her head. "No. Why?"

"I've just always had some unanswered questions in my head, since it happened. He said he couldn't hurt me, but was he just saying that because I had a gun on him, or did he really mean it? Did he really have a change of heart, or would he have gone back in the room and shot me if I hadn't gotten to him first? And then when I think about him leaving the gun where he did, and not turning around and trying to do anything even after I got it . . . I don't know. It's like he wanted me to kill him," Shyla said, the words sneaking out before she could think to corral them.

"Do you really think that?" Jinh said.

"Sometimes."

"Would it make you feel better if it was true?"

Shyla recalled the daze followed by dizziness that overcame her as she stared at Rodney's still body, the *pop-pop-pop* from his gun still in her ears like it planned to make a home there. It felt surreal, as did the aftermath of cleaning up the scene. It felt sickening and abhorrent, but also oddly relieving in a way that was still painful, like she had pulled a superfluous, pinching rib out of her torso.

Would it have been any better if she could have taken a second to consider whether he wanted her to kill him? That she'd given him the escape he'd hoped for but couldn't give to himself?

No.

"That would make it worse," Shyla said. Jinh flinched, but then moved closer to hold her.

"I'm going to need you to keep an eye on me, Jinh. If we run into something else like what's down in the basement, at that bar, or just . . . *anything* else . . . I don't know. I've got this side of me that bubbles up every once in a while. I keep it pushed down for the most part, and when it does come up I'm good at hiding it, but it's there. And it wishes I could have that night over so I could do it slower. Make him pay double, once for him and once for Linda. And learning about my mother–what you told me–that hasn't changed it. But without Rodney to kill again, that part of me will look for anybody it thinks is close enough, and I feel like we're going to be in enough trouble as it is without me looking for a reason to shoot when we might be better off running. So just look out for me, all right? In case it creeps back up on me at the wrong time."

"What if it's the right time?" Jinh said.

Not quite knowing how to answer this, or even whether Jinh really wanted an answer, Shyla fixated on the ceiling fan again. Her eyes followed a blade until it spun her to sleep.

18

Remy offered to drive to Yorktown because "If we were to get pulled over, I can deal with it better than you."

Shyla wanted to laugh at this, certain that Remy wasn't interested in being considerate, just in gaining control wherever she could. She woke up earlier than Jinh and Shyla that morning, and used Shyla's coffee maker to brew twelve cups. This felt like an immediate overstep, one disguised as a courtesy, no less.

"I just thought it would be one less thing to do before we got going," Remy had said when Shyla came out of her bedroom to not only see the carafe more than half full, but Remy holding one of her mugs with steam rising above the rim.

"I figured we'd get an early start, if both of you are good with that," Remy said next, then made her offer to drive. "I can even pitch in gas money." She took a fifty-dollar bill from her pocket, the same bill Shyla had given her a few days ago, and handed it to her.

So, she's a little petty and doesn't like to be one-upped, Shyla noted as she pocketed the bill, already trying to think of the perfect moment to return it to Remy—with a quip included—in the near future. She then cycled through her options regarding Remy's offer to drive, and decided there wasn't substantial risk to having Remy behind the wheel. At least she could keep an eye on her there, and, hell, hadn't she just let the woman sleep unsupervised under her roof overnight? She'd been a little too tired and overwhelmed by recent events, too distracted by the idea of spirits and remembrances of shooting Rodney, to grasp how careless that might have been.

Dwelling now on the potential mistake of leaving Remy alone in her living room overnight wasn't going to do anything to correct it. The sooner she found an answer Braith would be satisfied with, the sooner she could be through with him, with Remy, with all of the ghosts and weird shit. She needed to placate this man and then never see him again.

She agreed to let Remy drive them to Yorktown in Shyla's car, and Jinh didn't object. Before they left, while Remy was in the bathroom, Shyla told Jinh to take the driver's side backseat, and tried to give her a pocketknife. Jinh declined it, then let Shyla peek into her purse, past the business cards, lip balms, mints, and more, to see the folded, seven-inch knife—a navaja—at the bottom. Shyla pulled it out, opened it, heard the distinct ratchet-clicking of the pinions that locked it in place, then handed it to Jinh to see how to release the lock and refold it.

"When did you start carrying that?" Shyla asked.

"Had an incident at a meet-and-greet with fans in Pittsburgh," Jinh said, returning the knife to her purse.

"You know what to do with it?"

Jinh raised an eyebrow. "Yes. Different incident after an event in Denver. You'd know this if you hadn't blocked me on all the socials."

"Well, if it makes you feel any better, I haven't wanted to kiss you this badly since our first date."

Jinh's cheeks flushed rosy pink for a second, then the door to the bathroom opened and she reactivated her focused mode, soft hopefulness lifting from her eyes, replaced by unreadable blankness.

"Ladies, are we ready?" Remy said.

"Waiting on you," Shyla said, before handing Remy the keys.

Yorktown, Texas, was a ninety-minute drive southeast from downtown San Antonio. They stopped once at the edge of San Antonio's city limits to fill Shyla's gas tank and grab some energy drinks. The remaining drive was stalled only once, by an accident that reduced highway traffic to one lane for a five-mile stretch. When they made it to the scene of the accident, they saw one car with a barely dented fender and another—a minivan—that was upside down with its windshield half busted. Shyla glanced back to see Jinh briefly close her eyes and mouth what Shyla presumed was a prayer.

Once they passed the traffic jam caused by the wreck, they made it to Yorktown without incident, only seeing one state trooper in his Tahoe. He had pulled up beside them on the left, then slowed to match speed with them. Stealing looks without turning her head, Shyla thought she saw the trooper staring into her car, and at Remy specifically. Then after a moment he sped off like he was making a getaway.

Maybe Remy had been right about being of use if they ran into police. Hell, she or Braith might have made a call to every agency they could get ahold of to preempt any attempted stops. *Here are the two types of cars I'll be in, here's what I look like, here's who I will be traveling with, and here's what will happen to you, your career, and your parents' mortgage if you pull me over.*

They made it into Yorktown, a mostly flat area that covered less than two square miles. It had empty space to spare, nondescript homes and storefronts, and a higher pickup-truck-per-person ratio than Shyla had expected, even by Texas standards. Shyla had mapped her GPS to the address on East Main, and before they even turned down the street, it was evident that the building wasn't there any longer. A four-story hospital would have comparatively towered over the trees and other buildings in the vicinity and been visible from afar. When Shyla saw nothing looming over the treetops she readied herself to see a dollar store or local mechanic shop occupying the space where the hospital had been, perhaps accompanied by matching, oversized parking lots. What she was surprised to see, instead, was grass, strips of concrete comprised of a crisscrossed sidewalk connecting the opposite ends of the rectangular space, and a couple of relatively young trees. It looked like the beginnings of a courtyard that was abandoned before someone thought to add a few benches and maybe a small fountain in the center.

Remy slowed the car to a crawl as they came upon the open space. "This is it, right?"

"This is the address I have," Shyla said.

"You're sure?"

"I'm sure it's what I have, yes," Shyla said, annoyed.

Jinh asked, "Should we get out? Look around?"

Remy said, "Look for what? There's nothing here."

"But there used to be," Shyla answered, "and Jinh might be able to pick up on something."

"So she's legit?" Remy said, checking Jinh through the rear-view mirror.

"Just park," Shyla said.

Remy took a right turn at the next stop, passing a squat, white-painted bar with a letterboard marquee promoting a HALLOWEEN HAPPY HOUR ALL OCTOBER. Shyla thought Remy might circle the block just to delay following orders from someone she thought shouldn't be giving them, but she pulled into a diagonal parking space as directed. The three of them got out of the car. Jinh walked ahead, and Shyla followed a few steps behind her. Remy walked deliberately beside Shyla like she was aware of how Shyla would feel if Remy was in the back.

Three trucks, a jeep, and a sedan passed on Main Street as the three of them made their way to where the sidewalk intersected. Each vehicle appeared to slow down as they got closer, and Shyla could almost feel the drivers watching them, quickly determining that they didn't recognize them, and wondering who they were and what they were doing here.

This was presumptive on her part, but making such observations and assumptions was an essential part of her job. You never knew when some busybody would call the cops on you for looking "suspicious" at a public park, even with a book in one hand, a sandwich in the other, and headphones plugged into your ears. They might decide to confront you directly, ask what business you have here, *then* call the cops to claim you posed a threat—lying about you right to your face—when you refused to answer questions they had no business asking. Already, Shyla was preparing what to say in case someone came over to challenge them.

If it was a cop, she would present her private investigator license, quote a few court cases related to her rights to be where she was, and suggest that she was not only recording, but streaming live, if they tried to make her betray client confidentiality, or otherwise attempted to intimidate her, much less threaten her.

If it was just another citizen, she was prepared to turn their questions around to make *them* feel like they were being accused of something and needed to leave before they got themselves involved in a situation they wanted no part of. This had worked for her in the past, more than once. When asked what she was doing, Shyla returned volley by asking the person if they lived nearby. They would respond either with an arrogant “Yes,” an indignant refusal to answer, or just repeat their question. Then Shyla would flash her license and explain that she was hired to find a missing teenager. One time she’d said the teen had been taken by a parent, another time by an older boyfriend, and a third time by a cult leader. Each time, however, she made sure to insinuate that this nosy neighbor was behaving suspiciously, coming up and harassing Shyla to get her to leave. Something they might do if they were trying to hide something—or someone. She’d only tried this three times but was so successful at it she already felt she’d mastered the technique.

It didn’t look like she’d need to use it here. The gawking drivers kept going after apparently being satisfied with what they saw. For the second time that day Shyla wondered whether Remy’s promised benefits were actually paying off. Having a tall, fit white woman whose attire and posture declared *military overachiever* accompanying them couldn’t hurt. While it didn’t help them remain inconspicuous, that wasn’t an option for Shyla and Jinh, anyway. Not around here. But Remy probably made them look like they were on a mission that they had a permit for, and that would keep the average nosy neighbor away.

Even with all of this in mind, the openness of the space made Shyla impatient. The sky felt larger and lower than it ought to be, and the scant clouds looked to her like hiding places for floating, prying eyes. She couldn’t shake the sense of being surveilled.

“You getting anything yet?” she said to Jinh, who gave her a glare that could freeze fire, reminding Shyla that Jinh didn’t like that phrasing. Shyla realized the question was too vague and closed-ended, on top of Jinh finding it insulting.

"What's your first impression of the place?" she said.

"We haven't been here that long," Jinh said.

"I know." *I also know it doesn't have to take long,* Shyla thought, remembering how Jinh froze the instant she saw the door to the killing floor.

"Well, right now I just . . . I can tell something *should* be here. Or *was* here."

Remy scoffed. "The old pictures could have told anyone that."

"No, you don't get it. It's sort of like I'm staring at a spot on a wall where I know there used to be a picture hanging. And there are other pictures around that spot, and based on who's in those I can tell who's in the picture that got taken down. I can tell there's a reason that picture got taken down, like the person in it did something awful. That's how this feels. Like they took the hospital here down and left this spot blank for a reason."

"You sound like you're on your show," Remy said.

"Yeah, the show works because this is how I really am, and people can tell."

"Sure."

Shyla stepped between the two of them, as they had unconsciously come closer, and Jinh was getting visibly flustered. Which, to be fair, had started with Shyla asking a dumb question.

"Hey, you're here to help, right?" Shyla said to Remy. "You think upsetting her is going to do anything for us? Or do you have a better plan?"

Remy put her hands up just below her shoulders in mock surrender. "Sorry. I have a habit of rejecting certain things as a reflex."

"*You?* Knowing what Braith is? You ought to know better."

"I said I'm sorry."

"Okay. Listen, what if we all try to cover more ground on our own? I'll head that way." She pointed to the south end of the courtyard, toward the street they had come in on. "Jinh keeps walking the center here, and you've got the other side. How does that sound?"

"And we're looking for what?" Remy said.

"Anything. Whatever stands out, feels odd, or seems like it's worth a second look. Anything at all."

After a noncommittal side nod that looked like she was directing herself on where to go, Remy headed to the north end of the field. When she believed Remy was out of earshot, Shyla told Jinh, "Run to me if you need to."

"I'll be fine," Jinh said, patting her purse to remind Shyla of the impressive knife inside.

"I mean it," Shyla said, thinking that if Jinh had to pull it against Remy, the navaja had a one-hundred-percent chance of ending up stuck in its owner.

Jinh patted Shyla on the shoulder and said again, "I'll be fine."

With that, Shyla left Jinh to her section and tried to think of what "whatever stands out" actually meant to her. She wasn't living in a video game, where the meaningful artifact or clue would shimmer or give off a sound as she passed by. There were virtually no obstacles around that could hide something important. Only one tree stood on her side of the park. There weren't any hedges around the perimeter, no scattered bushes she could search, not even a pile of leaves she could kick through.

Only two things drew her attention. One was a grate near the elbow of the sidewalk closest to the old bar. The second was the bar itself, which didn't look like it was ready to host the Halloween Happy Hour it advertised, or any other event. It was checkered with peeled paint and exposed dark wood. Grime partially curtained its windows. Its CLOSED sign looked like it hadn't been flipped the previous night, but had been cooked into the glass door by a few decades of direct sunlight. Its name wasn't displayed anywhere on the outside, although some unreadable markings above the entrance appeared to be faded letters.

Shyla drifted toward the bar without realizing it until she nearly stepped over the grate placed in the ground along her path. It was square, covering a hole big enough for Shyla to sink into before her hips stopped her fall. It looked new and sturdy. Dark gray metal with thin, diagonal holes that exposed an oddly deep darkness. The blackness under the grate stole Shyla's attention, drawing a focused stare as she tried to process exactly what she was seeing.

She stepped on the grate like she thought it would turn out to be fake, a work of sidewalk art. A flat echo jumped up and died so quickly Shyla immediately stomped on the grate again to be sure her ears hadn't deceived her. While the blackness beneath the grate looked deep, the reverberation of Shyla's footfall was barely going underground before surfacing.

No longer self-conscious about being watched, Shyla crouched down on hands and knees for a better look through the gaps in the grate. Now she was close enough to be sure of what she suspected. Still, she took out her phone and used its flashlight feature to remove any doubt that she saw a black rectangular stone about five inches underneath the grate.

It made the hole appear deeper to anyone not close enough to see the grains of the painted concrete, or the four finger-width holes drilled through it, like air holes for a jarred, live bug. The reason the echo sounded surprisingly shallow was because the depth of the drain was a deliberate lie. There had to be a reason for that. Something was hidden, blocked from sight, deeper below.

Her phone buzzed twice in her hand. She'd received a text message from a number she didn't have saved, stating: *This is Remy.* A second after she read the message, her phone rang, coming from the same number. She stood, looked across the field, and saw Remy waving to her as a county patrolman's squad car crept behind her, and Jinh, between the two of them, looked alarmed.

Shyla motioned for Jinh to come to her as she answered her phone, "Hey. You've got something?"

"Yeah," Remy said. "There's something in the ground here. Looks like a drainage grate, but it's got something in it."

"Like a big brick or stone, right?"

"Okay, so that's what you were looking at over there, too? I was wondering why you were on the ground."

"Any idea of what it could be for?" Shyla said.

Remy chuckled. "I was going to ask you."

Jinh spoke up when she was close enough to be heard. "What's happening? What do you have?"

Shyla pointed to the grate and told her, "Look. Get close." Jinh blinked at her an extra second, expecting either additional direction or an explanation, then she dropped to get a good look and made a breathy noise. An audible question mark made of light smoke. She popped back up, brushing dirt off her hands and onto her jeans, and said to Shyla, "That's weird, isn't it?"

"It is."

Shyla looked back to Remy and saw her walking toward them, turning once as if to make sure the grate hadn't grown legs and scurried off, its cover blown. Shyla looked to the bar again. Aunt Teonna had told her to trust her instincts and she was taking that advice seriously now, focusing on the little twist in her gut that told her that building was as important and odd as the stone blocking the grate, she just had to figure out why.

Jinh's analogy about the missing picture on the wall guided her a little, helped her think not just of what was present, but what was absent. Or hidden.

She opened her phone again to pull up the saved digital copies of the books and articles they'd found about Yorktown and its dual old hospitals she had initially believed were one and the same. There was another "mistake" in that information that she was close to recalling, but it was just beyond her memory's reach. Something to do with the two different pictures, and the structure of this earlier hospital.

"You thought of something?" Jinh said.

"Maybe."

A moment later she found it. The black-and-white picture of the East Main hospital from 1919. In it, nine nurses dressed in white sat in the grass before four doctors wearing suits. Behind them all was a two-story brick building with smoky windows and gabled roofing. The caption beneath the photo, however, described the building as the *four-story hospital that would later become a health retreat*.

Shyla recalled one of the rumors Luisa's fellow churchgoers spread about the facility her mother and grandfather had checked themselves into, that a "death tunnel" ran underneath it, which Jinh said was likely an imported urban legend from Kentucky's Waverly Hills Sanatorium. But what if there'd been a kernel of truth hidden in the gossip?

What if the entire bottom half of the hospital was below the ground?

Tearing down and removing any trace of the two superterranean floors would be a fairly routine demolition job, but excavating and filling in the two underground levels would be more costly and difficult. Probably not worth the effort. So what to do instead? Pave over it, plant over it, plug any remaining gaps, and never expect a detective, her psychic friend, and her rich, immortal client's bodyguard to come snooping around decades later.

Shyla enlarged her screen and pointed to the caption accompanying the picture. She watched Jinh's reaction, the subtle squint of her eyes followed by an even subtler widening. Remy picked up on it from several feet away and she called out, "What is it?"

Jinh and Shyla peeked at each other as if there was a chance that they would keep what they'd found a secret, which, of course, they could not, and given the eagle eye Remy had demonstrated, now they couldn't even keep secret the fact that they considered keeping secrets. That was okay, though. Shyla thought there was at least a little benefit to reminding Remy that she was the uninvited, untrusted member of this trio.

"There are two more floors under us," Shyla said.

"What?" Remy reached for Shyla's phone, which Shyla did not hand over, instead just turning the screen toward her, and Remy stared hard at it like she was looking for fine print that was one hue off from the background.

"Damn, that's something," Remy said. "How do we get down there?"

"I want to try that place out," Shyla said, pointing her chin toward the closed bar.

"Why there?"

"Just a feeling."

"And that's what you normally go off of?"

"When I don't have anything else," Shyla said, already moving toward the building, cutting off any additional passive protest from Remy. Jinh followed her, and Remy trailed them, which was probably what she preferred, anyway. Better to keep an eye on the two of them simultaneously.

Instead of continuing toward the front entrance, Shyla veered toward the back, again guided by intuition more than any visible clues. It just felt like a better idea to try to gain entry through a back way, not facing Main Street. She rounded behind the building to an alley wide enough for a garbage truck to pass through. If one had come through recently, though, there was no sign it needed to stop at the unnamed bar, as there was no dumpster in back, nor even a small trash can. There wasn't so much as a scrap of litter on the ground. The site was being maintained but not used.

She stopped to take this all in, determine how meaningful it was, and was startled by someone's hand seizing her wrist.

"There used to be a door there," Jinh said.

The soft intensity in her voice made Shyla turn her way. In her periphery Shyla glimpsed Remy, strolling like she had until tomorrow to catch up, phone to her ear. Jinh's eyes were aimed at the windowless back wall of the bar, whose indecipherable, heavily faded lettering—greenish as far as Shyla could tell—was the only standout feature. Nothing else was there. But something *had* been, at some point.

A door.

Jinh could "see" it now, in the uncanny way that she saw things. Shyla wondered what it was like, and then wondered how it was that she had never asked her this in all the time she had known her. Was it a sort of corona? A glow invisible to the ungifted, ordinary eye? Ghostly?

Or maybe Jinh was fully immersed in a lost moment, the way Shyla had been in the killing room.

Why hadn't Shyla ever asked?

Because she had never wanted to believe. If the dead carried on in the places where they'd died, or where their remains were left, then that meant Rodney might be lingering near that well, or in the old house where she'd shot him. Or maybe he split time between both, trying to contact the living who came to either place, ready to tell them what Shyla had done. Paint her as an ungrateful, patricidal "daughter."

Far worse than that had been the thought of her deceased mother still suffering on earth, unable to move on, stuck in some basement, some makeshift, unworthy grave amidst the coastal dunes, or perhaps the trunk of her own car sitting undiscovered in a wooded valley of the Hill Country. Those were the final resting places she'd imagined for her mother, for years, before Jinh told her about the accident near the bridge. Shyla had to regularly fight off nightmares of her mother's wind-tossed voice calling to her from some desolate place. She never dreamt of her father doing the same, likely because, if both of their spirits were still bound to this world, his at least dwelt near family, as he had died at home. He could always walk or float—whatever it is ghosts do—two houses down from Aunt Teonna's if the loneliness of death became too much for him, or the guilt of letting his wife go to Texas alone to pursue a lead started to crush him. Her mother did not have that comfort. She was alone in a place unfamiliar to her. And before she learned the truth, Shyla's biggest regret about killing Rodney was not bleeding her mother's whereabouts from him before he died.

When they were together, Shyla never thought of Jinh as a charlatan, nor as legitimate. She just put it out of her mind, because there was no way she could convince herself that Jinh was a liar, and that left one alternative. She didn't think her mind could survive that. Her sanity had weathered the upending of her world, the realization that the people who raised her had also abducted her. Had talked over and planned for the option of killing her. She hadn't thought it could withstand the certainty of ghosts and psychics being real. Given how well it held up after seeing Braith survive Remy's attack with the poker, Shyla hadn't given herself enough credit.

So she had never asked Jinh anything about her gift, much less what exactly the world looked like to her when she had a vision—until now.

She asked Jinh, "What does it look like?"

Jinh shook her head like she didn't quite understand the question, or like Shyla had worded it improperly. Then she tilted her head a little as though gaining a new perspective and gasped weakly. "It's opening," she said. "Someone's opened it."

The odd squawk of a squad car's siren made Jinh jump and Shyla turn. Remy turned now, too, to see the county deputy stepping out of the vehicle that had pulled up nearby. A lean man who tried to carry himself like he was half-a-foot taller stepped out of the vehicle. He had gold-rimmed sunglasses, a stiff gait, and a wide stance. "Ladies, may I ask what you're doing around here."

"You may," Remy said before Shyla could get a word out, much less reach for her investigator's ID.

This summoned silence like a spell as the officer waited several seconds for an answer before realizing what Remy had meant. He gave them all a bitter smile, while Remy split her attention between him and her phone. Jinh turned her eyes back to the wall, while Shyla was already running mental laps around various scenarios that might ensue from Remy lightly bruising the deputy's ego.

"Well, what *are* you doing around here?" he said.

"Just out and about," Remy said. "We're not on private property, are we?"

"As a matter of fact, you're pretty close, and we got—"

"Pretty close isn't *on*."

"*And* we got some calls from some concerned people here," he said. "Told us they saw three ladies loitering."

"And asked if they could get that for the third day of Christmas?"

The deputy looked at Shyla, the invitation for her to intervene before Remy said something he *really* didn't like evident even behind his shades. Returning to Remy, he said, "I need your name and an ID, ma'am. I'm going to need that from all of you."

"Adrienne Remington. I just go by Remy, though. What's your name, Officer?"

"ID, please."

"Neal, if I'm not mistaken. And I know I'm not."

He looked like he wanted to shake his head no but had invisible bolts in his neck that prevented any movement. His assured smile curled curiously, like it had received bad directions and didn't know where to turn. Shyla watched his hand ease closer to his sidearm. Remy had to notice it, too, right? Despite the nonchalance she maintained as she scrolled through her phone.

He started to speak more quickly, losing any semblance of casual, leisurely control. "Ma'am, firstly, attempted intimidation of an officer is a crime, so I don't know what you think you're trying by guessing at my name, but be aware of that. Now, I'm going to ask one more time, and if you don't comply, you're going to be looking at an obstruction charge, interference, refusal of a–"

"Is this you?" Remy asked as she turned the face of her phone to him.

Shyla did not have the angle to see what the deputy saw, but his expression told her it was something personally, uniquely horrific to him. It might have been–and likely was–unsavory at best and terrible at worst to anyone else who looked at it, but for him it was a step or several beyond.

"That–that–that . . . that's not . . ." he stammered, sounding like a malfunctioning animatronic.

"Neal Bell, this *is* you, and your brother," Remy said, "and an unfortunate young man named Anthony Richard that you once knew. And this is a photo of what you did to him that's been in every phone you've had since you left college, because, I presume, the memory alone wasn't good enough for you."

"N-no. No. It's not . . . How . . . ?"

"I work for an unbelievably, *obscenely* wealthy man is how. And he is fully committed to me being successful at my job, which frequently means I need leverage over people like you. And I don't go anywhere unprepared. It helps that you're dumb enough to make the nickname you gave your first truck and the year you bought it your password. From there it was trial and error to find where you put the dollar sign, because of course your stupid ass used a dollar sign. You're hardly the only person in your department with a dirty secret, but yours *is* the dirtiest, and it's shit luck for you that you're the one who pulled up here right now. Because that means you get to be the one to tell me everything I want to know before this picture goes to your folks, first, then to every news outlet we're connected with, to make sure this isn't just a headline but a *sensation*. And not just you and your brother, but your parents, your sister, your grandparents, they all get dragged into it."

"It was just a joke," Neal said. "It was just a stupid joke, I swear to God."

"Oh, well then, never mind, forget everything I said. Just get out of here."

He looked at Shyla and Jinh for additional permission before stepping backward toward his vehicle.

"You stupid fuck, don't take another step," Remy said. "And drop that hand unless you're planning to shoot yourself. You raise your sidearm to me, this picture goes out, even after I take your gun and beat you half dead with it. Only reason I'll let you live is to deal with the aftermath. And if the devil's smiling on you enough to let you kill me, the picture goes out, anyway. It's called insurance, and being prepared, and being smart, and a bunch of other shit I know you don't know anything about. Now, drop that hand, Neal."

He barely seemed to register what she was saying, but his hand fell from near his waistband anyway, as if it had become sentient enough to make the decision for him.

"It was a joke," Neal practically whispered, looking like he'd aged, died, and dragged his dark-eyed, cold corpse out of a mortuary cabinet all in the last few seconds.

"Then why keep the picture? And even if it was, who'd believe you?" Remy said. "Anthony isn't here to say whether it was or wasn't, but this pic is going to convince people it's the reason he dove off that balcony. Now, I'm going to need you to shut up unless you're answering something I ask you. To start with, what's in this building?"

She pointed to the old bar. Neal's eyes followed but it was clear to Shyla that his mind was stuck in orbit now, a stranded astronaut hoping for a miracle, knowing nothing short of the hand of God could deliver him. Remy snapped her fingers in his face, causing him to flinch, which in turn made Shyla shift her weight, ready to tackle Jinh to the ground in case Neal was startled and stupid enough to just pull his gun and start firing. Instead, he awakened to the moment and answered Remy's question without her needing to repeat it.

"I don't know. Nobody tells us. They just say to stay out and keep people away."

"Well, what do people say is in there?" Remy asked. "Don't lie and say you haven't heard any talk. That'll just piss me off."

"Look, I'm sorry I upset you. I don't want anything to do with this. Whatever business you've got here, I'll just—"

"Neal, are you more worried about what you've heard is in there than you are about your parents seeing you and Gary with your pants literally down—"

"A church," Neal blurted out.

"In there?" Shyla asked, feeling a little more comfortable, re-entering detective mode now that Remy appeared to have cleared the threat.

Neal shook his head. "No, it's supposed to have a door that takes you to some stairs or a tunnel that leads to the church. A buried church, under all of this. But one for satanists or witches or something like that. That's just some dumb thing people say. They tell it to everyone who gets hired here just to freak them out. It's just a story."

"But nobody goes inside," Shyla said.

Jinh added, "And somebody covered the door that used to be here."

Remy's smile was almost flat, and spread like a snake stretching just to see how long it could make itself. "Deputy, would you be so kind as to show us the way in? All the way in, I mean, to help us find this supposed church."

Shyla had presumed Neal couldn't get any paler but it looked like his skin was trying to become see-through. "No one should go in there. I don't know what's actually there, but . . ."

"There's a reason you have to keep people out," Remy finished for him. "Which is exactly why you're going to take us in, to find out what it is."

"Please—"

"What aren't you telling us?" Shyla said.

Neal shut his eyes like he could turn off the world, reset it, make it better for himself, before reopening them. The defeat on his face when he saw that they were still there when he opened his eyes made Shyla think he might take Remy up on her suggestion to shoot himself. The prospect of stepping into this place genuinely unnerved him. Part of Shyla wanted to know what was in the picture Remy had shown him, but the rest of her thought she'd already seen enough horrible things and would need to save space in her mind to store whatever awful things would come with this job. No need to fill it with anything extra.

"What aren't you telling us, Neal?" Remy said, not asking so much as coaxing the way a hypnotist would.

"Just more bad stories," Neal said. "They warn us all that you'll see something you don't want to see if you go in there. People who've gone in have come back changed. It messes with your head enough that it can mess with your body, too, even if nothing really touches you. That's what I've heard. But it's . . . it's . . ."

"Just a story," Remy said. "And what you did to Anthony was just a joke. Keeping the picture was just a mistake. And you being here right now is just bad luck. That might be all true, half true, or a whole lie, but I can guarantee you it doesn't matter. You're coming with us. You're getting us inside."

"What about his car?" Shyla said. "People are going to see it out here. That's going to look suspicious."

"Yeah," Neal said, latching on to this life preserver. "She's right. Maybe I should move it."

Remy pulled her gun from inside her jacket now, smoothly and calmly, almost a sleight-of-hand movement. "I'll make arrangements for your car," she said. She needn't explain further, because Neal was too afraid to challenge her for details, and Shyla could piece it together easily enough. Remy had mentioned already that she had compromising evidence on others in the county sheriff's department. And she had planned for this contingency. She probably had the emails or texts prewritten, just like she'd had Neal's photos at the ready on her phone. A few quick thumb taps and one of his colleagues would see their own pictures, or some documentation, or maybe a video that would motivate them to do Remy's bidding, which would involve moving Neal's vehicle, at minimum, and possibly starting a story that made Neal seem like a rogue officer who got whatever was coming to him should the worst occur. Should Neal not make it out of the "church"–if it existed–with his sanity or anatomy intact.

Remy was proving more useful than Shyla could have hoped, and more dangerous than she feared. She could have admired her for it if she didn't have to recognize the threat she posed.

It occurred to her that she needed to check on Jinh, who still hadn't completely returned from the trance the building placed on her. Shyla grabbed her hand, squeezed hard, and coaxed Jinh to turn to her.

"Let's go," Remy said to Neal, and by extension to Shyla and Jinh, as well.

For a moment, Neal looked like he was ready to take the bullet rather than deal with what he'd gotten himself into. It must have been difficult for him to process. How routine had this interaction seemed when he first stepped out of his vehicle? Three women, probably overzealous sightseers or aspiring "paranormalists," like the others that visited town, had just gotten a little too close to a place that was off-limits for reasons he need not comprehend or believe in to respect. This was supposed to be simple.

Ladies, you're not allowed here.

Sorry, Officer. Our book just told us that there might be something of interest here.

I understand that, but you're not allowed.

Yes, sir. Sorry, sir. We'll be on our way.

Instead, he was under three points of duress, threatened with exposure, with a gun, and perhaps worst of all, with entering a place that was rumored to be an antichurch where nightmares could come to life and injure or end you.

Maybe taking a bullet here would have been better for him. But he was a little too dumb or scared to let that happen. Besides, some part of him must have realized he'd bought his ticket onto this train years ago, when he and his brother did whatever they'd done to make Anthony Richard kill himself.

He started toward the front entrance of the building, the others following close. When he reached the door he fished a small set of keys out of his pocket, fumbled to find the right one, almost dropped them all, then pulled a silver key from between two copper ones.

As the door opened, Shyla realized she hadn't relinquished Jinh's hand since she'd taken it, and Jinh was holding on just as tight. It should have hurt, but it was comforting.

When Neal opened the door, coldness and the dank stench of decay rushed out of the building, like an old rotting ghost had seized the opportunity to flee from inside.

19

There were dust-coated mugs and glasses on some of the circular tables. Old liquor bottles, some still full, some only half so, none empty, behind the bar. Someone had left a shoe under one of the small round tables where remained a tray of food so old it was unrecognizable, and unappetizing to the roaches. Nothing in sight looked like it had been touched, cleaned, or removed for years.

This place hadn't just been closed and abandoned. It had been evacuated.

"People left their lives here," Jinh said as she surveyed the interior. She didn't seem be looking at it, but absorbing it.

Neal was already trembling. Remy surveyed the place as though readying for an ambush. Shyla tried to take as many mental notes as possible, while also searching for the most logical way underground. Would it be a hidden, covered door? A conspicuous one, like at the Inspiration Sweet? Some kind of dumbwaiter left over from prohibition, good for bringing up or secreting booze as needed, but only capable of smuggling one crouched person at a time?

"How do we get down?" Remy asked Neal.

"I don't know. I told you, we're not allowed in here."

"But you've heard things," Shyla said.

"And you have a key," Remy added. In a different life, Shyla thought, the two of them might have made a formidable pairing. Tough and Tougher, the perfect investigative duo for when you needed a couple of war hawks people might mistake for doves.

"Right," Shyla said. "You've got a lot of keys. Is one of those for another door here? A way to get down?"

Neal shook his head, but looked like a boy saying no to a proposed parental punishment rather than a grown man trying to convince someone they were incorrect.

Jinh marched to her left, toward an old pool table with unracked balls and two cues still lying on top of it. She started pushing at it without asking for help, failing to budge it. Shyla, not needing any direct instruction, hurried over to assist. Together they started to slide the old, heavy, oak-legged table to the right. It moved a few inches before one of its ornamentally clawed feet caught a warped floorboard. Remy moved over to help, then stopped and motioned with her gun for Neal to give them some extra muscle. He was hesitant, and the sweat on his forehead made him look like he'd spent the last hour laboring in a field, but he moved toward the table like he wanted to sneak up on it.

Shyla wondered if he knew something they didn't. Well, *obviously* he did, even if he didn't completely understand it. Crucial, belated realizations seemed to be surfacing in him. Shyla saw them physically transform him.

His shoulders looked less broad, his arms looked like they had shrunk closer to his body, and he looked shorter. Fear burdened him like a brutal pregnancy, leeching his muscle mass and bone density from the inside. Shyla thought Neal might not be any better at helping move the pool table than she would be, given his present state.

He spoke a prayer so softly were she an inch farther away she wouldn't hear it. She wondered if he was trying to keep it to himself, worried any power it possessed would dissipate if it carried over to anyone else. He helped move the pool table.

Centered directly underneath it, largely untouched by dust, was a rectangular cut in the wood-tiled flooring.

Shyla dropped to the floor and turned her phone's flashlight back on to inspect the area, knowing what she was looking for. She probed with her hand for any inconsistencies in the surface, and realized the panel was laminate, not wood like the rest of the flooring. The first small divot she felt didn't give when she tried to dig her fingers under it, but the next did, revealing itself as a handle.

She stood as she started to lift it, anticipating it would be heavy, and that its hinges might be rusted from lack of use. Instead, it came up easily, assisted by a spring-action that suggested it was designed to be opened by someone weaker. Perhaps someone elderly. That, or it was designed for quick access, like an escape hatch.

Underneath the trapdoor was a ladder angled so slightly it almost appeared perfectly vertical. The darkness became impenetrable after the fourth rung.

Remy flicked her gun at Neal like she was shooing a gnat.

"You want me to go down there?" he said, almost breathless. He knew the answer but had to ask like it was the fourth wish requested of a genie.

Remy answered by walking past him, handing her gun to Shyla, then taking out a second piece from a holster at her back and flicking it at him. Neal stared into the hole in the floor.

Dust particles drifted just over the blackness, in the light shining from Shyla's phone. Shyla looked at Jinh for affirmation, and

Jinh managed to pull her gaze away from the trapdoor to meet the eyes of the woman she'd once said was the "love of my life," to tell her without words that they had to go down there.

There was a strange, fearful determination in Jinh's stare, like she was the first human to take a bite of something everyone else believed poisonous. Half certain, half concerned, but wholly committed. She would venture into this unseeable depth even without Shyla, but Shyla would not let Jinh go by herself, and Jinh knew that. It was strange how a moment like this, more than deep, long kisses, more than flowers and cards and anniversary celebrations, more than anything else could, told Shyla that she loved Jinh. And Jinh loved her. Enough for both of them to do something tremendously stupid for the other.

Neal took the first step on trembling legs. *A badly built attic staircase,* Shyla thought. She'd been in a few houses where the "stairs" to the attic were dangerously close to vertical. Rodney had asked her to wait at the bottom of those stairs—more of a ladder, really—once while he stored Christmas decorations that Linda insisted they keep with them wherever they went. It was, in hindsight, ridiculous of him. What was Shyla going to do at the bottom of those steps should he fall? She couldn't catch a grown man. Best she could do was break his fall. Maybe that was all he wanted. Maybe all he'd wanted her to be was a deflection. A cushion in case he fell.

She'd lost enough of her life to them to make her a little bit foolish in moments like this. To make her want to tell Remy, "No, I'll go first," because why not? She'd lost her real parents before she had a chance to know them. She'd lost a real childhood, never had any grandparents, never had a chance at a normal life. When she'd told Rodney, "You never gave her a chance," before shooting him, she'd been talking about herself as well as her mother, even if she hadn't realized it at the time.

Yet, what she'd been through had given her things others didn't have. She had tenacity, intuition, and courage that were hard to come by without certain life experiences.

Before Shyla could try to go in first, Remy told Neal, "Go. *Now*." And he went in. A few seconds later, he was up to his shoulders in darkness.

"Hold on," Shyla said, wanting him to wait so that they all could take a moment to talk through what might happen after he left their sight. What they would ask him when he made it to the bottom. Who would go next. What their plan was if it sounded safe, or the option if it was really bad.

The darkness enveloping Neal was like silt-saturated cave water. Something no one is meant to enter or emerge from.

Remy pushed the gun closer to Neal's head and he descended.

He was neck-deep in darkness now. A floating head. The light from Shyla's phone couldn't extinguish this surface of blackness, so she pulled out the pocket flashlight she kept with her. She clicked the button and pointed it down past Neal.

"What do you see?" he asked, wincing from how bright the light was. "Do you see anything?"

The words "nothing" and "no" caught in her chest, and it was as if the breaths she couldn't take leapt into Neal's lungs as he began to hyperventilate, understanding her lack of an answer *was* the answer.

The bright beam from her emergency flashlight met the blackness pooled just below Neal's head and lost the battle for supremacy. The darkness held like a wall.

"Oh fuck. Oh God," Neal said. Maybe the oddest start to a prayer ever, or perhaps an astonishingly common start to one given how many people must appeal to God when terrified. "Oh no. Oh Lord, Lord God, I am your humble serv—"

"*Down,*" Remy said, the threat in her tone securing an anchor to the base of Neal's spine. He continued down and disappeared.

"It's dark," he said. "It's so fucking dark. Oh my God. Talk to me. *Talk to me!*"

"We hear you, Neal," Shyla said.

"*Am I still here?*"

Holy shit, he can't even see us, Shyla thought. "Climb back up," she said.

"No," said Remy.

To Shyla's shock, Jinh added, "Keep going." Jinh anticipated Shyla's glance, her eyes ready before Shyla could look her way. "We have to know," Jinh said.

"I'm coming up!" Neal shouted. "I'm coming up! I can't even see down here. I can't tell where I am. I have to come back–"

Shyla barely noticed what Remy was doing in time to back away before she slammed the trapdoor shut. Neal's frantic cries of "What was that?" and "Please talk to me, *please*!" were muffled not only by the floor, but by a depth and distance impossible for him to have reached in the time since he'd vanished in the murk.

"Help me, please. I don't know which way . . . I can't tell . . . I can't tell where I am! I can't tell if I'm coming up. I think I am. Just talk to me. Please talk to me! *Please! PLEASE!*"

The ensuing silence was abyssal. It made Shyla feel as though the entire building was sinking. Then a crashing sound accompanied Neal's plummeting scream. Shyla jumped back from the shut door, while Remy reflexively pointed her gun at it in case something burst through. Only Jinh remained still, like she had expected it to come. The cacophony seemed not to end so much as fade, and the three ladies passed looks between one another. Shyla was sure they all thought what she did, that the ladder had collapsed. What else could have produced that sound? And Neal's scream had trailed like that of a falling man.

Jinh must have read Shyla's mind, because she shook her head and said, "No." Then she bent and took the handle of the trapdoor. Remy took an extra step backward and steadied her aim. Shyla could not help but creep closer for a better view. Jinh pulled the door open, and they all saw that the ladder was not only intact but seemingly less steep and, more important, visible all the way down to the next floor.

The impenetrable darkness was gone and had taken Sheriff's Deputy Neal Bell with it.

Jinh was already two steps down before Shyla thought to say, "Wait. Hold on."

Jinh did wait and held out her hand for Shyla to hold on to. "Come on. Just don't let go."

"We don't know if it's safe," Shyla said.

"We'll find out. We have to."

No we don't, Shyla thought. *We can go away and forget about all of this. I have enough money. We can go to Minnesota. Auntie T will take care of us. My family will mobilize and organize around us to keep us all safe. Braith would have to call in favors from every police officer he's pocketed in the state to match the guns they'll have on deck, and that kind of standoff will call too much attention. We can wait him out. He'll lose interest. We can be safe. We don't have to do this.*

She didn't believe this, though. Not the last parts at least. Not enough to put Aunt Teonna and the rest of the family's lives on the line because she was too scared to go underground.

If Teonna could talk to you now, you know she'd tell you to come home to her. Give them a chance to fight for you. The chance they never had with Jackie. They'd rather that.

And if you're too afraid to leave Jinh, just tell her you'll be with her—you two will be together again—if she comes with you. But it has to be now. One-time offer. She climbs out of that hole and you two leave together, or it's over between you forever. She'll go with you, then. You know she will.

Shyla took a few deep breaths that did nothing to dispel her nerves. Damn it, she was going in. This place had just pulled a man into nothingness. She'd seen it happen, right in front of her, and the only reason it wasn't a mind-breaking fright was because she'd seen things equally strange and horrible in the days leading to this. But now she was going to venture into a space where darkness came and went as it pleased, and, based on Neal's final cries, could take people with it.

As she took Jinh's hand, Shyla looked at Remy and said, "Don't screw us."

"What would even be in it for me?" Remy said. "I'm right behind you. Just watch your front."

Jinh went in, Shyla followed, and Remy held off until they were halfway down before coming after them.

As soon as Shyla's feet touched the floor of the sublevel, she heard an echoing bang above her. She looked up, as did Jinh and the still-descending Remy, to see that something had closed the trapdoor above them.

20

There was no latch from the inside of the door, no button or release that indicated it would be easy to push back open, but Remy hustled back up the steps to try. As she did, the sound of something grating across the floor above them filled the twelve-foot-tall hallway Jinh and Shyla stood in, and Shyla knew someone or something was moving the pool table back over the door. Not to where they'd found it, but to where one of its legs would pin the door shut. Remy had to know this, as well, but tried to push the door open nonetheless, even attempting to thrust her shoulder into it, as if she could generate enough force to dislodge the pool table and break through from below.

"Fuck. *Fuck!*"

Shyla thought the same thing Remy shouted, although less because they were stuck underground with no way out, and more because Jinh had already slipped her hand away while she was by the ladder. Shyla's high-beam flashlight worked decently, but the darkness seemed to swarm, compressing the edges of the light, lurking around its perimeter like an army waiting for the command to siege. If the word "shimmering" was an entity with a dark twin—not merely opposite, but anti—they were in that twin's belly. Within that strange dimness, Jinh looked more like a phantom than a living person as she stepped through an open doorway ten feet away from Shyla.

Shyla moved to follow Jinh and heard Remy call out, "Wait, hey!" She stopped, not because of what Remy said, but because she suddenly faced a closed door that she knew shouldn't even be there, much less blocking her entry. She tried the handle and it turned, but the door didn't give when she pushed it, opening when she pulled instead.

"No way," she muttered. Had the door opened inward, it was possible that she'd just been mistaken. Between the limited visibility and stress of the situation it would have been conceivable that she had just failed to hear the door close, despite its old hinges first squealing away the rust, then cracking as she opened the door now. It would have been hard to believe, but not unimaginable, that she'd failed to see Jinh open the door and—for some unknown reason—immediately close it behind her. But the door opened into the hallway. A safety measure, perhaps. Impossible for someone in the room, a troubled patient, for instance, to hide behind the door and attack. But that meant seeing it close would have been unmissable.

It just hadn't been there. Or it had, but was somehow cloaked. Or Jinh hadn't really passed through it, and was actually elsewhere? Just like Neal. Spirited away mysteriously, courtesy of the same witchery that Shyla had experienced at the hotel, only more intense now. Capable of doing worse than conjuring spirits. The two who had anticipated and outpaced her so far were here now, their evident power perhaps bolstered by an unknown number of allies, or by being in a place that formerly housed believers in such things.

Luisa had heard rumors of this being a secret satanic temple, and Neal had called it a "buried church."

Based on what had become of Neal, and the empty room before her, Shyla thought she had her answer. Jinh wasn't inside. Shyla went in, shining her flashlight on the cracked and filth-stained floor tiles, hoping to see signs of another trapdoor. A way down that Jinh might have taken and that Shyla could follow to get to her, but she saw nothing like that.

What she did see was Jinh's knife. Unfolded, long, unmistakable. She couldn't convince herself it was a different one that might have belonged to someone else, someone who'd either worked or been institutionalized here years ago, or a more recent "urban explorer" who'd broken in and was never seen again. This was Jinh's navaja. There wasn't a speck of blood near it. Shyla thought Jinh must have taken it out because she felt like something in here had threatened her, but whatever it was snatched her out of thin air before she could use it.

Shyla called out Jinh's name and heard nothing.

She scanned the dingy walls and saw faded brownish streaks too dark to be watermarks, but also too reddish to be fecal matter. People had bled here, and the staff from when it had been a hospital had either been unwilling or unable to clean it up, or even paint over it. Maybe they'd tried, but no matter how hard they scrubbed, no matter what bleach they used, no matter how many coats of paint, and even after they replaced the wall entirely, the stains resurfaced. Shyla remembered hearing a legend on one of the YouTube channels she used to follow in high school about a condemned innocent man who struck a wall in his cell prior to his execution, and how the mark of his handprint was unremovable.

Sometimes people leave part of themselves in a horrible place, creating an eternal scar. Shyla was sure that's what she saw on the walls now. She also saw faded writing that was not quite readable, although she thought she could make out the words "hell" and "hand."

As she tried to process what this meant, a hand clamped on her shoulder, and all that kept Shyla from blindly swinging and slashing away with the knife was the chance that it was Jinh. She pulled away and turned to defend herself–and saw Remy. The alarmed look on her face surprised Shyla. She had expected Remy to have a better lid on her fear. She'd been the one to insist Neal bring them inside. She'd behaved as though she had prepared for such an occasion. And she knew Braith's secret. She'd lived with knowing who he was for a while, long enough to be comfortable ramming a poker through his head without his explicit consent. Remy understood well, and had for a while, that there were weirder, grimmer things in the world, beyond explanation. She was supposed to be the one who could handle this. Between the two of them, Remy should have been the braver one.

Except she didn't have anyone to fight for down here but herself. Shyla was at least shielded by purpose. As easy as it would be for her to succumb to unrelenting terror or panic, she couldn't afford to, because Jinh couldn't afford her to.

"We've got to find a way out of here," Remy said.

"I lost Jinh. I don't know where she went."

Remy shook her head. "That's not . . . Look, we have to get out of here first, get a better idea of what this place is, then we can come back–"

"No. No fucking way. I'm not leaving until I find her."

"*Nobody's* leaving if we don't figure out how to get out of here," Remy said. "What's the point of finding her if we're still stuck here? Now, I can't push that door up by myself but maybe if we–"

Shyla brushed past her, headed out of the room. She wasn't going to waste more time talking. Jinh was down here somewhere, in one of the other rooms, or maybe a floor below. She had to be here and Shyla had to find her. She couldn't leave Jinh lost down here any more than she could tear her own heart out and drop it down a well.

From behind her came the sound of a gun cocking. Shyla turned, unexpected incredulity already furrowing her eyebrows. Remy had indeed pointed the gun at her, but Shyla could read on her face that this was less than a threat. It was an already shattered hope. And in spite of her fear, in spite of the situation, Shyla could not help but cough out a small laugh. Remy huffed at the sound but knew why Shyla had done it. They didn't have to share any words to know what both were thinking. If Remy needed Shyla so badly, she couldn't shoot her. There were a hundred different situations where menacing someone at gunpoint could coerce them to do what you wanted, but this wasn't one of them. Remy lowered the gun, and when Shyla left the room she followed.

Shyla folded the knife closed and pocketed it as she turned right in the hallway. She tried every door she came to as she walked the hall, but none of them opened for her. Two didn't even have knobs, and the other's handle broke away in her hand. Unable to pull any of them open, she tried more than once to slam through with her shoulder, assisted by Remy, and only ended up sore and exhausted. Breaking her shoulder to try to push through the surprisingly sturdy wood wasn't going to help, and Remy couldn't just shoot through any of the doors. Even if she could, what if Jinh was on the other side?

Shyla needed to find something she could use to either smash through the doors or pry them open. What that could be in a long-abandoned subterranean hospital, she could barely guess. Maybe an old wheelchair or gurney was around, with metal rods she could loosen and separate into makeshift crowbars? Or maybe, despite years of misuse, they'd still be solid enough to use as battering rams. She felt like old wheelchairs and hospital beds would have been made of stronger, more durable metals than they were now. She wasn't sure if that was true, but it seemed right.

More closed and likely unbudging doors were waiting after the first turn in the hallway. These doors were darker than the walls they were recessed into and appeared taller than the ones she had already tried. They made Shyla think of giant sentinels. Oversized men in robes standing guard, their watchful eyes and scowling faces cloaked. The beam from her light only made it far enough down the hall to reveal three doors to her left and two to her right, but she was sure there were more. The hallway might be two or three times longer than what the blackness allowed her to see.

Just have to keep going, she thought. *No other way to find her but to keep looking. Keep trying.*

A curious, short-lived squealing sound stole her attention. It came and went so quickly she couldn't imagine what might have produced it. A rat or other rodent? It hadn't quite sounded like that. Something metal? Old gears turning, long overdue for oiling, maintenance? That didn't quite match, either.

"You heard that, right?" Remy asked, her voice low like it was trying to crawl under the floor.

"Yeah," Shyla said, matching Remy's whisper, both afraid to be heard. But why? Whoever they needed to fear down here obviously already knew they were here. There was no point in pretending they could still sneak around. Shyla only now realized how quiet she'd been. She should have shouted for Jinh dozens of times already, hoping to get a response, but instead had only done it once, in that first room. It had been an unconscious choice, and she realized why.

To listen for anything else down here that I should worry about.

"It came from behind us, didn't it?" Remy said, referring to the squealing sound.

Shyla doubled back into the bend of the hallway and shined the light toward the first part they'd come down.

The doors were gone.

Over the pounding of her pulse deep in her ears, Shyla told herself, *Can't worry about that now. Just keep going. Keep looking. You can't find her if you stop looking.*

"It came from back there," Remy said again.

"I couldn't really tell," Shyla said.

"Shit. Me neither."

Shyla moved forward and shouted "Jinh!" as powerfully as she could, and the darkness around her seemed to ripple at her voice.

"What are you doing?" Remy said. She couldn't know that Shyla was shattering the relative quiet because it was the only idea she had for reclaiming a sense of power and reminding her what was real and what wasn't.

"Jinh!"

The squealing came back, sticking around longer this time. Shyla still couldn't tell whether it came from ahead or behind or, hell, overhead.

Remy said, "What is that? Did you hear—"

"Jinh! Where are you?"

There were no handles or knobs on the tall doors she passed. Shyla didn't try to push through them with real force, just enough to be sure none of them would open as she kept going. Up ahead, the end of the hall was lost either to distance or darkness.

The squealing got louder and, Shyla was sure, more mechanical than animal now. The loudness didn't necessarily mean it was closer, but . . .

"Hold on," Remy said. "Just wait a second. We have to—"

"Jinh! Talk to me!"

"Goddammit, we need to know what's making that noise."

The next bend in the hall revealed itself. Someone stood halfway in the beam of Shyla's flashlight, their other half obscured behind the end of the hallway wall. It was a Black woman in a floor-length white dress that had an unnatural sheen. She had a crescent moon smile. Her eyes shone like deep stars. She slid out of sight with insectile quickness.

Shyla sprinted toward where the woman had been. "Hey!" Remy yelled, although Shyla couldn't tell whether she was shouting at her or the woman who'd just been there.

The hall seemed to stretch with each step Shyla took, not quite at a rate that would outpace her, but close enough to suggest the possibility. She ran harder, ran like she was the one being chased. She rounded the corner sharply and what she saw gave her an extra gear.

The woman was at the back of a three-person train, facing Shyla and walking backward. Behind the woman was Jinh, marching like a convict bracketed by two guards. The person leading Jinh through the doorway and downstairs, based on how they lowered out of sight, was a tall, long-necked Black man with an untidy, small Afro. Shyla immediately knew he made up the other half of the tandem that had been stalking her. The pair she'd first encountered on the fourth floor of the hotel, who'd later gotten to Luisa ahead of her and Jinh. Who called this place home, at least some of the time, and whose presence here was so pervasive that understanding who and what they were was starting to permeate Shyla's being, making her feel like she was becoming one with the building. A brick in its walls, a fractured tile in its floors, a broken bulb so rusted into its socket nothing could wrench it free. Something that belonged to the people who owned this place.

Witches.

Why was that word dominating her thoughts now?

It's Jinh. She's trying to tell me. They're taking her and she can't talk but she's trying to tell me before they take her. Run, run, RUN, they're taking her! You're letting them take her! Get there, Shyla. GET THERE. Get to her. Don't let them take her.

You can't let them take her!

They should have been gone by now. They could have hurried down the stairs well before Shyla was even halfway down the hall and shut a door—or conjured one—behind them. But they moved like they were swimming through sludge and Shyla flew on her feet like she never had before, and she knew that this was deliberate. This was part of whatever they were putting her through, for whatever reason. The inverse of the usual nightmare scenario people speak of, where normally they are stuck in slow motion while the threat advances at hyper speed.

The forces of will, love, and desperation within her could have pushed her through many things now. Shyla thought she could take a bullet to anywhere but the brain at this moment and keep moving. A storm of bullets. She could run through a wall of fire, she could swim against a tsunami, she could jump from one mountain peak to another. She could defy nature to get to Jinh now, if she needed to.

But she was up against supernature.

Witches.

The man disappeared down the stairway, and Jinh followed. The woman backed into the darkened doorway until only her smile was visible, a disembodied entity unto itself. A part of her she left behind like a sigil carved in obsidian.

Still, Shyla ran. So hard she knew it should hurt. So fast she was barely able to stop herself from crashing into the end of the hall when she realized the image of the woman's floating smile actually *was* embedded in a solid, black blockade. She put her hands up and raised a knee to soften the impact somewhat, keep her face from smashing this phantasmic, materialized wall.

She probed the wall with her hands for a soft point, a secret panel she could press to open it, grant her access to the stairway she knew was there, that she had just seen. She'd *just* seen it, damn it. They had taken Jinh down those stairs.

You let them take her. You let them do it. You weren't fast enough. You're never fast enough. Always too slow. Always too late. You didn't realize what you were getting yourself into with Braith until it was too late. You're lucky Rodney got cold feet about killing you or else you'd have been too late to save yourself then. And it was still way too late to save your mother and father because you were too slow even when it came to spotting the clues that Rodney and Linda weren't your real parents. If you'd been faster by a few years, and more decisive, you could have gone to the police, or just a teacher at school, and told them enough to prevent what happened, and your mother would be alive, but you were too late. Always too late. Always–

This psychic assault on her confidence almost brought her to her knees. She put a hand down and crouched like a football player, knowing if she let herself fall completely, she might never get back up. The grief would bury her like six feet of dirt. She would believe what they wanted her to believe, the thoughts those other two were planting in her head. That everything was her fault, dating back to her childhood, when she hadn't been quick enough–*too stupid, let's face it*–to question why they had to move so often, why she didn't resemble the people who raised her, why she didn't have aunts, uncles, cousins, and grandparents the way other kids did. Why something about her parents made her a little suspicious.

Why, why, why?

The questions had been there for her to ask, and she *had* asked, but she hadn't really pursued answers until it was too late. Luck and mercy had spared her, and let her take a modicum of revenge, but she hadn't really saved herself. So what made her think she could save Jinh now?

"I have to," she said to herself, standing.

"What?" Remy said, reminding Shyla that she wasn't on her own down here, at least. Before Shyla could start to explain what she'd meant, or—more productively—start throwing ideas at Remy for how they could get downstairs, the squealing sound interrupted her.

It was stretched and lower pitched now, as though its source moved more slowly because it had its quarry where it wanted them to be. This was accurate. Shyla thought she saw the source of the noise behind Remy. Her gaze was pointed enough for Remy to follow it to what Shyla saw, and it startled Remy enough for her to raise her gun toward it.

A gurney. An old gurney with rusted wheels. There was a dirty sheet atop it, and a body fully concealed beneath that sheet.

Shyla looked to her left to see if there might be a different way back to the trapdoor they had come down here through. The last leg of the hallway ended with a brick wall. If they wanted to get back upstairs, they'd have to go through this thing.

Remy backed away from it to stand beside Shyla and said, "You see that?"

"I see it."

"What is it?"

"Just what it looks like."

Shyla's reluctance to draw either the gun or the knife she had on her fell away at last, and she pulled out her piece, although she didn't aim it at the gurney as Remy already had. It was like she was trying to present as non-threatening to an animal in its own habitat, hoping it would understand and back away if she stayed still enough.

The hall filled with the sound of Shyla's and Remy's asynchronous steadying breaths. Shyla soaked up the stillness and rhythm of the moment, remaining ready to react while granting herself an odd and essential piece of peace that restored some of her resolve. It helped alleviate the doubt that had nearly enveloped her.

Always too late. That's what the witches had just forced her to think, to break her. But too late didn't exist until you were dead, and based on what she'd recently learned, maybe even not after that. Jinh was still here, and she was alive. Shyla knew that much. She felt it. So, she wasn't too late to do something, not this time.

Slithery movement disturbed the sheet over the gurney. Maybe it wasn't a body? A bunch of snakes roughly shaped in a human disguise instead?

An abnormally long, pale arm slid out from under the sheet. Its heavy, oversized hand slapped the floor with an ear-popping echo. It looked like something an octopus might initially approach, mistaking it for kin.

On the other side of the gurney, the left side, the other arm slipped down. The fingers on this hand looked two inches too long, with an extra knuckle on each. The hands lay flat where they landed, but were they growing? The longer Shyla stared at them, the more they made her think of vines. Shyla thought they might be exploring the space before them, seeing what they could embed themselves in or ensnare.

The hallway felt like it was sloped in the direction of the gurney and those hands. Shyla struggled to keep her balance and a fog flooded her mind like it was being pumped in.

The right hand flexed, fingertips pressing into the floor. This gave it just enough purchase to pull the gurney forward. The familiar, off-key whistle of its old wheels filled Shyla's ears, and neither she nor Remy had to ask where it was coming from anymore.

The body's left hand lifted, landed, and dragged the gurney forward, followed by the right repeating this step. Then the left again. Faster now. Not enough to build momentum for its wheels to carry it without the assistance of the hands, but fast enough for Shyla to feel her chances of getting away vanishing, like blood draining out of her body.

Remy fired her pistol and the bullet passed through the corpse like it was tissue paper. She fired again, got the same result, then targeted the legs of the gurney. The shot was true and sounded like it should have broken the old metal and at least slowed the gurney's movement, but it did no damage, and the corpse did not break its freakish, hand-propelled stride.

Shyla grabbed Remy's arm to pull her away, down the next and last section of the hallway, so they could buy a little more time, come up with a way to evade this thing before it got close enough to do whatever the hell it planned to do. But when she looked left, toward where she planned to run, she saw it there, too. The covered body on the gurney, arms drawing it forward.

There was more than one?

Or one that could be in two places at once?

What difference did it make?

It closed the distance with one last, strong pull, bringing itself to within inches of her.

The body under the sheet raised at the waist. The white sheet slid down and Shyla barely recognized Neal's elongated face, stretched and thinned by anguish. He looked like an artist's impression of his pain. His mouth was agape as though he were trying to scream out more guilt than a human body could contain. A plea for help inflated his darkened, yellowed eyes so that the lids couldn't get around them. He was naked, with several fresh scars across his torso that only appeared in rows of four, suggesting fingernails had done the work. She recognized his paleness now as the color of old death. Forgotten death.

He'd been down here for longer than he'd been missing.

He'd been dead for longer than he'd been down here.

This place had consumed and killed him, then regurgitated him as this bizarre puppet it could do what it pleased with.

And now he was reaching for her.

She jumped back toward the door that had magically appeared in front of the stairway, only that door wasn't there anymore. An open space let her fall backward now. She had no hope of finding her footing as she stumbled, then tumbled, hit the stairs with her upper back and shoulders first. She extended her arms to break her fall and caught nothing but air, then instinctively retracted them to protect her head and also keep from getting an arm pinned or caught at a bad angle.

This defensive posture might have helped against the worst of the fall, but she still landed too hard on the crown of her head the next time she hit, and what little light was still visible from the bottom of the stairs blipped out, along with the echoing remnant of Remy's last gunshot, as Shyla dropped out of consciousness.

21

How could you have known?

This was not an honest question. It dripped with a bleak contempt that made Shyla want to shower and scrub raw the places where that sentiment might have gotten on her.

She opened her eyes to the bright, wicked smile of the woman from the hallway, but the remainder of the face looking back at her belonged to someone else. The eyes, the nose, the chin, the freckles. These all belonged to the woman who pretended for seventeen years to be her mother.

"You're not Linda," Shyla said.

"Call me 'Momma.' You used to."

"You're not her."

"Maybe not. Maybe so. How would you know? You didn't even know who your own mother was until you were damn near grown. Until then, I raised you. Me and Rodney, and what did you do? How did you thank us, you ungrateful thing?"

"Thank you for what?" Shyla said, despite the larger part of her holding to the belief that this could not be Linda Montgomery.

"For giving up everything just to have you. I risked it all and gave up my whole future, anything I could have been, just to have—"

"To *steal* me."

Linda shook her head. "To *love* you. I loved you so much, from the moment I laid eyes on you, that I was willing to do something horrible so you could be mine. Would she have done that for you?"

It took Shyla a moment to realize who Linda was referring to. "Don't talk about her."

"Or what? You'll kill me? Like Rodney? It's too late for that."

Linda's mouth moved somehow out of sync with the way her hair blew—almost floated—on the wind. Like it was an animated effect moving at a different frame rate from the rest of the film it was meant to be part of.

The sky behind her was gray despite being cloudless. Sunless, as well. A massive slate sheet hanging over creation, like the whole of the cosmos was an eternal storm. The water beyond the pier was choppy, thick with the darkest sand the bottom of the Gulf could belch up. The oil-stained sand from spills and leaks that permanently polluted the waters.

The wood of the crooked and leaning dock was dark, visibly broken in several places, and looked as though a crack of thunder, or just a loud enough scream, might shatter it to splinters.

None of this is real, Shyla thought. *This isn't really Linda. I'm not really here. I was just in . . . I was just somewhere else.*

"Where?" the woman said. "Do you even remember where you were?"

I was somewhere else, Shyla thought, refusing to answer the woman's taunt. *And I'm still wherever that was. They just want me to think I'm here. Wherever here is.*

"'Here' is where you'll stay, with me. Until the day you die. The way it was meant to be. I took care of you, didn't I? Maybe I didn't carry you and didn't go through the labor. Maybe I couldn't nurse you or give you any natural part of me. Eye color and complexion or anything of the sort. But I gave you everything I could. And you repaid all that love, *years* of love, by turning on me. Killing my man and making me go on the run, until I couldn't think of running anymore. But to tell you the truth, because you need to hear it, it wasn't really the running that tired me out, made me give up. It was being without you. That's what took me here. Your little girlfriend never told you that, did she? That I came here when I got too tired of being without you. Sat at the end of the pier, hummed a little bit of Otis Redding for a while. Let some tears fall, then let myself fall in after them.

"But maybe that wasn't the end of it? Maybe somebody fished me out and taught me some things. Some spells. Some ways to get back at the girl who let me down. And now I'm here to get you back, in one way or another."

Shyla shook her head. Not in denial, but firmly. Feeling as strong as she possibly could given the vulnerability of her position. "You're not Linda."

"How would you know?" the woman asked again.

"Because if you were, when I saw you in that hallway I would have shot you dead right there."

The woman held her glare for what felt like a day, and then the rest of her face faded, only to rematerialize in a way that matched her smile. She was her true self now, not the partial impersonation of Linda. Darker complexion, harder eyes, stronger features. Younger, too. Not that much older than Shyla.

"I'm surprised you weren't fooled," the woman said. "You let Linda and Rodney trick you all those years before you figured it out. I took you as more gullible."

"Get the fuck out of my head," Shyla said.

"And leave you alone in here? I'm tempted. But I'm not that cruel unless I really need to be. And I already had to waste some of my capacity for cruelty on that cop."

"What are you?"

"Don't play dumb now. I know your girl gave you the answer. Put it right in your head. I heard you thinking it."

Witch, Shyla thought again.

"Goddamn right," the woman said.

"*Who* are you?" Shyla asked.

The woman ran over the question with one of her own. "Why are you really working for Braith?"

"What?" Shyla said, genuinely confused by this more than she was by the unreality she found herself trapped in.

A hand slipped over her shoulder, meant to be soothing, but as comforting as a snake coiling around her neck. She glanced at it, shuddered, and froze. The hand was gloved with what appeared to be unnaturally preserved human skin. Its leathery scent sickened her. Its flesh was smoky dark, like someone tried to heal a bruise with a burn. It was just large enough to be noticeably abnormal. Its fingernails were missing, the nail beds exposed.

This was a hand inside a glove made of another hand. A dead man's hand.

Hand of glory.

The voice from behind her was silky and almost songlike, despite its weight. It belonged to the man from the hallway. The woman's partner.

"It's okay," he said. "Just answer the question. The other one can't hear you in here."

The other one. Remy. They were asking about Braith and isolating her from the person they were sure was loyal to him. When she'd first encountered these two at the hotel, they'd told her, *We know he sent you*. They'd warned her then who their real enemy was. But they hadn't been entirely sure about Shyla. They still weren't.

The money, she thought and almost said in answer to the woman's question, but that would have been a lie, and she didn't see how keeping the truth from them, or from herself, would help now. Part of her wanted to say nothing to these people, especially this woman—now sneering instead of grinning—who had just toyed with her mind. Petulance wouldn't help either, though.

So, she told the truth. "He scares the hell out of me."

"Because of what he is?" the woman said.

"What *is* he?" Shyla asked, glad she wasn't being asked to elaborate on what scared her most—that Braith might know what she'd done to Rodney and could take action if he wanted to.

The man responded, "He's what we are, but worse, because he's lesser, and envious, and that has led him to do horrible things. But he is still a natural, in his own way, and he has used that ability to make himself as invincible as he can, at the expense of others. Many others."

"I didn't know anything about that."

"How could you have known?" the woman taunted again.

"Braith is a murderer," the man said. "And an impostor. We know his true name, his real history. We know how to kill him. He knows that we know, and he sent you and Jinh to flush us out. So forgive my sister and me for treating you harshly. But we thought you were working for him just for his money, if not worse reasons."

"What could be worse?" Shyla said.

"To be like him. He's made that offer to others before, who've tried to accept. But it isn't just something he can gift to someone else. To curse someone else the same way, he has to precisely replicate the sacrifice that changed him, and every failed effort costs several lives. We can't make that kind of offer to you, and wouldn't even if we could. And we don't have a fortune to sway you with. So we have to resort to other methods."

"Well, now you know it's not like that," Shyla said. "So you can let me and Jinh go. We're not your problem."

The woman shook her head. "But you're scared of him. You just said so. If that's what's motivating you, how do we keep you more afraid of us than him?"

"All I'm scared of is that he has something on me," Shyla said. "The same thing you just pulled out of my head. I killed somebody once. I killed a man named Rodney Hewitt. You know why, and you know how. You know what I did with the body, I bet. You know it all."

The woman nodded, and her features surprisingly softened. "I do. You have some strong walls up, Shyla Sinclair. It's pretty impressive. But not as impressive as you having the guts and smarts to pull that trigger. I'm a little jealous, I have to admit. I've been dreaming of my own revenge for a long time. What's it like?"

"Not half as good as I wanted it to be. Especially since it came quicker than a gunshot. And you just told me Linda took a dive and killed herself. Is that really true, or were you fucking with me?"

The woman actually looked sad to deliver the news. "It was true. She did it just a few months after Rodney stopped returning her messages and went 'missing.' She never thought he would just abandon her, and that left you as the reason he was gone. I wasn't lying when I said she got tired of running, but it wasn't about the police. It was about you. She was scared that you would try to find her, to hurt her."

"She was right."

The woman laughed. "I know it. When she couldn't stand the thought anymore, she went to the pier and jumped."

It hurt Shyla to hear that Linda was dead. That she couldn't look forward to the possibility that one day she would catch up with Linda Montgomery, hold her at gunpoint, tell her what she did to Rodney. Make that woman weep and beg for mercy before telling her, "This is for my *real* mother," and shooting her dead.

That would never happen now. It broke her heart in half to know it, and tore those halves into strips to think about what this said about her.

"How do you know all this?" Shyla asked the woman.

Her brother answered, "We hear whispers from these waters. We're deeply connected to them. People we love have been lost to them for generations. We're going to break that cycle."

"How?"

"By killing the man calling himself Saxton Braith."

22

The sister reached out and touched Shyla's chin, and Shyla woke from the dreamscape to the sight of the woman's gaunt, weary face in the real world. Shyla scrambled away from her across the floor. The shock of returning to the grim immediacy of reality sent a pang through her chest. She glanced to her left and saw Remy seated on the floor, hands behind her back, legs straight out in front of her, bound by duct tape around the ankles. Dried streaks of tears lightly stained her cheeks.

The man—the brother—stood beside Jinh, to Shyla's right. Jinh wasn't restrained. The vacancy in her eyes made it clear that this wasn't necessary. This place had overwhelmed her. The wealth of agony and misery still present here must have been obscene. How many souls were pulling at her, and from how many directions? Shyla could not imagine what it was like for Jinh to be bombarded by so much history and bad energy, confined in such a relatively tight space. She'd seen Jinh need to take extra naps to recover from comparatively simple visions. Endure headaches that almost incapacitated her after spending the better part of a week sifting through the sights and sounds of the past and future that came to her. Now she looked like she'd been plugged into something that took *and* gave more than she could withstand.

When Shyla asked Jinh if she was okay—was she hurt—Jinh didn't move. Her only answer was a repeated muttering that Shyla couldn't quite make out at first. "Pray to her. Pray to her now. You have to sacrifice. You have to pray. You have to tell her. Tell her *now. Tell her now.* You have to sacrifice . . ."

The brother and sister looked like they were wearing a patchwork of skins sloughed off by older relatives. The crinkled spots on their faces appeared to have aged at different speeds. Some looked like they belonged to people just a handful of years their senior, and others like they had been pulled from a centenarian. They had certain matching features—the set of their eyes, the shape of their nostrils—that made it evident they were twins. The way their immense fatigue sagged their faces enhanced the resemblance.

Shyla suspected they'd brought her out of the dream state when they did in part because they'd reached a limit. Days spent conjuring spirits, manipulating minds, and bending the physical world to their whims had to take a toll, even in this place that they knew well, and was likely a battery for them. They could still burn out. Nothing could produce output indefinitely, inexhaustibly. Nothing man-made, nothing natural, or even supernatural.

Something (Jinh?) told Shyla to look at the man's hand. His right hand. Verify whether what she saw in the dream was strictly a construct of that space, or a carryover from this one.

He wore the glove, which looked just as it had when he'd been in her mind. A severed hand hollowed out, tanned, preserved, turned into a glove. Why?

This was the thing Luisa's mother and the reverend, along with others, had worshipped in this forsaken place decades ago. The stories Luisa had heard were at least partly true, and based on what Shyla had seen and felt, probably understated what actually took place here. At some point, the subterranean parts of the hospital had been made into a temple for a cult, whether by converted members of the staff, by patients, or some combination of both. They'd made believers of people with damaged psyches. Souls seeking solace or peace, or in Reverend Carol's case, forgiveness.

Because he'd ended up here after falling in with Garrett Schramm, the serial killer who died in a plane crash that Braith miraculously survived unscathed. Reverend Carol had trekked through parts of Mexico living as a pious pauper for years, but never found absolution there. When he arrived here, however, he became such a willing convert to the cult that he lured his own daughter into the same place. He found salvation in this place that the twins hadn't wanted Shyla to find.

The twins who wanted Saxton Braith dead.

Why?

Behind every fortune is a great crime.

That wasn't the actual quote. She knew that, but forgave herself in this moment, under these conditions, for forgetting what the accurate line was. What she thought of now was accurate enough, and appropriate for the moment.

Braith had known Schramm, a killer connected to the reverend, who was connected somehow to these two people. The witch twins, at least one of whom had spoken of a desire for revenge, and Braith was their target.

It was virtually impossible for Shyla to believe that Saxton Braith had no clue as to who these people were and why they wanted him dead. That could have been their influence on her, though, couldn't it? They had just been in her head, speaking to her there directly, making her see things, giving her a facsimile of her long-desired confrontation with Linda. How hard would it be for them to directly, psychically implant deeper suspicion into her? Especially considering the bias she already had against him, not just due to the way they had met and what he had revealed about tracking her even before inviting her to his home.

Shyla shook her head. She was weighing things that weren't that important right now. It didn't matter whether the twins were mentally manipulating her, whether her distrust of Braith was born solely of how he introduced his "condition" to her, whether he was as innocent as he tried to make himself out to be, or unequivocally guilty.

Right now, he was a bargaining chip for Jinh's life, nothing more.

Shyla knew already that she couldn't stop the twins from taking Jinh with them. Even so, she reached to see if she still had a gun on her.

"You understand why we're not ready to trust you," the sister said. "It's not a matter of want or belief, just necessity."

Without turning her head, Shyla tried to make quick eye contact with Remy, hoping to communicate the lie that she didn't mean what she was going to say next. Remy just stared ahead at the brother, however. That or through him. Shyla couldn't quite tell, but it seemed like Remy was looking at something beyond a horizon, as opposed to a man standing near a wall, less than ten feet away from her in a small bunker of a room.

Returning her attention to the sister, Shyla said, "Leave her with me." She stood slowly and pointed to Jinh. "Leave her with me. You don't have to take her. I'll bring you Braith, I promise."

"We know you will," the woman said, "because you'll want to see her again."

"Please . . ."

"We tried to warn you off," the brother said. "And if you had heeded, we would have had to resort to another method to flush him out."

Then do it now, Shyla thought, but she knew this argument—this plea—would be ignored. Still, she had to say something, had to hope this wouldn't go the way she knew it would, so she just repeated what she'd promised them a second earlier. "I'll bring him to you. You have my word."

"We don't even know you," the sister said.

"You were just in my head. You *know* I'm sincere."

"And if you weren't, you would tell us?" the brother said.

That just shows how well you know me, she thought. *So you know I mean what I say. I'll get him to you. I'll bring you his head if that's what it takes. From what he's said, he'd still be alive for you to deliver the killing blow, even then. Just don't take my girl. You were in my head. You know me. You know my heart. You know what she means to me. Please don't do this. Please don't make me turn on you for doing this.*

None of this, were she to verbalize it, would persuade them. They were going to take Jinh. They had her trapped in a semicatatonic state, unable to defend herself, barely able to get words out, and they had Shyla and Remy in a dusty, decrepit, windowless room, two levels underground, with no idea of how to defend themselves even if they could access their weapons.

"He'll tell you where to find us," the sister said. "Just ask him where it started. That's where we'll end it."

Shyla lunged for Jinh. If she could just grab her, hold on to her, they wouldn't be able to pry them apart.

She saw the sister's hand rise, wave toward her, heard whispers that rushed at her like a windstorm. Abruptly she felt a ponderous fatigue. She forced her eyes to remain open but blackness closed over her vision nonetheless. She blinked it away, and seeing her vision return so quickly startled her.

Jinh and the witch siblings were now missing from the room, and Shyla felt so sick she could hardly stand.

"Shyla, we have to get out of here."

She hushed Remy after hearing this a second time. She tried to listen for Jinh's thoughts, listen for a clue as to where the twins planned to take her, where they might stop along the way so Shyla could intercept them, and she thought she'd been close to hearing something–she would swear Jinh's voice was grazing the air an inch from her ear–when Remy's words cut through.

We have to get out of here.

She wasn't wrong, but Shyla still felt like she would be abandoning Jinh if she left too soon. That feeling dissipated as the suffocating silence lingered and the crushing truth of Jinh's absence pressed any hope of her return out of Shyla.

A new urgency spurred her to move now, as she hoped she and Remy could make it out in time to catch up to the twins. She considered leaving Remy where she was, not wanting to waste seconds on freeing her from her bindings, but figured that if she ended up needing Braith's help to rescue Jinh, leaving someone he cared about down here would make him less cooperative.

Did he actually care about Remy, though?

This wasn't something that occurred to Shyla until she was halfway through cutting Remy free, using Jinh's knife.

"Why the fuck would he send me in here?" Remy said quietly. "He had to know. I know he knew."

"Come on," Shyla said after cutting through the last of the tape and pulling Remy to her feet.

"What did they make you see?" Remy asked Shyla.

"I don't know," Shyla said, headed toward the only door in and out of the room.

Remy took a step to get close enough to grab Shyla's wrist, then stopped and said, "Tell me."

Remy's grip was strong, and Shyla could tell she'd had grappling training at some point in her life. But whatever she'd gone through while entranced had weakened Remy enough for Shyla to rip free with only a few scratches.

"You try to stop me again, you better be ready to fight for your life," Shyla said. She turned and got moving, hearing Remy follow her. There wasn't time for them to trade stories about what kind of world the twins had pulled them into. She barely trusted Remy enough not to let her stay tied up. She had freed Remy as a strategic move. She wasn't going to tell her—today or ten years from now—about the version of the Gulf of Mexico the twins had conjured in her mind.

I got too tired of being without you, the impostor version of Linda had said. Where had the sister pulled that from? Not Shyla's psyche. Shyla never imagined Linda as quite so pitiful. Only as a dark witch, like one from old lore. A child snatcher. A life taker.

Maybe the sister had made it up based on what she thought Linda would say, or what she thought would disturb Shyla most.

Or maybe she and her brother really could commune with spirits from the waters where Linda drowned herself, and she heard those words directly from Linda's spirit, or from other ghosts that eavesdropped on Linda's soul doing an unearned La Llorona impression, wailing over a lost child that was never hers.

That didn't feel relevant now, yet she banked the thought

nonetheless. Stored it in her mental junk drawer. It might be useless, and she couldn't explain why she wanted to keep it, but she still chose not to throw it away.

The bottom story of the old hospital was one long, incomplete rectangular hallway, much like the floor above, which made it impossible to miss the stairs after Shyla and Remy left the room and followed the only path available. Upstairs, they found their way back to the ladder that had brought them underground. Along the way, Shyla noted how many of the doorways were now missing doors entirely, and that the hallway was shorter than it had been before. The beam from her flashlight—which she'd found on the landing of the stairs—was far more effective now. She held it ahead of her at arm's length, like it was the world's oldest cross keeping a devil at bay.

The trapdoor above the ladder was open. If she'd had the time, Shyla would have hesitated to go back up to the ground floor, so she could talk with Remy about who might have opened the door and would now be waiting for them up there. Instead, she went right up, still clinging to the hope that she could somehow move fast enough to chase down a pair of witches who could spirit themselves away.

Outside the bar, Shyla and Remy were greeted by four white SUVs, trimmed in black and brown, the words SHERIFF and DEWITT COUNTY—along with corresponding seals—emblazoned on the grilles and doors. The deputies belonging to each vehicle stood outside without weapons drawn and with stances that projected zero confidence, like they were being forced to participate as practice targets in a live-fire exercise.

Much more relaxed, standing in front of the silver sedan that Remy had picked up Shyla in a few days ago, was a man in a suit tailored to make sure people knew how important he was. Shyla had only met him once but would recognize his face for the rest of her life.

Saxton Braith gave Shyla and Remy a window-wiping show wave, like he was the host of a public access program and it was his signature greeting.

"Glad to see you made it," he said. "I was beginning to worry. I was about to send everyone in."

Over her shoulder, Shyla heard Remy huff in response.

Shyla looked around for Jinh and her abductors but didn't even see any other vehicles parked near the courtyard or surrounding buildings. The bar had either been cordoned off for three or four blocks in every direction, or people in Yorktown sensed that the old underground church had become active and were keeping their distance.

Shyla stepped toward Braith to ask, loud enough for the officers to hear, "Did you see anyone else come out? Did you see where they went?"

He cocked his head to the side. "No to the first, so no to the second."

Remy, louder and more hurriedly, said, "There were two other people in there. Brother and sister. Black, twins, early thirties. They can–"

"They took Jinh," Shyla interrupted. "I need to get after them."

Braith whistled like he was mimicking the death music in an old video game. "Well, that's no good."

"We have to find them before they get too far."

Braith shrugged. "For all we know, they've already gotten too far. Jinh will be fine, though. You know her better than I do, but she seems like she can take care of herself. All these years with all of her crazy fans and stalkers, and she doesn't even have a scar on her so far as I can see. She'll be as fine as she's always been."

He wasn't taking them seriously. He believed her, no doubt. He'd spoken with Jinh before, knew she'd been with Shyla when he sent Remy to assist them. He likely knew enough about this place's history to have given them a proper warning when he found out where they were going.

He might have been lying about not seeing the twins leave the building with Jinh, but it was more probable that they still had enough energy to cloak themselves via some witchery. Either way, Braith's reaction felt designed to show how little he cared about what mattered to Shyla. How nothing she could say or do would influence him. A little more of his real self was peeking through, even here, which meant he was less concerned with hiding it.

Because he'd gotten part of what he wanted out of her.

"Who are the twins?" Shyla said. "The two that took Jinh. You know who they are."

Again, Braith shrugged. "Listen, these kind, upstanding members of the sheriff's office have set aside a private spot for us nearby, so we can talk. When we get there, I'll give you my theories."

His smugness was grating, and he had to know it. Deliberate and showy. He was purposely trying her patience when he had to know she was bordering on frantic. Did he want her to threaten him in front of these deputies so they could have a reason to shoot her? Spare Remy the bother of cleaning up after the deed, let the authorities handle it? Because he'd already gotten her to do something he needed her to do—maybe even *the* thing—and now keeping her around was optional, at most.

Braith approached Shyla with his hands flat, palms up, arms bent at the elbows, like he was offering to guide her into troublesome waters. When he got close he gently held her around her forearms and leaned in to speak directly into her ear.

"I know exactly where they're from, and what they have planned, but you'll have to come with me to hear it. Or you can go it alone. I won't stop you. But I like to think you would know better."

Shyla had a vision of stepping back from him and drawing the gun she no longer had on her, then telling every deputy present that if they helped her kill him now, they wouldn't have to worry about whatever dirt he had on them. She thought Remy would be too savvy to intervene, knowing she was outnumbered, and couldn't take half as many bullets as Braith could. Then she and the officers would empty their magazines into Saxton Braith, and that might not kill him, but it would cripple him long enough for one of them to stuff him into the trunk of his car. Then–

"And then what?" Braith whispered, startling Shyla out of this vision. "Did you know the deepest river in Texas only peaked at about fifty feet? And that was during a flood. You could try Laguna Madre, but that's a bit of a drive just to try to dump me and a car in less than forty feet of water. The deepest point of Lake Travis is more impressive and useful for your idea. Then again, if you're lucky, it wouldn't actually take that much water to keep me hidden. I'm sure you know that, given where your mother is."

At this, Shyla flinched and almost swung at him. Braith smiled.

"The big difference," Braith continued, "is that she was dead a couple of minutes after her car hit the water. She really didn't have a chance to figure a way out. I, on the other hand, won't be dead at all. I'll work through whatever you try to bind me with, I swear to that. It'll just be a matter of time. I'll find a way out. And then I'll find Jinh for you, and everyone in your family next, before I get around to finding you."

"Don't you ever mention my mother or anyone else in my family again," Shyla said.

"You know what, I can agree to that if you'll promise to stop thinking of killing me. Now, can we go, please? Talk this through? We're wasting time you'll need to get to Jinh before the Tarvers run out of patience."

The Tarvers. Shyla scanned Braith's expression and couldn't decide whether he was even aware of letting the name slip, much less whether he might have done it on purpose.

Tarver.

They were the ones who had Jinh. They had a vendetta with Braith that probably spanned generations, if the origin of it was tied to Schramm or the reverend's crimes.

They had a name.

That might be enough for her to go on, without Braith's help. Especially if she could parse out the clue she thought Jinh was trying to give her back underground, before she disappeared. *Pray to her. You have to tell her. Tell her now. You have to sacrifice.* That had to mean something. Had to be related to the cult, didn't it?

For now–for just a little longer–she was going to use Braith's resources. The influence and reach he exhibited just by having all these officers with him was a testament to what he could get done. For Jinh's sake, Shyla could keep her hands in the mud next to Braith's until she could figure out–

She cut the thought off. He'd read her mind a second ago, hadn't he? She had to be more guarded with her thoughts, although she wasn't really sure how to do that. She would focus on trying, though, figure it out. Learn on the fly. It was critical.

The Tarvers had said Braith was like them, but lesser, and it was apparent they had a commonality with Jinh. Shyla had always thought of Jinh as "psychic," and would have thought the same of the Tarvers if not for the word she was sure Jinh had placed in her mind. A more fearsome word, yet still appropriate. The term that, once upon a time, would have been quickly deployed to describe anyone with the abilities Jinh, the Tarver twins, and Braith had displayed.

Witches.

23

Two DeWitt deputies drove Shyla to a one-story building on the corner of West Main and Sellers Street. In front of the building, a sign read, YORKTOWN POLICE MUSEUM.

Remy had driven Shyla's car. Braith followed in his own car. One sheriff's vehicle took the point and another the rear, forming a mini-motorcade to the destination. The other two stayed behind at the old bar, likely to resecure it, dispose of Neal's vehicle, and maybe search the perimeter for signs of their missing colleague, but Shyla was sure that no one was going inside to really search for him. Braith had probably shown them whatever Remy had shown Neal on her phone. If that hadn't been enough to inspire them to treat him as a lost cause, then whatever sword Braith was able to dangle over each of their heads was enough to dissuade them from seeking "justice" for their fellow officer.

Really, though, the fear of what was rumored to exist in the old underground hospital was probably deterrent enough.

Neal would be forgotten by everyone except his family, and

Shyla. The look on his dead, animated face would be with her forever. Just one more thing she'd have to live with.

From what she'd seen and felt so far, the afterlife existed, and there was no evidence of it being pleasant. Maybe the equivalent of heaven, or even a peaceful rest, didn't exist, and the gloomy, torturous existence that she had glimpsed was the only version of continuance there was. That might explain why people were so terrified of death. Not because they were scared of no longer existing but scared of going into a world made of suffering. Unless you were someone like Schramm and found joy in the pain you could give others forever.

Why would Braith have ever been close to a man like that?

This weighed on Shyla as she followed Braith and the two officers into the Yorktown Police Museum. Remy entered after them. It was a small building that kept uneven hours, according to the text on the glass door. Today was one of the three days of the week it was closed, and it wasn't open any longer than five hours at a time on the other days. Its entire "museum" section was visible from the front entrance, comprised of glass-encased uniforms, service revolvers, and pictures hung on walls with contextualizing descriptions printed beneath them. It reminded Shyla somewhat of the tiny one-room history museum adjacent to a whiskey bar she and Jinh had stumbled into during a visit to New Orleans, in the early days of their relationship. Except the Yorktown museum, while a little larger, lacked the charm and upkeep. No bar, either. There was a small cell, however, that had a foldout cot affixed to one wall. A card table and four folding chairs were placed in the center of the cell. Mannequins occupied two of the chairs; one was dressed in old police tans, the other in prison stripes.

As Shyla came to the cell, following the others, she checked the floor, making sure it wasn't covered in a sheet of clear plastic.

If she died here, shot by any of the four other people in the building, Shyla wondered if her soul would get stuck in this place. That just didn't seem right. She thought of the many ghost stories she'd read and heard about, and of the few she had more familiarity with, and wondered what caused the variance in where one gets to spend the afterlife. Why did a bastard like Garrett Schramm get to haunt the Inspiration Sweet despite dying hundreds of miles away while Sarah McDaniels—the spirit who fully awakened Jinh to her abilities—had been stuck in the woods with her body? Was it because Schramm, a soldier, was buried at the Fort Sam Houston army base in San Antonio, less than ten miles from the hotel where he'd played in the band? Was it because Sarah didn't know exactly where she was, how she got there, and how to get home? Was it all random?

Shyla entered the old cell and thought she would hate to die here, and would hate even more to be *stuck* here. She took a deep breath, told herself that there were more sensible, practical places for Braith to kill her, if he meant to, then took the chair closest to the black barred door. Behind her, she heard Braith chuckle, recognizing why she had chosen that chair, closer to the exit. He did not try to move her, or ask her to switch seats, but sat in the chair opposite hers. Remy walked in and closed the door. The two officers waited for Remy's nod to dismiss them, then hurried away like they could outrun ever having been here.

Braith set his bag down by his side, reached into it, and pulled out a black thermos. He unscrewed a cup from the top and another from the bottom. Shyla watched the thumb of the hand he poured with as he filled each cup with a tea-colored liquid from the plastic spout of the thermos.

Shyla remembered Braith offering her tea at his mansion. The awkward comment he'd made about it being "home brewed." The emphasis he'd put on that, how she couldn't get it anywhere else.

Something had made her store that part of their interaction specifically, even though at the time she'd mostly dismissed it as a rich man showing off under a mannerly pretext.

He slid the first cup toward her and kept the second for himself. Right away he took a long drink, then refilled it.

When he had poured for her, she was sure his thumb had been higher up on the handle than when he poured for himself. The thermos being black made it difficult to see the hole his thumb might have covered, but she believed she saw it.

She was just one of millions of people—based on the view counts—who had seen more than one social media video showing how an "assassin's teapot" worked. It could hold two different liquids inside, one poisoned, one harmless. A vent over the handle could be surreptitiously plugged with your thumb, and whether it was covered determined if the poison or the decoy drink was poured. This way, the person hosting their intended victim could pretend to drink the same thing they offered their guest.

It has to be easier to just take me to the woods and have me shot, Shyla thought. But maybe it wasn't. Maybe he just wanted her dead here, in an old police station's cell, or he didn't want her shot, he wanted her poisoned, writhing as strychnine tightened her muscles into rocks, or thallium made her bowels boil while ataxia kept her from even cursing his name as she died. And then her spirit would be bound to this place she never should have come to.

It struck her then—not like a lightning bolt, but a cruder attack, a stone thrown at the back of her head—that her real mother, Jacqueline, could be stuck where Jinh saw her. Long dead, but still trying to open the door, roll down the window, or even just unbuckle her seatbelt. Still in her car, at the bottom of Moses Lake, just outside of Texas City. The site of her wreck was a little north of Galveston, where she'd drifted off the bridge after a meeting with

Rodney that didn't do anything but motivate him and Linda to move Shyla yet again.

Jackie Sinclair had driven twelve hundred miles in twenty-five hours through five states, including the fat of Texas, which should have counted as three or four states on its own. She'd stopped once to sleep for four hours and hadn't slept well in the preceding weeks as her investigation brought her closer to the answer of who had taken her daughter. She should have gone to a motel nearby after meeting with Rodney, but thought she was charged up enough by the angry "discussion" she'd just had to make it back to Houston, despite stormy conditions and the lateness of the hour lowering visibility.

Jinh had seen all of this and relayed it to Shyla years ago, altering their relationship forever. Shyla used to think that ending their romance was the least damaging thing Jinh's revelation had done. Maybe that was still true, but she wasn't so sure anymore, given what she felt now. How it would feel to lose Jinh permanently. How difficult it would be to reassemble herself from the incomplete pieces remaining after everything she'd lost already. At the time, however, all Shyla could think of was how Jinh had stolen some of her righteousness. Scratched out the back half of the sentence that Shyla would have had tattooed on her arm if it wouldn't have incriminated her: *I killed the man who killed my mother.*

An answer she never asked for made the last four words a lie. She could replace them with others that would justify the deed in many people's eyes, and her own, too, if she chose to look at things from a different angle.

I killed the man who stole my life.

I killed the man who ruined my parents' lives.

I killed the man who planned to kill me.

None of these were the ultimate reason she pulled the trigger, though. The clues she'd had available to her at the time gave her reason to believe Rodney had killed Jacqueline Sinclair. Silenced her, and then had the nerve to speak of her (*that woman . . . she didn't raise you*) as though she'd been a stranger. No, much worse. An absentee, unfit, uncaring parent. Shyla had shot him mostly for what he'd done, partly for what he'd said, and lastly, almost incidentally, to protect herself.

It felt important to her now not only to remember these details and distinctions, but to tell them to someone. Share her story with someone else so she wouldn't go to her grave with it.

What's happening? Why am I thinking like this?

Shyla looked down at the cup of "tea."

The liquid inside looked oddly clear, despite the black cup that contained it. Shyla saw her reflection vividly in it, but didn't view it as a mirror image, rather a depiction of herself deep under dark waters, with unidentifiable sediments drifting about her. She did not appear to be under duress. This image of her did not even reflect how tired and concerned she was, much less how frantic she would be if she were submerged, like her mother, desperate to get back to the surface again. This other version of herself was, instead, at peace, and as soon as Shyla recognized this, her reflection shut its eyes and slipped farther into the depths until it disappeared from sight.

Shyla gasped, and with the inhalation came recognition of the enticing pungency of the "tea" in her cup. Its flavor slid through her sinuses and into her lungs. Its feathery tickle stole into her heart and brain at the same time, and her hands moved to cradle the cup like a precious, rare treasure before Shyla could stop them. She strained to raise her eyes to look at Braith's confident, patient face.

"What is this?" she said.

"A home brew that you can't get anywhere else," Braith said.

"Herbal, mostly, plus a few drops of blood, a pinch of grave soil, and select fluids from a few different lizards."

Hearing this should have made her nauseous, but instead dried out her mouth and throat, making her more aware of how long it had been since she'd had something to drink, how refreshing it would be to have this brew at her lips. How good it would taste despite its disgusting ingredients.

"You may as well take a sip," Braith said. "I can see the smell already working on you. You know if you'd just taken a sip back at my house, I think we could be farther ahead in understanding each other. I'd have a complete understanding of what you've been hiding, at least. Or if you had just opened and read through the attachment I had sent you. The meditation techniques, remember? That could have done the same, made you confess the secret you're holding on to, although not as quite well as the brew here. Truthfully, if I just leave you with the aroma of the tea for long enough, it will have the desired effect, but one sip will expedite this, and then we can turn our attention to the Tarvers and get Jinh back. That's what you want, isn't it?"

"*What is this?*" Shyla asked again.

Braith said, "Well, to oversimplify, it's a truth serum. Although I'd say, more accurately, it deactivates the part of your mind that learned the benefits of deception, while also making you feel the full weight of lies, and encourages you to lighten your load."

"What are you? Are you a witch?"

Braith sighed, and the disappointment on his face surprised Shyla. "That could be the word for it, although I don't think I'm worthy of it. There are some like Jinh, and like the Tarvers, who don't need the concoctions and craftwork. No special blends or effigies necessary. They can, if they know how, more or less will things to happen, albeit at considerable mental and physical expense.

Nothing is free, after all. But I feel people with that inherent skill are the ones who deserve the distinction of 'witch.' The best I've ever been able to do is identify people who have that natural talent. I've mastered a couple techniques that aren't much beyond parlor tricks. Maybe I could pack a small theater with my mesmerism act, but only on the first night, before word got around that there isn't much of a show to it. But maybe I shouldn't underestimate it. At first I didn't know how much I could get out of spotting how gifted others are. Or, in a case like yours, sensing that you're the kind of person whose past makes them prone to the occasional 'power spike.' Speaking of, what exactly did you do that you were so scared of me knowing?"

"I k-k-k–"

Her throat constricted around the confession she impulsively wanted to give. The words sharpened, hardened, tried to scrape and grind their way free, and that just made her crave a soothing sip of tea more. She gagged and coughed until tears stung her eyes. Braith motioned to the cup and said, "Drink."

Shyla shook her head, responding to the internal voice that had answered him with a *yes*.

Yes.

It was going to taste good. It was going to feel good. She had worried it was poison when it was the opposite. The antidote to an affliction she didn't know she had. The unwelcome knowledge of and capacity for deception. She imagined a world where this "home brew" was a staple in every kitchen. Where the curse of lying was washed away every morning with just a few ounces of one of the greatest remedies humanity had ever created.

No more lies. No more secrets. It might not quite be a panacea, but it would instantly cure enough of what ailed the world to free people. A life without the ability to lie was a gift. What made her delay in accepting it?

This is *a lie. This* is *deception. It's part of a trick. He just wants you to tell him things. Tell him* everything. *He doesn't know. He suspected something. He "sensed" it. But he never knew. You could have called his bluff and walked away from moment one. You could have done it at any time and you still can now. Don't fall for this. It's a lie. It's not too late.*

"But it is," Braith told Shyla. He could already read some of her emotionally heightened thoughts even without the effect of the tea. The brew just amplified the signal.

He wasn't lying; it *was* too late, because the scent of the brew made her feel like she was close to dying of thirst. Her desire to bring the cup to her lips transformed from an ache and compulsion to a biological imperative. *Drink now, or never again drink or breathe or move or think or be.*

When had she raised the cup? It felt like her life was skipping frames of footage before her eyes. The cup was close to her mouth now, the scent of its contents more powerful this close to her nose. It was like a truer, better form of oxygen, something your body received and immediately relayed that you could no longer live without. And that was just the aroma. It would be so much stronger and better when it hit her taste buds. So satisfying when it settled in her stomach. And it would make for a perfect kind of inebriation when it traveled through her veins and into her brain.

Her lips were on the rim of the cup. She drew in one sip and felt as though a needle had pierced the tip of her tongue. She set the cup down, pushed it away, and straightened her arms against the end of the table, tilting her chair. She couldn't describe the flavor of the tea, or the flavor of just about anything right now. Hell, she wasn't sure she would be able to define the word "flavor" at the moment, but she would be completely honest about that inability.

The wrongness of this feeling made her want to escape her mind and flesh. In her own head she was bombarded with truths she didn't want to feel so intensely, how lonely she'd been without Jinh, how much more she missed her mother than her father strictly based on stories she'd heard about them, how isolated she still felt when she was around Aunt Teonna and her cousins. Almost like she had never found her family. There were just too many missed seasons and moments to make up for. This last truth almost propelled her into racking grief, but a truth more critical to the moment emerged as a byproduct of this emotion.

This was a mistake.

"What did the Tarvers tell you about me?" Braith asked.

The cup trembled at the tip of Shyla's fingers, some of the tea sloshing over the brim before Remy came and took it away. Shyla barely registered that there was someone besides Braith in the cell, or that she was even inside a building, much less a specific section of a building. All that mattered was the question and the drive to answer it.

"They said you were a witch. But lesser, and jealous, and that you've done horrible things. That you are a murderer and a fake. They said they know your real name. They said they know how to kill you."

Braith nodded, none of this surprising him. "And what did you tell them about me?"

"I said you scare me, and that's why I'm working for you. Not for the money. But to protect my secret."

His smile cast the darkest shadow, and when he leaned closer it spread easier than hate. Easy as a bad rumor. "You really didn't know that I didn't really know?"

"Not until a couple of minutes ago."

A small, prickly laugh crawled out of him on bug legs. "Well, that's something. So what precisely is your big secret, Shyla Sinclair?"

A deep breath did nothing to suppress her need to confess, and the delay only made her want to vomit so hard she'd never stand upright again. "I killed my fake father. A man named Rodney Hewitt. His girlfriend, a woman named Linda Montgomery, kidnapped me when I was an infant, and—"

"I know that part," Braith cut in. "I'm a fan of Jinh's show. Your episode was compelling. But on there you said Rodney Hewitt was still at large. And that's what the authorities still think, too, isn't it?"

"Yes."

"But they're wrong?"

"Yes. Because I killed him. And I dumped his body in a natural well that feeds into an underwater cave system near Wimberley, Texas. The same place he and Linda had picked out for me in case they had to kill me. It would be hard for anyone to find him, and risky, but probably not impossible."

"Not impossible." He shook his head at himself and shot a quick glance at Remy before telling Shyla, "You're going to be so upset at how wrong I was. I could sense you'd taken a life, like I said at the house. And there were aromatics in the house made from this same brew that could have made you tell me this back then, if I just kept you in there for a while longer, but then however much trust in me you've held on to would have evaporated. But honestly, I thought you had done something to Dante. None of my contacts have heard from him since you finished with his case. Given what I knew of him, I thought he either coerced you with the right price or figured out how to force your hand to grant his death wish. Then again, with what else I know about the man, he might be off the grid canoeing the Amazon, chasing his death, or followers, or both. The idea of you killing Rodney never crossed my mind. What about his girlfriend? What was her name? Did you do something to her, too?"

"No. I would have, but I never caught up to her."

"So she's still out there? What would it be worth to you if I helped–"

He stopped as Shyla shook her head. "The Tarvers told me–showed me–that Linda killed herself."

"And you believe them?" Braith asked.

"It feels true."

He made an approving grunt, as though he could relate to this sentiment. "Do you still believe me when I say I can't remember my past?"

"I'm not sure I ever believed you," Shyla answered.

A clap of his hands punctuated a machine-gun burst of laughter. Braith moved from his chair, pushed the mannequin of the prisoner to the floor, then slid that chair closer to Shyla before he sat in it. Seeing him with his back to Remy returned Shyla to the night they met. When Remy had reached for the poker and struck before Shyla could react, before Braith could even indicate that he was ready. Shyla pictured those large, dark portraits hanging high on the walls. All from different time periods, but of the same man.

That same man put his hand atop one of hers now, and his feigned gentility made Shyla jealous of Remy for getting to stab him through the head to shut him up. "Do you think I am about to lie to you?" he asked.

"I think there's a great chance," Shyla said.

"That's fair. But I genuinely don't 'remember' anything about my life before the crash. Having said that, I've been privy to dreams, every time I sleep, detailing who I used to be since my first night in the hospital after the crash. These are not memories—I don't consider them to be—just visions of my own life. That might sound implausible, but . . . it's a little bit like seeing yourself in photographs or film clips from events you don't remember. Here is evidence of where you were, what you did while you were there, who you spoke with and what your voice sounded like. But you have zero recall of any of it. It's strange. I have a theory on why that is. Would you like to hear it?"

"No," Shyla said, "but you're going to tell me, anyway."

"Oh, honesty with a little kick to it. There *is* a bit of pepper in the tea's recipe. Anyway, you are right, I've already made up my mind to . . . well, not 'tell' so much as inform you. It should make things easier, down the road, if you understand things as I do. Now look at me. Try not to blink. Listen for your heartbeat. I can feel it through your palm. Thump-thump. Thump-thump. There's a rhythm. That's your metronome. Tell me when you can hear it."

You bastard, she thought, remembering—nearly to the point of reliving—when he'd said something similar about listening to her heartbeat and spotting a rhythm to it back at his mansion. Right before he'd told her, "You can handle this." She hadn't immediately calmed down then, but she had started to entertain the possibility of accepting his offer.

He'd sent her that meditation guide with similar terminology bolded right on its cover page, keeping the suggestion in her mind even if she didn't look through the rest of the booklet.

He hadn't completely mesmerized her prior to this. That had to be true, because that's what she was telling herself now. She'd had more than enough free will to resist him, but she'd been ninety-nine percent too paranoid about what he knew and one percent too greedy to recognize how necessary it was to reject his offer when they first met. He likely would have tried to manipulate her some other way, but perhaps not. Maybe he would have taken the loss, trusted that she wouldn't tell anyone his secret, and that no one would believe her, besides, and then moved on to a different option. Instead, she'd taken the job.

"Do you hear your heartbeat?" Braith asked again.

Shyla thought she nodded, but wasn't sure if she actually did. She was going numb and felt a bizarre slowing sensation occupy the room. The dust particles that hovered around them, like confetti under the fluorescent ceiling lights, appeared frozen in place. Shyla stared into Braith's unblinking eyes for what felt like a time too long to put a number to.

When Braith spoke again, his lips did not move, and Shyla continued staring, unable to blink herself. Besides his voice in her head, all she heard was her heartbeat.

"Good," he said. "Finally. We're going to go away for a while, but it'll take much less time than you think. Just enough time for you to understand. The Tarvers are right. I was a killer. But never like Schramm. That's what led to the end of us. I wanted him to learn from me. I thought we could be real partners, but he was overzealous. I was practical. I had a goal whereas he had an addiction, so it just couldn't last. And I didn't have the patience to get him to realize what sacrifice truly is, and the power it can grant you when done the right way."

24

At the time, Galveston, an island off the Texas coast, was nicknamed "the Free State." A reference to its relative lawlessness, which it had gradually embraced in the aftermath of the Great Storm in 1900.

Before that, it had emerged as the jewel of the Gulf coast. "The Southwest's Wall Street."

Then it was blindsided by a hurricane that swept away at least six thousand lives, maybe double that. Somewhere between a sixth and a third of the island's population. Another storm fifteen years later killed any hope of a resurgence, even though it killed less than one percent as many people. Even with a new seawall, raised buildings, and infinitely better forecasting, the island was too vulnerable to invest much wealth into it. Unless you had some dirty money to spend.

Where better to bury some ill-gotten green and watch it grow than a place others viewed as a danger zone? Particularly if you want more of the spoils and fewer of the hazards that come with competition in cities like Chicago or New York.

Vice thrived, begetting a certain kind of tourism. If you make enough money while raising relatively little hell, it's easier to convince cops that bribes are part of their civic duty. The officers applying for sainthood don't have the manpower, public support, or ingenuity to undermine the dirty economy. Not even the church is completely on their side.

There's plenty of booze, gaming, and fucking to go around, and everyone's happy.

That old tarnished jewel gets polished with a little spit—and maybe a couple of other fluids not worth mentioning—and finds a different kind of luster. By the time I got there to do what I needed to, the city was feeling so delighted and defiant that its most popular casino, the Balinese Room, was built on a pier that went six hundred feet into the water. Like it was begging God to summon the Gulf to submarine it.

Back before they turned to sin, the Gulf once rose to drown whole families. People were battered to death in the water by the debris from their neighbors' crushed houses. Early in the storm, before the worst of the flooding, some were decapitated in the streets by asphalt shingles thrown in the winds. These were ugly deaths. Then the city embraced a playful, dark side, and nothing quite like that happened to it ever again. But other things happened. Gamblers who couldn't pay debts got shot and dumped in the Gulf. Witnesses to robberies and bribes lost their heads. The losers got sacrificed. This lasted until well after the First World War, after I came back from overseas in search of a place to call home. I sensed what was happening there, and realized it was the place for me.

Not the "me" that you've met, Shyla, but the me that existed then. The one telling you my story now.

Not the me who can't remember. The me who was there.

You see, I had learned about sacrifice.

I had a mentor whose name I won't mention, because some things are sacred. I might like to hear myself talk and tell stories, but I know where lines should be drawn. Everyone shares too much now. It makes nothing precious. The name of someone you owe everything to is something you should keep.

All you need to know is I first saw him in the Great War, soaking up bullets in no-man's-land. First he pulled me out of a mudhole I was sinking into, then he pulled me out of my shock when he told me that he could make me like him.

He taught me about sacrifice.

It's not as simple as most people think. Some fools take a knife to a baby that's not their own and think it's the most powerful act they can perform, but what does a baby know about what you're taking from it? What does the average person who would do that to a child know about innocence? Probably nothing, so what they're giving up is barely anything. They don't even understand what killing a child does to their own soul. So it's not a proper, meaningful sacrifice. Real sacrifice comes from self-awareness. If you can give part of yourself to the sacrifice, you can discover something truly special. If you can trick someone else into giving up something important within themselves on your behalf, even better.

I gave more of myself than I knew I had left to every person I killed, and there were dozens of them. Every time it felt heinous. Even more so because all but one of them was pointless. All I did was burden myself with guilt. I gained nothing, until I gained everything. Immortality. After that I was free. The sacrifice of another gave me exactly what my mentor told me it would, I just had to find the right one.

The first family I killed down in the Free State of Galveston were the Durbins. Their grandmother had potential in her. I felt that. But like the others I'd killed before her, she couldn't summon the necessary fury. Part of her was still hoping for a miracle to save her family, even as her grandchildren's blood spilled around her knees. She begged out loud for God to give her the strength to forgive–like there's any power at all in forgiveness–while her son and daughter-in-law writhed with their throats slit. I had my helpers pry her eyes open to make sure she watched them die while reaching for their babies. That still didn't incite the rage I needed from her. Grandma Durbin was just too good for this earth, so I gave her a quick exit. Two bullets in the back of the head. The first was probably enough, but bullets aren't diamonds. Might as well spend them.

My mentor taught me this process, and I've always thought that he learned from the old days of witch hunts, although he never admitted to it. But that's what I thought of every time I killed these people. All those old stories about witches being dunked or burned. I always thought the "hunters" should be able to tell they weren't witches, because if they really were, they would use their powers to save themselves. But now I could see that that wasn't necessarily true. Many people who possessed the power didn't know how to wield it. They didn't even understand the purpose I was trying to give them right up to the moment I killed them.

My mentor told me how much patience and perseverance were required to become like him, but no one can really prepare you for how many people you have to kill. All the crying, all the pleading, and then the waiting. To say nothing of the ineptitude. I can't express how frustrating it is to have your own talent limited mostly to being able to recognize people who have so much more of it than you, then watch them, time after time, fail to live up to their potential at the most critical point in their lives. Their last chance to do something amazing with something most of them didn't even know they had. It is uniquely hellish. More than sacrificing my own morality, I had to sacrifice my time, patience, and sanity to seeing this over and over again. If I had that much talent, I wouldn't need someone to murder my loved ones to bring it out of me, and if it came to that, I certainly wouldn't keep it dormant within me while my wife and children were butchered in front of me. But most of the people I killed didn't know what they had within them, or thought it was a cute little quirk. "I can predict storms better than the weatherman. I always know when family is making a surprise visit. I'm better than most at guessing the winning numbers." They didn't take it seriously enough.

A man I met in Nevada had seen his father and uncles die in a mining explosion one day before it happened, and just chalked it up to a bad dream, even though he'd been wide awake eating lunch at school when he saw it. Had he spoken up about it, who knows? Maybe they evacuate the mine and he saves the people he loves, along with the hundred and twenty other miners who also died. I should have guessed he wouldn't be the right one. His passion was gone. If I hadn't killed him, his guilt would have.

But what I'm getting at here is that all of these people had it in them, they just didn't dig deep enough to access it when the time called for it. And you can blame me for every life I took–I'd never suggest you shouldn't–but if the first or second one I tried this with had just done what they were capable of, just listened to what I told them to do, then I would have been done, and no one else would have died. Like I said, I'm not like Schramm. I wasn't going to keep killing for its own sake. I even tried to make sure every life wasn't taken in vain. You know how I built my fortune? By investing the money and property I was able to take from these people, because they rarely had their affairs in order, and their assets were easy to claim if you knew what to do and acted quickly. Which makes sense when you think of how these people wasted their potential.

Anyway, when I got to a man named Enoch Tarver, I got what I needed. He cursed me, and I didn't have to kill for myself anymore. At least not to obtain immortality the way my mentor had. I was done. And in that way, Enoch saved lives.

I brushed past him at a dime store, buying a doll for his youngest. One good thing about Galveston at the time was that segregation wasn't as much the standard there. A lot of people still stuck to their own, and it wasn't all harmony and kindness. But a man like him could walk past a man like me without lowering his eyes, so that was something.

It helped me see right into his soul and know that I might have found who I was looking for.

I followed him to his church, watched him sweat harder than anybody else fanning themselves in that building. Heard his voice climb over the tops of the others when everyone sang, "Let Jesus lead you all the way." I felt shock waves as he trembled through his prayers. He pleaded with God for direction, listened hard and prayed harder for a sign. Because to him he was either a prophet or a witch. Blessed or damned. This was a grown man in his late thirties, with a solid job and a good family, still scared like a child of getting punished for something he couldn't control. The idea of being something different, apart from everything his religion had taught him, never occurred to him until *I* did.

Hiring thugs to help with what I needed was never that difficult, but it was easiest in the Free State. There were a lot of men in debt. Most monetarily, but some owed favors, and some were working off a wrong they did to the wrong person. I got eight men to help me break into the Tarver home, tie up Enoch's family, and take them to a pier. We held them at gunpoint and I managed to quiet the family enough to talk to Tarver man-to-man.

He had a wife and four children. Two sons, two daughters. Perfectly balanced home. We cut the oldest boy's throat first. It's not really about letting people know how serious you are, not after you've invaded their home, beat them into submission, and dragged them to the edge of the sea in the dead of the night. Enoch understood what was at stake already, but that kind of kill provides a startling amount of clarity. You'd be surprised. Most people would.

You start with the oldest child to snap someone into a focus they've never had before, provided they don't get hysterical on you. Enoch had served during the war. I don't know what kind of action he saw, but he was at least aware of how quick death can visit you and your people, just through that alone. To say nothing of being a Black man in that time. You're aware of something like this being a possibility, even if it's the last thing you can afford to think about day to day if you want to stay sane.

I gave him the words to speak from a secret language. Some tortured Latin blended with ancient Greek and forgotten Celtic. I told him to say it slowly, phonetically, then gradually say it a little more quickly and confidently. Some of the boys I'd hired got antsy about this. It's strange, where people draw their lines. Tell them to abduct a family, murder them, and dump their bodies, and they're all in for the price of a few months' rent. But start a chant or admit that you're in touch with an energy they would classify as "dark" or "satanic," and now it feels like something they shouldn't be part of. Every time I felt that shift I wanted to shout to those men that they had already damned themselves, so there was no sense in getting worried about the fate of their souls now, but I knew it would be pointless. Belief isn't designed to be logical.

I don't know how it is that Enoch learned what I told him to say, for instance. I just know that he followed the instructions well, blocking out the crying from his family, the few nervous laughs from my men, and probably an inner voice warning him that something bad was going to happen. It hurt me to see him like that. A proud, strong man, a solid member of his community, down on his knees, hands tied behind him like a criminal. I'm sure he thought about trying to pop up and charge me, maybe to run me off the pier if he caught me just right. But I had a knife under his wife's neck to keep him motivated and compliant. You always threaten the spouse after killing the eldest child, if they have one. Trial and error taught me this was most effective.

I watched Enoch closely, saw his eyes go from pleading and desperate to almost blind from anger, and I felt the beginnings of a charge under my skin. It made me scratch my arm hard enough to draw a little blood, like I was trying to free that new, uncomfortable energy, but I kept my focus on Enoch. When I thought he might be hitting the last wall between ignorance and understanding, I slipped that blade through his wife's windpipe. He almost got to his feet and completely broke his concentration then, but I reminded him he had three kids left. The three most vulnerable. He could probably tell there was barely a chance in hell I'd let them live at that point, but any decent parent is going to go for that chance, however small, over just letting their kids die.

We had to push the knife hard enough into the next son's cheek to make the boy squeal. Then it finally clicked for Enoch. He was sweating harder than he had when I observed him in church, and he cursed me and my team in English every half-sentence, or thereabouts. But I saw it in his eyes, the moment when he realized the nature of the curse I wanted him to put on me. The nature of the sacrifice his curse required. And the charge got stronger.

I'd learned how to coerce a curse out of someone from my mentor. The specific prayer curse that I learned was: *You will die by my hand or never.* That's the best English translation of it, anyway. An old revenge curse. It damns the one who speaks it to a restless existence, and residually condemns their descendants to the burden. But these are just words unless the person speaking them is capable of making them a pledge. Something they mean so sincerely they no longer care what the consequences of it are to themselves, to anyone they love, or anyone not involved. They don't care whether it's realistic to believe what they're saying or not. All that matters to them is their promise, and the hate that fuels it.

You will die by my hand or never.

I needed him to mean it like the first time he said, "I love you," to his wife. Like the awed gasp he uttered the first time he held his newborn. Like when he said, "Thank you, I'll miss you," standing over his father's grave.

You will die by my hand or never.

I doubt his gums ruptured from the force of his passion when he declared his love for his wife, but they did when one of my men pushed that blade through his surviving son's neck. The words came up thick and covered in a bubble of blood after we stabbed his daughter to death. His lungs ruptured from the force of his hate, like we'd put blades to him instead of his wife and children. His rage was so severe it cut up his windpipe and split his lips. He shouldn't have been able to speak through his coughing, but he did.

Most of the men I hired were repulsed by this. One even ran away, and that let me know I wasn't imagining anything. Not in any way. The itch I'd felt in my arm wasn't an itch, but a different, wonderful sensation I couldn't define. I wasn't deluding myself because I wanted this so badly. It was really happening. The curse was coursing through me, and I was becoming unkillable, unless the man to kill me was Enoch Tarver.

He fought through the damage and pain the curse caused him to say it as forcefully as he needed to.

You will die by my hand or never!

You will die by my hand or never!

The energy of immortality spread from my arm and engulfed me.

It can't be compared to anything. I could tell you that it felt like I was made of light. Like I could suddenly feel the true speed of our planet flying through space, circling a sun that was also flying through space, circling a galaxy that was *also* . . . You get it.

I could say I felt like the father of giants and the brother of God. I could say all of that, but none of it really tells you what it felt like.

There are things inherent to the curse that my mentor told me about but that I wasn't prepared to immediately experience. Like knowing that you not only can't be killed, but that any harm that comes your way will be healed. Some things are inferred without needing to be said. It's like the opposite of that old story "The Monkey's Paw," where if you're not overly careful about what you wish for, and how to get it, what you didn't say will get used against you. A true, pure curse, spoken by someone with a real gift, fills in what you forgot to say with what it knows you really want. Enoch's curse wouldn't let me die unless he killed me, and also wouldn't let me stay broken, burned, crushed, gutted, peeled, or anything else that could happen to me. He wanted to take my life when I was whole, healthy, and happy. Anything else would be less satisfying, and the curse, the power behind it, understood this.

A wave of energy almost brought me to the floor. One of my boys saw this and caught me before I fell. He asked if I was okay. I just told him to do something for me.

Cut off both of Enoch's hands.

He stared at me like I'd asked him to stab someone's child,

except he'd already done that, so I couldn't understand what the look was for. Again, the lines some people draw. Strange.

A different man heard the command and obliged. He pulled the big bowie knife he'd just used on the older Tarver daughter, went behind Enoch, and cut off his hands without touching the rope that held him. That man was Garrett Schramm. This was how we met.

Enoch never stopped praying and barely even winced when Garrett started working on him. He never looked back to see what Garrett was doing, and never tried to move away. His eyes were fixed on me. It was like he thought he could keep me from going for his youngest daughter as long as he didn't stop watching me.

Garrett tossed the hands toward me one at a time, and they twitched after they landed on the pier. Then they started really moving. Crawling on their own toward me, slow and staggering like they were drugged, trailing blood like slug slime. I can't even blame the others for being alarmed by this, but none of them ran until I started giggling, and even then only two of them took off. Garrett smiled like a kid seeing his first rainbow. One of the others took out their gun and shot the left hand three times, and it looked like he "killed" it for a second, before the bullet holes closed up and the hand reattached the part of its ring finger he'd blown off, then it kept coming at me.

I made a very bad mistake then, but it was that feeling. That charge and recognition coming over me. It made me feel giddy, and a little childish, too, I suppose. I walked up to the hand my man had shot–the left hand–and stepped on it. Then with my other foot I kicked the right hand toward the eager gunman. Like a joke. Like putting a worm in a little girl's hair. Stupid. Childish. Frankly unbecoming of me, and disrespectful to Enoch, given the moment, but . . . that feeling. My head was far above the clouds. I was on a high no one else has ever felt, unless they had this thing happen to them.

The hand landed on the gunman's face and clutched him reflexively. He screamed, ripped the hand away, and flung it right off the pier. Right into the water. He didn't realize what he'd done, of course, but it still pissed me off, and I think I've established how far past controlling my emotions I was by then. So I took out my gun and shot him in the face until there was nothing left to hit. That got all the others, except for Garrett Schramm, to run away.

I locked eyes with him then, and really thought in that moment that we understood each other and would be perfect together. How wrong I was.

While I looked at Garrett, Enoch's surviving child dove off the pier into the water.

She was about six years old, and the only one we hadn't tied up. Honestly, we just ran out of rope. Enoch was a big man, and his oldest took after him, so we used extra on the both of them, which left us short for the kid, but there wasn't any scenario where we really thought that would present a problem. She couldn't outrun us, and any of us could snatch her up with one hand if she tried to make trouble. She was a kid, and she was about to die after watching her mom and brothers and sister die. I took it as a small blessing. The absolute least we could do for the kid was not tie her up. So I don't consider that a mistake, just an unfortunate consequence of my earlier mistake, which was kicking Enoch's right hand like a brat. The sequence of events that followed that let the girl escape.

I barely even heard the splash when she dove into the water. Garrett noticed before I did. He went to the side of the pier where she went in and fired into the water with his pistol. I figured out why a second later and joined in, but I only had two shots left in the magazine after shooting the other guy. I let Garrett get off about seven or eight shots before I told him to stop so we could listen. I didn't hear any splashing, and didn't see any signs that she had resurfaced, so I figured we got her, or that she couldn't swim, so we didn't need to get her. I didn't find out until much, much later that I was wrong.

Anyway, it occurred to me that I might have made another mistake by turning my back on the hand that was left, no pun intended. When I looked back at it, it was headed toward me, moving a little more quickly and steadily, and Enoch had gotten from his knees up to his feet even though he was bound at his ankles, which kept him from walking toward me. Garrett went right over and pressed the heel of his boot into the back of the hand to pin it down. He wasn't the least bit afraid or bewildered by seeing a severed hand moving of its own accord. It was remarkable. Can you blame me for becoming enamored of him? He asked me if I could tell him what all was going on. I told him yes, if he'd do me a couple of quick favors first.

I asked how many bullets he had left, and he checked and confirmed he had three. I told him to put one in Enoch's head, and the shot was out and true before I hit the last word. Then I asked him to shoot me dead center in the chest, and tapped my finger on the target in case he needed a visual aid. He hesitated at this for a couple of seconds, but didn't make me repeat myself. He fired, the bullet punched through, and it hurt, but it also felt kind of good, because I could feel the pain become a ghost as I immediately healed. Right before the wound fully closed, I unbuttoned my shirt and wiped the blood away so he could see the hole closing up. I don't know if he got the best look, but he caught on to what happened pretty quickly, because he pointed the gun at his own chest next and said, "Does this mean I can't die, either?" I had to rush to tell him no.

He asked if there was a way this could happen for him, could I teach him, and I said maybe, but it would probably take a long time and a lot of killing before he found the right one. The way he smiled then should have told me that we weren't a good fit. He was the wrong kind of killer.

But you aren't the wrong kind, are you, Shyla Sinclair? You understand sacrifice. You understand necessity.

Now, you may dislike me, or even loathe me for what I've done, but I'm not the one who took Jinh from you. The ones who have her are the ones who want to kill me, and have been trying to draw me out. They're using her as bait to force your hand. All they're offering in exchange for helping them is Jinh's safe return. I can give you a lot more than that. So much more than the money we've already agreed to.

Firstly, I can give you my word that I won't tell anyone about what you did to Rodney Hewitt. But that honestly doesn't feel like a fair exchange for ensuring that the only thing that can kill me is neutralized. I believe in doing good business, and I think you do, too. You took my initial offer, after all, even after seeing what I was. That was only money. This is so much better. Shyla, I can give you eternity. I can point you to two people who we know can say a prayer with enough conviction and skill to bring this same "curse" down on you. This amazing, perfect curse.

If you help me kill the Tarvers, I will help you live forever.

25

Shyla shuddered and gasped for air when Braith freed her from the trance he'd put her under. She looked toward Remy to be sure she was still there, and started to stand and reach for the cup Remy held, desperate for a drink of water. Then she remembered what was in that cup and remained in her seat, swallowing the few drops of spit she could muster instead.

Braith patted her hand and said, "Well, he told you everything, didn't he?"

"He?" Shyla said.

"The old me. The one who killed all those people."

Shyla shook her head. Yes, he sounded a little different now than he had when speaking directly into her mind, but that didn't mean anything. "There's no 'old' or 'other' you. There's just *you*."

"Not true. I'm surprised the tea let you say that. You must sincerely believe it."

"It's the truth."

Braith smirked. "I guess it's unfair to expect you to grasp this.

But I genuinely am a different man from who I was. A 'changed' man, let's say. I wasn't lying about my memory loss and having to connect to my past through these dreams. I basically just plugged my old dream self into your brain now to let him explain himself. My theory on it is that every time I suffered some brain damage, from a bullet or knife or having my skull crushed in a plane crash, the healing was a little imperfect. Rebuilding countless cells from scratch leaves ample opportunity for tiny, tiny mistakes. There are going to be some alterations over time. I think that the old me might have realized this and done it deliberately to try to hide his identity and his past. It could have been a way to try to escape the Tarvers. I've asked him in dreams if any of these possibilities are true, but he won't confirm or deny any of it."

"Are you really going to keep referring to yourself like this?" Shyla said.

"If it keeps it simpler for you, I'll refrain, but–"

"You still want to kill the Tarvers?"

"Well, they want to kill *me*."

"What did you do with the hand Garrett stepped on?"

Braith sucked in a hissing breath through his teeth, his patience visibly thinning before Shyla's eyes. Then he shook this off and slipped his affected affability back on. "It's in a safe, inside a vault, buried in a bunker on my property."

"And you . . ." *need the other one,* she was going to say, but caught herself. Did he know about the other one? The hand of glory glove that she saw on the brother's hand? "You're afraid they'll dig it up or something? How would they even know where you have it?"

"That's a great question. The only people I've told about it are Remy and you, just now. Well, and Garrett, but I'm confident he took it to his grave. But several months back I started receiving threats in the mail. Cryptic messages and packages that my screeners brought to my attention. Old newspaper clippings about unsolved murders that I was responsible for, and disappearances with the words 'we know' or 'we remember' or 'we're coming' handwritten on them. Actually, the first such article was the story of a young girl who was found washed ashore. The paper called her a 'miracle child,' like they were so wowed and impressed, but the half-column they spared for her tells you how much of a damn they actually gave about her. Anyway, the last one they sent was the one I showed you. Just the story of my old . . . of *me* surviving the plane crash. The people who sent it never identified themselves, and we couldn't trace them, but I knew who it had to be. And if they were bold enough to send me those messages, that meant they were up to something, but also that they needed me to act. I suppose I could have just waited them out, but passivity isn't in my nature."

"I guess not. You could have done more than just waited them out, you could have lived a completely different life. If you really didn't remember your past you could have done a thousand different things that didn't draw attention, anything except make yourself a billionaire with a mansion you can see from the moon."

"Come on, you make it sound like I pursued an acting career or something," Braith said. "Or like I've been posting online, making a spectacle of myself, hunting cameras and microphones everywhere I go. I could have run for office or made public appearances with politicians. I've indulged, I'll admit, but how much attention have I really called to myself?"

"Too much, apparently," Shyla said.

Braith laughed. "Hard to argue that."

"You really expect me to help you?"

"I expect you to weigh your choices and make the only sensible decision in front of you."

What happens if I tell you to go to hell? Shyla wondered. *If I spit in your face and say that's for the families you killed. They all want me to tell you you're not forgiven, you never will be, and you can't buy or trick your way out of judgment.*

What if I shoot my thumbs into your eyes, get you off balance, and slam the back of your head into the floor? What then?

"Then you screw yourself and Jinh over for nothing," Braith said, still eavesdropping on her thoughts, although she didn't feel the weight of him in her mind quite so heavily now. Nothing was inexhaustible, Shyla remembered. Reading minds had to take up some energy, and he'd spent a lot just now on putting her in contact with his "old self." He had to be tiring out, at least a little.

"You can't kill me," Braith went on. "You don't have Enoch Tarver's hands. And Remy will pull you off of me before you even get a good hit in. Let's not pretend you have much of an option here. I'm your best hope to get Jinh back safely. And, to be fair, I think you can help me, too. I need something from you, and I can help you in return, so let's just keep working together, hm?"

"There's no way I can trust you, and no way you really trust me."

"Shyla, if you haven't learned anything else through all of this, you should know by now that there's *always* a way."

"I've learned there's always a lot more to the story than I've been told," Shyla said. "And I've learned that you're a liar and a piece of shit, not in that order."

"I don't doubt you feel that way, but it doesn't change what your choices are. And whatever you may think of me, I can assure you I'm telling the truth now. What incentive is there for me to lie to you?"

Before Shyla could rebut him, Remy said, "What about to me?"

He turned to her, the wrinkling of his brow belying the confidence of his steady smile. Once he faced her, Remy threw the tea from the cup she still held into his face. Braith flinched, recoiled, stood, then snorted and coughed. He'd accidentally inhaled and swallowed some of it. At least a few drops, which was enough for it to be effective, according to what he'd said earlier.

Remy stepped toward him and took a fighting stance. Shyla seized the opportunity, while both of them were focused on each other, to stand and move toward the cell door.

"Did you think I would die down there?" Remy asked Braith. "You're done with me, like Garrett? Is that why you sent me with her without telling me what all was down there?"

"I didn't really think about what might happen to you, just whether you'd do what I needed you to. Apart from that, I didn't care." A dazzling, almost impressive degree of disdain saturated Braith's tone. It was like he was addressing a roach that dared ask why it was so reviled. Unable to lie, he doubled down on the truth, and said more deliberately, "I. Didn't. Care."

Shyla didn't know Remy well, but she knew that this wasn't a woman who considered herself glorified, expendable help. She might drive when needed, assist where needed, and go where she was asked, but if she could find offense in an offered gratuity, she wasn't going to take well to hearing she'd been sent into a deadly situation, unprepared, as an afterthought. She might have responded better had Braith told her he planned for her to die because it was part of his grand strategy. That he had to give her up to achieve bigger goals. Instead, she wasn't even worthy of that. Braith had sent her to assist Shyla because she and the Tarvers mattered far more than Remy did. Her survival was immaterial.

He didn't care.

Remy lunged at him, throwing her whole body into a punch that Braith barely slipped enough to minimize the impact. Still, his head rocked back, spit flew from his mouth, and he almost lost his footing. He grabbed Remy's extended arm and spun her into the wall, but she kneed him in the groin and stamped on his ankle before he could strike her, the latter move generating a distinct crunch. Braith did not scream–he'd endured considerably worse pain many times over–but he gasped at the snapping of his ankle, which gave Remy space to fishhook the inside of his mouth with two fingers of her right hand. He put a hand up to guard his eyes, knowing she would go for them, but she pulled down with her full weight to throw his defense so she could sneak the fore and middle finger of her left hand past his guard.

She pushed her fingers deeper into Braith's eye socket than Shyla had imagined herself doing, like she would win a prize for touching the back of his brain. Now Braith squealed, and instead of trying to pull away, he reached around to Remy's back, scooped her up with surprising ease, and slammed her hard enough on the table to bend its legs.

All that kept Shyla from running from the building was that Remy still had the keys to her car, and as much as Shyla needed to get away from Braith, she also had to think ahead to how she would get to Galveston.

What kept her from rushing to help Remy was how stunningly crisp–almost choreographed–her fight with Braith looked. There was little wasted movement from either. Attacks, counters, and counters to the counters. Shyla had seen her share of fights, and it was rare even for professionals to be this efficient when engaged with each other. This looked more like a movie playing out before her, with one person so committed to the role that he would give an eye for it. Then again, that wasn't much to give when you knew it would quickly grow back.

What if this was just an act to lure her in? To what end, she couldn't imagine. They already had her trapped. Still, she was programmed to distrust everything she saw and heard now.

Another few seconds helped her realize that Braith—a man who'd been to war, albeit over a century ago—and Remy, a professional mercenary and bodyguard, likely sparred together. She probably kept him on his toes, trained him to anticipate certain actions. And he knew her moves, as well. And, regardless of how solid their relationship might have once been, how much they might have trusted each other, each likely had a move or two that they saved and practiced in private, just in case the fight between them got as real as it was now.

Shyla jumped in, throwing her shoulder into Braith's as he raised a hammer-fist to bring down on Remy's face. Her own muscle memory and jiujitsu training all but failed her then, as she wasn't sure of what to do besides hold on to Braith's arm for a moment that felt longer than it actually lasted. Then, barely thinking, she mimicked Remy's plan of attack, although instead of poking with her fingers, she pulled Jinh's knife from her pocket, flicked it open, and plunged it into Braith's good eye. When she tried to yank it out to use it again, she felt it scrape and then get stuck against the bone of the eye socket.

At last, Braith screamed, although he sounded more aggravated than pained. Shyla wiped the blood on her hands onto the floor while scrambling to her feet.

Remy got up as well, and stood over the blinded Braith, who curled into a defensive shell. Remy raised her foot to stomp on the back of his skull, but he sensed it somehow—heard it, or knew what her go-to would be—and flipped over to catch her foot as it came down. He spun her quickly into a kneebar, and Remy shouted in pain as weight and leverage threatened to hyperextend the joint. Shyla leapt and crashed down on Braith's temple with her elbow, landing so cleanly her first thought was *That had to kill him,* before she remembered who this was.

He let Remy go and reached back for Shyla, who barely evaded his grasp. Remy stood again and went for the cell door, shouting, "Come on."

Braith roared, first with anger, then laughter, as he ripped the knife out of his eye. Shyla followed Remy out of the cell. She took a look back before exiting the building and saw Braith groping for the exit from the cell. The eye that Shyla had stabbed through was becoming whole again, although it had no pupil or iris yet.

"Remy!" he called out as the women fled. "*Remy!* I didn't care. I *didn't* care if you lived or died. But I do now.

"I care now."

26

There wasn't time to think, to plan, to debate, just to go. Braith would be out of the door soon, and on the phone with cops he'd pocketed soon after, possibly while on the road, giving chase. He could try to run Shyla and Remy off the road with no regard for his own safety. If he pushed them over a railing with his own car, and both vehicles in the wreck flipped and caught fire, only one person involved in the crash would emerge intact.

But he wouldn't be able to chase them immediately, not in his own car, because at some point in their scuffle, Remy had pick-pocketed his keys. When they got outside she went right for his silver sedan, and Shyla followed. Before Shyla made it to the passenger side, however, Remy tossed Shyla the keys to her own car and told her, "Rockport. El Chaparro."

She didn't give Shyla time to ask any questions or repeat the name of the location for clarification. Shyla didn't even catch her keys when Remy tossed them. They bounced off her chest, she bent to pick them up from the pavement, and Remy had already started

Braith's car by the time Shyla stood back up. Shyla hustled to her car, got inside, and took off.

In her rearview mirror, as she peeled out of the parking lot, she saw the door of the small museum open. She returned her eyes to the road.

He would send officers after them, starting with the DeWitt County sheriffs, which was probably part of why Remy said to meet her in Rockport. It was basically a straight shot south, the fastest way out of the county, and not where Braith would expect them to go first, since Galveston was more directly to the east.

Shyla was sure Braith had some form of GPS tracking on his vehicle, but also thought that Remy must know what she's doing. She surely had access to disable or misdirect the tracking within Braith's car given she was his driver. Hell, his confidante. Probably a little more. Shyla got the impression based on an exchange they had at Braith's manor that the two weren't above a dalliance. Maybe Remy had genuine affection for him and thought he'd had at least a modicum of it for her.

Then he'd said what he said.

I. Didn't. Care.

But I do now.

He could talk about there being a difference between his former and current self, espouse his ideas on the personality-altering effects of brain damage, but based on what he said and what he'd done, Shyla was sure it was complete bullshit. Remy had accused him of being done with her, *Like Garrett.* He must have confided to her exactly what happened with the crash.

He'd alluded to it being something other than an accident, perhaps unknowingly, and Shyla had picked up on that. He spoke of him and Garrett parting ways as though it had been his call, but why were they in that plane together? If he'd come to think of

Schramm as unworthy, someone he couldn't rely on anymore, why put his health—if not his life—in Garrett's hands, thousands of feet in the sky?

Because he'd trusted Schramm with his secret, then needed to guarantee Schramm wouldn't be able to tell another soul.

There are different kinds of serial killers. Pop culture presented the idea of men who killed for pleasure or some other dark compulsion, but some killers were simply greedy opportunists. Killers for profit who racked up a significant body count chasing one relatively meager payout after another, because they weren't the evil geniuses that films and modern myths made them out to be. Braith had been the closest thing to a twisted mastermind that Shyla had ever heard of, and even with his preternatural gift for spotting the likelier candidates, he still had to murder an unknown number of families before he hit his jackpot.

Jesus Christ. The man had wiped out entire families. He had ended bloodlines in his quest to never die.

Braith's supreme avarice—determined to hoard lifetimes instead of gold or dollars—eventually conflicted with Schramm's sadism. He'd found it useful for a while, and maybe enjoyed Schramm's company during that time as well, but eventually decided to rid himself of the only man who knew his past.

Next in line was Remy. She knew Braith's secret so well they had practiced a routine for how he would showcase it to a skeptic. She'd practiced it so often she'd gotten comfortable with getting ahead of the script, like she knew better than the man who would take a blade through his head. Shyla could only imagine what Remy thought as she watched Braith put Shyla under hypnosis, then snap her out of it seconds later, having shown her at least as much as he'd trusted Remy with, if not more. If he'd already told Remy that he'd deliberately caused the wreck that killed Schramm when he became a liability, she must have sensed what was coming for her. Not in the way that Braith could sense things, with the privilege of ESP, but in a far less reliable way. With gut instinct that penalized gambling and hoping as much as it rewarded it.

Remy had rolled the dice on believing Braith had set her up to die, discovered he'd only been indifferent to her fate, and was now on the run from him. And what had led her to this belief? Something in the way he'd spoken to and looked at Shyla. The offer he'd made her.

Braith must think he had a promising protégé in Shyla. Perhaps, with Remy, he'd repeated his trial-and-error process to replicate the "sacrifice" that had granted him immortality. Or he'd held off for want of a surer thing, in the hopes he'd only have to do it once or twice. But things hadn't shaped up well enough with Remy, as opposed to the situation he found with Shyla.

He had real leverage over her. Initially, just because he knew she had something to hide, and could bluff about knowing more than he did. He'd sensed she was a killer, and that this was a secret, but didn't have details—and Shyla didn't know what he didn't know. With Remy, all he could do was pay her off, or maybe manipulate an emotional investment, if Shyla wasn't wrong about the nature of their relationship. With Shyla, however, he could lord knowledge of what she'd done over her to extort loyalty. But what she'd done mattered less, at the moment, than what she needed. She needed Jinh back. Braith presented this as a chance for them to help each other.

Someone Shyla loved was held by people he wanted her to kill. Descendants of a man who cursed Braith with immortality. People who could warp minds, create, open, and close doors with their thoughts, and commune with the dead.

Shyla pictured his plan so clearly she wondered if he was still in her head, even at a distance, showing her how it would work for both of them. He wanted her to kill one of the Tarvers to inspire the other to curse her. Jinh's survival was only incidental to this. Braith just wanted what, company? Yes, because he'd lost his mentor and didn't have anyone else to relate to. Because even though he'd signed himself up for an existence that demanded a certain level of isolation, he didn't accept that, because he was that kind of person. Rich, entitled, self-important. Having to choose, and live with the choice, was limiting. It was for plebeians, not someone like him.

Braith fancied himself as the "smartest man in any room." A guy who imagined himself a grandmaster at 4D chess when in actuality, at best, he was the guy who cheated to get a higher ranking online, then showed off his score even when no one asked. This would explain how he'd been arrogant and foolish enough to make a play for Shyla to be his new mentee right in front of his current one, as if Remy wouldn't piece it together and react accordingly.

Tracking the motives, moves, and history of Braith and Remy helped distract Shyla enough to keep her calm as she found and merged onto the first highway marked "south"—State Highway 119.

She hadn't plugged her phone into her car's USB to map herself, and didn't do so until she saw a road sign indicating that Rockport was eighty miles away. She checked that her speed was at sixty-five miles per hour—squarely in the range of not fast enough to draw a ticket, or slow enough to inhibit traffic and draw attention.

She zoomed out of a map to Rockport to see which side-road alternatives there were for her, in case she ran into enough squad vehicles on 119 and junction highways to make her paranoid in the hour that remained before she made it to Rockport. She was over halfway to her destination before she saw her third different SUV with "exempt" plates. Each time it was a fight for her not to take the first exit, or slow down so quickly it would prove conspicuous. But when she thought of venturing into one of the even smaller, more-out-of-the-way areas these detours would take her through, she saw herself falling into Braith's next trap. A small town would be harder for her to speed out of, easier for him to find cheap hoodlums in.

These were the places she'd avoided during earlier, far simpler jobs from her initial days as an investigator. Back when she didn't have a reputation, didn't have credentials, didn't know about licensing.

There were places where she would be too memorable, and where the consequences of getting caught could be more dire if the person she was tailing was connected or liked by enough of the locals. She'd read and heard too many stories about everything from asset forfeiture schemes to abduction and trafficking rings to risk venturing into these quieter areas unless it was an absolute necessity.

Those rules didn't loosen until Massimo Dante offered enough for her to make an exception. It hadn't just been about the money, though. His personal investment in her success gave her a sense of security. If she got stonewalled, hemmed in, or, God forbid, went missing, Dante would follow up, and the people trying to inhibit her, or worse, would find out she was almost certainly better connected than they were, and that they'd made the kind of enemy everyone could do without. Rich, influential, and possibly insane.

Working under Braith gave her the same luxury, but now that they were all-but-declared enemies, she wouldn't be going to any places similar to Yorktown unless she had to.

With that in mind, overriding the fear she felt every time she passed a state or county trooper on the highway, she stayed on 119 until it turned into a series of farm roads that wound through territory she would rather not venture into but couldn't be avoided.

Periodically she passed through towns that demanded she slow to thirty-five miles per hour or less. At each stop her peripheral vision caught the wholesome, guilt-inducing glare of a man or woman selling something at the corner. Watermelons, assorted flags, fresh peaches, and in one case homemade barbecue plates, which even without signage told her they were fundraising for either a Little League sports team's trip or a funeral. She kept her eyes forward and focused on the road ahead.

Pray to her, Jinh had said. *You have to sacrifice.* Shyla recalled those words now that she had enough distance from Braith to feel somewhat safe.

Tell her now.

The Tarver twins had cut Jinh off before she could elaborate on this. What had she meant? What did Shyla have to sacrifice, and to whom?

Without knowing, she nonetheless started to pray. Jinh had told her to do so "now," back when they were still in the ruins of the hospital. That was a couple of hours ago. Shyla was on her way to a place that hadn't been on her mind this morning. Now the afternoon light was going extinct. The day was dwindling. She was losing time. Jinh had told her to pray *now.* How long ago was that, exactly?

She checked the clock on the upper corner of the dashboard console and saw that it wasn't noon yet. That didn't feel possible.

The road was comparatively tranquil given how hectic and horrible the day had been. She thought about changing her destination, partly just to keep driving. She could go to Galveston directly and bypass Rockport. She didn't have to meet with Remy. She wasn't even that confident that Remy was on her side. Remy's anger and fight with Braith had been real, but she surely had her own motives and priorities that might not align with Shyla's. In fact it was all but guaranteed that rescuing Jinh wasn't very important to Remy.

Shyla did expect Remy to have additional insight on Braith, and possibly the Tarvers, that might be useful.

Her thoughts returned then to the prayer, and what Jinh could have meant by saying she had to sacrifice. Shyla couldn't say she believed it would be useful right now, but she didn't see how it could be harmful, either.

Shyla only knew Jinh had told her to pray, so she did, or started to. She was so repulsed by the first four words that came to her that she cut herself off. It had to have been a slip of the tongue brought about by things that had been forced into her mind just this morning.

"Momma, are you listening . . . ?"

She'd meant to say "God" not "Momma." Neither word had occupied much space in her vocabulary for years, but the latter tasted like acid when she spoke it, and felt like a shock of torture when she thought it.

Anytime Aunt Teonna or Shyla's cousins spoke of her mother, they used that term: "Mother." So that was how she thought of her. It helped her more easily distinguish Jacqueline from Linda. Because "Momma" is what she called her kidnapper in the years before she discovered the woman deserved no honorific. But that was the only person she would ever reserve the word for, because she had no intention of using it for anyone ever again.

Her actual mother would be Mother, Linda would be Linda, and "Momma" would be verboten.

So why had she said it now?

No, no, she wasn't going to dwell on that. She'd misspoken, and that was it. Her energy would be better saved for something productive.

It occurred to her that she hadn't tried to call Jinh's phone yet. There hadn't been a chance before now. The Tarvers might have taken Jinh's phone from her, but it was equally plausible that they were awaiting Shyla's phone call. That seemed to be how hostage takers typically operated, although Shyla didn't really know if this was true, or just the way it played out in stories. This was entirely new territory for her.

Nonetheless, it was worth trying. Shyla tapped the phone icon on the console's touchscreen. Her most recent contacts came up, and Shyla tapped Jinh's name, then waited for the ringtone.

The CONNECTING message, with trailing ellipses, appeared under the red-and-white phone icon on the screen. The timer underneath started even though it was only supposed to start tracking the length of the call after the connection was made. Following fourteen seconds of silence, a series of clicks sounded, chased by another, deeper stretch of silence. It seemed to insulate Shyla from the hum of her engine, the rush of the air moving around the car, the rasp of other vehicles speeding past her as she unconsciously slowed on the two-lane highway. The silence flooded her ears and made her feel like her head was swelling.

Another series of clicks dotted the air like Morse code and relieved some of the pressure building in Shyla's skull. Something else drew her eye to the counter on the console, and she couldn't tell what it was at first, but after a couple of seconds she realized that it was the seconds themselves. They weren't moving on the timer. It was stuck at thirty-five seconds. This wouldn't have been the first time her console had locked up for no apparent reason, just like every other device she relied on did from time to time. But that wasn't the case here, and she knew it.

The clicks came again, this time introducing static, and through that white noise came a voice like a face rising out of sand.

Shyla heard Jinh tell her, "You have to let go . . . You have to give something up."

Her voice was clear and emotionless. Distant and monotone.

"Jinh? Jinh, can you hear me?"

"Pray to her . . . Tell her . . . Sacrifice . . . Pray." She sounded like a recording. A phantom voice coming through on an old tape being played on an even older stereo. The static rose like it was fighting to force Jinh's voice back down. "Pray to her . . . Tell her . . . Pray now . . . Tell her now . . . *Now.*"

"Jinh, tell me if you can hear me."

No response.

"Jinh? Jinh?"

The blare of a horn startled Shyla into focusing on the road. She'd drifted from the right lane almost halfway into the passing lane. The truck that honked at her as it passed maneuvered onto the shoulder to avoid a collision. The truck's driver shot their left hand out of the window to flip her off, and seeing this made Shyla so angry she couldn't have spelled, defined, or pronounced "rational" to save the world. She had been at fault, could have run another motorist off the road, and had infinitely greater things to be upset over, and that combination made her briefly angry enough to kill a stranger, to redirect her rage at someone she could more easily hurt, to pass along her pain and fear. It was a selfish, ghoulish thought, but one that lingered uncomfortably.

She pulled over to the side of the road, only wanting a few seconds to gather herself. There was no way she had imagined Jinh's voice, but did she physically hear it, or had it been beamed like a psychic signal into her mind? For God's sake, the last things she needed at this point were more questions, but here they were.

Here *she* was. On the roadside, alone, needing to save her friend from two witches while trying to evade another one, and the best advice anyone could give her was "pray." That was it? Pray? And she couldn't even do that right. She couldn't even get the word "God" out, instead praying to one of the two people she hated most.

Momma, are you listening . . . ?

She may as well be praying to her personal devil.

Why not "Mother"? What made her ask if Linda was listening, and not the woman who gave her own life in pursuit of her lost child?

Because she already gave everything. Jinh keeps saying to sacrifice. Give something up. There's nothing left for my mother to give. I can't ask her for anything more. I won't do it. But Linda . . . she owes me. She took everything. Not just from me. She and Rodney took me from my family, and took everything my mother and father could have been. She took my life, and theirs, and then took her own life because she was too scared to face me.

And then . . . then she still tried to tell Jinh about what she'd "given up" to take me. She wanted Jinh to tell me that.

"Tell her now."

She'd repeated that to Jinh. Replaying what she heard of the conversation Rodney'd had over the phone with Linda, Shyla remembered hearing it then, as well.

"Tell her now."

She didn't even have to imagine what Linda wanted Rodney to tell her. It was the same message she'd wanted Jinh to give her. That she'd given something up to take Shyla. That she'd made a sacrifice. She was like the people Braith had talked about, the ones who didn't understand what a sacrifice really was. The ones who could bleed a baby without any real appreciation for who was really giving up more in that situation.

Linda thought she had surrendered something, when she'd actually incurred a debt.

She owes me. She owes *me . . .*

It had been years since Shyla had cried about this. She couldn't remember what exactly triggered it back then, only that she'd been thinking of the years she'd lost and relationships she would never get to have because of what Linda and Rodney did to her, and her usual resentment for them unexpectedly turned into an immense grief. It happened much too quickly for her to fight it, and she felt that same pressure now. All that held it back, even for a few moments, was her familiarity with it. It couldn't completely take her by surprise this time. But it would outlast her attempt to fend it off. She knew that. Letting this feeling pass wasn't feasible. It would be like trying to wait out the flow of a river before crossing.

A car pulled up and parked behind hers, and panic allowed her to push the grief down. She saw the trailing car in her periphery, through the side mirrors, before looking up to see it in the rearview. In the instant before she got a clear view of the vehicle she assumed it was a cop car, and readied herself to speed off as soon as the officer got out and walked close enough to touch the trunk of her car.

But it wasn't a squad car behind her. It was a silver sedan.

How the hell did he find me? Shyla thought and felt the urge to escape even more urgently than she had a second before. A half-beat later, as the door to the shiny Lincoln opened, she remembered who had actually taken Braith's car.

Remy exited the sedan, rushed to the passenger side of Shyla's car, and reached for the handle just as Shyla almost absentmindedly hit the button to unlock the door.

"Why are you pulled over? What happened?" Remy said.

"How did you catch up—" Shyla started, but stopped when she saw the gun in Remy's hand.

27

We need to go. Now," Remy said.

Shyla shook her head. Remy's appearance struck her as a little too surreal and coincidental not to be a setup. Remy noticed her staring at the gun, huffed in frustration, and turned it around to offer it to Shyla grip-first. "You want it?"

"Where'd you get it? I thought you lost yours at the hospital."

"It's the spare from Saxton's car. And I caught up to you because apparently you've been driving like a grandma. We need to go before a cop comes by and wants to know what we're doing here."

Shyla put the car in drive and merged into traffic, still holding on to a few more questions.

"I needed to buy some time for you, and throw him off," Remy said. "I headed toward Galveston until I could deactivate the GPS, then I came back around to the way I knew to Rockport. Then I just saw you on the road here and I got scared for a second that something happened to you. That's why I walked up with the gun out."

Shyla kept an eye on Remy as she drove, like Remy was a phantom hitchhiker liable to disappear the second Shyla completely looked away from her.

"What?" Remy asked.

"What do you mean, 'what'? You know what," she said, not fully buying Remy's explanation.

"I just told you, okay? Focus on the road."

Shyla did as advised for a while, long enough for the silence to get to Remy, who turned the radio to the first station playing music. Shyla turned the volume all the way down from the buttons on her steering wheel.

"Why Rockport?" Shyla said.

Remy just shook her head and put the pistol, a smaller caliber than the one she preferred to carry, in the glove compartment. Shyla started to repeat her question, then pivoted to something Remy might be more eager to answer, based on the anger and hurt burning through her face.

"Why did you do it?" Shyla said. "What made you turn on him?"

Remy's lips receded and she partly bared her teeth as she contemplated whether to answer, as though she'd rather bite her tongue off than confess anything to Shyla.

"Because I know him. I've done things for him. One really, really awful thing in particular. I got a reminder of it back in that hospital, or 'church,' or whatever it was. The Tarvers showed it to me. That's what they put in my head while they were doing whatever they did to you."

"What are their names? First names."

"Alan and Ava. Why are you asking that?"

"I just want to know how much you know," Shyla said.

"Just what he's told me," Remy said. "No, that's a lie. Fuck, we're in this together now, huh?"

"Looks like it. No more sense in lying to me."

"I guess not. I *mostly* just know what Saxton told me," Remy said. "But I did a little bit of research into them on my own for him, and told him what I found because I thought . . . I used to think he could appreciate things. I thought if I showed him I really cared, then *he* would care. I learned their names from obituaries about all of their family members who passed. I had some suspicions based on the frequency of those old obituaries, and some of the wording. Plus a couple of stories about weird suicides that coincided with certain time frames."

Shyla raised her eyebrows. "'Weird'?"

"Yeah. Just two stories, about twenty years apart, but too out there not to be connected. Both times, it was a suicide in pairs. Somebody saw two people at night walking out into the water, into the Gulf. Each time was under a full moon, high tides, pretty strong surf. Just walking out until their heads disappeared. The witness would report it, but the authorities wouldn't follow through until a few days later when the bodies were found. In the first instance they washed up on the beach. In the other one they were each found by different boats. In both cases, the people in question were twins. Looking at the obituaries, it looked like twins ran in the family."

"You think they all killed themselves like that?"

"I do."

"Why, though?"

"Because they burn out. And it's their way of honoring their dead and making peace with not being able to get revenge for Enoch and the others."

"You *know* that?"

"I'm guessing. But I feel like it's a pretty good guess based on what I do know, and Saxton agreed. I think he did, anyway. I could be wrong about that. He lied to me about what was in Yorktown.

That hospital. He knew what was really in there. His mentor told him about it. The Tarvers showed me that while I was down there."

"And you believe them," Shyla said.

Remy nodded. "They showed me something else that I know is true. They could've been lying about what Braith knew, but I don't think they were. It's deeper than a doubt. I know how he treats his 'friends' when he's done with them. Don't know what made me think I would be different. Well, I *do* know, but it's stupid."

Shyla played "One of These Things Is Not Like the Others" in her head to see what the most obvious difference between Remy, Schramm, and the mentor—based on the little she knew of him—was. It popped to mind right away and made her look twice at Remy. She struggled to picture her as lovestruck, but it became easier when she realized what she might really have been in love with. Not Braith himself, but the promise of his power. And Braith might have only wanted her for sex. Or maybe Shyla was wrong and they'd shared a genuine, warped romance, and fantasized about living eternally together after making enough sacrifices for Remy to find the one who would curse her properly.

"Don't judge me," Remy said.

"Don't judge the aspiring serial killer?"

Whatever Remy planned to say next got blocked on its way up, and she just sighed and turned her head toward the window. "Fine. Judge."

"So he killed Schramm."

"Yeah. He told me he set Garrett up. Agreed to fly out to kill another family with him, but he took the plane down instead. He thought Garrett was too much of a liability. Then I guess he got a little lonely, because he went and found his mentor again. The man he won't name, because I think that makes it easier for him. I'll name him because it doesn't make as much difference to me. It's always going to be hard to think about. Now it's just fresher because the Tarvers put me right back to where . . . Anyway, his name is Weldon."

"'Is,' not 'was'? He's still alive."

"Yeah."

"Braith couldn't kill him."

"Not for lack of trying," Remy said, her voice darkening. "And then, *completely* for lack of trying."

"What's that mean?" Shyla asked.

"You don't want me to tell you."

"I want you to tell me everything. *Everything*. I don't know what's going to help me save Jinh and what won't, so I just need to know as much as I can."

"You're not going to be able to save her."

"What?"

Remy didn't respond to this and didn't turn to look at Shyla until she slowed the car down and started to pull over again.

"Whoa, what are you doing?" Remy said.

"That's why you want us to go to Rockport," Shyla said. "This isn't about misdirection, you just want to run."

"You *can't* kill him, Shyla. The Tarvers won't be able to, either. They got too impatient. They were burning out, and probably started thinking about passing their responsibility on to the next generation, and then the next and the next forever, so they got aggressive and overplayed their hand, when they might not even have one to play. Not the one they need, at least."

"We're going to get Jinh."

"Look, let's just get to Rockport, get some rest, and whatever we do next—"

"What were you going to do when we got there?" Shyla said. "Take my keys while I was asleep?"

"If I wanted the car, I could have just made you get out when I had the gun out back there. Together we can watch each other's backs, and even win a fight if we have to."

"We're *going* to get Jinh," Shyla said, almost bringing the car to a complete stop.

"Damn it, we can't just be on the side of the road," Remy said. "I told you–"

She opened the glove box to retrieve her gun, and as soon as she opened the compartment door, Shyla stepped on the gas, lurching the car forward and sending everything in the compartment–paperwork, old napkins and sauce packets from fast-food restaurants, and Remy's gun–spilling out. Anticipating her move while catching Remy off guard, Shyla snatched the gun as it fell in Remy's lap and pointed it at her head.

Remy stared down the barrel, a smile almost coming to her.

"That was pretty good," Remy said. "You don't mind if I use that one day, do you?"

"I'd rather us be more like partners," Shyla said, "but you know I'll kill you if I have to. I've done it before."

"I'm aware," Remy said. "Now, this is the second time you've pointed a gun at me. There's not going to be a third."

"Bitch, are you trying to sound tough *while* I've got a gun on you for the second time? Because I can make that whole won't-be-a-third-time thing happen right now."

Remy sucked air through her teeth. Shyla went on, "I'm not going to make you come with me to Galveston, but you're going to tell me everything I want to know, right here. You're going to answer every question I have, and I don't care if you think I asked something stupid, I don't care if you think it won't help me, and I don't care if I have to drive like this the rest of the way. You're going to tell me everything. *Every fucking thing.*"

28

Turning toward Galveston put them in the path of a storm that looked endless, its sickly gray clouds covering every inch of the sky. Shyla guessed they wouldn't reach the storm for twenty minutes. From this distance, the visibly sliding wall of rain looked like an enormous curtain hiding a secret world. She could have taken this as an omen, and wondered if she ought to, but opted to view it as an empty threat. An attempt to scare her off that couldn't even produce lightning.

In actuality, she knew, it was just a weather system pushed inland from the Gulf. It had no preternatural origin and wasn't meant exclusively for her, but it was hard not to see herself as the center of a world at odds with her right now. She was privy to grim knowledge that would have shattered most people's minds, and seemed to be alone in wanting to put up a fight, regardless of how hopeless her cause appeared to be.

With more time to think about it, she found Remy's plan to run from Braith—presumably for the rest of her life—increasingly surprising and disheartening. It weighed on her enough to make her hopes sag, and she was already struggling to keep them aloft. There was zero chance that she would leave Jinh on her own with the Tarvers–relying on them not really wanting to kill her and eventually letting her go when their plan fell through, as Remy kept insisting since Shyla had gotten the gun from her. Her future self could have appeared as an apparition in the road now, screaming for her to turn around because she couldn't win, and Shyla would have accelerated to run that specter down. She didn't want to be so trite as to believe that the difference between saving Jinh or getting them both killed might come down to simple optimism, but she didn't see how pessimism bettered her odds.

She refocused on the conversation she held with Remy. The gun rested on Shyla's left thigh and under her left hand while she steered with the right. She felt comfortable with this after opening the passenger side window, having Remy stick her right hand out, then raising the window up to pin Remy's wrist. If it was too tight, enough to cut circulation and numb the hand, Remy didn't let on, and Shyla didn't care either way, as long as Remy couldn't make a move.

"He wasn't lying about still having one of the hands?" Shyla asked.

"No. I've seen it. He has it in a vault. Same place where he keeps Weldon."

"What?"

"Weldon. His mentor. The man who–"

"I know all that. I remember that," Shyla said, "but what do you mean, he keeps him in a vault?"

"I mean what I said. There's a space under the basement in his property, and calling it a 'vault' is probably generous, now that I say it out loud. It's barely bigger than a coffin, which would be more than enough space if he only kept the hand in there, but he's got Weldon locked down there."

"Jesus. Against his will, I presume."

"Most people don't sign up to get locked in a metal box underground forever."

"We're not talking about 'most people.'"

"Against his will, you're right," Remy said.

"You saw this yourself, or just heard–"

"I saw it," Remy cut in, agitated and curiously defensive, like she could anticipate what Shyla was about to accuse her of.

"And that didn't bother you?"

Remy sighed through her nostrils and shut her eyes, but only for a moment. Her eyes popped open like death was waiting behind her eyelids. She stared ahead, and Shyla could see her resisting any urge to blink for several seconds. "Weldon's done really, really bad things," Remy said. "He probably killed twice as many people as Braith. Hell, he coached Saxton through half of his kills. And he had a head start of about a hundred years on doing the worst he could do."

Shyla said, "And you know that because of what you learned or what Braith told you?"

"I know Weldon has the curse, because I saw it in action," Remy said somewhat defiantly. "I know he must have done something to earn it. Whether Saxton lied to me about everything Weldon did or not, I know he earned that curse. He killed someone to get it. He wronged someone bad enough for them to wish that he'd never die, or get old, or stay injured, just so they'd have a chance to kill him at his best. That's enough for him to deserve everything that Braith did to him."

"Talk to me about it."

Remy gritted her teeth, shuddered, then found it in herself to tell all. "Of all the things the Tarvers could have shown me to get under my skin, I would have guessed they'd pick something else. I'm not a saint, myself. I've hurt a lot of people in my life, and worse, way before I met Braith. I got a pretty early start. I took a fight a little too far when I was in high school and left a girl half blind. I realized then that I had it in me to do things most people wouldn't think to.

"Soon as I left home I joined up with a little survivalist group strictly for the opportunity to learn how to weaponize myself, and thicken my skin around men who I knew all hated me just for being harder than them. When they started leaning toward becoming a militia, and started talking like they wouldn't let me leave if I wanted to, I set a fire at the encampment that killed a few of the people I had called friends, and injured a few more. Only one I felt bad about was a guy who was fairly sweet to me, because he liked me, and so I ended up getting close to his daughter. She was almost like a little niece to me, and I know it must have hurt a lot to lose her dad. But I did what I had to do, and after I learned what I was really willing to do, it was easy to say yes to different jobs a lot of other people would turn down.

"I'm saying all of that because, getting back to my point, the Tarvers didn't show me a reminder of decent people I've done things to, or the former friends that I trapped in a fire while they slept. They showed me Weldon. They knew what really bothered me, because it . . . it's not natural."

"What did you do?" Shyla said.

"I put gloves on. Like the one Tarver had on. You saw it, right?"

Shyla nodded.

"Gloves like that, made from the hands that hold the curse. Weldon kept his just like Saxton kept the one that he didn't lose after killing Enoch. Saxton had those hands deboned, skinned, tanned, and turned into gloves. Hard to believe there are people out there who will do that for you, right?"

Shyla shrugged. "There are people out there who'll make you a book cover out of human skin. And they aren't even shy about it. They put up videos online showing it off."

"True. Maybe not as crazy as I think."

"I didn't say that."

Remy managed a tight smile and continued. "Right. Anyway, I put the gloves on because Saxton asked me to, and I took a knife in each hand and carved Weldon up like I was trying to make something new out of him."

"And that killed him," Shyla said, hopefulness sneaking into her voice. She grimaced when Remy shook her head no.

"It wasn't the first time, either," Remy said. "Saxton had put the gloves on himself before, opened the vault to take Weldon out, and done all sorts of things to him to see if he'd die. He stabbed him, shot him, set the man on fire, strangled him. None of it killed him, but it did keep him from healing completely the way Saxton does. Too much of it has built up over time, and Saxton's cut him and hammered him too often. His jaw is at a pretty nasty angle. He's holding on to a lot of scars. He's in a lot of pain. When I pulled him out he kept trying to talk to me but his vocal cords hadn't fully healed from the hundred times Saxton cut his throat while wearing the gloves. He was wheezing hard like he had a leak in his lungs. I can't say whether he was trying to ask me to put him out of his misery or what. I only found out for sure that I couldn't kill him. Like it was physically impossible, not that I didn't have the nerve. At that time I was doing anything for Saxton. He asked me to do it because he wanted to be sure Weldon wasn't surviving because he was holding back. That's what he told me, at least."

"Sounds more like he wanted to test you," Shyla said. "See if you would actually do it."

"Or that. Or he's just sick, which makes me whatever I am. I don't know. I don't know what I know anymore."

"Do you have any idea why the gloves didn't kill Weldon?" Shyla asked.

"Not sure, but I talked about it with Saxton and we think that it's because the gloves aren't really doing the work. They wouldn't be responsible for the kill. Someone else's hands are actually holding the knife or the gun, or putting the pressure on his neck. The gloves aren't doing the killing."

Shyla nodded at this. She couldn't quite say it made sense, because nothing really did anymore, but it tracked as an explanation. She wondered if there was a way to fix this, so that the glove, and not the person wearing it, was the real killer.

"I don't think the Tarvers realize that," Remy added, "but they're the reason Saxton got the idea to make gloves out of the hands Weldon had kept and test them on Weldon. After Saxton killed Garrett he got in touch with Weldon again. Partly to fill in some gaps in his memories. That whole partial-amnesia thing he was talking about, from repeated brain damage, seems to be legit. So Weldon came back to him and helped him, and agreed to retrace Garrett's steps and find some of the people he ran into, in case they might know something Saxton wouldn't want them to know. He couldn't be sure what Garrett might have said to anyone. Saxton had trusted Garrett the way he trusts . . . *trusted* me. He's a lonely man. Which is weird because he made himself that way.

"He used to talk to me sometimes about how he saw the world, and how he thought everyone else saw it. How no one would ever have sympathy for him, no matter what he might go through, even if they never learned anything about him, because of his money. Whatever people first think of when they hear about you, or see you, that's what you are to them, and he was rich first. Not human, not male, not white, not a son or friend to anyone, not anything but rich. 'Rich first.' But he was fine with that, he said, because to him, eventually all of those people would be dead, and he'd go on.

"Everyone else alive now, or born tomorrow, or born a thousand years ago, was 'dead first,' and they'd be that way for way longer than they would be alive. That was going to happen to almost everyone else in the world, except him, and whoever he decided to bring along with him. He'd say that, then talk to me about how much more we'd be able to do together when we . . . Well, that doesn't matter. We never got around to it. I mean, really, how was I supposed to fully trust him after seeing what he'd done to Weldon, and knowing what he'd done to Garrett? And how was he supposed to trust me? It was impossible, but he liked talking about it. I don't know if he ever really wanted that for me, though. I don't think he really knows what he wants in life, except more life."

"Poor guy," Shyla said.

"Hey, I've still got some of his eye drying on my fingers. Whatever feelings I've had for the man are pretty far gone. I'm just pointing out what I think. You wanted to hear everything, right?"

"Sure. So Weldon comes back, helps Braith track down people Garrett Schramm had been in touch with."

"Right," Remy said. "Eventually he gets to this psychiatric hospital in Yorktown, where there's allegedly a secret church. Weldon gets himself admitted for long enough to find out what's really happening there, and when he gets away he goes to tell Saxton that Enoch Tarver's surviving family members have created a church dedicated to his lost hand. The hand of glory. They found it easier to convert people who were going through some kind of mental struggle, and tried a few different recruiting methods in different towns before locking in on the hospital.

"At first they kept the hand on an altar, under glass, but after some time they made it into the glove that the preachers wore during services. He didn't hear about why they did that, but Weldon thought that the Tarvers probably just figured it would be easier to use the hand that way. If the glove worked, then they wouldn't have to try to trap Saxton in a room with the hand and hope it got to him before he could just toss it or kick it away or something. They could try to catch him out in the open someday, then snipe him from a hundred yards away or something."

"But it doesn't work. You're sure?" Shyla said.

Again, Remy shook her head. "I mean it didn't work on Weldon, at least. Maybe the Tarvers know some different magic than what Saxton used to make his gloves. But I can tell you that he's convinced the Tarvers' glove won't work on him."

"Shit. So he really can't die? Why does he even care about the Tarvers if that's true?"

Remy looked at Shyla like she'd asked if there was an *s* in "stupid." "You heard what I said about the condition Weldon is in. The whole not-healing thing. There's . . . there's a reason the Tarver twins knew remembering Weldon would mess with my head. He's far from the first person I tried to kill, but he's the first I really *wanted* to kill. I still want to. I dream about it. I need that man to die to know he's not suffering anymore. As bad as he might have been, as many people as he probably killed, it still bothers me to know he's stuck like that. The fact that I couldn't kill him, that I damn near pulled a muscle from stabbing and beating him so much, and all that did was make it worse . . . I . . ."

Remy choked a little, then made herself retch like she needed to throw up a key to uncuff herself. Shyla considered raising the gun, in case this was a ploy to throw her off guard. Maybe Remy wanted her to pull over—despite her earlier admonition against this—so she could take Shyla by surprise. She felt more at ease when Remy grabbed a stack of napkins that had spilled out of the glove compartment and spit a blob of whitish saliva into it. Afterward, Remy looked sheepishly at Shyla for a place to put the napkins and Shyla nodded toward the back. She'd been ready to stain her upholstery with this woman's blood for a while now. She wasn't going to get dainty about a bit of not-quite-vomit in the backseat.

Shyla gave Remy a moment to collect herself before saying, "Maybe the Tarvers know something Braith doesn't. Maybe they did something different."

"Or this could be hopeless," Remy said. "If you had to bet on something, I'd go with them not really wanting to hurt Jinh. Worst-case scenario, I'd bet that they would basically adopt her and try to bring her into their fold over killing her. Probably try to train her to weaponize what she can do, the way they do it."

"What makes you think that sounds good to me?"

"It's not about good. It's about not getting yourself killed—and me, while you're at it. And Jinh, too, when you could just leave her with people who'll probably just take care of her."

An acidic sensation burned through Shyla's veins. She thought of her mother knowing that her baby was out there somewhere, snatched by people who would "probably just take care of her." Jackie Sinclair could have told herself it was futile to pursue Shyla, that someone desperate enough to risk their freedom to commit such a crime wouldn't mistreat the child they valued enough to take. Chasing down the daughter she never got a chance to know, and removing her from a situation that she might be comfortable in, wasn't worth it, especially considering the danger she might put herself in.

If Jackie ever heard a voice—internally or externally—that tried to convince her the pursuit wasn't worth it, however, she ignored it. Or she shouted it down, insulted that it even thought she would consider it.

"I wasn't made by people who abandon people," Shyla said. There was more authority in her tone than she could have aspired to, and it stunned Remy into silence.

The patter of raindrops on the windshield made up for the absence of conversation between them. Remy leaned toward the center of the vehicle as water came in through the cracked window pinning her hand in place. Shyla didn't care about water getting into her car any more than she cared about the messy napkin in the backseat, but she did think it was a little unnecessary to force Remy to soak up the rain where she sat. She wondered if she'd learned as much as she needed to from her passenger. She tried to draw out another pertinent question to ask her and came up dry.

Given how averse Remy was to going to Galveston, Shyla doubted she'd be of much help to her when she got there. She wouldn't be able to switch sides, exactly, after what she'd done to Braith, but that didn't make her a reliable partner. Although it felt wrong to venture into this alone, she couldn't find a good reason to keep Remy with her.

Just before the rain intensified, they came upon a rest stop. Shyla exited the highway and pulled into it. It was the middle of the day and middle of the week, with rain beating down, so there weren't as many cars on the road, and just three at the stop. No one in the other vehicles would have reason to pay attention to them. How much that mattered, Shyla couldn't say, but it felt a little bit serendipitous, like the world was telling her that this idea she'd caught was a solid one.

She pulled to a stop on the side opposite of where the other cars were parked, under a canopy of trees planted to provide shade above the benches. She rolled the window down enough for Remy to free her hand before rolling it up again.

"Get out," Shyla said.

"You're making a mistake," Remy said. "You can't kill him."

"Get out of my car."

"At least let me have the gun."

Shyla raised the weapon, letting the gesture retort better than words could. Remy sighed and looked through the window like Shyla was telling her to dive off a cliff, then glared at Shyla bitterly.

I'm giving you a chance, Shyla thought. *I could have just driven somewhere out of the way, shot you, and dumped you, just to be sure. Don't think I didn't consider it.*

Still, a part of her understood why Remy was treating the situation Shyla was forcing her into as though it were dire. She would be on her own, without a weapon, with whatever credit cards she might still have in her pocket, which were probably all either Braith's directly or connected to accounts he had access to. She would have to get creative and be extremely resourceful to find her own way without a car, a gun, or income that couldn't be traced to the boss she'd attacked and temporarily maimed. But she was resourceful. An ex-survivalist. Temporary militia member, albeit unwillingly. Killer for hire. Full-time criminal. The only thing that gave Shyla pause about letting her out of the car now was slight concern for who Remy might come across, and what kind of harm might come to them, what she might do to get their car and their wallets. She couldn't worry about that now.

Jinh needed her.

That had to be her sole focus.

When Remy opened the door it almost startled Shyla into pulling the trigger. She was beginning to think that she'd have to issue more threats and possibly risk whipping Remy across the face with the butt of the gun before she moved, but Remy exited with no show of force needed.

Holding the door open and standing under a mini-waterfall spilling through the gaps in the branches and leaves, Remy told Shyla, "I hope I'm wrong. I hope you kill him."

Shyla nodded. Then it occurred to her, the absolute least she could do to try to give Remy a better chance at keeping ahead of Braith.

She went into her pocket and brought out the fifty-dollar bill they had traded back and forth. Remy cracked a smile that looked like it made her face more fragile. She shook her head but took the bill from Shyla's outstretched hand.

The car was rolling as Remy shut the door. Shyla almost made it all the way out of the rest area and onto the on-ramp without looking in her rearview mirror. When she did, at the last available moment, she caught sight of Remy entering the building, where the restrooms, vending machines, maps, and brochures were. Shyla wondered what Remy's plan was. Whether she would try to overpower someone, or just try to steal their keys.

The windshield wipers barely kept the road visible as Shyla pulled back onto the freeway to Galveston. A few drivers had pulled over to the side and put their hazard lights on rather than brave the downpour.

A road sign stated that Galveston was forty miles away. Her GPS told her she could make it there in under forty-five minutes, although it wasn't factoring in the storm. She felt an urge to get there fast, but didn't want to risk getting into a wreck.

She thought of how slick the roads must have been the night her mother died.

Her mother deserved so much better. A better life, a better death. A better daughter.

I'll be that now, Shyla thought. *I'll show you, I promise.*

The rain fell like its mission was to smash the windshield. She thought of an old local legend she'd heard in grade school about a haunted car or haunted road, she couldn't remember which. It might have been both. A story about a man who accidentally ran over his wife and daughter with his truck. His wife and daughter pounded on the undercarriage with their fists to get him to stop while he dragged them along, but he didn't understand what the banging sound was at first. He kept going until he got to the stop sign at the end of the street, then got out, checked, and saw the trail of blood that went from his driveway—near his daughter's crushed backpack—to the legs sticking out under his truck's rear bumper. The idea of the mother and daughter beating on the bottom of the car with their fists for any amount of time was, of course, ludicrous, but Shyla didn't realize that in fourth grade. Now she thought of the blows coming down from above, as opposed to up from below, hammering a vehicle in the hopes that its driver would stop.

She wondered if all waters carried spirits. The Tarvers said the Gulf contained spirits that spoke to them. Could those ghosts be absorbed or diluted in water over time, and rendered particulate? Maybe every drop of rain contained just a bit of someone's soul, or several smaller bits of different souls that were all just a strange mass within the sea.

These were bizarre thoughts, the kind she assumed people had when they were a little higher than they meant to get. She was running on a dwindling supply of adrenaline, and what sleep she'd grabbed over the last few days had been troubled at best. Dread and desperation fueled her decision-making and compromised her reasoning. On top of that, she had been drugged with an arcane truth serum just a couple of hours ago. Of course odd concepts were creeping into her mind.

She wanted to call Teonna for some direly needed normal conversation. Not even encouragement, just a reminder that there were parts of the world where ghosts, witches, and curses didn't dominate life. Where she could take comfort in the mundane or even the tedious. Indulge in the silly debate her auntie kept trying to drag her into over what's more overrated, Whataburger and Buc-ee's in Texas, or the Mall of America and the "Juicy Lucy" in Minnesota. That sounded like peace to her right now.

It would have to wait.

If she spoke to Aunt Teonna now she wouldn't be able to suppress the tremulation of her voice. And she would be compelled to beg her forgiveness for the prayer she had started to utter. For the reverence she would give to a woman who didn't deserve it.

Many people's "prayers" ought to be called "wishes," Shyla believed.

People typically didn't surrender anything of themselves or of others through their prayers. They didn't take on any risk or pain. They didn't make any real sacrifices. Many couldn't even be bothered to say the words aloud. They whispered what they wanted to come true, or simply thought about it and moved their lips without any sound coming out, before they got into bed every night. They never prayed so hard they gave themselves a headache. Never said something that was as sickening as it was necessary.

They wished. They hoped. They did not truly pray, and damn

sure didn't sacrifice. But Shyla did now. Just trying to commune with Linda, or even think of her without also picturing a bullet or knife ending the woman's life, was difficult for Shyla.

Over the sound of the beating rain and traffic, over the distant crack of thunder, she reopened her prayer with words that loosened her teeth and made her gums sore.

"Momma, are you listening? Because I need you . . ."

29

It was hard to picture Galveston as either the desolate wreck it had been post-storm, or as the emerging gem of the southern United States it once was. What it looked like to Shyla was a casino resort town that wasn't legally allowed to operate casinos. A city that felt incomplete without a greater degree of open vice. Its family-friendly carnival on the water was called "Pleasure Pier," an old term born in England that, when exported overseas, especially to a place that once thrived on quasi-legal criminality, sounded salacious.

The island was busy and colorful. Not nearly as crowded as it would be in the summer, but still more active than one might expect in October. Then again, it was still hot enough to be hurricane season, so people could go to the beach as long as they didn't mind that the jellyfish were washing up in the thousands at this time of year. Shyla figured everything from the hotels to the cruises that departed from the bay side were probably cheaper now. And some of the "Winter Texans" who came down from the North to escape the cold might be here early to get a jump on the others while prices were down.

This all accounted for why the island wasn't as empty as she would have liked, even as the rain proved relentless. Storms along the coast often swept through quickly, pounding the area with water for half an hour and then releasing day as though nothing had ever interrupted the sunlight. This was a larger storm system, it seemed, though not big or strong enough to be a flooding concern. Shyla checked the local weather on her phone and saw that the rain was expected to continue, but there weren't any warnings of hazardous conditions.

The rain must have felt more intense to her than it was in reality. The island was equipped to deal with a downpour. Coming from drought-ridden San Antonio, where heavy rain was sometimes a salvation, but also a threat due to its capacity to summon flash floods over dry ground that couldn't soak up the water fast enough, she had a different view of dark skies and cloudbursts.

A few people still walked between stores advertising T-shirts in their windows that ranged from cute to crude—I'M A GALVESTON GAL to I NEED HEAD ON THE 1ST DATE. Shyla checked the hotel app she had on her phone for short-notice vacancies and found several, many with marked-down prices, indicating they weren't in high demand. Perhaps the island wasn't as populated as she'd feared.

Now that she was here, she had to think of her next step. The question of *What then?* had lingered in the periphery of her mind since she had made it to the road after escaping Braith in Yorktown.

Get to Galveston.

What then?

Find out where Jinh is.

What then?

Save her.

What then?

Because even if she found a way to get Jinh from the Tarvers, there'd be the question of what to do about Braith. He'd pose a threat, and not just in the short term, while they were still in Galveston or in Texas, but for the rest of their natural lives, and possibly beyond.

Shyla figured she was the only person in the world who had to fear that an unkillable man might exact revenge on the descendants of people she loved, years after she was dead. It made her think of the old movies about mummies, witches, and vampires she used to catch on local television stations with Linda and Rodney, how she always found it selfish of those witchfinders and priests in prior centuries to invoke a curse that someone would have to suffer hundreds of years later. There had to be a way to do better than that.

She had to think of a way to kill him. To let Enoch Tarver's hand do the work.

Shyla drove in a snaking pattern through the island, detouring down side streets, then looping back to the main street to progress, passing the Pleasure Pier, the historic district, the cruise ship docks, the aquarium, and much more while she wondered what to do. What she *could* do. She decided she needed a place to rest, recharge, and prepare.

Of the many places to choose from, she picked a motel on the west end of the island—the generically named "Waterfront Inn"—that appeared to be as removed from the multitude as you could get without camping on the beach. It also seemed like the kind of place where adding a night wouldn't be much of a hassle. She had no idea how long it would take to either find the Tarvers or for them to reach out to her. She presumed they or Jinh had already sensed her arrival, but it still might be hours or days before they contacted her, or she tracked them down.

She cruised through the city, slowing and dipping through large puddles. It was barely past two o'clock, which struck her as nearly impossible. She called the motel to request an early check-in. On her first attempt the phone rang for twenty seconds before her call was directed to a generic voicemail announcement that didn't verify she was dialing the Waterfront. When she redialed the ringing continued for half a minute before Shyla hung up and decided to go to the place and ask whoever was behind the desk when she got there if they could accommodate her.

The congestion and relative urbanization of the island faded after she made it to Seawall Boulevard and continued west. To her left she spotted two determined souls running up the beach in waterproof fitness gear, but no one else was braving the elements. The surf did not look menacing, but anyone familiar with the island's history–or who had a general understanding of what a storm surge was–knew that it could come up to take Galveston like an occupying force under the right conditions. While she had lived in nearby Texas City when she was young, Shyla had never been to the island before. Just hearing of its history spooked her back then. An entire city where upward of ten thousand lives were washed away in a single night struck her as uniquely terrifying. Even now, if she stared at the waves for long enough she could give herself a minor panic attack.

She thought of people living decades before the invention of radar, before authorities could provide consistent updates on the path of a storm via radio, then later television, and now through alerts pushed directly to a computer in your pocket that people still called a phone. Not that far back–one great-grandparent ago, depending on how old you were–the storm of the century could ambush a growing metropolis in one of the most prosperous nations in the world. People trusted the local expert who had long assured them that a hurricane couldn't impact their community, so they woke up that morning without even thinking it possible that the sea could swell, engulf the island, and reshape their reality in a matter of hours.

Shyla tried to imagine what it must be like for Jinh to be here. Had she ever come to a place like this? Not to Shyla's knowledge. There was plenty of death and despair to go around in any other place in the nation, to be certain. Every place in the world, in fact, was the site of a murder, or accident, or natural disaster, or outbreak of disease, or something else that killed people violently and suddenly. But there had to be something about the concentration of destruction and death—the density of it—present here that amplified the "energy" Jinh was unwillingly tapped into. Shyla thought she could feel it a little bit, or was at least cognizant of its presence, the way she could see evidence of electrical currents moving all around her without feeling the conduction. And she had no "talent" for such a thing. She wasn't inherently tuned in the way Jinh was.

Part of her wished this hadn't crossed her mind. She was worried enough for Jinh's safety. Now it occurred to her that Jinh's sanity might be at stake, as well. Even if Remy had been right about the Tarvers not wanting to deliberately hurt Jinh, they might be devastating her mind, just by bringing her to a place that could psychically overwhelm her.

Shyla called Jinh's phone again, bracing herself for a phantom version of Jinh to answer like she had earlier. The call went unanswered, as did the next, and the one after. Shyla sent a text message, one not exclusively meant for Jinh.

I'm on the island. This would hopefully be enough to get a response. They would know she was here, and obviously what for.

So she had every reason to think—or at least not disbelieve—that despite being visibly weakened, Alan and Ana Tarver were still capable of seeing that Braith wasn't with her. They might be waiting for him to come after her.

The sign for the Waterfront Inn was oversized and had pale cursive lettering against a grayed wood-paneled placard. It looked quaint, especially compared to the brighter, newer plastic and metal signs of the franchise hotels and motels that preceded it. Chain-linked placards underneath the sign advertised BREAKFAST, POOL, and BEACH ACCESS in bold letters like it had invented these amenities.

The building was two stories in the shape of a squared-horseshoe, and was close enough to the water to make you think, *Is it safe to be this close to the water?* When Shyla pulled in there were only two other cars in a parking lot made for a few dozen.

This was the right place for her. It would be quiet enough here for her prayers to be heard without having to weave through so many other thoughts and voices. People pleading with the Maker of their choosing for a better job, a sexier partner, the winning lottery numbers, a cure for the disease killing their mother or father. A hundred different things, some important, some not, all competing for space in the ears of whatever deity might act on what was heard. The Waterfront took her away from them, and she felt like that mattered.

Jinh had told her to pray.

She parked, stepped out of the car, and tucked the gun in her waistband and under her shirt before she walked inside. There was no one behind the desk as she approached. Before she could ring the bell to announce herself, however, a woman with a wealth of wrinkles and ink-black hair came out from a door to a back office. She had a smile that looked like it was part of a cheap disguise.

"How can I help you?" the woman said.

"Hi. I just booked online. Wanted to see if I can check in early."

"Sure, sure," said the woman. "This is our in-between season, so we won't have to bump or rush anybody. Heck, apart from me and some of the staff, you'll hardly see anybody today, especially with the weather how it is. You're liable to feel like you own the place."

30

Room 103 was along the back of the motel and had a view of the Gulf from the balcony window. A rattling noise persisted from its floor-unit air conditioner, just loud enough to be distracting. Likewise, a steady drip striking the bathroom sink with the rapidity of impatient footsteps made it immediately challenging to think and would fight any effort to sleep. Shyla cut off the water valve in the cabinet under the sink, then unplugged the AC. This let her listen intently to the muffled sound of the surf's duet with the rain. It was interesting to her how the sound of countless water droplets falling from a mile high onto glass was so much more pleasant and comforting than a single drop tapping porcelain.

The room smelled of age under a veneer of cheap cleaning products. Something else, too. Something unpleasant. She tried not to think of it. If she figured it out, she might have to leave. Try her hand someplace else where staff and fellow guests alike would give a second look at someone who was harried and arrived without luggage. To say nothing of any other hotel probably having security cameras.

Was any of that really important, though? She was still thinking of this as a "case" where being inconspicuous mattered, when it was something else altogether. A rescue mission, or hostage negotiation. Possibly even a setup, if the Tarvers or Braith were using her for a purpose she hadn't predicted yet.

Shyla removed the gun from her waistband, set it on the nightstand, then sat on the bed. The thought of people having died in this room, on this very mattress, rushed to her mind. Not many, but at least a few in the decades since the Waterfront first opened. That didn't make the room more ominous than virtually any other motel or hotel room that had been open for a similar length of time. Hell, she'd spent time in a hotel with ghosts downstairs and witches upstairs just a few nights ago. The fact that someone might have passed away in this room was comparatively mundane. People of various ages and stages of health must have stayed here, and on a few occasions the date that they were ordained to have a heart attack or aneurysm coincided with their vacation. It happened. Nothing to worry about.

She lay back in the bed and immediately sensed the impression of an extra body lying beside her. Stiff, cool, and a little damp to the touch. A little leathery. The feeling kept her closer to the edge of the bed, rather than its center.

The bedsprings groaned and the mattress sighed weakly as whatever was next to her evaporated, and she wondered if acknowledging its presence in her mind had placated it.

Shyla considered how much time she'd lost and wasted by not being more curious about Jinh's ability, and even more so about Jinh's personal stories. She could have asked; she could have learned.

She could have stayed.

It was too late to blame or be mad at herself for leaving, but she couldn't deny how different things would be for them if she had stuck around after finding out what really happened to her mother. She had told Jinh that part of why she left was to protect her from any culpability. That hadn't been a lie, but it had been an excuse.

The risk of embroiling Jinh in Rodney's potential murder investigation had existed *before* Shyla learned about her mother's car accident. She had just ignored it. When Jinh told her that her mother had driven off a bridge and died there in the water, she had inadvertently ripped away the sense of justice and righteousness Shyla comforted herself with after she shot Rodney. Shyla couldn't think of anything to do with all of the anger she felt after that, except take it away with her. So she left when she should have stayed and worked through her rage and pain with Jinh by her side.

There was no way to make up for those lost moments now, but this time she was going to stay when she wanted to leave. And she would listen to Jinh. Do what she told her to do.

Pray to her. You have to sacrifice. You have to tell her . . .

Tell her what?

Shyla thought she knew. Braith, loath as she was to admit it, had been right about at least one thing. The value of sacrifice.

"Momma, are you listening? I'm not . . ."

She started to lie and say, *I'm not angry anymore. I don't hate you anymore.* Lying did not make for anywhere near an adequate sacrifice, however, because it lacked value. People everywhere surrendered their truth regularly, multiple times a day, sometimes so readily it became second nature to them. Some people were quicker to lie than tell the truth even if there was no benefit to lying.

The truth was inherently more precious, and the truth was that Shyla still hated Linda. She hated her even more since she'd found out she was dead. The woman who stole Shyla's life also stole her revenge.

"Momma . . . *Linda* . . . are you listening? Do you know how much I still hate you? Can you feel it? Did you know it back then? Is that why you jumped in the water? Because if you were going to die anyway, after everything you took from me and my real family, you should have let me have my moment. You didn't deserve to take your own life. You took *mine;* you should have let me take *yours*. After everything you stole from me, that's the only thing you could have given me to make up for it. I wanted your *life*. I still want it. I want your motherfucking soul."

A rush of power shot through her, the words she spoke summoning the tangible force that was hatred.

One of the things that divided the metaphysical from the physical was the inability to even recognize, much less measure and weigh, the energies that created and fueled ghosts. The same energies that created and fueled consciousness. You could not put hatred or grief or longing on any kind of scale. They had no mass or weight. That made these things incorporeal, but they were nonetheless felt and *real*. They could consume and absorb and catalyze the way flames and acids and oils could. They were, in effect, elements, and Shyla understood that so clearly now it almost obliterated any other thought that had ever occupied her mind. It was a pure, dark epiphany that told her she was doing at least one part of what Jinh wanted her to do.

Tell her . . .

"Linda, listen to me. When I say your name, all I feel is hate. If God told me I had to wait a million years in hell for the chance to make you and Rodney suffer, I'd take the deal. I want your whole existence, forever, to be the same fear of me that made you take that last dive. I *want* that. But . . . but I need something else now. I need to save someone, so I'm willing to let that go. Do you hear me? Are you listening?"

Linda did not answer her, but there were other spirits near that were drawn by her prayer and energy, who just wanted to be heard.

There was an older gentleman who had renewed his stay in the room for three weeks in anticipation of the catastrophic heart attack he knew was looming. He had dreamt of dying on the beach, ideally while facing east during the sunrise, but his death had arrived as he dallied in this room, rethinking whether he should just go back home to his family to be with them instead. So here he was now, eternally reaching for the door, convinced that if he just repeated this act, he would find the strength or luck or grace from God to get out of here, and then he would be able to work on getting down the hall, step by step over decades, before someday making it to the water.

The water, Shyla thought, would make it to this room first if enough years passed. She shook her head. This was a distraction. She needed to keep the channel she had now opened clear so that Linda could come through to her.

She fought to block out the other consciousnesses trying to speak to her. Some slipped through briefly before she pushed them away, and in the glimpses she received their tremendous fear and desire to be heard. The emotions that let them carry on. Many of these were the dead from the Great Storm. A century and a quarter removed from their lives, they couldn't remember much of themselves beyond trying to survive. They remembered the push and tug of the sea, the battering they suffered as beams and even entire walls of felled houses slammed into them. Some seemed only to want it known that they hadn't merely drowned.

I was slashed open by glass from broken windows.

I was gored by a broken beam flung by a wave.

I was beaten to death by wood, water, and other bodies.

Shyla was too new to this experience to know how to suppress these consciousnesses and clear a line to Linda Montgomery. It felt easier to do the opposite instead. To relax and let them all pass through. She exhaled and listened to the voices of the past until newer ones started to come through. Each asked her, *Are you listening?* Then told her, *This is my story.*

One of the spirits told her that they had been shot in the back of a vehicle for gambling debts unpaid, then dumped in the bay, and they just wanted someone to tell their sister what had happened, and her name was–

Another said that they'd run afoul of corrupt police who wanted them to change their testimony to frame an innocent man. These officers tied him up, placed him a dinghy on the water, then shot holes in it from their own larger boat. They shared a cigarette and watched as the dinghy sank, and–

The next spirit told Shyla, *My father was killed by a man who made him pray until he spit blood.*

Shyla went stiff like she'd been struck by lightning. This wasn't Linda, but it was someone who might be able to help her, or who would at least want to, because they had a common enemy. She locked in on this voice, which made the others try harder to be heard, and in turn made her more determined to be deaf to them. There was only one voice she needed to hear. The strain of her focus almost exhausted her, but she felt renewed when the remaining spirits finally faded while the one she fought to isolate remained.

My father had to watch my mother, brothers, and sister die. I jumped into the water to save myself. My father's ghost watched over me in the water. Both of his hands had been cut off by the man who killed us, and my father's hand . . . his hand that used to hold mine when we crossed the street, his hand that gave me ice cream cones and candy pops . . .

That hand helped me stay afloat and then it pulled me to shore.

That hand was with me when I was found by a preacher. When he saw my father's hand move, he thought it was a sign from God.

The preacher reunited me with my family and I told them about the sacredness of my father's hand. It was a terrible burden to put upon my family, but it had to be done. My father's spirit cannot rest until the promise he was forced to make comes to pass.

The man who killed my family will die at my father's hand, or never die. My father swore this. And his hand embodied this and defeated the ravages of time for this. The burden and obligation of finding the man who needed to die to give my father's spirit peace has tortured and shortened the lifespan of every generation in my family. I suffered, my children suffered, their children continue to suffer. We have been cheated out of our lives, but we would not have lives at all were it not for my father's spirit, and his hand.

Our curse was actually a blessing. We formed a church to honor this.

Faith helped keep my father's hand alive, and more than that, vital. Faith birthed new ideas, so that my father's hand could be used in new ways.

My father's hand can be wielded now. It will not wither.

The killer, the murderer, calling himself Saxton Braith.

You know him, Shyla Sinclair, as I now know you.

Deliver him to the children of my great-grandchildren. Deliver him to the weapon they have made of my father's hand.

Deliver him to them, and deliver them from him.

"How?" Shyla said, but Enoch Tarver's daughter didn't answer. She wanted to ask if the spirit understood what her descendants had done to Enoch's hand. They'd turned it into something they thought they could more easily use—a glove—but had instead weakened it, according to what Remy had said.

Remy said Braith even knew how ineffective the glove would be. He had tested his own version of it on his mentor, Weldon. He'd planned ahead for this since before any of the other parties involved were born. This was the supreme benefit of being unkillable. Shyla was scrambling to come up with a plan based on new information learned in the past few hours while Braith had decades to prepare for every contingency.

"How do I kill him?" Shyla asked again, and Enoch's daughter remained silent.

Boiling from beneath the darkness of her closed eyes, silvery and shadowed like a monochromatic print, Shyla saw the horizon. Oversized celestial bodies hovered above the line, and waters that shimmered but refused to reflect the stars waited below. A figure she shouldn't be able to make out ascended from the water and walked stiffly over it, toward her. For a moment she thought it was Enoch's daughter, coming to answer her question. Then she realized this spirit was, itself, part of the answer.

"Linda . . . is that you?"

"Don't call me that. I raised you. I'm your—"

"You were never my mother! Haven't you been listening?"

"*You* listen to me. I gave up everything for you. I *loved* you."

Linda's voice was a serpent coiling around Shyla's mind. The word "loved" struck her like a venomous bite.

"I wish I could have killed you," Shyla said.

"What did I ever do to you but raise you and love you?"

"You were going to have Rodney kill me."

"No, no. You're wrong."

"You picked out a place—"

"You're wrong. I loved you," Linda said, her denial palpable. "I only wanted you to hear us out. I don't deserve this. I deserve peace. After everything, I even gave up my life for you. I bore that sin so you wouldn't kill me, your own momma. I made sure you didn't double your sin. I did the best I could for you. I gave up so much."

"Everything you gave up was a lie," Shyla said, and thought she tasted a drop of blood on her tongue. "A lie you told yourself to make yourself feel better."

"No. No, no, that's not it."

"Stop talking, *Linda*. I need you to do something. I need you there for me for once, and if you do it . . . I'll . . . I'll help you. I'll give up the thing I've lived with since the day I learned the truth. But only if you help me—"

The hotel room's phone rang, jarringly loud. Shyla's eyes shot open and her mind rushed back into her body from an unfathomable distance. A place well past the many thick barriers dividing life from the planes of death.

31

It took her a second to remember how to breathe again. She sat up and felt dizzy. The ringing of the phone stretched in her ears, then became a spiral, forever descending while rising to a fresh crescendo at the same time.

The sound faded into a tinny bell, then disappeared.

It took her another second to notice how dark it now was. She didn't quite feel like she'd just been asleep, but she had been, and time had jumped ahead while she was under. She'd lost hours.

She stood from the bed, circled around it to get to the window and touch the pane. It was cool against her palm, and she knew this wasn't a dream or trance. She was in the Waterfront Inn, in Galveston, where through the square double windows she could see the flat sand and, past that, night encroaching on the sea.

Shyla searched the dimming horizon for the shape she'd seen last in her vision. She looked for the sign of Linda Montgomery's corpse in the Gulf of Mexico crawling over the waves.

The phone in the hotel room sounded off again, making Shyla

jump. Things were coming to a head, and her nerves weren't holding up. Maybe she'd spent too much of her cold composure on killing Rodney all those years ago, and her reservoir was depleted. Now, at the stony bottom of it, there was only uncovered anxiousness that made her jumpy. Shit, maybe she should have just listened to Remy and made a run for it while–

No. No, hell no.

I wasn't made by people who abandon people.

Shyla walked around the bed and answered the phone.

"Hello?"

"Hey there," said the woman from the front desk, sounding relieved to have made contact, and reserved about bad news she had to deliver. "I'm glad I got ahold of you. Sorry to bug you. How is the room? Were you napping?"

"Room's fine. Were you calling for something?" she asked.

"Right, yes. I was calling because you had visitors. I told them I couldn't give them your room number without permission, but they had your name. They told me it was urgent and I told them I'd give you a call to call them back."

Alertness broke through the remains of Shyla's drowsiness as her heartbeat sped up. "They? How many people? What did they look like?"

"Um, well, there were a few of them and . . . Hon, I have to say, I've seen my share of strangeness try to come through the door here over the years. Now, I'm not judging, but if you're involved in something, I have to ask you not to have it going on here. You understand, I hope–"

"Ma'am, I'm just asking who it was. I don't know what the problem is."

"Uh-huh. You think it's normal for people to ask 'how many' and 'what did they look like' when they get unexpected visitors at a motel? When they came in with a last-minute booking and no luggage? Don't take me for a fool. I'm trying to be reasonable. I could have just called the police on you."

Shyla sighed. "Whatever you're worried this could be, I promise it's not that."

The woman remained quiet for several seconds, then said, "There was one man who was pretty clean-cut, good looking, with a couple of larger boys along with him. Do they sound like friends of yours?"

"Yes," Shyla said, slightly impressed with how she kept the tension from cracking her voice. She thanked the woman for the description, then hung up the phone.

Her visitors weren't the Tarvers. Braith, then. How had he found her?

Shyla looked for her phone, saw it on the nightstand beside the gun, and it clicked for her. She thought of the ads for GPS trackers she'd seen when she'd researched what gun would be best for a private investigator.

She picked the gun up now, properly inspected it, and realized that the discolored bottom inch of the magazine *was* the tracker. Inconspicuous, unobtrusive, more easily fixed or upgraded without taking the entire gun out of service if needed. Fairly clever.

Shyla cocked her arm back and almost threw the gun through the window before dropping it and growling out, "Motherfucker." She should have let Remy keep the gun.

She set it down and picked up her phone. There was an unread message from the contact line Braith had given her.

Hello Shyla!

Wait an hour after you read this, then drive east until you hit Boddeker. Go left. Past San Jacinto. Ignore any "closed area" signs. The water isn't that deep, you'll make it. There'll be a turnoff on your left. It will look like a foot trail but your car will fit. Drive until you see another car. That will be my guys. They'll take you the rest of the way. Let us know when you're leaving. I know I don't have to tell you not to do anything dumb, but don't do anything dumb. I'm not in the best mood. When you watch the video below, you'll see why. You'll get another message after I see you've read this.

See you soon!

Beneath this was a shortened hyperlink. She tapped it with her thumb and downloaded a web browser she'd never heard of to her phone, which then opened to a video that played automatically.

The video was dim and grainy, but Shyla could still tell she was watching a side view of Remy from several feet back. Remy was on her knees in sand. A broken, stony shore was between her and the water. She had to be facing the bay side. On a better, brighter day, during a busier time of the year, cruise ships or the ferry would pass near enough for passengers to see her, but not in rainy, dusky October.

Her hands were bound behind her, and the rope around her wrists was also looped around her ankles. She looked so still that for a moment Shyla wondered if the video had frozen, or never started, despite the time bar moving across the bottom of the screen. Then Remy took a big breath as something moved behind her, and Shyla gasped along with her.

From the right, Braith stepped into view. He held a knife in his left hand. Jinh's navaja. He placed the blade flat on Remy's shoulder, a mockery of knighting her, and she shuddered in a way that told Shyla she was at least as furious as afraid.

Braith glanced at the camera, then he looked at Remy. He caressed the back of her head with his free hand and asked, "Shall I wait for you to say that you're ready?"

"Go to hell–" Remy said, barely getting the words out before Braith stuck the knife into the side of her neck. When she tried to pull away, he held her in place, withdrew the knife, then stabbed her again, this time through the back of her neck. Shyla thought of Remy jamming the poker blade through the back of Braith's head, how it felt like she'd visited four or five different worlds since then.

She thought of Braith killing Garrett Schramm, his previous would-be protégé and confidant, and how he'd apparently maimed Weldon in a self-serving experiment. And now he wanted Shyla to be the next person he could eventually find disposable.

Shyla watched Remy fight for final breaths. When Braith was satisfied she was either dead or close enough to it, he let her fall to her side, nearest to the camera, though, not away from it. The person holding the camera lowered it to catch death stealing over Remy's eyes before he raised the view to show Braith. Shyla waited for him to say something, knowing he'd done this for her to see.

Just as he opened his mouth to address her, a gunshot sounded and Braith's head jerked back. Dots of red spattered the camera lens as it dropped into the sand. The video ended and the browser closed.

Shyla tried to click the link again and received an error message.

A second message came in, as Braith had said. But this one didn't come from the same line. It came from Jinh's phone.

As fast as Shyla's heart already beat, it found a higher gear that almost snatched her out of consciousness when she checked Jinh's text.

It was exactly the same as the one sent from Braith's phone.

He had her.

32

Killing time for an hour was the hardest part. She was afraid to start praying again. The last time she'd done so, she'd self-induced a trance without realizing it. If that happened this time she might miss the window Braith had given her to arrive in.

I'm not in the best mood. An understatement given he'd sent that message after getting shot.

She brought the gun with her, thinking that even if a bullet couldn't hurt Braith, one could still drop any of the thugs he'd hired. Of course, they'd likely frisk her and take it from her, but she thought it was worth bringing.

She drove toward the lights and activity of the island, and stopped at the nearest gas station to refuel. Based on the instructions she'd received, a full tank of gas would be useless to her, but in case she was able to get Jinh to the car and they needed to haul ass across the country immediately, she thought she should fill up, anyway. She then went inside and bought two sixteen-ounce cans of Red Bull, finishing one before she even made it back to the car, and the other when she returned to the road, driving back toward the Pleasure Pier.

The rain had become a drizzle, almost a mist, which was still enough to keep most people from coming out. The island looked more desolate now that night had fallen, especially as she approached the Pleasure Pier, knowing it was largely, if not entirely, empty. The neon blue and red lights of a large Ferris wheel, a scoliotic roller coaster, and a drop tower shone through the shroud of precipitation. Galveston felt apart from the rest of the world, instead of a short bridge away from the rest of Texas. It barely felt like a real place, but like something that used to exist. An amusement park foolishly built on a glorified sandbar, abandoned, and left to nature.

This wasn't where she wanted to die, or where she wanted to let Jinh die. A fleeting, frightening thought almost ran her off the road: What if she was already dead? What if everything since she'd helped Remy attack Braith in the cell was a final hallucination? Braith had gotten the better of both of them somehow, smashed Shyla's head on the floor, and she was leaking out there still.

She checked the time. Forty minutes had passed since she'd read the first message. Close enough.

She drove east until Seawall Boulevard came to a T-intersection with Boddeker Road. The world darkened quickly, like God had thrown a curtain over Shyla's life. In the summer, or the spring, or even during certain seasonable days of the winter, there might have been a line of cars along the way to East Beach. Tonight she passed only three cars on Seawall when she made it past the last hotel and gas station, and didn't see any other vehicles as she crept down Boddeker.

The first large "puddle" took up most of the road for several feet. Shyla wondered whether Braith had lied about the water not being that deep in order to trap her. She took her car around the perimeter of the water as well as she could without venturing too far off the paved road. She was entering the marshland of Galveston Island now and didn't want to get stuck in the muck.

She made it around the first puddle, then the next, and drove through a third that was too wide to circumnavigate, growing concerned when her headlights briefly dipped below the water. She gunned the gas and got them above the surface again. The engine sputtered briefly but kept going.

Less than a minute after this obstacle she saw the trail. The grass around it was tall, but not higher than the roof of her car. She hesitated a second, steadied her nerves with a couple of breaths and one quick prayer.

"Linda, I'm going in. I'm going to need you. And you owe me."

Then she made the turn. The trail was obviously not built for cars, and the vehicles that had disregarded the warnings were likely pickup trucks and ATVs. The path they made was especially uneven, but she kept her foot on the accelerator, just enough to preserve her momentum over the bumps and dips. The trail was relatively straight for a few minutes, then made a sharp right turn. Her headlights almost immediately illuminated Braith's favorite silver sedan lying in wait.

She pulled to within about twenty feet of it, then stopped, put her car in park, and got out.

"Headlights," called a gruff voice from near Braith's car. Shyla turned her headlights off but didn't cut her engine.

The sedan's high beams flared up. Shyla raised her hand to shield her eyes, so didn't see the men exiting the car, but heard two doors open. Passenger's and driver's sides, she guessed. So there were only two of them.

"You were supposed to message us when you were on the way," one of them said. The same one who had barked at her about her headlights. The one designated to speak. He sounded seasoned, authoritative, professional. A guy who was a little bit tired of this work but who didn't think he was good at anything else, so here he was. Probably the driver, then. Shyla decided she shouldn't go for him, but for the other one instead.

Other one. She hoped it was just one and that she wasn't wrong. Hope wasn't quite all she had right now, but it made up a large part of her arsenal.

The rest was comprised of one bullet.

She had banked on Braith and his thugs tracking the gun. To count on her not to trying "anything dumb."

Braith knew she didn't have any other gun on her and would guess she couldn't procure another quickly. So, with the tracker showing the gun back at the Waterfront Inn, Braith's two goons would assume she was unarmed.

But the tracker was on the magazine, not the pistol.

Before Shyla left the inn, she'd racked one round into the chamber, then dropped out the magazine into the nightstand's drawer. She would go back for it later to clean up that evidence.

She had one bullet in a pistol these men didn't expect her to have.

Shyla lowered her hand as she saw them come around the front of the sedan. They looked like solid silhouettes in front of the high beams. The one on the left was tall, lean. The one on the right stockier. Somehow, in her mind, his shortness matched his voice. She hoped she was right about that.

Shyla drew the gun from her waist and aimed at the man on her left. She targeted center mass, not aiming to kill, not aiming to maim, just aiming to *hit*. To *stop*. The shot was loud and sudden. Close thunder from a cloudless sky. The lankier silhouette to her left let out a stifled cry and dropped while the crack of the gunshot still held domain over the moment.

The shadow to her right froze just long enough for Shyla to turn the pistol on him next and keep him in place. The man on the left grunted, shifted, then was still. Shyla barely heard this over her own voice shouting, "Don't fucking move. *Don't fucking move*."

The shorter man had one hand behind his back, but the other raised in surrender. They both remained frozen long enough for the deafening effect of the gunshot to clear, so Shyla could speak to him in a quieter, more controlled tone.

"You know I could kill you, right?" she said. "You know why I haven't?"

He waited to answer, and Shyla wondered if the aftershocks of her heartbeat could reach him, alert him to how scared she was, despite how cool she felt on the outside. So cool she was numb, while her chest was the epicenter of an earthquake.

Finally he shook his head, a small movement, and told her, "You don't need me to take you there. Just follow the trail until you see the old fort. Big square building. You can't miss it."

"Are you making a case for me to let you go or put you down?"

He made a frustrated, throat-clearing noise upon recognizing his mistake. "Well, I guess that's your call."

"Sure," Shyla said. "On the ground. Flat. Hands out."

Again, he stalled, and she thought that if he brought his hand around from his back too quickly, she'd throw her gun at him, aim for his head. Either hit him or make him raise a hand to deflect, one was about as good as the other as long as it made him miss if he took a shot. She would charge as soon as she threw the pistol. Take an angle toward his left shoulder, away from his gun hand, and get there before he could recover. She thought she was close enough. She never really put a lot of stock into the old "twenty-one-foot rule" of distance that asserted a person with a knife could close a twenty-one-foot gap on a person with a firearm before the latter could draw and get two shots off. It presumed the person being charged was a statue and wouldn't move. Besides, she didn't have a knife on her. But she was less than twenty-one feet away, and didn't see another option, so she would put faith in it now.

The older goon slowly dropped to one knee, then the other, and withdrew his hand from behind his back just as carefully, keeping it low and spreading his fingers wide to show his hand was empty.

When he flattened himself out Shyla went to him, hiked up his tan Members Only jacket to see the handgun tucked in back of his pants, and pulled it out. She had a good look at him now. He wasn't quite bald, but close, and had more gray than brown hair on his pale scalp. He had a scar on the back of his head and a cauliflower ear. Tough old dude. Survivor. He'd played it safe with her. She tossed Remy's gun away, toward her car. It landed in the dirt of the trail with the hollow end of the grip facing him.

He groaned and said, "Shit. I knew it."

Shyla kicked his ankles to check for a spare gun, then told him, "Turn over."

He did and faced the muzzle of his own gun pointed at him. A defeated look softened his eyes. It almost made Shyla proud to see it. She had a chance. This had worked. Only a few larger, more hazardous hurdles to go.

Should she kill him or not was the question. She listened for the other man and heard nothing, and thought he would at least be struggling to stifle groans if he was alive. She'd caught him with a good shot. She'd killed him without having seen his face. She'd shot Rodney in the back. Any time she'd put her gun in someone's face, it had been in the heat of the moment, under stress or duress, like at Braith's mansion. This would be different. She'd have to stare into this man's eyes and pull the trigger right now.

She was tempted to do it just to prove that she could. He was the enemy. Either he or his partner had been behind the camera when Braith killed Remy. He would let Jinh die if that's what he was hired to do, and probably would have been a half-second quicker to pull on Shyla if Braith hadn't wanted her alive.

That was reason enough to hate him, reason enough to kill him. The one thing that kept her from pulling the trigger was the thought that she might need him for something, starting with making sure she found the exact place where Braith was keeping Jinh.

"Up," she told him, taking a few steps back to be sure she was out of his reach.

As he stood, he flicked his eyes over her shoulder as though something behind her caught his attention. Shyla trusted her senses. She hadn't heard anything, and even if someone or something was there, if they were on his side he would have been too smart to give away their presence with a glance. Seeing that this didn't work deflated him.

"Look," he said, "I'm just doing work. I don't have anything against you, I'm just here for hire. I just told you where to go, and you've got my gun. I'm no threat. I don't have to be involved anymore."

"Yeah, you do," Shyla said. "You took the work. You involved yourself. Let's go."

The walk wasn't far, but was enough to make Shyla feel that they were going someplace remote. Again, she thought of her and Jinh dying here, in an unfamiliar place, their bodies hidden and never found, their spirits restless and homesick.

She thought of her mother driving off the road because she was too tired and ending up in a lake, with no one knowing what happened to her for years, despite the fact that she was traveling between populated areas.

She thought of Linda finding some unused old pier and deciding it was a good enough place to die. She'd had something to live for, though. Not the "daughter" who was never hers, nor the partner she'd never see again, not on this side of existence, anyway, but retribution. Responsibility. She'd had that to live for, and she had opted out of it. If she'd ever had a sliver of genuine love for Shyla, she would understand that and try to make amends for it now. Even if she didn't really understand it, Shyla hoped Linda could at least grasp what Shyla was offering.

"If you're listening, I'm going to need you," Shyla whispered.

"Who are you talking to?" the man said, anxiety cracking his voice. This wasn't the first time he'd asked, because it wasn't the first time Shyla had whispered her prayer during their walk. Shyla continued to ignore him. She wanted him to think she was a bit crazy. He may have been through enough gunfights not to be thrown off by being escorted at gunpoint to a showdown, but how accustomed was he to weirdness? Based on his tone, not very.

He hadn't lied about the old fort. It wasn't visible from the road and wasn't accessible unless you were willing to get your shoes wet, and probably the cuff of your pants, as well.

Shyla's pants were wet up to her lower shin after splashing through a few unseen puddles. She wished for a moment that she'd worn shorts, then remembered that rattlesnakes enjoyed the warmth of the Texas coast and was glad to be in jeans.

As they started the last, shallow descent toward the fort, the building appeared to grow. It was actually three buildings in one, connected by a few short hallways. All she needed was for this man to bring her to the entrance that would bring her closest to where Braith was holding Jinh. He could try to mislead her, but she doubted he would. She imagined he would want to get to Braith immediately to get away from the girl who'd outwitted him, taken his gun, and was now talking to herself.

Maybe that was wishful thinking. That was okay. It was more than nothing.

There was a large, open entrance to the main body of the old fort, and the man walked her straight to it. She saw a flickering light inside and knew that whoever was near that light would hear her approaching, even if they couldn't see her.

She stepped a little faster to get closer to the man as they approached the pried-open wooden boards that had barricaded the fort's front entryway.

The light came from a road flare in the center of a narrow concrete chamber. Braith stood over the small, persistent flame. Before him were the Tarver twins, on their knees and bound with their hands behind their backs. Their faces were wrapped nose to chin with at least three layers of duct tape. Behind him, also tied up, lying on the floor, was Jinh. She was so still that Shyla's first instinct was to scream her name. She saw Jinh's chest rise just before this cry could get out.

Braith turned to face Shyla and the man she was effectively using as a shield as they walked through the entryway. There was a large, unhealed wound that split his cheek open on the left side of his face. A brutal, bloody grotto that broke part of his jaw and burrowed all the way to an exit wound in back of his neck. When the right side of his mouth curled up to smile, he looked like two conjoined theater masks, with the tragedy half broken.

"Hello, Shyla," he said, barely moving his lips. He waved at her with a hand that held Jinh's knife, a hand now wearing the hand of glory.

33

Shyla was struck with sudden flashes of how this scene came to be, and couldn't tell whether they came from Jinh, the Tarvers, or even Braith. Maybe they came from all of them. The disjointed replay of what happened gave Shyla a stabbing headache.

Braith had tracked Remy's gun to the rest area where Shyla dropped Remy off. He must not have been too far behind them. He'd caught up to Remy and taken her to the shore and killed her on camera to show Shyla how cruel he could be. She'd heard stories, but he needed her to see it. But he'd left himself vulnerable. The Tarvers sensed him on the island and weren't lying in wait with a trap, like he expected. They came to him.

Alan, wearing the glove on his gun hand, shot Braith, which was why Braith hadn't yet healed. Unfortunately, Remy had been right. The gloved version of Enoch Tarver's hand was not enough. Braith's men—professionals—had returned fire, gotten the upper hand, forced them to take Braith to Jinh, and now here they all were.

Shyla shook off the headache and half ducked behind Braith's goon, who stood with his arms up. Braith raised his other hand, his ungloved hand, to point a pistol toward them, although not exactly in a threatening manner. Almost like he forgot he was holding it. "Shyla, if I wanted to kill you I'd just shoot through him. Step away, please. And put the gun down, you know it's useless on me."

It was, she thought, a pretty good bluff, but if he was actually willing to shoot his man, he could have done that already. Plugged him in the leg to drop him so Shyla couldn't hide behind him. But then Braith would be alone against her, and two or three other hostiles if she could incapacitate him long enough to free them.

He hadn't been lying about not wanting her dead, however. He had a plan for her. He couldn't really think she would go through with what he wanted. To become cursed like him. He must want her to kill one of the Tarvers. That's why he had left them alive. Force her to kill the sister or the brother to see if the other would curse her the way Enoch had cursed Braith. But there was no chance in hell that would work. The Tarvers looked like fragile, half-cracked shells. If they had the energy left to summon a curse, they would use it to conjure something to help them.

But their mouths were sealed, so they couldn't pray, and prayers, spells, and curses had to be spoken. Thought was the domain of clairvoyance, communication, seeing and speaking to spirits, but not manifestation. That required a voice, and Braith had deliberately robbed the Tarvers of theirs. So what was his plan?

Braith had said something back in the cell in Yorktown. He'd said that while others had gifts they didn't recognize, Shyla was capable of what he'd called a "power spike." He'd immediately followed this by asking about her secret while she was under the truth serum's influence, and she'd focused on that, so she hadn't thought about who he'd been comparing her to, until now. The others who had the dormant gift, like Enoch Tarver, were the ones he sought to inflict the curse. But the ability to tap into a dangerous, supernatural ability, to create a power surge, that was also useful to Braith.

"Oh my God," she whispered.

"Shyla, I hate having to repeat myself," Braith said. "Put the gun down and step away from my man. Or did you forget the part in my message where I said I'm not in the best mood?" He leveled the gun with Jinh and fired a shot into her thigh.

The duct tape on her mouth muffled Jinh's scream, but Shyla heard it louder in her mind, and staggered like she'd taken a punch. Braith's goon turned on her and grabbed for his gun, but Shyla still had the presence of mind to hold it tight and pull the trigger twice. It had a stronger kick than anything she was used to. Higher caliber despite not looking much bigger or feeling heavier than guns she'd carried before. Both shots more or less gored the man. Exit wounds smoked like fumaroles in his back.

Shyla had the gun trained on Braith before his goon dropped, but Braith had a clear shot at her now and fired first. The bullet struck her on the right shoulder, clipping the end of her clavicle, and her arm promptly felt like dead weight. She lost her grip on the gun and it clattered to the floor. She dropped to retrieve it with her left hand, but Braith fired two more shots, this time at the gun. One shot missed, but the second struck and spun the pistol a few feet beyond her reach. As she dove for it he fired yet again, hitting the heel of her foot. The pain set her bones aflame, but she kept crawling toward the gun.

"Shyla!" The stone acoustics amplified Braith's voice as much as it had the gunshots. The sound of her name cut through the ringing in her ears. He fired again at the gun she was reaching for, pushing it farther from her and making her wince, her nerves finally shredded.

"Shyla," Braith said again, cooler this time, his fury falsely subdued, a demon behind a broken door. "Look at me."

She turned over, expecting to see the gun in her face, but he held it to his side. She struggled to define his expression, because she'd never seen someone so happy and simultaneously deranged before. A dancing, psychotic, lonely light shone in his eyes. The light of the last star at the end of the universe, overjoyed to be the only thing left. Everything else that ever existed was no more. Dead first. Only the survivor mattered.

That he had kept this light hidden until now was an impossible, wicked miracle.

Realizing that he had revealed himself, that Shyla now *saw* him after he'd blown away the remnants of his façade, Braith moved closer to Jinh, stooped, and pushed the tip of the knife into the bullet hole in her leg. Hearing Jinh scream again skewered the two hemispheres of Shyla's brain. It was debilitating, worse than the pain in her shoulder and heel. Through blurred tears she saw Braith twist the knife back and forth as though he were unsure whether or not to screw something in.

Jinh wasn't bleeding too much, as far as Shyla could tell. Braith hadn't hit her femoral artery. That was good. But Braith seemed to be teasing at doing just that. Or maybe he wanted Jinh to suffer. Maybe that was the point, something he'd learned how to do–and to take some delight in–from Schramm.

"Stop! Stop, *listen,*" Shyla pleaded. "Stop. Do it to me."

Braith did stop and eyed her suspiciously, though not without interest.

"Do it to me," she repeated. "You've already got a start. Just kill me, and have Jinh say the prayer."

Braith scoffed. "Why? To give her an extra minute to live? You know I'm just going to kill whoever says it, don't you? I have to."

Shyla swallowed. This confirmed it. The idea of wanting a new protégé, a companion, was a lie. Or maybe he'd changed his plans after Shyla attacked him. Either way, he didn't want to replace Remy with Shyla. He wanted Shyla to curse him the same way Enoch Tarver had. In a moment like this, with her anger and desperation and sadness and pain boiling over, he knew she could do it. Her power spike would only intensify as he continued to torture Jinh.

A second curse might make him truly immortal. Two hexes effectively competing against each other. Not canceling each other out, but battling to a stalemate, with Braith the beneficiary. Two different people couldn't share the sole supernatural claim on killing him. Even if Enoch's other hand ever got to Braith, Shyla's curse would keep him alive, and vice versa.

Braith stood and started toward the Tarvers. "If you think I'm hurting her now," he told Shyla, "you have no idea."

Alan Tarver tried to pull away as Braith came closer, while his sister tried to move toward him, as if she'd be able to prevent him from doing anything if she could actually get between the two men.

Braith stabbed Alan in his left eye, then set his gun down to hold Alan's head steady. Ava groaned for him, like doing so could alleviate some of his pain.

Braith slashed Alan's right eye. Ava tried to inchworm toward him, and Braith stood to kick her away. Shyla glanced back toward the gun while Braith was distracted. She judged the distance and wondered if she could get there in her condition before he got to her.

"You know, I'd really rather not do all of this," Braith said. "I'd rather trust you to do as you're told. Then it could just be this." He pulled Alan up by his shirt collar and pushed the blade in just under his jawline, then adjusted his grip to crank it around to the opposite side of the man's head, like he was operating some obsolete machinery, pulling a stiff old handle to pop off a lid.

Braith couldn't contain his laughter as he looked at his hand in the blood-soaked glove. The thing that was supposed to be the instrument of his overdue death. He had used Enoch Tarver's hand to kill one of the man's descendants. There might have been some dark magic to that, but Shyla thought that any power Braith felt was the simple rush of sadism and barbarity. That was the sole reason he had put the glove on. To have this moment.

As Alan's head slumped and his life flooded down his chest, Ava wept and tried to screech through the tape shutting her mouth. She made a repetitive sound that Shyla understood to be a single, two-syllable word. For a second she thought it was part of a spell, something that would help her—help them all—survive this if she could just say it a certain number of times. But no. She was trying to call her brother's name.

The Tarvers were going to die. Alan for certain, as the final seconds of his life spilled onto the floor before him. Ava, as well, if Shyla didn't try something.

Tell her. Sacrifice . . .

Shyla started again, softly, so far under her breath she could barely hear herself, although the continued ringing in her ears might have contributed to that.

"*Linda* . . . are you listening? Help me."

Either not hearing her over Ava Tarver or not caring because he was too enamored with the gore in front of him, Braith said, "Now, wasn't that pretty fast? After I got past the eyes, I mean. I can skip that part when I get back to work on Jinh. It'll be mostly painless. A couple of long slices up her forearms, and she'll barely feel a thing after a few seconds. I'd love to go that route, but that wouldn't work with you. The anger is your engine. Really, it's your entire purpose. And it's necessary for this to work. The sooner you understand that, and give me what I need, the sooner I can put Jinh out of . . . Shyla, are you listening? What are you saying?"

"Linda, I hate you," Shyla whispered, and tiny cankers surfaced on her tongue. "You did this. I wouldn't be here if you hadn't taken me. You owe me."

"Shyla," Braith said, trying to get her attention. "I appreciate your enthusiasm, but I haven't told you what to say yet."

She closed her eyes to him and kept on. "*I hate you*. If I had found you I would have killed you. I would have shot you and watched you die, just like Rodney. You don't deserve peace. You should suffer forever for what you did. My real parents—my *real mother*—died because of you. You wanted to kill me when I found out what you were. *You* wanted to kill *me.*"

A force rumbled through the fort hard enough to make Braith momentarily lose his balance.

"Shyla! Whatever you think you're doing—"

She shut her eyelids tighter like she was trying to squeeze her eyes into the back of her head. She heard Braith move, and next heard Jinh both trying to scream and fighting to suppress her own scream.

"Whatever you think you're doing, you're just going to prolong this," Braith said, "and put Jinh through that much worse. I've just scratched the surface of what I could do. Imagine when I put the flames to her."

"I wish I could do worse than kill you," Shyla said to Linda, and an image flashed through her mind of what Braith's mentor, Weldon, must look like in his coffin prison, at Braith's mercy, tortured forever, and Shyla felt sickening glee at the idea of being able to keep Linda in such a state. She barely registered that Braith spoke to her now. The taste of blood from her seeping gums told her to keep going. This was how you could tell you were praying with all of your soul. Praying so hard it hurt, it damaged.

The building trembled again and a cold wind pushed through, carrying Linda's faint voice with it. "What did I ever do but love you?"

Quickly, out of urgency and a need to drown out Jinh's cries, Shyla continued, "*I hate you* and I wish I could have watched you die. You never loved me—"

"You're wrong. I—"

"You *never* loved me but I will try to forgive you. I will forgive you. I *will* forgive you if you help me now and stop this help me help me now because you did this you put me here you owe me *you owe me my whole fucking life* and if you help me now, if you prove you ever had any love for me and help me now, I will forgive you. I swear I'll forgive you, I'll dig out all of the hate I have for you and throw it away and give you peace if you help me."

Her tongue bled. The roof of her mouth was tender and blistering. She felt like there were little spikes floating in her lungs, making it painful to breathe, and bits of her throat came up as she spoke. She spit it all out as she continued the prayer loud enough to shout down whatever Braith was doing to Jinh.

"I will forgive you, are you listening? *Are you fucking listening? Linda!*"

Two of her teeth cracked and the pain almost made her pass out, but Shyla's eyes snapped open as she heard:

"Yes." Linda's voice boomed. Its agony was deep and hollow.

"What was that?" Braith said, startled not just by the voice, but by the fact that something had happened he couldn't account for. He tried to hide his fear when he asked Shyla, "What did you do?"

He rose from where he stood over Jinh, blood dripping in a thin, almost unbroken line from the tip of the blade. He looked around the fort as if he could find where the voice came from. As if it hadn't come from all directions, through every open window, through the open entrance, down through the holes in the ceiling.

"You can't take her," Linda said. "She's *my* daughter. I gave up everything to have her. She's mine. You can't take her!"

The wind assembled all the moisture in the room into a whirling mist. Shyla saw it blow toward Braith and flood through him. He went stiff for a second, then he bulged from within. Linda's invasive spirit lifted him onto his toes and stretched his arms wide. For half a second it looked like he might keep expanding and burst.

His eyes narrowed in concentration as he appeared to flex every muscle in his body to regain control with noticeable but frighteningly simple effort. He dropped to his knees, propped himself up with his hands, and vomited a couple of buckets of water.

Linda's weak spirit splattered on the floor as Braith chuckled between retches.

"I'm sorry," Linda said, her voice fading, not from growing distant, but from its exhaustion. "I tried. I tried . . ."

Braith wiped his mouth, looked at Shyla, and started to say, "Nice try," but a bullet clipped his chin before he got the words out. The next shot pulverized the bridge of his nose.

Linda didn't have the strength to incapacitate Braith for more than a handful of seconds, but that was enough time for Shyla to get to the gun. She'd needed an extra moment to aim with her off hand, since her right didn't have the strength after the bullet she'd taken in the shoulder.

She remembered what Braith told her about the times Remy had done this to him as a test. That literally blowing his head off with a barrage of bullets had left a "hell of a mess," but more important, that it had taken him some time to recover. She'd seen the holes this gun had put in his thug, and trusted that enough shots, well-placed, would essentially behead Braith.

She fired until the remaining thirteen bullets were spent. Ten of those shots hit their target. Braith's face went from punctured to fractured to obliterated. Even then, Shyla fired the last three rounds at the broken dome sitting atop the ruin of Braith's lower jaw, and with that he finally fell onto his back.

Shyla hurried over to Jinh. While she had been praying to Linda, Braith had cut deeper into Jinh's thigh, but still hadn't hit the artery. He had also poked over a dozen surface wounds in her torso. Her shirt looked like an old smock owned by a painter who only worked in red.

Shyla helped Jinh turn onto her stomach so she could get to her tied hands. There were multiple knots in the thick, black rope. She couldn't see any separation in the fibers to determine where she should begin to untie them. She looked for the knife and saw it close to the outstretched fingertips of Braith's blindly groping right hand. Shyla heard the sucking, popping, and cracking sounds of his skull reassembling.

She grabbed the knife just before he could and used it to cut through the rope, freeing Jinh. In her periphery she saw Braith trying to sit up. His lower jaw and the back of his cranium were already remade. He was a ways away from full reconstruction of his face and crown, but not as far as Shyla wanted him to be.

He lunged and Shyla pulled Jinh away while stabbing at his arm. The blade sank completely through the underside of his forearm just under the cuff of the glove. Seeing the hand of glory this close reminded Shyla that it had to do the job. She could shoot him with every bullet in Texas and he'd just keep coming back. Even if she put the glove on, it would permanently scar him and keep him in some degree of pain, but it wouldn't end him.

Enoch's hand had to do the work.

This had been in the back of her mind since Remy had told her about the nature of the hand and all of the things she and Braith had tried on Weldon. The glove couldn't just hold the instrument intended to kill Braith. It had to *be* what killed him.

She started to slip it off Braith's hand. When he tried to pull away she drew the knife closer, into his wrist bones, then downward, as she rolled over to get on top of his arm to trap it, and removed the glove.

Shyla looked into the gory crater that was Braith's reconstructing face. The upper jaw was returning, a few back molars in view, but for the most part she was staring dead into his sinus cavity. An open space with plenty of room for her hand to fit.

Using his tongue as a helpful marker of where his throat would be, she stuffed the glove into that space and pushed hard, until the constricting muscles in his neck gave out under the pressure. Her triceps spasmed and almost cramped from the effort, and she leaned forward as he fell back to be sure the glove was lodged deep where she wanted it to be. Right in the back of his throat, blocking his airway as his head regrew around it.

Braith reached up to pull Shyla's hand away, but Shyla grabbed the handle of the knife still stuck in his wrist and used it to wrench his arm. She allowed him to sit up so she could shift behind him. She pulled his arm with her and stabbed the knife into his back to pin his arm in place, while locking her legs around his waist.

He reached toward his face with his free hand, but Jinh sprang to life, grabbed his arm, and wrapped herself around the entire left side of his body to help immobilize him. He bucked, twisted, and writhed, and came close to freeing himself twice, but Shyla and Jinh adjusted and repositioned themselves, and held on.

Braith shook more violently and tried to force up screams that remained in his chest with no way of escape.

It was happening.

This was not another hand doing the killing, pulling the trigger while the glove was merely worn. This was Enoch Tarver's hand. Transformed, yes, but his hand nonetheless, preserved through generations, and thrust down Saxton Braith's windpipe, fully obstructing it. Choking the life out of him.

Seconds passed slowly, like each dragged a century behind it, but seconds *did* pass, enough of them for Braith to grow weak, and then become still.

"Hold on," Shyla said to Jinh after Braith stopped moving, and Jinh did so. Shyla didn't think he was clever enough to play dead, not in the moment, but she wanted to be sure his heart had finally stopped before she let go.

After another minute she felt for a pulse in his neck, then again at his wrist, and finally put her hand on his chest to feel for a heartbeat. There wasn't one. Shyla let Braith go hesitantly, and Jinh followed suit to peel the duct tape away from her face.

Braith's eyes were wide and still clouded. One sat deeper in its socket than the other. The gash the Tarvers had put in his cheek was matched by several other wounds in his face. His lips looked peeled, the tip of his nose was missing, and there was a dent in his forehead. None of these injuries were healing. They had all stopped partway through restoration. At the moment Saxon Braith was, at last, dead. All the way dead.

Muffled crying behind her reminded Shyla that she and Jinh weren't the only ones alive in the building. She turned to see Ava Tarver struggling to free herself. Shyla walked over to help her and saw that she had scraped her wrists and palms raw against the rope from how hard she had worked against it. Ava had loosened her rope just enough for Shyla to spot where to untie it. As soon as she was free, Ava grabbed the gun Braith had dropped, walked to his corpse, and fired four shots into his heart. She stood over him and watched these newly placed holes stay open, then dropped the gun and returned to her brother to cradle his body.

"It's over," she told him. "He's gone. He's dead."

Shyla started to put a hand on Ava's shoulder, to tell her she was sorry for not saving some of Braith for her, but instead turned away and limped to Jinh. The adrenaline was starting to wear off and all of her pain was coming back to her now, which meant it had to be hitting Jinh, as well.

"Are you okay?" Shyla said.

Jinh responded, "Are you?"

Shyla didn't answer. She moved closer to Jinh, knelt beside her, and hugged her tight, almost as tight as she'd held on to Braith moments before, and as tight as she wished she could hold on to what was departing her now.

The pain and rage hadn't completely left yet, but their edge and fire were disappearing with Linda's vanishing spirit. Shyla wanted to renege on her promise to Linda but couldn't. Linda didn't deserve her forgiveness. She never admitted to the harm she'd done, and had tried to claim Shyla as her daughter even as she stormed in to help.

But she *had* helped, and Shyla had promised to let go of her hatred for her if she did.

"I loved you," Linda said, as softly as possible while still being heard. "I showed you how much I love you. I did everything I could. I gave—"

No, you didn't, Shyla almost screamed. Linda's spirit sounded so frail. So pitiful. Shyla wanted to shout—loud enough to be heard across the water—that Linda deserved nothing but scorn and turmoil forever and ever. But she couldn't.

Linda's spirit drifted into a solace that Shyla could sense, but not touch, and certainly not have herself. She had prayed for this.

Letting go of her anger was the sacrifice she knew she'd have to make in exchange for help. She had tried to prepare herself for this moment, but part of her wished she could take it all back. She wasn't sure she'd needed Linda's help, as dire as things had been when she called on her. Shyla would rather Linda had arrived just to witness what Shyla could do on her own, powered by actual love that Linda knew nothing about. That, and the animus that had shaped and hardened Shyla into who she was.

Shyla was entitled to her hostility toward the people who had abducted her, but it wasn't hers to hold on to anymore. Linda's spirit had absconded with it, and left Shyla with a ragged emptiness in the space it had occupied.

Sacrifice can take many forms, and Shyla had made hers, giving a woman she hated the grace she didn't deserve.

"I'm sorry," Jinh said. She was too close to Shyla now not to draw in her emotions. "I'm so sorry."

Shyla pulled back enough to kiss her, then held Jinh's gaze and told her, "Don't ever say that again. Not about this. I'd do it again a thousand times for you."

34

Sometimes, being up against someone so well connected and powerful that they didn't care how many enemies they made, and never had to bother with actually being good at things, can work out for you.

Saxton Braith paid for people to clean up his messes after he made them, even if that required bribing or blackmailing cops, so he didn't care about being sloppy in advance. He'd brought his own vehicle all the way down to Galveston to do his dirty work, never changing it out for a less conspicuous, less comfortable option. And when he needed a place to store Remy's body after the Tarvers attacked, he'd just opted for the trunk of said car, where he had also stuffed Jinh for transport, while he sat in the backseat with the Tarvers, keeping watch over them on their way to the fort. It was as if he'd been trying to track as much evidence through the car as possible, and Shyla wondered what the older professional he'd hired must have thought of it.

He might have wondered how nice it must be to know you

could buy twenty new cars after having this one shipped overseas to cover your tracks. How nice it must be, not having to be cunning or clever, not having to think ahead. What a luxury.

In Braith's entirely unearned defense, dying was the primary thing that made his shortsightedness stand out as glaringly stupid, and right up until he felt Enoch's hand crammed into his neck, he likely didn't believe it was a genuine possibility.

Shyla had no proof of this, but she also believed Braith's tactic of blackmailing law enforcement around the state worked in her favor. She imagined some police stations, DA offices, and even elected officials, from council members to mayors to judges, popped champagne bottles or turned up their favorite songs when they learned Braith had died. Shyla and Jinh had cleared many ledgers. A few hundred of the state's most powerful and influential people owed them a personal thank-you. While that wasn't forthcoming, or practical, behind the scenes they would apply pressure to make sure a case against Shyla wasn't pursued.

Before her three-day hospital stay was over, Shyla had already received confirmation of this. She, Jinh, and Ava Tarver were being viewed as victims. To the select few in the know, they were heroes.

If there was a service for Ava's brother, Alan, Shyla received no invitation to it. She took this as a sign that Ava wanted to be left alone, and respected that, although it was hard not to think of her frequently in the following weeks. Especially with the regular dreams Shyla had of Ava carrying her brother's wrapped body into the Gulf, the two of them disappearing beneath the water forever.

She woke up from these dreams with tears in her eyes. In the end they had been on the same side, and Shyla could empathize with their loss more deeply now. She'd never quite appreciated—or accepted—how much her resentment of Rodney and Linda had shielded her from the despair of losing both of her real parents. The weight of this new grief kept it from being cathartic. It felt like she had a sinkhole where more productive emotions used to be, and every day she had to worry about falling all the way down into it. She cried more in the weeks following the sacrifice of her rage than she had in her entire adult life prior.

It helped to have Jinh with her. They stayed together after returning to San Antonio. At some point Jinh would have to return to her life in Washington, and Shyla would need to visit Teonna and the rest of the family, but they didn't discuss these eventualities for two weeks. Instead, Jinh was there to wake Shyla when her dreams were bad, there to remind her where she was and that she was alive and okay when Shyla woke up.

Shyla had anticipated needing to do the same for Jinh, given what she'd been through, but Jinh said she felt disconnected from her gift, like a television with no inputs plugged in. On, ready to receive, but with nothing to see or show. She wondered how long this would last but didn't sound worried that it was gone permanently. This sort of dormant period had happened to her before. Shyla took her word for it. If Jinh was lying about this, and just masking her own nightmares, she was doing a remarkable job.

They helped each other get around on crutches and made jokes about who was milking their injuries more. During the day, Shyla felt she had a decent handle on her anxiety, but as evening approached and the world darkened, she grew tense.

The first half-normal day she made it through was spoiled by an unexpected knock at her door after five o'clock that sent her scrambling to her bedroom for her gun. Jinh had to talk her down, and convince her to look through the peephole to confirm that it was just a deliveryman carrying a vase of flowers.

They were sent by Massimo Dante, along with a longer-than-necessary letter, first thanking her for helping him find his "true self," then apologizing for being away for his "self-discovery" while she dealt with Braith ("Had I known, I surely would have intervened"), and, lastly, inviting her to join him on an investigation into something that had dominated the news cycle recently, which partly accounted for why Braith's death hadn't made more waves. Apparently, another wealthy person had beat him to the headlines by dying, only her death was caught by a news camera, and was related to something called a "spite house."

Dante promised to pay Shyla "enough to buy yourself a little island like the one I just visited (pictures enclosed)." He couldn't imagine doing this with anyone but her, he wrote, since she knew the real him, and had proven she could deal with evils "like no other."

Shyla trashed the letter.

That night she did not suffer the dream about Ava and Alan Tarver. Instead, she dreamt of a woman rising from a body of water so still its surface resembled glass. The woman was wrapped in shadows that blocked her features and suppressed her voice, but Shyla could tell she was trying to find her way, crying out in the dark, one word over and over again that Shyla couldn't understand. Shyla tried to walk toward the spirit, forgetting that the solid-looking surface beneath her was water, and she promptly sank to a terrible depth where darkness never ended.

She woke up to Jinh jostling her, a look of terror on her face. "You weren't breathing," Jinh said.

Shyla got up, marched to the bathroom in case she needed to vomit, and checked in the mirror to make sure she was still there. She took several deep breaths like she was storing them for later use, then walked back to the bedroom, where Jinh was waiting.

"Can you take me to my mother?" she asked Jinh.

It took Jinh a moment to realize what Shyla had asked of her. "I think I can. I won't be able to see exactly where it is, but I think I remember the bridge. I remember what's nearby. I can get you there."

"I need to go. She needs me to get her home."

Jinh nodded. "There's a guy I've worked with before who does dives. Helps find . . . helps give closure–"

"Helps find bodies?"

Again, Jinh nodded. "I'll give him a call in the morning."

"Okay. Thanks."

Shyla returned to the bed and only got under the covers so that she could be the little spoon to Jinh. She wouldn't be able to fall asleep again tonight, and that was a blessing.

Jinh kissed her three times on the shoulder and for a moment Shyla thought she was back in her life before she'd left Jinh, and well before she'd been forced to accept that there were unpredictable horrors in the world, not so easily prepared for or controlled. Back when she felt she could eventually, somehow, find peace without surrendering her anger. That hope was gone, and something sadder, but more important, was in its place.

Seeing her mother's remains wasn't going to be easy. She almost couldn't bear the thought, but she had to. She wasn't made by people who abandon people.

"Are you going to be okay?" Jinh asked her.

"If I wasn't, I'd tell you."

Acknowledgments

Thanks to my editor, Daphne Durham.

Thanks to everyone at Penguin Random House / Putnam who helped this book see daylight.

Thanks to my agent, Lane Heymont, for handling business.

Thanks again to my parents for the stories they watched and shared with me that helped influence my storytelling tastes.

I'm far, *far* from the only adult who was impacted by Edward Gorey's animated opening for *Mystery!* on PBS as a kid, but even beyond that brilliant intro, something about the stories themselves got under my skin, even when I didn't really understand them. Especially the stories of Sherlock Holmes, who is probably my mother's favorite fictional character. I have her to thank for introducing me to those gothic stories—I don't think I would have watched them on my own.

The Norliss Tapes is a little-known TV movie intended as the pilot for a mystery horror series that never materialized. I only know of it because my father told me about seeing it on television for the first time while hanging out with one of his college buddies, Mack. They were sitting around listening to music and talking with the TV on in the background, but something about what was on the television made my pops get up, turn the music down and the TV up.

Mack told him, “Man, if you wouldn’t have done that, I would have.”

My pops told me about that moment, and about the movie they watched that night on the TV, and that–along with the *Mystery!* episodes–hooked me on creepy, mysterious stories forever.

About the Author

Johnny Compton is the author of *The Spite House*, which was nominated for a Bram Stoker Award, and *Devils Kill Devils*. His short stories have appeared on *PseudoPod* and *The NoSleep Podcast*, and in *Strange Horizons* and several other publications. His fascination with frightening fiction started when he was introduced to the ghost story "The Golden Arm" as a child.